CONVERGENCE

C.J. CHERRYH

THE FOREIGNER UNIVERSE

FOREIGNER
INVADER
INHERITOR

PRECURSOR
DEFENDER
EXPLORER

DESTROYER
PRETENDER
DELIVERER

CONSPIRATOR
DECEIVER
BETRAYER

INTRUDER
PROTECTOR
PEACEMAKER

TRACKER
VISITOR
CONVERGENCE

THE ALLIANCE-UNION UNIVERSE
REGENESIS
DOWNBELOW STATION
THE DEEP BEYOND Omnibus:
Serpent's Reach | Cuckoo's Egg
ALLIANCE SPACE Omnibus:
Merchanter's Luck | 40,000 in Gehenna
AT THE EDGE OF SPACE Omnibus:
Brothers of Earth | Hunter of Worlds
THE FADED SUN Omnibus:
Kesrith | Shon'jir | Kutath

THE CHANUR NOVELS
THE CHANUR SAGA Omnibus:
The Pride Of Chanur | Chanur's Venture | The Kif Strike Back
CHANUR'S ENDGAME Omnibus:
Chanur's Homecoming | Chanur's Legacy

THE MORGAINE CYCLE
THE COMPLETE MORGAINE Omnibus:
Gate of Ivrel | Well of Shiuan | Fires of Azeroth | Exile's Gate

OTHER WORKS:
THE DREAMING TREE Omnibus:
The Tree of Swords and Jewels | The Dreamstone
ALTERNATE REALITIES Omnibus:
Port Eternity | Wave Without a Shore | Voyager in Night
THE COLLECTED SHORT FICTION OF CJ CHERRYH

C. J. CHERRYH
CONVERGENCE

A *Foreigner* Novel

DAW BOOKS, INC.
DONALD A. WOLLHEIM, FOUNDER
375 Hudson Street, New York, NY 10014

**ELIZABETH R. WOLLHEIM
SHEILA E. GILBERT
PUBLISHERS**
www.dawbooks.com

First Printing, April 2017

1 2 3 4 5 6 7 8 9

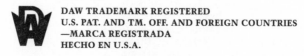

DAW TRADEMARK REGISTERED
U.S. PAT. AND TM. OFF. AND FOREIGN COUNTRIES
—MARCA REGISTRADA
HECHO EN U.S.A.

PRINTED IN THE U.S.A.

For Jane, always.

Table of Contents

Chapter 1	1
Chapter 2	35
Chapter 3	54
Chapter 4	67
Chapter 5	82
Chapter 6	124
Chapter 7	140
Chapter 8	186
Chapter 9	199
Chapter 10	207
Chapter 11	222
Chapter 12	231
Chapter 13	240
Chapter 14	243
Chapter 15	250
Chapter 16	257
Chapter 17	269
Chapter 18	282
Chapter 19	297
Chapter 20	306
Chapter 21	323

1

Home again. But not, immediately, to the Bujavid's third-floor residency. Tabini-aiji had sent a request to the Bujavid's train station, hand-delivered by Assassins' Guild, to meet with him in his downstairs office . . . uncommon venue, but likewise safe from eavesdropping, even from servant staff.

And from immediate family. Which, in the situation they had in the world, might be a needful consideration.

Such considerations applied, even in the narrow confines of the lift car that rose from the underground train station. Bren Cameron, paidhi-aiji, translator, diplomat—and carrying, in a document case, the outcome of an encounter that still had the world anxious and unsettled—also carried a secret. His four atevi bodyguards, Guild themselves—black-skinned and golden-eyed, head and shoulders taller than most humans—all knew it. The aiji-dowager, Ilisidi, diminutive for an ateva, armed with a cane that lent stability to aged bones in the long, rapid rise—she knew the gist of it. So did her two bodyguards. The third of their company, Cajeiri, aged fortunate nine years, Tabini-aiji's son, did not. His bodyguard, Guild, but still in their teens, did not, and Bren had been extremely careful to keep it that way.

Three hours back on Earth and they were all still suffering, to varying degrees, the effects of the express shuttle flight from the station.

The lift stopped, opened doors on the ornate lower floor with its travertine columns, its plinths with ornate porcelains and its tapestries and hand-loomed carpet runners. This corridor, this area, was at a T intersection with the main entry hall, the public areas, the audience chamber, the public museum and state library, the office of records—places where the public went.

This hallway—no. A black velvet rope on four gilt stanchions provided a gentle security. Two black-clad members of the Guild stood there, armed, a less gentle reminder that, no, these were not public lifts, and the upper and lower floors were not on the tour.

Bren and company crossed the hall. The guards at the office doors, Tabini's own—on loan from his grandmother the aiji-dowager herself, in point of fact—opened the doors without a word exchanged.

The three of them entered. All the bodyguards but the dowager's two, Cenedi and Nawari, remained outside; and Bren walked hindmost—mere court official here, if not in the heavens. Tabini sat at his desk, isolate in a very large office, a place of towering windows, immense tapestries, carpet far more ancient than that bearing traffic outside.

There were chairs, felicitous three. Cenedi arranged the endmost for Ilisidi, would have taken her cane, but she retained possession of it, and Cenedi and Nawari withdrew from the room entirely.

Tabini turned his chair to face them as Cajeiri settled into the chair beside his great-grandmother, and Bren sat down . . . feeling a little plainly dressed for the executive office, for the aiji of the majority of the world—very little cuff and collar lace, which tended to float in lack of gravity, plain coat and trousers, a ribbon that might be a little askew: Bren's bodyguard had re-tied it on the train.

"Grandmother," Tabini said. "Son of mine. Paidhi."

That was the greeting, for three who'd just come from the heavens, with a document guaranteeing the world's survival, at least as regarded the kyo presence up there. It was not want of concern. Concern was evident if one read atevi, and Bren did. Half-rising, he laid the all-important document case on Tabini's desk.

"One worried," Tabini said then, "regarding the weather."

Ilisidi waved her hand, dismissive. "It would not dare storm. We were assured we would land well ahead of the front. As we did. The pilots were quite confident, or we might have stayed circling the world indefinitely, we were assured. Read the document, grandson. It took considerable effort to obtain it."

"Not only among the kyo, as one hears," Tabini said, making no such move. "One trusts they are departing."

"Far more rapidly than they arrived, aiji-ma," Bren said.

"Without further communication."

"Without a word," Bren said.

"And Gin-nandi is now in charge," Tabini said, "of both Mospheiran *and* Reunioner folk up there."

"Yes, honored Father," Cajeiri said.

"Gin-nandi will request atevi assistance to land the Reunioners."

"Yes, aiji-ma," Bren said. "They have not fared well on the station. There are security issues."

"One understands that the Presidenta of Mospheira considers them all his people. But that we will receive a request to transport numbers of Reunioners on atevi shuttles. Have we seals on that?"

"We shall have," Bren said. "Likewise we shall have requests for landing zones for parachuted capsules."

"Not bearing Reunioners."

"No, aiji-ma. Only cargo displaced from the shuttles. This was Gin-nandi's idea, and it will move that population to safety without a shuttle-building campaign."

"The Presidenta is not about to suggest that we subsidize settlement for these people."

"He will hope only for your cooperation in the program. They are a human problem."

"You have the children and their parents lodged with Lord Geigi. It is your intention to land them on the next shuttle flight . . . an earnest of things to come."

"A pleasant, an innocent face on the undertaking, aiji-ma—representative of most of these people. They have suffered very heavy losses—in the kyo assault on Reunion, few households were left intact. The kyo themselves regret the attack. They have expressed that. They misinterpreted the presence of the colony. They have expressed sorrow at the situation, and they have absolutely no inclination to do harm to atevi or to Mospheirans or the Reunioners. This document is a resolution of disengagement, with the provision that, should we wish to contact them peacefully, there is an appointed place and procedure."

Tabini nodded. "At Reunion. Which they will retain."

"They are doubtless sifting it for every morsel of information they can gain from it," Ilisidi remarked dryly, "and since we have accorded humans an island to live on and half a station orbiting over our heads, we have *some* interest in their interest, but *we* have observed the kyo representatives, and we find them reasonable folk."

"One was Prakuyo's son," Cajeiri said. "And we talked, honored Father. We spent a lot of time talking. I, myself. And their security played chess with mani."

"One can only imagine," Tabini said, equally dryly, while the document case lay untouched on his desk. "Chess, was it?"

"A very interesting opponent," Ilisidi said. "I shall play you a round, grandson, using *his* style."

One had absolutely no doubt that that would be an interesting game . . . and no game, but a distillation of observations that didn't fit neatly in the vocabulary they'd collected. Bren had his own set of notes he'd taken since, and on the way down—to preserve the immediacy of the information. Likely no one else could read those, either: circles, diagrams, arrows, and lines of relationship and relevance: non-words that had no equivalent in the languages he dealt with, words that might combine concepts humans and atevi didn't see as related, and that he had to commit to more readable notes. It was an architecture atevi might have to deal with—someday. Not soon, however. The document in that case saw to that.

And left him questioning his own sense of right and wrong.

"I shall look forward to it," Tabini said, "once we have resolved the lingering problems, such as onto *whose* land Lord Geigi proposes to drop the equivalent of rail cars from the heavens, and *how* we shall secure the safety of these children Lord Geigi has as guests."

"We might bring them and their parents down on *our* shuttle," Cajeiri said, "and they might be at Najida, honored Father, at least until there is a place for them."

"No," Tabini said.

"Honored Father—"

"They are human. They are Reunioner. Someday, as we suspect, they will be of service to you, as nand' Bren is to us. When you came back to us, *you* benefitted from atevi associations. You began to feel man'chi, you had the chance to form associations in a normal way . . ."

"They have man'chi to *me*, honored Father."

"Nand' Bren may argue that they do not. They may have a profound sentiment, but a *human* sentiment, son of mine, which, since they are not adult, is still forming. They have lived in fear much of their lives, have been uprooted from their home, transported across space in less than comfortable circumstances, subjected to Tillington's ill-run administration, entertained in great luxury on Earth and finally dropped into Lord Geigi's household in the heavens—but they have never seen humans live as humans live on Mospheira. Now they will see all their people brought down to the world to become Mospheirans—yet one more experience in their young lives. You may ask nand' Bren what his opinion is. But consider that you have the satisfaction of man'chi in this household. What connection does their birth fit them to feel? And should they not be given the chance to discover it, and should not their parents have that chance?"

Cajeiri was silent a moment—not an angry silence; not an entirely happy one.

"They should," Cajeiri said then. "One understands. One did not feel, then—all that one feels now. One hopes—one hopes the same for them."

A human had no precise idea what Cajeiri was feeling at that moment. A human could imagine—but dared not inject too much that was human into it. Or too little. Pain was involved, pain of separation. Massively frustrated instincts figured in it.

So did human attachments on the other side—matter. The children needed the ability to judge human folk accurately, the ability to judge people—and trust people—and *distrust* with accuracy. The ability to form those concepts like self-worth and selfless love . . . feelings that could go hurtfully sideways in the interface between human and atevi. He himself had had his human sensitivities well-developed, if a bit over-developed in some cases—before he took on the paidhi's job, and learned that when atevi committed, they committed profoundly, potentially for life and death.

He *had* that devotion, in those four outside this room: in Banichi and Jago, Tano and Algini—a connection so close as to *be* self, an upward flow of loyalty that didn't ask questions in a crisis and didn't want reciprocity from him, no, not in the least. An aiji's role was to *be* protected, so he could use his skill to keep them all *out* of crisis in the first place, or to pick up the pieces when things went wrong. That was how atevi felt centered and heart-sure.

No, Cajeiri didn't want to *be* one of those kids. He wanted to steer their lives for them, in a good way. In the best and most devoted and atevi way, being what he was, which was literally born to lead. While they took care of him. And right now doing that meant giving them up, which was, for Cajeiri, as painful as unrequited love for a human. It was a lot to ask of a nine-year-old whose privilege was absolute, and who, in his highly securitied world, had absolutely *no one* who wasn't adult and taking care of *him*. His teenaged aishid, his bodyguard, was only a few years older than he was. That relationship would deepen over time. One sincerely hoped it would. There was nothing wrong with that foursome, nothing lacking but the profound experience that had welded young Cajeiri to four human kids in a voyage before that atevi foursome had ever had a chance to affect him.

Damn, Bren thought. Just—damn.

"Our son," Tabini said, nodding slightly, "our *heir*, satisfies all expectations. Go upstairs and please your mother."

Dismissed. Atop it all.

But the young gentleman knew there were secrets. He waded hip-deep in secrets, only some of which he was privy to. A year ago he might have protested his not knowing what had gone on, when messages had come from the kyo ship and his great-grandmother's door had shut, sealing one kyo and Cenedi, her chief bodyguard, into conference—and not him, and not the young kyo who had sat with him, equally excluded.

Secrets. Damned right there were secrets. Even the dowager didn't know all of them.

"One is gratified, honored Father." Cajeiri quietly rose, bowed—Bren likewise rose, Cajeiri's rank demanding it. His actions just now demanded it.

Cajeiri left, quietly.

Tabini took up the document case and opened it, extracting a piece of paper or its analog never made on Earth, and bedecked with seals and stamps of some substance not wax, written in various colors not ordinary in atevi documents. Three languages, three forms of writing, one of which evoked sounds neither human nor atevi could duplicate . . .

"You have read this," Tabini said.

"Only the paidhi can read all three," Ilisidi said with a wave of her hand. "He believes they are identical enough."

"One can decipher key words," Bren said, "to indicate that the substance is the same. *Read* it, no. One was obliged to take their word for it."

"Under the circumstances," Tabini said, perusing the document, "understandable." He scanned it for a moment. "Your hand, your seal, is set to all sections but one."

For the Ragi version, and the Mosphei', it was his signature and his imprint. The kyo version, Prakuyo an Tep had written, by hand, and signed all three documents. As he had signed, for the President of Mospheira, and the aiji of the aishidi'tat, and the four *Phoenix* captains, all of whom he had represented. One document was headed out of the solar system at the moment. One was on Tabini's desk. One remained to deliver to the President of Mospheira, to whom the kyo imputed all human authority, on Earth, on the station, and over the ship that served it—a point it had not, at the time, seemed safe to contradict.

"It seems a very simple document," Tabini said. "I know you, paidhi. Did you gain all you wished?"

"I gained all I wished."

"In these simple words."

"Complexity and subclauses seemed only likely to complicate matters. In essence, the kyo will not advance beyond Reunion in our direction—one has to understand that, while everything in space may be reckoned as a sphere, and boundaries are difficult to define, there are paths in the heavens, routes dictated by the avoidance of hazards and the availability of resources. Reunion is a place between us and them. Reunion is our agreed boundary in their direction."

"They may visit it but we may not."

"It is not in our interest to visit Reunion, aiji-ma. They have claimed it. One believes they are studying it. But they are promising not to go closer to us than Reunion so long as they are at war with anyone. And we promise not to go closer to them than Reunion, which we may do, from our side, if we wish to contact them while they are still at war. We are given a signal to use to identify ourselves should we make that choice. But one does not advise we seek that contact."

"Which leads one to ask—why?"

"Their enemy is human," Ilisidi said.

Tabini looked at her in a shock he never would have shown outsiders.

"The ship *Phoenix* came here hundreds of years ago," Bren said, merging facts Tabini well knew—with things they had just learned. "It had lost its way in the heavens. It first found itself near a dangerous star, which killed many of its best and bravest. They then worked their way toward *this* star, *this* world, and built Alpha in our heavens, the station from which all Mospheirans descended—before the ship moved on to build Reunion two centuries ago, at a place with resources but no green planet. When the ship left Alpha the first time—the ship-aijiin declared they were trying to find their way home. One now believes—and I have said this to very few, aiji-ma—I believe at least one among the captains had a good notion in what direction to look. Alpha was a first stepping-stone after their original disaster, and when *Phoenix* left, it never meant to come back to Alpha at all, unless it met extreme difficulty.

"Reunion was the next stepping-stone they built, and they were preparing to leave it behind, too. Unfortunately . . . the third stepping-stone they planned to make was at a kyo star, perhaps *the* kyo star. What the ship did not know—was that, on the other side of kyo space, the kyo had been at war with humans. Who these humans are, whether they are a splinter, or the world from which all humans come, I do not know. How this war started, I am not at all certain, either. I am certain that *Phoenix*, years ago, setting out from our star, and then from Reunion, had no idea the kyo even existed. *Phoenix* may have detected a civilization of some sort at the star it proposed to visit next—they have instruments that can see that sort of thing. They may well have thought the civilization was human, and they seem to have been cautious, aware that time may have worked profound changes. The senior ship-aiji, Ramirez, on his own, had prepared paidhiin, Jase-aiji and Yolande, schooled in languages of the Earth of humans—so he could talk with other humans after so long an absence. He had done everything generations of ship-aijiin before him had done, advancing and searching. But this time, I think anticipating a meeting with other humans, he had prepared people to speak in whatever language they might need."

Tabini listened silently. Some of the history he had long known; but that the captains might have searched with the means to *find* others out in the heavens—that was news; and that there were humans fighting the kyo—that was very grim news indeed.

"They arrived at this next star," Bren continued, "and immediately met a kyo ship. Ships, aiji-ma, have a distinctive *voice*, an electromagnetic voice, that clearly, the moment *Phoenix* heard it, said—this is another ship and this is not human.

"Ramirez ran. He ran for another destination than Reunion, trying to lead this ship off from Reunion, but the kyo, who had been at war with humans for a hundred years, had been watching Reunion, which was giving off its own electromagnetic voice, a voice virtually identical to their enemies' voice. And once *Phoenix* made its move from that station into kyo space, the kyo attacked Reunion."

"This *voice*," Tabini said, gold eyes intense in thought, "this distinctive *voice* ships and stations have . . . Would not this kyo place give a kyo signal to Ramirez-aiji? Should he not have known there were inhabitants?"

"I also have wondered, aiji-ma. Jase-aiji said that a planet's voice is detectible at a vast distance, and a ship's voice is generally lost in the star's noise. But a planet's voice, Jase-aiji says, can be muddled, and hard to read—especially—this is my surmise— if one is expecting something of a certain nature and listening for that."

"As the kyo mistook Reunion's voice."

"Exactly so. A quiet voice. And once struck, Reunion did not retaliate—it had no ability to do so. This, apparently, was not what the kyo expected. The kyo drew back to wait and see what would happen—whether *Phoenix* would come back with reinforcements.

"*Phoenix* did come back, but alone. And left again. It very likely was tracked, which may have brought kyo to observe this solar system, again, watching, waiting, all the years that *we* were building the shuttles and rising into space. What they may have seen, even at great distance, confused them—because we would not have the pattern of a human world—we would not have the pattern that high technology would give us. We were not what the kyo expected.

"And when Ramirez-aiji told at least half the truth on his deathbed and when *we* traveled aboard *Phoenix*, looking for survivors on Reunion, then the kyo sought contact."

"Could they know atevi were aboard?"

"If they were watching this world, they would know we are different. They would know that, in the ten years after Phoenix came back to us, the world's voice changed. The station came alive and we flew in space, but only in a small way. They knew we were the same ship, surely. But maybe the fact that *Phoenix* is old gave it a slightly different signal. And maybe, too, we were in an odd direction, a place that did not fit with what they knew. Something made them wonder and made them signal. And when they signaled, we signaled. We began to communicate. We asked to take the Reunioners. And they set a condition."

"The prisoner they held."

"Exactly. They wanted him. Or his remains. And it was our good fortune he was alive. *Our* kyo, Prakuyo an Tep, whom we rescued from Reunioner detention, had learned a little shipspeak—and he picked up Ragi very fast. *He* introduced us. *He* spoke for us. And the kyo said they would come visit—to see what we look like close at hand, we assumed. And surely that was no small part of their visit. But the more important thing—

they brought a prisoner of their own, a human—and let me meet this person in secret—to see what would happen, certainly. To see if I could talk to him—and, one is certain, aiji-ma, to know where my sentiments would lie.

"I was indeed able to talk to him, which they had not been able to do. I learned his name. I learned he was a person of some integrity, and I took a chance, aiji-ma. I taught him *how* to learn their language. I took it on myself to *give* the kyo a human paidhi. In seven days—I taught him basics, I restored him to a better appearance, I told him about atevi, but very little about this world. I let him believe, if he would, that ship had met ship in deep space. And in those seven days, I gave him the structure of the kyo language. I gave him words that would let him gain other words. I set him in communication with Prakuyo an Tep, and with influential persons who also had come on the ship. I gave him the best instruction in the paidhi's office that I could give in the time I had, and told him it was his burden to find a way to talk to his humans, and to the kyo, to find out the causes of their war. And to end it."

His voice shook, nearly to breaking. Above all else, with Tabini and Ilisidi, he did not want that. Tabini needed facts. He needed details. "I told Prakuyo not to tell this man where I came from, and not to let him go to other humans, either. For one thing, I fear his own people might not let him return, and would not let him end the war. For another, on our side of space—I decided that neither the ship-folk nor the Reunioners nor Mospheirans should learn that the kyo's enemy are other humans. Not until the kyo war ends. His name is Guy Cullen, but the kyo cannot pronounce that. They call him Ku'yen. Ku'yen is what he will be. I gave him everything I could. Except the truth. Which I have withheld from all our allies but Jase."

There was a small silence.

"Tea," Tabini said, into that hush in the room. That was the atevi custom, when passions rose. Tea. And calm.

"I shall pour it," Bren said, being, in the room, least in rank.

Tabini pushed himself back from his desk. "We need the exercise," Tabini said.

Home. It *was* home in Cajeiri's mind, now, though it was spooky, being let out of the lift upstairs, alone, with his aishid.

And he had to ask himself why his stomach felt tense, and tell himself there was no reason.

But Father, downstairs, in his office, had things to talk about with nand' Bren and mani, which confirmed what he had thought, that there were things mani and nand' Bren had to say that he should not hear, regarding the kyo, regarding that document nand' Bren had brought back.

He did not think he had deserved not to be trusted.

Possibly—possibly, he thought, his father had just happened to be in the downstairs office for other reasons, and *possibly* his father had sent him upstairs because his mother really was all afire to see him.

It was possible. His mother wanted things to be in their place, and people to be in their places, and she had not wanted him to go up to the station at all. She might, in her fierce way, be anxious to see him.

But it was also possible he had been sent up simply because secrets were about to pass downstairs, and if that was the case, his mother might not even come out of her suite to meet him. That had been the way of things since his baby sister had arrived, well, mostly, and the situation did not make him sorry. Perhaps his mother would pretend not to have worried at all, and take her time about seeing him, once she had word he was indeed back. That was very possible. She kept her displeasure cool, and easy to bear. She had made one or two moves to bring him closer, but such moods came and went, and her detachment— that was a breach never quite made right. He had been brought up by mani, on that long trip through space, and his mother had let him go. She had had to let him go. For his safety. But any reminder of his absence with mani upset her to this day.

So, well, if that was the case, they only had to slip in quietly; the major domo would let them in, and then they only had to head to the inner hall and his own suite as quietly as five people could.

"We shall try to slip in," he said to his aishid.

"Your mother is expecting you," Antaro said, in electronic communication, constantly, with other Guild, inside and outside the apartment.

"Oh," he said, walking toward the apartment door. There was no help for it, then. Expecting him. And doubtless upset. "You need not be there. Go on to the suite."

"We should hear," Antaro said. Antaro and Jegari, sister and brother—they were the oldest *and* the youngest of his bodyguards. Taibeni—his father's clan—and younger in years, but longer with him.

"So we should," Lucasi said. Veijico and Lucasi, another sister and brother team, several years older, but still in their teens. They were *his* household, along with Eisi and Liedi, who were grown-ups, and patient with his wants, all the same.

It was loyalty. Man'chi. Whatever his troubles, they shared them. *They* were his household, these six, his advisors, his protection, his better sense on most occasions.

And that better sense advised him now to go directly to his mother. He wished his stomach were not in a knot at the prospect. There was no reason for it. He knew nothing he should not know, so there was nothing he could do wrong. He just did not expect an easy meeting.

He had met with the kyo, who all the world feared could just blow up the space station with the push of a button. And he had been nervous at that. But there was a peculiar kind of nervousness his mother could set into him—wanting to please her, and absolutely convinced he never would. Not quite. Not in the way he imagined he should.

Maybe it went both ways. Maybe his mother viewed *him* with the same nervousness, dreading to *be* upset by a situation neither of them could have helped. He'd been able to figure out alien words. He'd learned to talk to the kyo. Could it possibly be harder to figure out what his mother meant, in the language they shared?

He had no chance to set his hand on the door. He never tried. The major d', inside, whisked it open, also electronically fore-warned, and expecting him.

"Your mother," the major d' said, "is waiting in her sitting room."

"Yes," he said. *Her* sitting room, not the main one. He slipped the top button of his coat, seeing his own servants, Eisi and Liedi, there to provide him another. The travel-worn coat slipped away. The lighter coat went on, cool from the depths of the closet, and his aishid shed their baggage into the hands of other Guild, who guarded the apartment. "Is everything well?" Cajeiri asked the major d'. "Is she happy?"

"One believes she is relieved, young aiji. As always, when you return safely."

"Who knows about this, paidhi-ji?" Tabini asked, when he had set aside his cup.

"The aiji-dowager," Bren said, with a respectful nod toward Ilisidi. "Cenedi, I believe."

"Cenedi and Nawari," Ilisidi said. "Cajeiri does not."

"Jase-aiji. No one else, of the ship-folk, though he may have told the ship-aijiin."

"Is that not a danger?" Tabini asked.

"The ship-aijiin, Jase-aiji says, were driven by their original mission, to find an answer and find out where they were. But now they have a base at Alpha. They have all other directions to explore but one, and the original mission is now satisfied. It is Jase's sense that the crew knowing at this time might not be desirable: it is too close to Ramirez' lifetime, and loyalties are still active. But that the four ship-aijiin should know—and un-derstand this document—makes it *less* likely that they would willingly take the ship in that direction. Even subtracting the fact that the kyo have armaments that could destroy the ship, they have just freed the ship from the governance of the ancient Pilots' Guild, which they had come to detest, in the person of the Reunion stationmaster, Braddock. They have no desire, now that they know where they are, to go where some other authority may seek to direct them. Their freedom lies in all directions but that one. They are safe, they are in command, they see their future clear, and they have no problems except the difficulties of Alpha Station—all of which we can resolve. We have new science—which we gained at Reunion—which will increase our own prosperity. We have every possibility of having the kyo as *our* shield from any attempt of other humans to come here. There is every hope for a good future . . . in which the notion of the paidhi-aiji as the dispenser of human science is becoming obsolete. I see no future for restriction. The whole of the human Archive should be open to Mospheira, to Alpha, to the Reunioners, to the ship—and to the aishidi'tat, without restriction. Our science is one science. Or it will be, in not so many years."

"Amazing," Tabini said, who was not one to use that word. "We have come a long way, paidhi."

"A very long way," he said.

"But *we* shall not have highways," Ilisidi said firmly. "We shall not *become* Mospheira."

"No," Bren said. "I shall never urge we should have highways."

The building of a railroad through a string of clan territories and hunting ranges centuries ago had set up the supremacy of the Ragi atevi and created the Western Association, the aishidi'tat, which now stretched from shore to shore of the monocontinent and set the capital at Shejidan. It had put Tabini's dynasty in power, and despite the advent of air travel, the development of a space program, and the dowager's recent campaign for ocean traffic, rail remained the primary mode of long-distance travel . . . thus preserving the unique cultures, the traditional patterns, dialects, and market communities essential to the atevi way of life. Mospheira had developed traffic, and highways—and the mainland had rail. They were two different lifestyles, two cultures which, after two hundred years sharing the world, still couldn't speak each other's language. Which was probably still a good thing.

"And have you told this secret to the Presidenta on Mospheira?" Tabini asked.

"Not yet. I am asking myself whether I should."

"Gin-nandi does not know."

"Gin-nandi does not know. Nor does Lord Geigi. Only my aishid. They were with me. No one else on my staff. No one else on the station. No one on this earth but the aiji-dowager, her closest guards, and now yourself, aiji-ma."

"How is the Presidenta's security?"

"Subject to elections . . . not themselves, but in terms of the Presidenta they serve, so that, over time, their service is mutable. It worries me. I would not tell the leadership of the Reunioners, and I am far from certain I should tell the Presidenta, who is my oldest ally, older than Gin. I am inclined not to. It could ruin them, should it become known that they knew and kept it secret. But likewise, the Human Heritage Party, that brought so much trouble to the world, will use any argument it can to promote fear of outsiders. The kyo's attack on Reunion is something they will certainly try to use. If they found out this secret, they would try to argue the kyo cannot have the same interests, that the distant humans are our natural allies— to which I certainly cannot agree—and that we should launch a campaign to join them against the kyo. That it would be extreme folly, that it might be factually wrong, that it might destroy everything we have built—that is an acceptable risk to them—an acceptable risk, if one thinks a few thousand humans with no ship and no weapons could attack a people who could wipe out our presence in space with one strike. Heritage Party leaders would not be the ones to set out across space and risk their lives. What they *would* do is stir up fear, use the public outcry to get elected to office, and immediately put through measures to be sure relations with the aishidi'tat are continually disrupted and that the Reunioners, another variety of outsider, are kept unemployed. Their vision is mostly for present gain for their party. Troubles they might cause in the future are not on their personal horizon."

"They are the clanless who cry fire in the shop and make off with the till."

"That does describe them, aiji-ma. They would find profit in the situation."

"You say the time of the Mospheiran paidhi is ending."

"So far as the dispensation of technology is concerned, yes. But as a mediator, that, I shall be, as long as you wish, aiji-ma."

"We agree. And toward that end, perhaps, that time when all science will be held in common, paidhi-ji—perhaps it is time Mospheira *met* the paidhi-aiji."

"Aiji-ma?"

"Mospheirans think the paidhi is simply the arbiter of technology—giving small gifts to appease the aishidi'tat and keep us happy. Let our human allies learn the true value of our paidhi-aiji, firsthand, and in a needful instance. These young Reunioners are under our protection. Go to Mospheira. Make that clear, by your presence, by your dealings. Set up adequate protection for them and assure their proper education by sensible people. If the Presidenta is your oldest ally, and we are likewise your allies, you should use those circumstances to declare how these children will be treated, and why they should be treated so, and assure that *all* these Reunioners who will be landing also become Mospheiran, with all their benefits of science and knowledge at the world's disposal."

"They are not all scientists, aiji-ma."

"Yet they are humans like other humans, are they not?"

"Not all in the most fortunate way, aiji-ma."

"Gin-nandi is in charge, is she not? Human authorities surely can screen them before sending them down. And the Presidenta can act with authority, as he did with Tillington."

"That is so, aiji-ma. But—"

Ilisidi swung her cane down and set it on the carpeted stonework with a distinct thump. "We *approve* our grandson's notions. Go to Mospheira. Let them see they are not dealing with a market squabble, but something far beyond their shores and likely beyond the lives of their grandchildren. We have finally gotten sense from the ship-aijiin. We have established order on the station, granted we move these people off with some dispatch. Let us not leave this decision to the Mospheiran legislature to send to committee and committee and committee. We know their ways. Let us cast this matter into *treaty* law, in which, if we recall, the Presidenta has an aiji's power, so he need not refer to the legislature and its committees."

"Approval from my grandmother," Tabini murmured. "When we two agree, the sun runs backward."

"Look to the sky, then," Ilisidi said. "The world is in for a long afternoon."

"I shall go where I am sent," Bren said. Images flashed through his mind, Port Jackson. The University. The Department. Occasionally the halls of State. His mother's apartment and the downtown traffic—but that wasn't there anymore. She'd died while he was at Reunion. Everything had changed while he had been at Reunion, and he hadn't been back to any of those places since.

Everything . . . had changed.

"You will go to the island as paidhi-aiji," Tabini said, "and with your aishid. Wherever you stand, you stand *in* the aishidi'tat."

"Aiji-ma." That was an order, as direct and specific an order as Tabini had ever given him.

And as simple and as complicated as the last one, to go up to space and deal with a kyo ship.

In some ways—that one had been more straightforward.

Mother's suite had the really nice windows . . . a row of them, with beautiful lace curtains that stirred in the northern breeze. And Seimei slept, in her crib, opposite them, serene in her little world. Cajeiri paused on his way to his mother's sitting room, stood by Seimei's crib, nudged a little dark fist. Seimiro was her name, but it was too big a name for so little a person. Seimei was how he thought of her. Her hair was more abundant, black as his. She had plumped out since her birth, and he supposed that was healthy in a baby. And she was a determined sleeper, fist clenched, her mouth so strangely like their mother's. She could frown. She did so, in her sleep, probably because of his shadow falling on her face.

He had no desire to wake her and have their mother upset. He had left his aishid to relax with Eisi and Liedi, and see Boji, and to settle down to a quiet cup of tea with the first chance to tell Eisi and Liedi at least the surface of the adventures they had had. *He* would have to answer his mother's questions, and be careful what he said.

Well, there was nothing for it. Mother's maid was waiting at the door to Mother's sitting room. He left Seimei and let himself be ushered in.

Mother was waiting for him, in her chair. He gave a little bow. "Honored Mother."

"Son. Sit down."

He took the chair that was sometimes his father's. "Seimei has more hair than when I left."

"Do you think so?"

Saying something nice about his sister was the fastest way to get his mother in a good mood. It proved he had looked. Which proved he had cared. And he did care, actually; it was just that it did work, and he knew it. The fact was that, no matter what he did, he would never be as much as Seimei, in his mother's eyes.

Her concentration on Seimei gave him peace, at least.

"I think at least a third more," he said, and added: "She sleeps a lot. Is she all right?"

"She wakes midway to morning," his mother said, "and goes to sleep in the sun. You were a sun child, always awake by daylight. Which you could not quite do on the ship, I fear."

"No," he said. "There was only artificial light there. But one trusts she will change."

"Babies do," she said. "And did you have a good trip?"

As if he had only been to Tirnamardi and back, on an outing. "We did. We had no trouble on the shuttle."

"But on the station. Your father says you had to pull your young guests to safety, and Lord Geigi has them."

"Yes."

"Have you eaten? Would you like teacakes?"

He had had an absolute excess of teacakes, dealing with the kyo. He did not think he would ever like them again. "I think I would like a sandwich, honored Mother."

Mother gave a nod to her maid, and another servant, standing beside a buffet, began to prepare tea.

"Tell me," his mother said, "how these strangers were."

"Prakuyo an Tep, Hakuut an Ti, and Matuanu an Matu . . ."

"Such strange names."

"We have pictures of them," he said. One had to be careful, warming to any topic with Mother. Some stories alarmed her. "Prakuyo-nandi remembered me. Remembered us all. Matuanu was fairly solemn—we think he was a kind of bodyguard. Or maybe he was old."

"Could you not tell?" His mother seemed interested, in astonishingly good spirits.

"With them—they have no hair at all, they scarcely have any wrinkles, their faces are bony, but fairly pleasant, and we never could tell. I felt a closer association with Hakuut—he was always the one to try things—but I had no idea until the last that he was young. Like me. Well, like Veijico. We spent a lot of time working on the tablets and pictures. And he turned out to be Prakuyo's son. Prakuyo brought his *son* to see us. None of us expected that!"

"I would not have expected it," his mother said. The maid served tea, and he was not sure he should go on. It was never proper to discuss business over tea, but he was never sure, with his mother, what constituted business. "So did we get all we wanted from them?"

"I think we did." He had his own reservations, all in that conference downstairs, but he did not think he should mention that to his mother. He was supposed to be ignorant, and sometimes that was safest. "They are going away now. They are way out from the station and going fast."

"But still here."

"I do not understand quite how it works," he said, "but they will go, soon, quite suddenly, and we will not see them. They go faster than light. And light goes faster than thunder. By quite a lot."

"Well, well, these are things we will be obliged to understand, one supposes. What did they want? To look around? And for what? What were they looking for?"

"They are fighting a war, far on the other side of where they live. And nand' Bren says they are probably very glad to see we are not strong and warlike."

"They are not seeking us as allies, then."

"Maybe they would have wanted to have allies, but mostly they just wanted to have us stay out of their territory. They evidently think they can deal with things. They just did not want a powerful enemy on their flank."

"On their flank. When did you learn such warlike things?"

"I think from Father. Or mani. Or maybe Banichi."

"Well, my son is back. And we shall not have a war in the

heavens. And one hears your young associates will be living on Mospheira soon. You are *not* to take a rowboat, son of mine."

It was humor, and from his mother. But it happened to conjure an all-too-vivid image. "I have had my adventures with rowboats, honored Mother."

His mother instantly went solemn. "We should hope so. But you will know they are safe."

"I shall."

"Your tutor has missed you."

Lessons. And routine. His brain hurt, from all he had learned above, and he did take notes, and he was still taking them.

"I think I should like a little holiday, honored Mother. I studied and studied up there. It was a *lot* of study."

"You are tired."

He hesitated to answer. He wanted no quarrel. But he nodded.

"We were very worried," she said. "Your father was on edge the whole time. I confess the same. The major d' was under orders if anything came at any hour, we were to know, and word was very scarce, until the last few days."

"I am sorry."

"We understand that there was a time when the human in charge interfered with the orderly transitions. We hear that there is now a new person in charge of the Mospheirans."

"There is, honored Mother. Gin-nandi. She is a very nice person."

"With other qualities, one would imagine."

"Very many, honored Mother. She is excellent. I know her from the ship."

The servant arrived, with little sandwiches. And he wanted one, but only one. He drank his tea unsugared, now, and it was strong. His stomach was all in knots.

"Please take all you want. Maeta, take a tray to the suite, with little cakes. My son's aishid will surely be hungry."

"Nandi," the servant said, departing. Cajeiri took down his little quarter-sandwich in two bites, and washed them down.

"Are you sure you want no other?"

"No, honored Mother. Only to settle my stomach. I feel as if I have run for days."

"And left your associates up there. Are they well?"

"They are well. They and their parents."

His mother nodded. "I have you back. I have great reason to be proud of my son."

He stopped in mid-motion, setting the teacup down on the side table. He did set it down. The click was loud in the room. He had stopped breathing for a moment.

"I am glad to be back," he said, and added, thinking fast, as desperately fast as he had ever thought, trying to communicate with the kyo. "I really am."

In the next room, Seimei began to fret. It was, in a way, a rescue, because he had no idea how to proceed from where he was, and he was relieved when his mother got up, and gave him a chance to go and take off the coat and greet his little staff and fall straight into bed for days. He was tired. He was so very tired of a sudden.

But his mother put out her hand, expecting his, and he gave it.

"You have done very well," she said. "I have the report from nand' Bren and from your great-grandmother, and from Lord Geigi . . . well, they were your father's reports, but I shared them. Go. Rest. Your father has a thing in mind, but I told him he should give you a night to rest."

"What does he have in mind?"

"Nothing of concern at the moment," she said, and let go his hand. "Go."

He did go, out past his sister, in the arms of the nurse. Seimei was lying against the nurse's shoulder, but she looked at him— opened her gold eyes a slit and actually looked at him for the first time, a small frozen moment.

He said nothing. He thought, outside the door, that possibly he should have said her name. First meetings had omens.

But he was exhausted, and wanted to be in his own quarters, and his mother had said she was proud of him, had given him a holiday from his tutor, and said he should go rest.

That was the best encounter he ever remembered.

It was a quiet ride up the lift to the third floor. The dowager was momentarily pensive, and offered no advice or opinion, and Bren carefully confined his own thoughts, steering his mind onto simple things, things that had to be managed *before* he could leave—things as simple as wardrobe, as simple as a diplomatic pass, the procedures of which were ordinarily a phone call. Customs was usually inspection of fruits and vegetables— not people.

Clearing his aishid to step onto Mospheiran soil—had no precedent. Not to mention their bringing over their equipment, which was classified. It was not the matter of a simple phone call.

And he needed to move fast, before Mospheirans started getting anxious about their copy of the kyo document, which he would, under ordinary circumstances, have sent over by air, by courier.

The lift door opened. The dowager, with Cenedi and Nawari, exited first. He followed with his own bodyguard about him, into the third floor residency, a corridor as ornate as the one they had left. The dowager, Lord Tatiseigi, the paidhi-aiji—and Tabini himself—occupied this restricted section of the third floor, only four apartments, in the whole wing—only four, since the renovations. The other residencies, on second and fourth and off in other wings, were generally occupied seasonally, a prestigious nearness to the legislature, the audiences, the offices and conference rooms. Living in the residencies and not needing the hotels at the foot of the Bujavid's high hill, was a jealously maintained privilege of the oldest clans, the largest clans—and one human official who had started his career in the basement, sharing an across-the-hall bath with not-so-powerful functionaries and servants.

He'd made his trips back to Mospheira to consult, in those early days, in a little five-seat passenger compartment on one of the few planes that carried passengers at all, typically ahead of a load of seasonal fruit or fish on ice. He'd changed to Mospheiran dress, hired a taxi at the airport—stayed wherever he had to stay to do the business he had to do.

His passage to Mospheira was going to be a little different, this time.

"You will go tomorrow?" Ilisidi asked, as they were about to part company.

"As soon as possible," Bren said. "Tomorrow morning, if staff can manage it." Wardrobe was an issue. Transporting it fit to wear was another. He could not unpack a suitcase on Mospheira and turn out in anything like the state Tabini expected. Moving him in his official capacity needed wardrobe cases. Staff to deal with it. Security—his aishid was enough. But they had equipment. They had a whole other level of security concerns. He had used to stay with his mother—one suitcase. Her apartment. That was gone.

Toby wasn't. Toby was here—at Najida, at least, maybe hoping to hang on just a little longer, that they might manage a meeting . . .

Thump. The dowager's cane.

"You are staring at things absent, paidhi."

He focused on the dowager, shaken, still, by the prospect. By the things she knew, and didn't know, even yet.

"We do not release you to the Presidenta's service," Ilisidi said. "Be firm on that point."

"I shall be, aiji-ma."

"Well, well, take care." And with a sharp glance at his aishid: "Protect him."

On Mospheira.

That was going to be a first.

He went his way from the lift, she went hers, but he was not alone. He was never alone. Banichi and Jago were right beside him, Tano and Algini at his back. Comfortable. Familiar. Here on the mainland—he had them with him, near him, constantly.

On Mospheira—he'd taken his chances.

Now—there were risks he could no longer afford, for the sake of people who relied on him.

"Has our baggage arrived upstairs?" he asked, already estimating what it was going to take to turn everything around and go again.

"Yes," Jago said, and: "Everyone has arrived."

A few staff had just come in from Najida, resuming duty in the Bujavid apartment, which had been running on minimal staff in his absence. Everybody would be justified in assuming he would stay at least a day—maybe make a flying run out to Najida to spend a day with his brother, and then settle down to normalcy. All plans would operate on that assumption. Country clothes. Maybe one court appearance, considering all that had gone on. Time to sort everything into order again.

That was not going to happen. The treaty he had—best that *not* go over by courier, though the more delay there was about it reaching Mospheira—the more speculation might attend it.

Which might not be a bad thing—since he had the fairly simple facts of it in his possession. And if he delivered it personally, the document would get full attention, but his presence could also loom over any debate on the specifics.

His presence—in full force—would certainly get cameras—cameras when he wanted them, and when he didn't. Full attention of the Mospheiran news services.

He was an issue over there. He could tip the balance of public opinion in either direction. It *was* a chance to say to Mospheira—I *haven't* forgotten you.

Things are changing. Things not only *have* to change—things have *already* changed. But I haven't forgotten.

The door opened ahead of them: Narani had arrived back in his place, and resumed his duties as major domo, no question at all.

"Nandi!" Narani greeted him, and there was a mild, decorous uproar of welcome from inside. There was food, there was the whole staff back together again, the ones from the station and the ones in from Najida and the ones who had stayed to keep the apartment in good order during his weeks of absence. There was an astonishingly empty message bowl—likely his secretarial office had handled anything that had to be handled: rare the person who had missed the news that the paidhi-aiji was not on the planet.

And there was wine. He let himself take a glass, and, amid the celebration, took it to his office, and picked up the phone, and asked the Bujavid operator to put him through to Najida.

Right before dinner time. No way would the staff send off Toby and Barb without one festive supper—and no way would Toby leave the harbor until he knew that the shuttle was safely down and that there would be no need for him to serve as emergency contact between the President and Tabini.

Getting to Toby before he did leave dock was, however, imperative.

"Is nand' Toby still there?" was his very first question, impolitely abrupt, but there was a noisy party outside his office attempting to find him, and he needed to know that one fact from Najida staff before he took any congratulations from anybody on anything.

"Yes, nandi," was the answer. "I shall find Ramaso."

"Find Ramaso and find nand' Toby, nadi. I need to speak to him." He took a sip of wine. He needed to be in three places at once. Here, instructing his staff. At Najida, talking to the President on the most secure communications available. And on Mospheira, dealing with the situation and presenting that document before politics could muddy the waters.

A mild outburst from the hallway, followed by calls to hush, nand' Bren was on the phone to his brother.

"Bren?"

Toby himself was on the line. Out of breath.

"Toby. Good to talk to you."

"Good to hear from you. *Are you home?"*

"Home, and everything's in good shape." Never trust that a Bujavid phone was absolutely secure. Guild could get a message to Guild in security, and he could have gotten a message to Ramaso, but it was Toby he needed.

"Need you and that boat, brother. How's the bilge pump?"

"First rate," Toby said.

"Fuel full and stock the galley," he said. "Me and four. Meet me on the noon train. Bring the baggage truck."

"Got it." Toby couldn't possibly have a firm notion why he wanted a truck as well as the bus or why on earth he made a special note about the aishid that was always with him, but Toby had to be making guesses, and fairly accurate ones, that he was going out on the boat, that the probable interest in his boat had to do with the communications gear it carried, with accesses to President Shawn Tyers, and that if they were fueling full up, it was not a day trip or a fish dinner he had in mind. *"Everything's ready."*

"Put Ramaso on." He was sure his Najidi major d' wouldn't be far from the phone, and he was not surprised when Toby immediately handed the phone off.

"Nandi," Ramaso said. *"Are you well?"*

"I am exceeding well, Rama-ji. Nand' Toby will tell you everything he knows. I only wished to be sure you were in the current, and I thank you in advance. Nand' Toby will explain. Please congratulate and thank the staff."

"I shall, nandi. Welcome home!"

"Thank you, Rama-ji. I shall go now. They have given me wine and I believe there will be supper."

He hung up, with due courtesies. Toby was there. Toby would meet him. That was an immense relief. He wanted contact with his brother. He *needed* contact with his brother. He needed to be grounded—with what was Mospheiran—before he tried to slip back into that mindset.

Now he had to break it to Narani and Jeladi that he was leaving and this time might *not* take them with him—Narani was an elderly man. Along with Jeladi, he had already voyaged to Reunion and back and dealt with the kyo on two occasions. But a Mospheiran venture . . .

He rose and opened the door: Tano and Algini were out there, guarding his privacy even in the midst of festivities. From the sitting room, from the dining room, there was activity, laughter, even a waft of music.

"Call Narani and Jeladi," he told Tano and Algini, and retreated again into his office; and when Narani and Jeladi arrived: "Nadiin-ji, you have *earned* a homecoming and a rest. The aiji's orders send me and my aishid to Mospheira, for at least seven days of meetings and dealing with the Reunioner problem. We shall go by boat. I can take Koharu and Supani . . ." Those two, his valets, had served in Narani's place here, while Narani and Jeladi had gone with him aloft.

"One has always longed to see the island," Narani said.

"If you do wish it." It was a heavy load for the old man, seeing to court wardrobe with no assistance. But Narani's good sense and calm demeanor was an asset.

"We shall manage," Jeladi said. And Jeladi was a young man.

"If you wish, then," he said. "I know you are up to the duty. Koharu and Supani may continue to manage the household here. We do not know what we shall face in terms of services, but take a cleaning kit and a press: we shall manage the press in baggage, one benefit of the sea passage. Arrange the red car, if you can, or something apt, to arrive at Najida at noon. Advise the three I named. I fear staff will be up all night dealing with the cases we brought down. It all must go again."

"It will," Narani said.

"Yes," Jeladi said. "We shall manage it, nandi."

"Bring blankets, for the boat. And enjoy this evening. Please. Simply give orders. I plan to enjoy the party and get some sleep. Everyone else has at least just come back from holiday."

"Do not fret for staff," Narani said. "One recommends at least two glasses of wine, possibly three: medicinal, nandi. A good supper, and *sleep*, nandi, at an early hour. The rest will happen on schedule. A sea voyage. What could be better?"

Clearly a good many things could be better. They could not be facing Mospheiran politics, for one. But the old man bowed, Jeladi bowed, they left, and there was, truly, not much else for him to do. If there were a dire message in the letters in the hall, Koharu and Supani would have told him, since they had been handling his mail. If there were a problem in the household, they would have handled it or brought it to him, and he had heard of none.

The back end of the apartment, staff quarters, the laundry, the storage, would be a busy place for the next number of hours, and he was sorry for the short turnaround. But what needed to happen would happen, clothes would be cleaned and re-packed, right back into the cases, the cases that had just come up from the train station would be sent down again, and he, meanwhile would have dinner, enjoy the happiness of one homecoming, have that second glass of wine—and he and Jago would find a very pleasant finish to the evening, abed.

Guild reports? The Guild Observer who had come down with them, and the dowager's head of security, Cenedi—they would deal with such details. Even his aishid could relax for one evening.

Tomorrow would be mild chaos, but once they got there—they could get away fairly expeditiously. There would be some little to-do porting the heavy cases down the winding stone path to the dock, and getting everybody's baggage canvased and secure on the deck, but deck cargo was no novelty for Toby. They would manage—himself and Toby and Barb, Banichi, Jago, Tano, Algini, and now Narani and Jeladi. Seven plus Toby and Barb. *Brighter Days* could sleep that many, easily, even in bad weather.

Which he also needed to check. A storm front was just rolling through the midlands. That usually gave them five days' grace before another, in this season.

God, he was looking forward to the front end of this business—the familiar routines of a simple train trip, the chance to see his household at Najida—he should warn them he would not stay, that they would load on their cargo and go.

But Toby would do that. Trust Toby for it. Toby knew Ragi enough.

Thinking of language, however, and what he had to communicate, and to whom—that advised him there was some personal packing he had to see to before he had that second glass of wine.

The document, above all. Electronic tablets, station technology, with Ragi and the kyo language.

One was his. One he would give to the University.

He also had his own computer—the Mospheiran original, poor battered machine, had finally senesced beyond rescue. He had a new one of atevi manufacture, with a keyboard that could flick from one set of characters to the next and might someday, with a little effort, deal with kyo.

It was also half a kilo lighter, with four times the storage. The old one languished on fading batteries, viable, but nothing he was going to take to Mospheira—there was far too much on it that he had no desire to have meet electronic intrusions on the other side of the strait.

There were people he wanted to meet. Shawn was one. President of Mospheira and likely one of the best ones they'd ever had. Kate. Who'd worked with him building the space program. Tom. Ben.

Industry had wanted them—badly. He'd had that from Gin. Industry and commerce had wanted what they knew, wanted their management skills. Wanted their expertise, during the ship's absence, when they'd needed to communicate with the station, and with the mainland.

But the whole year before this one had been a crisis—one

that had set the Reunioners ashore on a space station that didn't want them, and one that had started with Tabini in exile and a puppet in charge, a front for some people who wanted to take the aishidi'tat back from every agreement with humans.

The people of the aishidi'tat had had a voice in that, once they knew Tabini was alive and the aiji-dowager and the heir were back on Earth. They'd fixed things, and there'd been a few adjustments since . . . principally uncovering how conspirators had managed to overthrow Tabini by force, and hang on to power for as long as they had. It had boiled down to one little old man in an antiquated Guild office, a man who'd moved Guild assignees like chess pieces, putting them where the conspirators wanted. He'd been Ajuri clan, related to the aiji-consort, Cajeiri's mother. Cajeiri's grandfather had gone down, assassinated, possibly while trying to warn his grandson . . . they might never know.

It had been a busy year and a half. But that evil time was behind them.

And to his mild surprise—the atevi-human entente hadn't fallen apart. The most dyed-in-the-wool conservatives in the aishidi'tat had worked with salt of the earth Mospheiran fishermen and coasters, smuggling, sharing information by sign language and a handful of words like *fight Murini* . . . had gotten information to orbit—passing notes the University could decipher and getting information up to Lord Geigi, who had kept the conspiracy discomfited, building a satellite network, informing the rebel underground, and in a few instances, getting communication equipment into rebel hands.

He didn't know what he'd find, in that regard, whether new people had made headway with the old attitudes in the University, or whether new people had had no such luck. One thing offered a little clue to that—that Gin Kroger, attempting to deal with the Reunioner resettlement situation, had found herself profoundly ignored. She'd been ordered home from the station, her visa expired and not renewed, and, damn, he wished Geigi had stepped in to grant her one from *his* side of the divided station. But Tillington. Tillington. Tillington . . . stationmaster on the human side . . . had simply declined to renew it, and ordered space for her on the next shuttle downbound.

An atevi shuttle, as happened. But that had been the transport available.

She'd gone up this time on an executive branch appointment— the approach of the kyo and Shawn's declaration of an emergency had enabled that move. And with a Presidential fiat in hand, she could issue her own visa.

He really wondered whether it was all Tillington—or just how Gin's dismissal had played out. He had his suspicions who *might* be agitated about Tillington's case, or who might find it convenient for their purposes.

Which was a very good reason to delay getting Tillington down to the world.

He had not wanted to involve himself in that.

But Tabini had picked up a chess piece and moved it. Onto the other side of the board.

2

Nand' Bren was *leaving* again. Nand' Bren had only just gotten home yesterday, and Veijico had heard it from Guild communications that nand' Bren was sending baggage *back* down to the train station and he would be taking the Red Train.

Today.

So maybe, Cajeiri thought, nand' Bren was going to the coast, because nand' Toby was there, or he had been, and probably still was, so it was *very* likely nand' Bren was going to see his brother and go fishing.

Well, no, probably not for more than a day, but if it was going to be a short run out and back, maybe *he* could go along, maybe his father would let him.

But then Veijico said, when the thought was only forming in his mind, that nand' Bren was taking the same big wardrobe cases he had brought down on the shuttle. Court wardrobe.

That made no sense at Najida, especially out on the boat. So *something* was going on.

"*Is* he going to Najida?" he asked Veijico, and Veijico said, "What they say the paidhi is doing and what he is really doing may not be the same thing. The cases are not what one would need at Najida."

Veijico's sources were not necessarily telling all the truth. But if nand' Bren was going anywhere *but* Najida, or even if he was, certainly Father would know about it.

And Father was in his upstairs office this morning.

So he went there, knocked softly and opened the door.

Father looked up from his desk and gave him an acknowledging nod.

He came the rest of the way in, bowed. "Nand' Bren seems to be going to Najida, honored Father."

"He is, but Najida is a waystop. He is going to Mospheira."

"To Mospheira!" That was a little scary. Nand' Bren had not gone to Mospheira, ever, that he could remember.

But nand' Bren was on good terms with the Presidenta, and there *was* the treaty he had brought down.

"Is he taking the treaty, honored Father?"

"An excellent guess. Yes, son of mine. He is. He will relay our good will to the Presidenta, and he will prepare the way for your young associates to come down, and do all that needs to be done to make a safe place for the rest."

That was very good news, though far more remote than the trip to Najida he had hoped for. He regretted not going. But it sounded like more than a day or two. It sounded like something that could take a long time. He hoped not. He truly hoped not.

"One thought, if he were going to Mospheira, he would fly there, from here."

A nod from his father. "Indeed. But nand' Toby and he have a little to discuss. He will wish to know how Mospheira is, what currents run there. They will make a fairly leisurely crossing, and Port Jackson affords an easy access, so he says."

"Will it be long?"

"A number of days, one would think. And he wishes to give this return to Mospheira a little *leisurely*, but respectful approach, with the treaty, with the meetings to come. If he flew, it would all be in great haste, with high security, with an atmosphere of modern haste and perhaps a sense of pressure. I think nand' Bren knows exactly what he is doing, and the tone he sets. Do you not?"

Toby's boat pulling into Port Jackson, just like coming in at Najida—was a great deal different than coming in at the airport—

Cajeiri had actually set foot on Mospheira, very briefly, when he and mani and nand' Bren had come back from space, and that had been hurry and worry all the way to the harbor, where, among a forest of masts of little boats, they had just gotten on nand' Toby's boat and been away and safe—at least for a while. The airport was a confused memory, haste, and worry—a great deal of worry about security.

He understood, maybe better than his father, why nand' Bren had wanted to come in on nand' Toby's boat—for quiet, for security, because there would be no need to watch his back for however long it took. The kyo were going away. And everything was safe. But he well understood why nand' Bren chose what he did, just to have a few days of rest.

"I think so," he said to his father. "One only wishes one were going along. Except not to Mospheira. I would not like to be there."

His father gazed at him a moment in a way that said he had bad news. "There *is* an obligation, son of mine, regarding where you have been and things you have seen. Your great-grandmother will host a dinner, to which she will invite certain persons, like your great-uncle, who will listen to her. So it falls on us to host one for those who will not."

That required a little second thought. A dinner party. One of those that did *not* include mani, and probably included absolutely nobody he wanted to deal with.

"So I should be there," he said.

"You are the one who can explain these things," his father said. "Some of these people are skeptical that things in the heavens even exist in the way we say. But you have seen these strangers, and you have talked to them."

"I have," he said unhappily. "When?"

"The day after tomorrow. Giving certain of these people time to come in by train. You are tired, you have more than merited some days of rest, but the opportunity to meet these people and bend their opinions in a good direction—"

"Is important," he finished for his father, with a deep sigh. Completing his father's sentence was impertinent, and mani would never tolerate it. So his father would not, under ordinary circumstances, but he had just lost an imagined chance to go to Najida, and now discovered he had a dinner party with people he wished did not exist. It was not going to be a good evening, and his father was trying to make him happy in the situation.

"Son of mine, . . ."

"I shall do it," he said. His father was always telling him being aiji often consisted in doing things one had far rather not be doing, and he only wished *he* could take a slow boat trip toward *this* obligation. "I shall, honored Father. May my aishid see the guest list?"

"Your aishid. Do you expect daggers?"

"I wish to learn what I can, honored Father, about their opinions. And if senior Guild will *talk* to them, I would like to know these people."

"We *are* getting clever."

"I know *you* will know. *Your* bodyguard reports to you. So should not I ask?"

"Yes," his father said. "Yes, you should. Well asked. But these are not people easily convinced of anything. Do not press them too hard with reason. Reason is not among their motives."

He thought about that, and thought it did explain several disagreeable people he knew, none of whom would be at mani's table.

"Are the dinners the same night?" he asked, hoping to the contrary.

"Yes. They are deliberately opposed. Strategically opposed. *We* get the honor. *Our* invitation is the higher one. But your great-grandmother's guests are not the sort to think they are second in our esteem."

Politics, politics. He restrained a second sigh, but he understood what was going on, which was better than he had been two years ago.

"One understands," he said. "I *do* understand, honored Father. I shall do my best."

"Yes," his father said, not giving him *good lad* or anything patronizing. Just *yes.* Which was some sort of a reward.

So he missed Najida. He missed nand' Toby and Barb-daja. And he missed mani's party with Uncle Tatiseigi, and got—

Oh, he imagined the head of the list of lords and ladies. Darbin. He fairly well imagined it.

But Father *had* given him respect. That was something.

And he would find out the names and find out things about them, what they deemed important and what they disparaged, and he might find a way to persuade them that there was *not* a massive conspiracy of deception in the heavens, and that the ship was not secretly running everything and that Lord Geigi was honest and loyal, and had been on his way to setting his father back in power even *before* he and mani and nand' Bren had come back from a place some of these folk believed had never existed.

These people were not responsible for overthrowing his father in Murini's conspiracy, but they had not been of great help restoring the government either. And he did not know why his father even cared about these people.

That was the question he wished he had asked when he took his leave and walked back toward his suite. Somewhere there was a reason, and it might just be keeping these people as quiet as possible, or it might be there was something his father wanted to do that was so narrow a vote these people mattered.

There was nothing his father *currently* wanted to do that he knew about. But there could be.

Maybe it *was* to do with the Reunioners, and his guests, and Father's willingness to land cargoes on the mainland, and to have Reunioner passengers landing on atevi shuttles. That could well stir up some legislators, but these people were going to be stirred up no matter what.

Was it just that the aishidi'tat had taken so many heavy

blows that they had to pay attention to these districts—because certainly there was going to be some disturbance.

He understood some things he had not understood two and three years ago, but there were other things just dark to him.

Boji, in his cage, was quite sure anyone who left the apartment was coming back with eggs for him. Cajeiri opened the door to his suite, and Boji immediately set up one of those fusses, leaping about and rattling his big cage, spilling some of his water dish.

"Hush!" he said, thumping on the cage wall. "Boji! Behave! Did you think I had gone away for good? Come here."

Boji screeched, the sort of sound that could wake his sister and make itself heard in Father's office.

"Hush! Scoundrel! You were getting better before I left!"

Liedi came in from the back rooms with an egg—probably, he said to himself, Boji had gotten eggs every time he had pitched a fit all the time they had been gone, since his orders had been to keep Boji quiet and not let him wake Seimei.

He had remarked last night that Boji was quite happily plump—*he* had thought it lack of exercise.

Boji took his egg, pierced it, began quite happily sucking on it.

"I think when he does this," he said, "we are going to have to find another answer."

"We have tried, nandi," Liedi said.

He contemplated the little thief, thinking how Boji had been his idea, a very inconvenient idea, that his parents had tolerated, and that had more than once complicated things, and been, over all, a comfort to his loneliness, but a trial to the household.

Then his guests had come down to the world, and with prospect of having them resident on Mospheira—he was not as lonely as he had been.

So did he feel less attachment to Boji?

Boji had man'chi of a sort, to him, and depended on him, and he could not just send Boji off to some forest to try to live—Boji probably had no idea how to get an egg that did not come from a kitchen, so he could not even live as tame parid'ji had lived for thousands of years, finding nests for their masters, and getting an egg for a reward.

He knew now his notion of having Boji sit on his shoulder would never work. It was not the sort of adornment one had, with court clothes. And Boji loose in an apartment was a disaster.

Liedi was just looking at him, having offered his one excuse for an inexcusable creature.

"I think he has become a problem in the household," he said. "You have far more important things to do than seeing to this rascal. Are you attached to him?"

"We do not mind," Liedi said, who regrettably had several scars from Boji's teeth, and whose traveling about with him had been in the baggage car, seeing that Boji did not panic. Liedi and Eisi both had been more than understanding.

"He is not a toy and I am not a child, not so much, any longer. He deserves better than a cage he cannot climb in and you deserve better than riding in the baggage car with a spoiled parid'ja. I wish I might find a place for him, but he is too bright for his own good and too stupid to find eggs in the wild. Ask about, Liedi-ji. Talk to Eisi. See if anywhere in the Bujavid anyone has an answer for him. I should miss him, but I should not like to see him getting fat and miserable in a cage without enough room for him."

"Nandi." Liedi gave a little bow. "One will ask."

"I am amenable to keeping him," he said, "if only there were a place. But he needs trees, and he needs eggs. He is a thief. And he bites."

"We shall make every effort," Liedi said, without, one thought, too much regret in the proposition.

Boji had finished his egg, and dropped the shells to the bottom of the cage, where they would have to be collected, to another fuss as the tray was pulled. He did make a mess. He was a problem.

He had very intelligent eyes, and he looked back like a person. He caught moods, and hung on the side of his cage, staring back very solemnly.

"I think you would like to be free," he said—silly thing, to be talking to a creature. But he did, sometimes. He had, on lonely occasions. "But I think you would also like to be safe, and fed."

Nothing but a solemn stare.

"I took responsibility for you, and I have no idea why, now, I should send you away. But I should. I think I should."

Boji chittered at him, still with that quizzical stare.

"No, I have not another egg. Fat creature. You need trees. Tall ones."

He had no idea why he had suddenly made that change of mind—except Boji was so silly a creature, and so easily hurt.

He had been lonely, he had found associates on the ship, he had established ties to them and he wanted them back. He had not, when he had met them, been mature enough to really see how complicated it was. He had not cared about consequences. He had only just learned about consequences, in the real sense—he'd only begun to understand how far they could reach, and how long they could go on . . . much, much more complicated than he had thought, much more complicated than he had known. He had filled the empty spot with his aishid, with Boji, with his patient servants. And he was not alone, but he was still lonely. His aishid and his servants took care of him—and he took care of Boji, some of the time—being a child. Being foolish, and not understanding really *how* to take care of Boji.

He'd been a child when he'd left Earth for the first time. Travel to another sun? Of course. The ship did that. Talk to an alien species? Oh, of course. He could figure it out. Associate with humans? That could not be different than dealing with nand' Bren. Could it?

Young, he said to himself. Young. Foolish.

He'd come back from *this* trip with a sense of things much, much wider than he had realized. So many things looked scarily different now. They had no idea when the kyo might come back, and with what changes of their own. They had no idea what was out there around other stars. He had no idea how Reunioners would mix with Mospheirans, but in their situation, they had to. He had no idea how the whole world would get along in years to come. Or what would happen when they did build an atevi starship, and where they would go and what they would do.

Most of all he had no idea what would happen to Irene and Gene, Artur and Bjorn.

He had left them in a better situation, this visit. At least they would be coming down to the world to live. His human associates could fend for themselves on Mospheira. And would. He knew that Mospheira could be a scary place, a place as dangerous as the Marid on occasion: he knew he had singled them out by his association with them, and they would have no bodyguard with them. But that was what nand' Bren was trying to set up, their coming down to Earth, among other things. And definitely—their safety.

They would be living so close, and always out of reach. They would grow up human. That was right. That was proper. That was what would satisfy them. They would run risks he could not predict. And that was where they could be human.

Boji was no different in essence than any parid'ja in the wild, but he had had a young silly boy try to make him a sort of safe associate, which had served the boy for a while, but now the boy had grown past reaching out, and begun to think how to *protect* his associates, when there was no way to do that.

He had caged Boji. He kept him in, he kept him safe. But it was such a small cage. And Boji needed to be what he was, too.

He had dreamed about nand' Bren on his boat last night. He had almost felt the sea under him. It was a favorite dream, being on the boat.

But he had an uneasy feeling, a question where the boat was going, and what nand' Bren was going to do, and what it would mean to his associates and all the world—about which he could do very, very little at the moment—

Except sit at table with people who hated the very idea of association with outsiders, and smile, and try to make them understand something about the universe.

He sat down and he thought about it—how he could talk to these people *he* had to deal with and get them to see what he had seen, and to understand that the kyo were indeed a danger, but also that they could be allies, too.

He called Antaro in, of his aishid.

"My father is giving a dinner tomorrow night and wants me to attend. My father says we may see the guest list. Ask particulars on all the people." That was how mani would say it: *particulars* covered everything they possibly could get. "And ask to borrow the clan book."

"Yes," Antaro said, and immediately left.

When Antaro came back, this time with her brother Jegari, she had a sheet of paper, the requested list. He took it, he read it, and he knew some of them by reputation, and yes, Darbin, the one he detested, was on the list. He took the sheet and he went to his office, where he had a wall map, with pins in it to denote clans and territories where he had associates.

Could he put a pin on the very edge, for a ship traveling outbound from the solar system?

Or several more, along the top, for people up on the station, pins for his associates and their parents?

In not so very long, he *would* have a place on the map to put them, pins on Mospheira, on solid ground, where horizons bent around the world—instead of up.

Unfortunately, he had no pins of help in the dinner situation, not even acquaintances in the regions these people ruled. The clans on the guest list were scattered mostly toward the mountains, the continental divide, and to the northwest, where he had no pins.

Well, except Lucasi and Veijico, whose clan was a little more to the north. He actually had one lonely pin up there—but Lucasi and Veijico did not maintain close ties with their own clan, and had no inclination to do so.

They were all little clans, these troublesome dinner guests, but together they represented a large area of the mountain region, and with their votes all together, they could pad out the conservative vote if it was close, tipping the balance against a bill. They were some of them clans with no real master clan, just a local association of families tucked in little valleys. Such areas had legislators who, when they did come to Shejidan, would usually just stand up and cast a no vote on just about everything unless somebody traded them something for it. There was flooding in the west? They thought the west should pay for it, when, of course, the west could not pay for it, because their houses were flooded. That was the reason there was an aishidi'tat, so that they all could pay a little and help people when they needed it. Well, that, and being sure the guilds did what they should, and that districts were fair to each other.

But these sixteen almost-clans and two real ones from the mountain districts were not interested in anything outside their own areas and kinships—except to vote against it.

They were also all from the old traditional areas. So was mani, but these people generally were not fond of mani, because along with the old traditions, there were old feuds, and one of those feuds involved the dividing line between the west and the east, right up at the top of those mountains. These people absolutely believed in the numbers and in omens. They practiced kabiu in everything. And one had to use proper language and keep everything fortunate, with no missteps. These clans were not happy with having the space station, but they certainly did not like sharing it with humans now that they had it. They wanted their own starship, because humans had one, but they would not want to pay for it.

And they would not at all approve of nand' Bren, and certainly would not approve of his own young associates, so he ought not to mention them, either, or get into anything that he wished they *would* understand. No. They had rather carry on an argument with mani, because Easterners were wicked.

It was a big map, covering a whole section of the office wall. It had always been one of his favorite things. He had been so proud to put pins on it. But they had gotten harder to acquire, and they had proven all too easy to lose.

When he had first come back to Shejidan from space, when Father had retaken the government, his map had once had a pin for practically everyone he had ever dealt with, and the north had held a cluster of them, a place where he could claim his mother's Ajuri clan and Great-uncle's Atageini clan and all their subclans and townships, right along with his father's Taibeni. Now all he had was the Atageini association and the Taibeni, who had stopped being at war with each other for his sake—a good thing.

But because of a great-uncle of his, Shishogi, who had been in the Assassins' Guild and in charge of Assignments, he had had to pull out every pin up there *but* the Taibeni and the Atageini, and now there were little pits where Ajuri and its subclans had been, a gap between Atageini, where Great-uncle Tatiseigi was lord, and his several pins in Dur, over on the coast.

Grandfather, mother's father, lord of Ajuri, had *tried* to break out of that situation—or at least he hoped that Grandfather had been on his way to contact Great-uncle Tatiseigi when he had been assassinated. And he was relatively sure that it was Shishogi who had done in Grandfather, and not his mother, his father, or Great-uncle Tatiseigi.

Shishogi was dead now. Mani and nand' Bren had taken *him*

down. But it was just a mess up there, and Ajuri still had no lord until Ajuri came up with a candidate and actually not until Father approved it. He had Great-aunt Geidaro left in Ajuri. He had met her. And second-cousin Meishi. But Geidaro was no one he would trust, and Meishi was, well, she was nice enough, even kind, but she was not the sort to hold a pin. As an ally— she was safe in Ajuri only because she was harmless.

It was just a mess up there . . . with another great gap in his pins to the east of Atageini, but that area of the map was not scarred with pinholes. He had never had associates in that region—Kadagidi and all its subclans.

Dinner tomorrow night he was sure would not add any pins—no associations among those people in the mountain districts. He certainly had pins on the *other* side of the mountains, in the East, where mani had her estate, and several more besides, but the people coming to dinner tonight would think *mani* was a particular problem, because she was an Easterner, from the *other* side of the mountains. And *Easterners* were foreigners.

Father wanted him to be there, he suspected, because *he* was just back from the space station and the meeting with the kyo and all that strangeness was in the news and upsetting to these people—who sometimes sold their votes, and who were certainly going to be flattered by an invitation and a private hearing.

He had no idea what sort of thing was up for a narrow vote. He had not even thought to ask Father why—but on another level, it hardly mattered. Father asked. He had to do it, and do it with good grace.

No pins tomorrow night. Not at all likely.

The Red Train pulled up to the Najida station, with slow steamy puffs that eased down to one long sigh. It had been a quiet trip, nothing so exciting as the shuttle ride and landing. There had been work to do. There had been the rare chance of just putting one's feet up and relaxing as the scenery flowed past.

And there would be no more work to do here. Staff would want a celebration, and they were due it. So, for that matter, was his brother and Barb due a little celebration of their own, sheer relief, after what could have become a disaster in the heavens.

Banichi and the rest were on their feet. Guild was talking to train crew, and to the several Guild who would exit the train to the platform, meet whoever was there to meet them, ascertain that everything was in order, and supervise the offloading of the baggage.

One didn't expect trouble—one was gratified to see, almost immediately, Banichi's signal that they might disembark. Bren stood up, straightened his coat—Tano took up his personal case, which held his computer, the tablets, the personal items he might want before baggage could be unpacked; and the heavier small case which had two changes of clothes, a pair of deck shoes, and, which he had not taken aboard the station, his small pistol, Guild issue. He had a pocket com. He was never supposed to be separate from his bodyguard, or vice versa, and he was not supposed to need one—Guild forbade it, for security reasons. But he did carry one in recent years. There was also, in the wardrobe, several bulletproof vests, in a variety of brocades. That was his bodyguards' insistence, and he'd agreed.

But not for the Najida train station, which sat as a lonely waystation on a gravel road, on a ridge between Taisigi hunting lands and his own district of Najida.

Banichi and Jago opened the door, Tano and Algini stood behind them, and as they walked out there was far and away more noise than he expected at the lonely train station. A lot of voices. All shouting, and shouting as he walked out, and there was the wooden platform full of people—his people. People so many they more than filled the platform and stood on the ground, and Toby and Barb were there, and Ramaso, and the estate staff, dayshift and night, and the Edi grandmother, and her council, Edi folk, the elders, and standing round about, mingled with Najida village folk. The estate bus was there, tall and glossy red and black, as modern as buses came; there was the baggage truck, and indeed, his luggage cases were coming out of the baggage car, with Guild help, and with staff help, for this very short train—but there were market trucks, there was the village fire engine—God only knew how so very many people had gotten to this remote train station, or how they proposed to get back, but here they were.

He bowed. He gave a profound, lengthy bow, and the people fell silent and bowed. He looked up and the solemnity remained, all around him.

He touched his heart. "One is profoundly affected, nadiin-ji. This is my *home.* This, above all other places, has become my home. Thank you. Thank you all." Toby and Barb were in front of him. The human in him had planned, in the privacy of the bus, to give them both a hug. That was *not* going to happen. His aishid would see strangeness enough on Mospheira, and the villagers would be profoundly distressed. So he gave a second shorter bow.

"Brother. Barb. Long road to get here. Let's get to the bus, and give these people a head start getting home."

"Good to see you," Toby said. "So good." Toby didn't touch him. Toby knew better. Barb looked agitated, but happy.

"Bus," Bren said, and switched to Ragi. "Jago-ji. As *soon* as we offload at the house, send the bus and trucks back for whatever people are walking."

"Yes," Jago said. But never left his side, even so, on a relatively smooth progress to the edge of the platform and the steps down to the bus. Narani and Jeladi tried to pitch in to carry baggage, but Ramaso, Narani's second cousin twice removed, and quite likely dying for a direct account, would not have them carry even their own bags, not a one, no.

They waited there, Bren and Toby and Barb, an impromptu reception line as Ramaso marshaled Najida staff aboard as rapidly as they could move, familiar faces, known names, a second family, hurrying by with great excitement and shy salutations, and one somehow suspected they were not going to escape at least a standing buffet back at the house while the baggage loaded.

"Boat's ready," Toby said in Mosphei'. "Weather's clear. Wind out of the southwest. All we have to do is load. I took her out last night for a check. Did you know the navy moved in this morning?"

"Navy?"

"Two," Toby said as the bus started up. "One gunboat, one little pursuit running with it. I thought it might not be unrelated."

Bren drew in a slow breath. "Tabini's orders. I'd hoped to move this quiet." He said this, on a bus so crowded with staff they were standing in the back of the aisle. Not mentioning the trucks. "I think I failed to realize the degree of attention."

"Everybody was scared, and now they're just relieved," Barb said. "We're so glad."

"*I'm* glad," he said.

"You're taking that treaty over," Toby said.

"Exactly." The rest of it—he couldn't say, even among these nearest and dearest. Some were *too* innocent, and trouble didn't deserve advance notice. "The navy isn't taking any chances with us springing a leak midway. But I'll be calling the President, pretty soon after we leave dock—to let him know."

On Toby's very high-end communications gear, that was, on a system which Shawn's office had set up, and maintained, and which didn't have the Messengers' Guild's fingers on it—or private interests tapped into various offices on the island. Things had improved since the upheavals in the last year or so, but security of messages was still not optimum—and depend on it: upheaval in the heavens was going to have certain ears listening intently.

Toby and Barb both could guess that. They asked no more

questions, and the bus rolled briskly on the gravel road, headed down the long rise, now, toward the coast, toward Najida.

Cajeiri passed the word to Eisi and Liedi about the dinner, too, at the next opportunity, with specific urging. His closet was still uncommonly empty, while all those massive cases they had flown up to the station and back again were probably being gone over in due course, with no sense of emergency— and they might all be hanging together in some recess known to the staff. But they were not hanging in his closet, which he was quite sure was because nobody on staff was hurrying on his account. *His* domestic staff was only his two valets, who were below Father's staff and below Mother's, even if *they* did not have most everything they owned needing cleaning.

"Court best," he said. "In the cases I brought back. I shall need it tomorrow night, but definitely nothing better than my father's and mother's."

"Yes," his valets said, duly authorized to raise a protest, and went off to the depths of the suite, to the routes staff of whatever level used to make things happen.

Staffs worked out such details among themselves. Eisi and Liedi would pass the word to the major d', someone would talk to someone, and his closets would have clothes again.

Domestic details. The world could rock on its hinges, but the cleaning staff would follow its routines and priorities, of which he was still a small one.

He would *so* much rather run off with nand' Bren, have stowed away on the boat and not come out until morning, when they would have no choice but take him with them.

But that was only imagining. When he was younger, he might actually have done it. He *would* have done it. But now—

Being a whole year older now, and a lot wiser, he simply opened the book Antaro had brought along with the guest list, the history of all the clans and subclans in the aishidi'tat, so he could be prepared, at least, to know these guests better than they knew him.

He was *not* going to be what they expected. He was going to be better.

The house sat overlooking Najida bay, rustic stone, with its new addition's roof all tiled—Bren had to express delight and surprise at that: and it was real delight and surprise. Staff had put great energy into finishing it while he had been gone. A further surprise, Ramaso proudly informed him: Najida had its new windows in, the beautiful stained glass work that was the aiji-dowager's special gift—one at the end of the entry hall, the old main hall, and the other at the end of the dining room in the new wing. And of course one had to go inside, see it properly.

"I am amazed, Rama-ji," Bren said, hearing about the windows, in the little interval as the baggage was set down. "A moment to set the loading underway, but we are not that rushed. I would wish very much to see them before we go."

"We would be delighted, nandi," Ramaso said. "And by no means should you or your staff deal with the crates: we shall deal with everything."

"Then I have every confidence."

The gate of the truck banged down on the cobbles. Ramaso's aide and Banichi both moved to give orders for the unloading of the baggage truck and for the transport of the wardrobe cases— the correct end up, look for the emblem!

The massive cases had survived space flight. They would certainly survive Najida's careful handling.

His own precious hand baggage was accounted for in Tano's possession, and nothing would separate Tano from that charge. Jago had the document case that contained the treaty, and would not relinquish it.

"Go," Toby said with a wave of his hand. "We've seen the windows, and Ramaso should go with you. We'll get the crates down to the boat. We'll all manage out here. Go. Ramaso has been burning to show you."

So he himself had no burden at all, and they all, including Banichi, walked with Ramaso through the restored doors and down the rustic hall, which looked again as it should look, with stained glass at the end, lit by daylight outside and casting colored beams into the hall. There were, on either side, two vertical companion panels, each with a tall oval inset, to afford a clear view of the bay—it was a new and welcome touch.

"Excellent, Rama-ji!" he said, and let Ramaso and a small number of excited house staff escort them to a door which had used to lead to the garage and storage, but which now had a wood-paneled arch, and led to a hall with more rooms, and a stairway. And at the end, a grand entry to the dining room framed the second of the new windows, a pattern in reds, to catch, were it the hour, the setting sun, with the same sort of side insets.

That sight came with the waft of food from this new dining hall. It was an ambush, a delightfully prepared one, and they would not escape unfed: Najidi dishes in a hall that still smelled faintly of new varnish—home made new, and no longer bearing the scars it had taken in the upheaval of last year.

"We have set up tables in the village," Ramaso said, "and there will be visitors to the village from Kajiminda." That was Lord Geigi's estate, neighboring theirs, and served by folk with ties both to Najida village and to the new Edi establishment on the wooded promontory. "All the houses are bringing food, like spring festival."

It amazed him, and made him wonder whether anyone in the village had gotten any sleep last night. His phone call and a word from Toby had launched it. There was *very* likely a picnic box in the yacht's galley at this very moment, a supply which would carry them a distance out to sea and possibly all the way to Port Jackson.

3

There was a crowd at the pier as well, when, under a warm sun, well-fed, they headed down. Bren's own *Jaishan* rode at anchor, in from her current job ferrying construction materials to Kajiminda Peninsula, in service to the locals, and with her brightwork shrouded in canvas—wearing her work-clothes, as it were. Toby's *Brighter Days* had the only proper mooring spot, and now had a canvassed object lashed to her deck, ahead of the mast. Toby and Barb quietly inspected that with a walkaround, and then came back to the console, ready to go.

"Thank you!" Bren called out to the gathering of staff and bystanders, waved to them as Toby fired up the engines and called for the mooring lines to come in. There was no shortage of hands to do that service, and Tano and Barb hauled up the lines and coiled them as *Brighter Days* began to move.

The good wishes ashore faded under the sound of the engines as they drew away from land. It was more convenient to rely on the motor until they passed the point and reached the wider bay. Then the sail rose and the boom swung over and *Brighter Days* steadied down at a slight lean.

Barb took Toby's place at the wheel, then. Bren stood at the rail, waiting, with bodyguard around him and Narani and Jeladi waiting to be instructed.

"Rani-ji," he said to Narani. "You are officially on holiday until we reach port. I have my warm coat in hand luggage, and absolutely no need else. I do not yet know our sleeping arrange-

ments, but there will be a cabin, rely on it, and I am equally
sure our larder is full of small surprises from Najida's kitchen.
Go be at leisure, both of you."

He needed to talk to Toby, point of fact. He needed to have a
long, serious conversation with Toby.

But ahead of that, ahead of everything:

"Toby. Need you to contact the President. Tell him I'm coming in at Port Jackson. Which I trust we are."

"Wherever you need me to go," Toby said. They reached one
of those little quirks of wind in the bay, and the sail thumped
and filled again overhead, the boat steady under Barb's hand.

"I'm coming as Tabini's representative. Court dress. All of it.
Tabini's orders. That's likely going to upset some people."

"There'll be a fuss about it. There's a fuss about everything.
Why should this be the exception?"

"That's kind. But I've reached a point it doesn't matter if I
make certain people unhappy. I'm not representing them. *You*
might, someday."

"God, no."

"Things are going to change for me. I'm over here to make
that clear, and to settle some issues. First thing—we've got a
crisis situation on the station, not active at the moment: Gin's
using up supplies hand over fist, and that can't go on: the Reunioners need to come down. There's no Maudit colony in the
works. That was never practical and everybody up there knew
it, even if the world didn't. Now five thousand people have got
to go someplace, and they've got to *start* coming here in the
next couple of weeks."

"Weeks. Good God, Bren, is it that critical?"

"It's critical not to lose the momentum. We can do it now.
We can't stall out. Not significant numbers at first, maybe not
for most of the year, but they have to start, and we'll start with
the three kids and their families. That's one thing. We also have
a prosecution on our hands. Or Gin does. The treaty that got
Mospheira into space in the first place says clearly the popula-

tion up there has to be equal, atevi to human. Tabini's put up with a situation that couldn't be helped; but we now know the human-side stationmaster made a thorough hash of things, and Gin's launched a probe of misconduct that may go under corporate doors and involve more than the stationmaster's office. Tabini's official reaction to that situation is one reason he's sending me as he is—which is, let me say, a very serious move on his part, when the paidhi goes out 'caisi linieiti,' with instructions. That means I go in with a message—not a bad message, not a threatening message, but a serious one, meaning the aiji is pressing for action."

Toby gazed at him soberly. "So what *is* the opinion of the aiji?"

"That we have a very narrow window to do things right, as regards the Reunioners, and he wants some changes. I know that my appearance here as an atevi official may stir up some resistance, but I'm to make it very clear that Tabini's patience with human politics, going back to the mess that sent us to Reunion in the first place, is finite, and that something sensible has to be done, and quickly, without the Mospheiran legislature tying things up in committee. That's the point. I know Shawn actually wants what Tabini-aiji wants. The world has just had a major scare because of human actions. We've managed to send the kyo away believing we have gotten our house in order—which makes it a very good time actually to *set* our collective house in order, and to cash in on whatever credit we all have gathered from the kyo treaty. I have to apologize—to you and Barb both—for whatever heat may spill over to you from the situation. And I hope—sincerely—that you'll take it seriously and protect yourselves. If it gets hot, say anything that you need to say to distance yourselves—"

"No way in hell."

"Listen to me. You know the people on the opposition. Some of them have a political point to make. That's one thing. But the issue attracts unstable people, and it just takes one. We can put the kids in a security bubble. You're out there coming and going—"

"Bren, Bren, the isolationists are nothing. Bigger threats than that have been after us. We dodge."

"Take it seriously. Please. Unofficially, I'm offering you harborage at Najida any time you need it, as long as you need it. Lord Geigi would offer you the same over at Kajiminda. We could keep trading you back and forth, every forty-nine days, and stay within the regulations. I don't think Tabini-aiji would officially notice. And if I have to ask permanent asylum—I think I can get it. Not for the Reunioners. But for you and Barb."

"You're serious."

"I'm serious. I'm absolutely serious. Our handful of home-grown problems haven't met the ones who may have survived Reunion, and we don't know how or when their issues may manifest. That's one thing. I'm also worried about the consequences when the criminal investigation up on station begins to reach under certain corporate and personal doors down here. On the good side of the ledger, I know for damned certain that Gin Kroger won't bend to threats up there, and Lord Geigi will certainly take his stand for what Tabini asks—not to mention the ship-captains, who know where *their* critical supply comes from. So no, I have no great fear for the station under current management, and Shawn's capable of weathering the political storm down here. But I can't be blind to the exposure you have. I came this route for several reasons, one of which is that it solves logistics and keeps us away from any official fuss with airport officials, police, and, well, you can imagine my aishid and the customs inspectors. But the other reason is seeing you. And Barb. And a thing—I'm asking myself if I want to tell you. And I think I do. But I'm not sure I want to tell Shawn, I'm warning you."

"You're being mysterious. Is it something with Tabini? Or something that happened up there?"

"Up there," he said. "My mind is stuck somewhere between

the kyo—and atevi—and ship-folk and stationers. I need this passage. I need to take a few slow breaths and reconnect with Mospheira. I need to speak Mosphei', and hear the accent."

"We don't have an accent," Toby said. Old joke. Toby was trying to drag him back to sense. Which was what Toby could do.

"Unfair to ask you," he said to Toby. "Unfair to involve you."

"Don't even consider it. You know damned well I'll involve myself."

And Barb? he asked himself. And Barb?

Barb hadn't understood *him* when they'd been lovers, hadn't understood the involvement in politics, hadn't wanted to understand. Now she was his brother's partner, face going weathered with the sun and the wind, those kind of lines that came with the sea and constant travel. There was no nightlife, there were no glittering parties, there was not even a house or an apartment— just Toby, and *Brighter Days,* and the attachment that never had quite gone away, but had never been unfaithful to his brother, either, never said no to a risk or a crisis—just somehow stood her ground, in her own way, staunchly attached to Toby, who was the soul of calm, not a shred of glitter about him.

Separate them? No. He couldn't. What he did to Toby, he did to Barb. He couldn't claim otherwise. And he was sorry, at least as sorry as he needed to be.

"I'll warn you, if I do tell you—it *is* something you can't tell Barb."

And what did Toby do to that? He gave a silent little laugh. "There's a raft of those. Barb says, you fix it. That's what she'd say, if I offered to tell her. You fix it. No, she knows. There are things I do for Shawn, for the government—I had that discussion with her back when we began to take our boat on little trips to the mainland, back when you were off at Reunion. I'd say, Barb, this is what we've got to do, and she'd say, Are they going to shoot at us on this one?"

"God."

"They did, now and again. There was a time we had a pursuit

on our tail and she was at the helm. Someday I'll tell you that one. But tell me your secret, brother. And I'll keep it even from the President. If it's the sort of thing you lose sleep over, she'd hit me if I told her."

He let go a long, slow breath. "I met the kyo's enemy. They're human."

Toby frowned. "From where, for God's sake?"

"From the other side of kyo territory. They're original human—they're what *Phoenix* went out to find. *That's* why the kyo hit Reunion. *Phoenix* went nosing into kyo territory from that station, and the kyo mistook them and their origin as their enemy running around their flank. Likely they had Alpha under observation, too. I don't even want to think how close we may have come here, on this world, to seeing a kyo strike."

Toby considered that in a long moment of silence. "What's in the treaty?"

"A firm promise to keep out of each other's territories. They won't come here until their war is over. And we won't go there. The ship-folk have agreed. They're relieved to have an answer. And not to have to take on the kyo bare-handed."

"And you *got* this."

"I got the treaty. We won't go that direction. The kyo won't let those humans come here. And humans on our side aren't to know what's on the other side. The man I met—one man—" Deep breath. "I told the kyo not to let him go. Not to let him tell the humans beyond their territory that we're here. I took that on myself, my decision, solo, on their ship. I didn't like my choices. But I taught him the basics—how to talk to them. I gave him that. And the kyo have every interest in keeping their agreement with me—not to release him. The last thing *they* want is humans trying to make contact with each other in kyo space."

"God."

Bren gave a shrug. He wasn't sure the burden was lighter, having put it onto Toby's shoulders. But the world seemed a little saner, given Toby's predictable reactions—entirely predictable. Like the next question.

"So are you going to tell Shawn?"

"Tabini knows. The dowager knows. And Jase knows. I *think* he may have told the other three captains. At least two of them. His reaction is simply—now we know. Now we know. The ship's overriding question is answered, and there's no reason to go there."

"That doesn't make sense."

"They don't want to be under some authority. They don't want to go wandering into a place where they'd be a historical curiosity. They're a ship designed to seed colonies. That's their mission, as Jase sees it. That could move them from here again next year—though I don't think it will. There's that other starship we're building, and this colony, in their view, is still a work in progress. So there's reason for them to stay a while. Maybe a hundred years. Maybe until the kyo end their war out there and come calling again. That's what we hope, at any rate. I gave the kyo a human who wants to communicate. And what they can build, I don't know. What they *will* build, I don't know. But far more than two hundred years separate us from original humans. They don't know us. We've got our own troubles. And we don't want their war."

"We damned sure don't want their war, no question."

"So that's it. That's the thing I don't know if Shawn needs to know. That's what I can't decide. Does he really need to know it? Does he need to factor it into his decisions? I don't think so."

"But you told me."

"In case I start factoring it into *mine*. In case . . . they don't settle their war. Right this moment—I'm more at peace with what I've done than I have been. Far more at peace."

"Did you have to ask me to know you were right? Of course you're damned well *right*, brother. We don't need their war. We've already got two species who've worked long and hard to cooperate as well as we do. There's no way we'd ever want to leave here and go somewhere else. I'm not even sure that atevi at this point would like to see us go. We're not what we were. Either of us. And what we are, we haven't even explored yet. So, no. Whatever they are, we're not quite them. And don't want to be a drop in somebody else's ocean. No. You did the right thing. What do the atevi say?"

"That I did the right thing. I think—I think I wanted to hear somebody born on Mospheira say it."

"Well, I do say it. How was this fellow you met?"

"I can't say I know. But smart. Thank God. Motivated. Mentally resilient, or he wouldn't be sane. He's on that ship out there, leaving us without ever knowing there was a world or a station involved in that meeting. I told him we're a small group of humans that happened among the atevi, who, like the kyo, don't want to have visitors who bring a war with them. He understood that." He leaned on the rail, looking out at the sunlight dancing on the water. "He'd be a foreigner here. We'd be foreigners there. And whatever his people are, they need him. I get the feeling they may be outmatched. The kyo's technology is way above ours. Fortunately for all of us, they're not keen on this war, either."

"So there's hope of settling it."

"There's hope." Water raced under the hull. The offshore wind helped them along. "But telling Shawn—who can't choose his employees, who has elected officials with relatives in certain posts . . ."

"Shawn's office has leaks. He knows it has. *You* know it has."

"He has a legitimate right to know, on the one hand. On the other—what good can he do with the information? Mospheira as a whole may find out someday, in which case they'll curse my name . . ."

"That's not a given. On either count. That they'll find out. That they *need* to find out. I'll give you your question back: what good can they do with the information? And if these alien humans do come, we'll likely see the kyo first—or the kyo may bring them. And how much like us will they be then? People will take a look at that technology and say, It's a real good thing they didn't come here shooting at each other."

He laughed silently, imagining that day, with Prakuyo an Tep and Guy Cullen in the mix. But not likely in their lifetimes or his.

Need to know? He felt more at ease with the decisions he had made. As long as the atevi, who didn't have a hand in that fight, knew that the kyo's quarrel was with humans, and that they hoped to find a settlement—that gave them a record, a history, to start from at whatever time the kyo contacted them again. And they would start with a knowledge of the language—and possibly, if Cullen did what he hoped, the kyo would understand humans . . . and make peace.

"In that case I'm carrying," Bren said, "I've got the language records. The beginnings of a grammar. A vocabulary. I'm going to turn it over to the University—and hope."

"For the Linguistics Department?" Toby's tone was not respectful.

"Have they given you trouble?"

"Oh, not so much. Nothing direct. I'll have the usual report to fill out, for my little stay at Najida, for any communication I may have had—did I pick up any new words? Did I exchange any goods? Did I have any personal relations with atevi? Give their names. I don't fill those out honestly. Presidential orders. But Shawn can't exempt me from them without blowing my cover."

"As a harbor rat?" Bren was amused.

"An unemployed harbor rat, with funds enough to maintain a yacht. The tax folk are sure I get my funds from you. And they're sure I don't report all of it."

"I think this year's gifts amount to free lodging, boat services, and a bilge pump."

Gentle laugh. "Port gossip is, I'm smuggling. The fact I fill out the University forms keeps the tax people and the harbor police off my case. I really don't want to have Shawn have to pull strings."

"So am I going to blow your cover?" He was a little distressed about that.

"Not in the least. I'm your brother. I was replacing a bilge pump at Najida. You wanted passage for yourself and your people. Perfectly reasonable you'd commandeer my boat."

"I do want you to make that call for me."

"No problem. What do you want me to say?"

"Tell Shawn the treaty's coming. That I'm on a state visit, with my aishid, with staff, that I need a secure residence, no news folk, no cameras chasing us every moment, but I will accept a request for a news conference, but conforming to arms regulations, and having monitoring in my quarters is right out. When I officially represent the aiji, I need the same protocols the aiji would receive."

"I think I can convey that idea."

"Tell him he has to decide where to put us. Wherever he can manage those things. And we need to make that call as soon as we clear the bay. Catch Shawn in prime office hours. Give him time to set things up."

"You're going to create a sensation, you know that. What do you want me and Barb to do while you're getting all the attention?"

Bren dipped his head slightly, toward a gray shadow out across the water. "Pull out of port for the duration, out beyond the harbor. That gunboat, and that pursuit ship—will be under Tabini's orders. They'll respond to Guild inquiry. My aishid will be in contact with them, either directly, or through Shejidan, before we leave the bay."

"Over there, their communications won't work."

"We'll manage, at least in our immediate vicinity. That's also a question of protocols. No interference with our communications. Add that to your list for the President."

"Will do," Toby said, and looked up at the sail and the rigging, squinting in the sun. "Good wind for the passage. Forecast is in our favor. Just laze about and enjoy the sea air. I'll tell Barb as much as she needs to know. And make that call. Fishing gear's in the locker. Fair weather. Sunburn lotion might be a good idea. It's with the fishing gear."

The sun slipped below the sea-flat horizon and the stars spread out across the sky, suns like so much dust. The mind reeled when one remembered traveling that void, and seeing them *as* suns, which one did, in the heavens. Now progress was measured much more slowly, on an earthly wind, on a finite stretch of water, such a little distance, seen from the space station looking down. Now that gap took time to cross, and the closest stars on either hand were the lights of two naval ships, one on the portside horizon, the larger one to starboard . . . doing nothing, never contacting them, just there, watching.

Ramaso *had* sent them food, plenty of it. "We won't even need to pick up supply at Port Jackson," Barb said. "We'll be well-set to wait it out and fish."

They sat about the benches at the stern, with three bottles of wine to go about the nine of them—even Guild could partake, thus isolated, guarded, and running under clear skies. It was, after the haste, hurry, and desperate tension of the station, a time to relax, and not to think too much, at least for a while.

The call to Shawn had gone through. Toby had delivered the message that he was coming, and had the treaty in hand, and would be a party of seven needing a place to stay, and a place for conference with him. Not to mention adequate security for their docking, which would not allow news to get near him, and transport with high enough overhead for atevi.

Shawn had, Toby said, taken all that without objection, and said he would call back.

The Grandview was Bren's estimation of the best solution. It was the largest hotel in Port Jackson—at least it had been some years ago, and if the usual situation held true, corporations, one of which owned the hotel, held several top floor suites, very frequently unoccupied, in order to move high level personnel about. He'd be very happy to find out what one of those looked like.

But he trusted Shawn to figure something out, and what Shawn did figure out would set the tone for the visit. That part wasn't his to do. He wouldn't demand, not in that matter. Shawn knew his own political climate, what was best to do for his own survival. He'd have time to warn people who needed warning, and time to prepare a response.

He told himself he should put on a heavier coat, go up to the bow by himself and think, for a while, of what he *would* say when he did face the inevitable Mospheiran cameras.

But Barb asked him, "What were the kyo like?"

He looked across at Barb and Toby in the slight glow of the running lights, and thought that, too, was something people wanted from him. Common sense. Eyes on the problem. What were they like? What did you see, representing us? What can we expect to happen now? What does this mean for us and our kids and our future?

In all the hurry and necessity of political entities, that question, the needs of ordinary citizens for reassurance, should not fall by the wayside.

"Reasonable folk," he said. "But different. Large. A little taller than we are. Heavy-set. I helped rescue Prakuyo, back at Reunion. He got upset during the trip and I felt it . . . a boom that went through his body and mine, like a shock, like an explosion. Several kyo together could make a whole room uncomfortable. So they're never unarmed, so to speak. But once they knew I had trouble with it, they muted that, considerably. They like sweets. They're real fond of sweets."

"We've got that in common," Barb said with a laugh.

"Prakuyo brought his son," Bren said. "The lad's twice Cajeiri's age, but they got along quite well. Filled out the dictionary, between them, while I was organizing the treaty. The department's going to owe a bit to that kid."

"Kid," Toby said with a gentle laugh. "That's a surprise."

"Surprise to us, too. I have pictures of them. I'll show you."

Showing involved the computer, and a lengthy session, and another bottle of wine.

It was, in its way, stranger than where he'd been—showing his family pictures of a trio of kyo, while sitting on the deck of a sailing ship crawling its way over the strait between the atevi mainland and the Mospheiran island. In this strait, old conflicts between human and atevi had set the boundary, back before airplanes, before computers—because a lost starship had arrived in that sky up there, and left off colonists who flung themselves down to an Earth they didn't own . . . and could not then leave.

They'd had to find a way to coexist, and they had.

Humans had likewise flung themselves into kyo territory, with a less happy result . . . now mediated, they sincerely hoped.

Their kyo visitors hadn't stayed. Might not ever come back. But they'd always know the kyo were out there, more advanced than they were, able to have done them terrible damage, and choosing not to.

It was a vast universe. But they couldn't think of neighboring space as empty any longer. There was a border up there they must not cross, a direction they must not go.

And that changed the way they looked at the sky at night.

4

The gathering was in Father's dining hall, twenty-seven guests, fortunate three times fortunate nine. Kabiuteri, the arrangers of felicity and good auspices, had done their best, with the arrangements, the china, the arrangement of dishes. But it did not produce happy faces.

They were old people, most of them, without spouses, and the food was plain, very plain, starting with, of all things, porridge. For supper. For an important dinner. And without sugar.

Cajeiri sampled it. Which was a good thing, because the porridge was better than the boiled vegetables of the next course. He pushed that offering slightly under the bones of the ammidet, which he had never eaten, and was not sure would ever be eaten in the midlands, but his reading had warned him these folk were much on traditional fare, and were intensely observant of kabiumaro, meaning they would never seat four at table and that they would be keenly aware of every flower in the centerpieces, whether it was a fortunate arrangement or whether it carried some hidden and insulting message.

Well, yes, it did. It carried the message that their kabiutera had worked hard to impress, and the flowers were chosen to offend no one's heraldry. They were expressive of good will, and the aiji's power. He was *not* a kabiutera, but it all looked good to him. The service was good china, not extravagant, fine crystal, not the most extravagant in the state collection. And instead of the usual presentation of special utensils and special goblets and all the fuss of a state dinner, the settings were what one would have served on a tray. It was, as state dinners went, austere, with very few sauces, very plain food, and a few dishes—the ammidet and the vegetables—of which he had had enough for a lifetime.

Light talk ran to hunting. Father could talk about hunting and mecheiti for hours, and Mother said nothing at all, just smiled and nodded.

He had his own mecheita. He did. She was resident with Great-uncle, in his herd, out of mani's breeding, a granddaughter of the great Babsidi. And if they wanted to talk about mecheiti, he would be very happy to discuss that. He almost made a comment.

But very rapidly they were on to trapping, and the proper way to set snares, about which he knew nothing. It was interesting, in a way, but talk about bait was not what he had ever heard at a state dinner.

He managed hardly three words that were not to his mother during dinner, when it was not proper to discuss business. His mother smiled, discussed the weather, decried the heat, and suggested the public gardens might be pleasant. That was all, while his father discussed the merits of high country hunting.

There was, at long last, the brandy session, in which the guests repaired to the sitting room with Mother and Father, and in which Cajeiri, with a fruit juice he judged to look as little like a fruit juice as possible, managed to observe to the elderly lord of Musuri clan that he had seen pictures of the Musuri clan hall, and found it quite interesting.

"Drafty place," was the old lord's comment, before he launched a question to Father regarding an appropriation bill.

Frustrating. He made another attempt with the lord of Darbin, asking whether they fished in Darbin Lake, since fishing was something he knew at least a little about. "In winter, yes," was the unexplained answer—unexplained, since the lord of Darbin immediately entered his own objections to his father regarding the appropriations bill and the shift of policy toward the south, notably the Marid.

"I know something about that," Cajeiri said, and found himself outright ignored as the lord addressed himself to a fellow lord, and both directed their questions to his father, who Cajeiri hoped would back his assertion.

His father was dealing with two, however, and the *numbers* would be infelicitous if he put in his own opinion, besides that his father needed no help. He drew a deep breath, then sipped his fruit juice and tried to find another conversation.

Conversations eluded him, one after the other. He was seated out of position to reach others, and simply got up and walked over to introduce himself personally, and to hear and mark names, but one flatly turned his shoulder to him, and that was unbearable.

There was, however, a call for silence, as his father called for attention, and summoned him with a gesture.

"We have heard a question," his father said, "as to the disposition of these foreign visitors, and whether we may look for peace in the heavens. Son of mine, you were there."

He walked near, bowed, properly, and faced the company with a placid expression.

"We did meet them," he said, "and there is a treaty."

"We have heard," the lord of Darbin said, "that the paidhi-aiji wrote this document entirely on his own, without reference to the hasdrawad or the tashrid, scarcely even consulting the aiji-dowager."

"No, nandi," Cajeiri said. "He did not. We all talked to the kyo, and we all talked with nand' Bren, and nand' Bren and Lord Prakuyo an Tep wrote the document."

"A child, a human, and the Lord of Malguri," someone said, behind the lord of Darbin. "This is not a consultation with the tashrid."

"Would you have gone up, nandiin?" Father asked, in that voice that could ring through arguments. "We saw no rush to

the port to help deal with this situation. We received no requests to mediate. These three individuals managed to avert
war in the *first* encounter with the kyo, and these were the
individuals most reasonable to meet with them a second
time."

"The kyo asked for us to come, nandi," Cajeiri tried to say,
but:

"There is still," Lord Musuri said, "the necessity to pass on
it. Only the dowager could legitimately sign it."

"The paidhi-aiji representing *me* could well sign it," Father
said sharply, "*as* could my invested heir, speaking for the future, nandi, though he did not, and left that decision to my
representative. The tashrid may ratify a treaty. The tashrid *will*
ratify this one, at my request. And the fact that we are not, at
the moment, standing in smoking ruins . . . is to the credit of
our negotiators and our allies. We are *not* capable, with four
shuttles incapable of defense, of standing off these visitors were
they less well-disposed."

"It was folly ever to venture up there, into affairs which do
not concern us."

"Because you decline to defend your valley, nandi, because
you do not choose to see the shadows in the woods, do you
think this protects you against those shadows should they come
with weapons? Whoever looks down from the space station sees
everything, and might *take* everything, were *we* not the ones in
charge. We *are* in charge, we *do* have a presence watching over
the world. And our people are up there able to deal with such
things sensibly. And instantly."

"So do these folk come from higher in the heavens?"

"Farther, nandi," Cajeiri said sharply, this time determined
to be heard, "and at great speeds. And over great distances. They
are at war, far distant from us. They came to be sure we were
well-disposed to them, being at their backs, and nand' Bren has
written that treaty so they are a border defending *us* from whatever lies beyond them. They are polite, they are different from

anything ever seen, and they may come back some day, when their war is done, to visit us. That is also in the treaty."

"Aiji-ma," the man said, glancing instead at Father, "does a *child* assure us these foreigners will regard them as binding once they have no war to distract them?"

"For that," Father said, "we rely on the written and signed word, as we have on treaties throughout our history, treaties negotiated by paidhiin centuries gone. The words live. The words bind the aishidi'tat together. And define our holdings. Gods less fortunate, nandiin, what do you demand of visitors who could light up the world in fire? We have talked reasonably, we have concluded a mutual agreement not to intrude in each other's affairs, and they pronounce themselves satisfied. That looks like victory to me."

"Then what is this talk of them coming back?"

"We can initiate a visit," Cajeiri said, "if we desire, nandi."

"Well, there is no sensible reason to do so. *I* can think of none."

I can, was the retort Cajeiri wanted to give. He hesitated two heartbeats, and Father said, instantly, and sharply, "The point is, nandiin, that there are many *more* foreign sorts out there, some of them perhaps near enough to worry about. Do we think that because the heavens have delivered us humans from one star, and kyo from another, while we are born from a third, that there are no more foreign folk out there in a heaven so crowded with stars? The Astronomer Emeritus comes from your district, Lord Heinuri. Ask him how many stars there may be. And does it not suggest to us that *any* meeting that concludes in a document in three languages makes us more, and not less, apt to survive? We are not in the situation of our ancestors, who sat in fortresses walled about, and fought over wells and fields. We are land-rich. We have every rock and hill in every world that circles our sun, and there are five worlds, nandiin, not to mention the moons. But what we need, nandiin, is not more land. We need allies out there beyond our boundaries, good allies, who have their own lands to manage, and who do not see any advantage in having ours."

"How are we to know what they think, aiji-ma?"

"Because we have talked with them," Cajeiri said, out of turn. "Because we have played chess, and exchanged gifts, and because they are sensible people. I have talked with them. I *can* talk to them, and I intend to do so if they return."

There were two heartbeats of unpleasant silence. Then his mother said, "We are *far* too worried about things which will not happen soon, or perhaps at all. Brandy, nandiin, and perhaps a wafer to go with it."

That was the last sensible conversation, as mani would put it. When a dinner turned out contentious, or particularly happy, either one, the brandy might flow, and the anger would settle. Most of the time.

It worked well, generally with these folk, one of whom had to be helped by his bodyguard. But it was just an upsetting evening.

"You did well," his father said, after their apartment was their own again, and his father met him in the hall.

"I did not," he said. He was embarrassed, he was angry, and he was very little from swearing vengeance on the lord of Darbin, futile as it was.

"It is to the good of the aishidi'tat that we hear unpleasant things. That way they are said to us, where the light shines, and sometimes the light shines brightly enough that a thought gets through. You had a good influence."

"They simply do not see. They think the kyo have a large city somewhere a little more distant than the moon."

His father laughed. "They think the moon is a ball about the size of Shejidan, and they simply are not clear where humans came into the region. From over some celestial hill, hitherto invisible. I confess my own imagination limps on occasion. Your mother says it makes no difference where they come from so long as they do not want to deal with us, and she is quite content with that. If only all the districts were so sensible."

"Mani says if we site a space industry in their district they will become great supporters of the ship. Perhaps we should give them a contract."

"Change, son of mine, should be applied like salt to a dish—best taste it, understand it, and then decide."

"Is that your saying, honored Father?"

"It is your great-grandfather's."

"Well, one has tasted that dish," he said sullenly, but his father did not deserve the sullenness. "Perhaps a block of salt."

His father laughed. "Like the ammidet?"

He made a face. "That was awful."

"Cook calls it an authentic recipe, with ingredients shipped in at some difficulty."

"Did you like it?"

"If we host this association again, I think we shall have a choice of meats." His father set a hand on his shoulder. "Well, we have survived it. Well done. We all had rather have been at your great-grandmother's table."

"Even Mother?"

"All of us. Porridge for an appetizer. There is a reason no conqueror has ever subdued that association. But we have survived it and they now have an inkling that there are things among the stars a little more complicated than their assumptions. We have sown a seed. There was a time, you know, when your great-uncle thought humans were all barbarians."

"Great-uncle is easy."

"Oh, son of mine, if you had seen the distress when I invited nand' Bren to Taiben. I might as well have set the Bujavid alight."

"Mani said he came to see her."

"Mani invited him. *I* provided him a bodyguard. Two of my best."

"Banichi and Jago."

"Yes. And a good choice it was. Nand' Bren stirred up *mani's* neighbors, far, far more than we disturbed our guests this evening. We honored them, we made them slightly inebriate, and we sent them home safely, with no offense against them. So they were at risk, and knew it, the deeper they drank. We dared them, and they did, and now they are obliged to our hospitality— by the custom of their region. So it was a small gain, but it was not a loss. Do not reckon it as such. Recall that I won your great-uncle, who was *trying* to win your great-grandmother away."

"Indeed." That was a large new thought.

"So. Go to bed. Rest. Tomorrow I have another thought for you."

"What thought?"

"That you have a mecheita you have not ridden but a day or two."

Two years ago he would have been delighted and distracted. In the present conversation, he had more sober thoughts. "Why?" he asked.

And shocked his father.

"You *are* your great-grandmother's."

"I am yours, too," he said. "Am I not? What is the problem with Uncle Tatiseigi?"

There was no sleep, not after the short conversation in his father's office.

Cajeiri dismissed his staff to sleep, even his aishid, and went to his own office.

The map on his wall had used to be a matter of pride. He had put pins in it with every meeting.

Tonight—definitely there were no pins to add. The mountain districts were still what they had been, unswayed. And the north . . .

Uncle Tatiseigi was going home. Uncle had spent the evening with mani, an association which was very strong, and there was no doubt of Uncle's loyalty, but the evening had not ended as pleasantly as it might. It had started, Father had said, when some of the guests at mani's table had shown up determined to see a new lord appointed for Ajuri. Two of Uncle's staunchest supporters had had words with mani, and more, declared the kyo treaty of less import than the vacancy of two ancient lordships in the midlands, and Uncle, to quiet them and prevent a quarrel that might have involved mani, had agreed to put forward a candidate they approved, and set the weight of his reputation behind it.

It had clearly not been the most pleasant evening over in mani's apartment. Mani had arranged to fly to Malguri in the morning, to spend a number of days on local issues and brief her own association on a number of issues. Uncle Tatiseigi and all the guests had been well aware of her schedule, but the conservatives, who never liked to consider space at all, had been caught without a policy and without a position on the kyo emergency—*they* had been preparing to launch a campaign to fill the vacant lordships in Ajuri and Kadagidi, and suddenly the whole world had shifted attention to the heavens.

Suddenly, again, there was *no* threat, which disturbed them quite as much. So the Ajuri and Kadagidi situation had predictably— his father's word—*blossomed forth* at last night's dinner. The conservatives' power had been concentrated in the seven oldest western clans, two of the seven original western clans were now lordless and threatened with being broken up, which would utterly change the balance of power—and in a little surcharge of brandy, one old lord had used language that had not been heard about the East, since the East, namely mani, had joined the aishidi'tat.

Uncle had immediately stepped in to cut off the argument. Uncle had named a name, one of his own relatives, with Ajuri ties, and *some* claim on the succession, and that had let the party end with a plan, instead of mani Filing Intent on the man who had drunk too much, or excusing it, neither of which she would want to do.

"Who is this person?" he had asked.

"The name is Norigi. A scholar, your grandfather's second cousin. And one cannot expect the problems within Ajuri to yield to a theorist. If I approve the appointment, the man will be dead before fall, or taking all his orders from your aunt Geidaro, which is close to it. I have to say no. Your great-uncle knows it. He knew it when he did it."

Ajuri had a very unhappy succession of assassinations. If it was a proper Guild Filing against the man, Father could stop that. But that had been the problem. Ajuri just killed people and nobody was sure even yet they had found everybody responsible.

"So your great-uncle Tatiseigi," Father had said, "is going home for a while to save us both the embarrassment when I reject the appointment. He knows. But he is not happy in his situation. He is particularly not happy that your great-grandmother had already announced her plans to go to Malguri, and now she cannot go to Tirnamardi to support Tatiseigi without lending the situation of the distress in the conservative party far more attention than it already bids to have. So *we* have this ridiculous nonsense going on with Tatiseigi covering for a drunken fool, at a time when the liberals have scored a victory with the kyo treaty in our hands and the paidhi-aiji negotiating with the Presidenta. The conservatives are very afraid I may let Ajuri and Kadagidi fragment both into several minor parts, take out two of the Seven Ancient Clans, and change the balance of power in the north—I have no such intention, but they feel vulnerable and see their crisis ignored while their opposition prospers—and the very last thing we want is for the news to pick up any rumor of conservative disarray. We need a distraction, a pleasant one, to keep Uncle's spirits up and to keep him shining in the eyes of the people. So would *you* like to go see this mecheita your great-uncle gave you? Just go. Smile. Go riding. Your visit will engage the news services, and *you* will provide images for the news. Your great-uncle will have the favor of your visit, markedly *above* the honor of these recalcitrant folk we hosted at dinner, and your great-grandmother may spend a few days at Malguri and come back to us with sunlight and flowers all about, your great-uncle's power intact, and *no* candidate sitting in Ajuri."

What could one say? He barely followed what he was supposed to do, except attract attention and have the news of his presence as Uncle's guest be far noisier than the rumor that Uncle's influence had not been enough to get his faction's candidate put in as lord of Ajuri.

Mother might be upset about him going to Tirnamardi. Mother and Uncle were on good terms now, but that situation was not reliable—and everybody knew that the candidate for lord of Ajuri most directly in line of succession—was Mother. And him. But he was his father's invested heir, so *he* was out of the question.

His going up there, however, reminded everybody that his father's household had a strong connection to Ajuri, and Ajuri had a strong connection to Uncle.

Everybody was married to everybody. That was how everybody got into trouble up there.

"Of course," he had said, with, in his mind, the *last* time he had tried a subterfuge of guesting in Tirnamardi—which had ended with *Kadagidi* going down in fire and ash, *and* Grandfather being assassinated.

"Good lad," his father had said.

So here he stood, contemplating the map: Uncle's estate at Tirnamardi, where the Atageini pins stood in a desert of missing pins.

Ajuri, and all of Dursai province, which it dominated, with its subclans: Jaibon, Seigin, and Muri. Pins all gone.

Kadagidi— Well, Kadagidi had *never* been one of his pins, and Kadagidi was responsible for that gap around Uncle Tatiseigi being so very large. Kadagidi was another of the seven oldest clans in the aishidi'tat, and it was the *other* clan missing a lord, having connived with the Marid, down south, in one part of which he *did* now have a pin. Kadagidi had also connived with Ajuri, the foundation of all troubles, and all that had led, finally, to a Kadagidi with roots in the Marid rebelling against his father and killing all the staff he himself remembered in his youngest days—poor old Eidi, his father's major domo, who had been a kind old man, and who had died right in the foyer trying to hold back the people trying to take over the government.

Father and Mother had not been home when the cowards had hit the Bujavid apartment. *He* had been up in space. Father and Mother had been in Taiben, on holiday, and the Kadagidi had tried to find them there. Their attack had killed all Father's aishid, and no few of the Taibeni, but Father and Mother had gotten away, all the same, and lived to take back the aishidi'tat, because the people—the *people* of the aishidi'tat had had enough, and supported Father, and Great-grandmother, which was the position his father was in right now, a strong position. There was no doubt of that. They had taken down the Shadow Guild, which had put a Kadagidi lord, Murini, in power.

But while they'd taken care of the Shadow Guild and Murini, they had not quite dealt with the Kadagidi's bid for power. That was one problem. They had arrested the new Kadagidi lord, Aseida, who was still supporting the Shadow Guild, so there was no lord now over the Kadagidi. And it had turned out the reason there was a Shadow Guild at all was because of a little old Ajuri man, one of Mother's great-uncles. That little old man, Shishogi, his own twice-great uncle, had held an important post inside the Assassins' Guild, and he had been putting people where he wanted them for decades and decades. And when Great-grandmother had found it out, and Banichi had, and Father had, then they had taken down Shishogi.

But not before somebody, maybe some unknown Kadagidi, or maybe Shishogi himself, had assassinated Grandfather, who was the Ajuri lord.

He had pulled all the Ajuri pins. And there sat Uncle Tatiseigi, with two of his three neighbor clans not having any lord, and with his conservative allies all upset because the conservatives had lost two lordships they were scared they were going to see filled with liberals.

What Father *might* do was dissolve Ajuri and dissolve Kadagidi all into smaller clans, who then would lose all their seniority, and become something new, losing some of their subclans to Atageini and other neighbors.

Father could also just let both clans go along for another year with no lords, which meant nobody representing them in the legislature, nobody taking care of hospitals and fire and schools and such, which was terrible for the people, besides creating continual upset around Great-uncle, whose situation made the map in that region look very sad, and really upset the conservatives.

So Father wanted him to go see his mecheita, and say just a few words for the news services, quietly indicating the aiji's *approval* of Tatiseigi himself, and showing that Great-grandmother's departure to the East was *not* a gesture of displeasure.

Will Mother be upset? he had asked, and his father had said—

"At cheering up her uncle? No. At my sending you into this region alone, yes. She might be."

"With my aishid. With my servants."

"That is the exactly the point. Eisi and Liedi are two excellent fellows, cheerful and willing and very happy to be in your service, and they would fling themselves between you and any hazard, but with little else they could do. Your aishid is remarkably able for their age—but they are not senior Guild. They will be, someday. But they are not yet."

"Casimi and Seimaji—"

"Are going with your great-grandmother. No. I am assigning

someone more permanent to you, and I am moving in added protection for your great-uncle. And do not give me that face, son of mine. I am giving you, permanently, someone both Banichi and Cenedi approve . . . granted they are willing to stay."

So he had agreed. He would have more bodyguards. What else could he do? He was given a responsibility, he was given a thing to do for his father and for his mother. *And* for mani and Great-uncle. He was given a chance to ride. And he *had* always traveled with senior Guild in charge of the party. The difference was that this time Father was sending him off by himself.

The difficulty was in his upside-down aishid, in which the youngest were first, because he had promised them always to be first, before he had had Veijico and Lucasi handed him during the situation in the south. Now they were all to be outranked by somebody permanent and high in the Guild.

He had not even told them. He had to, in the morning. But he also understood why it was necessary for his father to add that protection—not just for him, but for his household and for everybody around him.

He had no idea where he would even *put* four senior Guild, in the confines of his little suite.

But being grown-ups, and senior at that, they probably would not appreciate the silliness that went on in his suite. They probably would be grim, and serious, and they would be much happier operating out of the regular Guild office for the whole household. That would be better for everybody.

But . . .

He had to get up early and pack in the morning, and at noon, after lunch with his father and mother, he was to go down and take the Red Train, which was back from its trip to the coast, and after that, he would be on his own, with his staff.

And he would take Boji, he decided. He was taking Eisi and Liedi, who were the ones who cared for Boji, and he could not ask regular staff to do it.

If he was to have new staff, they would just have to get along with Boji and all his nonsense. It was the way his house was. His aishidi had to have some patience with *all* his associations, which *were* not what everybody would have patience with.

And that was the way he would have it.

5

The sail came in, with no shortage of hands to help—but Bren was obliged to stand clear of the action and watch in lordly dignity as they came in sight of the harbor. Narani and Jeladi had, an hour ago, extracted and opened the smallest of the wardrobe cases. The locker in the cabin had received the comfortable deck shoes and the casuals from the luggage, as well as the traveling clothes he had worn on the train. He was kitted up now in pale beige with collar and cuff lace, his queue was done up in a fresh white silk ribbon, and the pale blue silk vest, glittering with gold embroidery, was bulletproof—but not up to handling rope.

Toby fired up the motor while they were still underway, and eased them into the harbor under power.

They had an appointed berth, which Toby's communications had assigned them this morning, number seven, a politic choice, a number which humans and atevi alike found fortunate . . . not a marina berth, but a massive floating dock used by the ferries, the water taxis, and the small Mospheiran Navy craft, which doubled as sea rescue.

A police boat lazed slowly along, turned, and began to pace them at a respectful distance, escorting them in, one supposed—acceptable so long as it kept its distance. Bren's bodyguard was close by him, Tano and Algini paying attention to that presence and Banichi and Jago watching the landward side as they came nearer. Vehicles and people were gathered there, up on the pier, and on the dock a police boat sat at mooring, while the other hovered off, turning now.

A band struck up, tinny with distance.

God. He *hadn't* expected that.

News trucks up on the landing. He saw the emblems. He saw the murky green and black of Mospheiran military vehicles, and black ones, officialdom at very least.

Deep breath. "It is possible," he said in Ragi, "that the Presidenta is meeting us in person. If he is, there may well be news services. Expect too that some persons may attempt to touch, without ill will. Concealed weapons are the danger. The Presidenta may have people to spot any such, and not all will be in uniform."

"One hears," Banichi said, never taking his eyes off their landing.

Nearer by the second, across the green water. There were metal barricades up top, yellow warning banners that secured the stairs. One thing they did *not* have was their own baggage handling, and he was not going to leave either pair of his aishid to deal with it, or expect Toby and Barb to do anything but get the crates off their deck as rapidly as possible and move out beyond the territorial limit, where the atevi navy would be waiting. Narani and Jeladi had volunteered to stay and deal with the problem.

"Narani and Jeladi cannot move the crates ashore," he said. "We shall have to have local people boarding."

"They are sealed," Algini reminded him. Which was so. Nobody in an ordinary time frame could open the crates without leaving evidence. They would know. What they could do about it was limited. But the things snoopery would truly want to know about were not in those crates. They were in the black leather bags, much more portable.

And he simply had to trust that Narani, with Jeladi assisting, would be safe, and unmolested, in their getting the baggage moved.

They were close enough to distinguish individuals. And to

see, standing down on the dock itself, a man in a dark blue suit among other people in gray business dress. Shawn, one would bet on that stance, that familiar way of moving, Shawn with aides and a security detail, waiting right down on waterside, and with a handful of other people in suits at the stairs that led up to solid land. Those black vehicles up above likely were the trappings of the presidency.

Toby slowed their progress, began to work with the local currents, which Toby knew well—it was his home port—and carefully brought them in against the buffers, and indeed, it was Shawn, with security, and aides. Barb and Jeladi flung out the mooring lines as Toby reversed and held the boat steady.

Algini and Tano ran the gangway out, thump, resting with necessary give on the heaving dock.

Bren gave a little nod to Toby, one to Barb.

"We'll be waiting," Toby said.

Safer, Bren thought, for being under atevi guard. Jago had the treaty in her keeping, but he took the document case into his own possession, slung the strap from his shoulder, then said quietly, "We shall go." He could see Shawn waiting with anticipation, surrounded by his own complement of security, same dark suits, same short haircut, women and men alike.

Banichi and Jago went across first. Bren went second, Tano and Algini following, with Narani and Jeladi staying aboard. Shawn walked forward to meet them, and bet on it, there were cameras on them. Bren gave a little bow before Shawn could extend a hand, lifted his head, smiling—as much breach of atevi protocol as he was going to afford.

"Good to see you," he said to Shawn. "Very good."

"Good crossing?" Shawn asked.

"Smooth as silk."

"Surprised you came by sea."

"Massive baggage," he said, indicating the cases on the boat. "And after the station, I frankly wanted the sea. We all did. I also wanted to give you a little lead time on this."

"Useful. Yes. There's been, you can imagine, a stir of one kind and the other."

He was well aware as to which kinds. "I need to get my wardrobes ashore. My two staffers will go with them."

"No problem. Your message said baggage. We're prepared for anything.—You'll be my guest at Francis House, I hope."

Not the Grandview, but the local presidential palace, one of three official residences—one at Port Jackson, one at Bretano, and one on the Southern Shore, that the President used in a several month rotation, keeping current with various sections of the island.

"Honored," Bren said, already parsing the politics of it. Advantage to Shawn for receiving a first atevi delegation, for the reflected glory of the mission that had turned aside the kyo threat, for *getting* a direct visit from the aiji in Shejidan—and disadvantage, in certain quarters, for dealing with atevi on sacred Mospheiran soil, for letting atevi handle the kyo negotiations, because Bren Cameron didn't count as human; and for *receiving* atevi officially in the Presidential residency.

Everything anybody did on Mospheira was subject to dual interpretation, depending on the political party. What counted was the disposition of the audience and majority sentiment, and what determined *that* was where the attention of the Mospheiran people, who had lately been highly agitated by a threat in space, happened to be focused. The Mospheiran people en masse rarely awoke from their own concerns . . . rarely took a long view or a wide one about an issue; but when they'd been scared by it, they had opinions, loud ones. And that awakening had happened several times in recent history—when *Phoenix* had turned up in the heavens and reoccupied the space station; when *Phoenix* had left the world again, looking to find out the fate of a colony at Reunion, giving Mospheira no vote in the decision; when Murini's conspiracy had overthrown Tabini and Mospheira had found itself facing alliance with atevi counter-conspirators on the one hand and hostilities from the atevi side of the strait on the other. Now they'd just seen an alien ship capable, so they'd been told, of wiping out civilization arrive in the heavens, had had to sit quietly as it talked with the atevi, leaving Mospheirans to accept whatever deal atevi made with them—and it was still here, in the act of departing.

So were the Mospheiran people currently focused on foreign relations?

They were. But being Mospheiran they wanted nothing more than to leave the fearsome issue behind and sink back into their own habits, their own domestic concerns.

He could give them that chance. He wanted to give them that assurance that all was well and would be.

Unfortunately, what he also had to give them was five thousand human foreigners, some of them with issues of their own and others with ambitions. Not as frightening, perhaps, but dangerous? Possibly. Disruptive? Absolutely.

Shawn led the way up the steps. Bren let Shawn and his people go first, he and his followed. He had to trust Barb and Toby and the Mospheiran government to see to the offloading, and the Mospheiran government and Shawn's security to get it to Francis House.

He and his aishid mounted the last steps up to the wooden pier, where cameras and onlookers abounded, spilling onto solid land, behind flimsy yellow barriers. Mospheirans who didn't work at the airports or the shipyards were getting their first-ever firsthand look, not only at atevi, but also seeing one of their own, the human paidhi who had served Mospheira, who had walked the streets of Port Jackson looking no different from themselves, turning up in full-on atevi court dress—which everyone knew he wore, but Mospheira had never seen him in that mode. That he was here now representing atevi interests, as they could well guess—that was what the paidhi-aiji was *supposed* to do, but Mospheirans had never had that called to their attention—until now—and they had to figure what to make of it—along with the news that atevi had done the negotiating with the kyo. Atevi weren't exactly enemies. But they were the majority. They weren't enemies. But they notoriously didn't understand the word *friendship.*

And atevi hadn't set foot officially on Mospheira in the last two centuries.

So what did it mean? they might ask themselves. The paidhiin had been the go-betweens for them for two hundred years, the only go-betweens, and here was *their* paidhi not going between any longer, but coming ashore with an armed atevi guard, and getting an official welcome from *their* President, to talk about what had just happened up in the heavens? What did it mean for them?

He couldn't *be* what he had been—not when he wore what he wore now. He maintained the demeanor of an atevi official, the solemnity of an atevi official. He walked closely behind Shawn, and behind two of his aishid, the rest following him. He had not planned to intersect the cameras as anything but image.

But the crowd was not unruly and the cameras were close enough to catch a word—casual or not. He made up his mind on the instant and paused, with a little, a very little bow, and a pleasant look acknowledging the crowd. News services moved directional microphones so quickly he saw his security twitch, just slightly. Shawn delayed.

"The aiji in Shejidan," Bren said, fully conscious of the physical risk an unscreened crowd posed, pressing hard against the barriers, "sends regards, and wishes you to know you are safe. With the cooperation of Gin Kroger, Lord Geigi, and the *Phoenix* captains, the aiji has secured a treaty with the kyo. President Tyers—" He glanced toward Shawn, but spoke loudly enough for the microphones. "We are glad to say the kyo are satisfied that we mean them no harm, and they assure us they mean none to us. They are leaving the solar system as they came, and wish to remain unvisited for some time to come, since they are at war on one frontier, and hope to resolve that conflict without others' involvement. We wished them, in the

President's name and in the aiji's, likewise to respect our territory, and assured them we are peaceful people and good neighbors, which they were very glad to confirm." He unslung the document case from his shoulder, and held it aloft, in public view. "I have with me one of the three documents that gives us all that assurance, with no real concessions on our part." He handed it to Shawn on the spot—impromptu, but perfectly opportune, and in full view of the cameras. "This is the kyo's promise, their recognition that this is our solar system, and they will honor our boundaries as we honor theirs. One copy is in the hands of the aiji, one copy is aboard the kyo ship outbound from this solar system, and the third copy you now have in hand, Mr. President, with the aiji's good wishes."

A barrage of questions followed from the reporters. He said nothing. Shawn simply held up the document case, potent visual that it was, and said, "We shall be studying the document and hearing the paidhi's report. We will report to the people the precise provisions of the agreement in due course, but in our understanding, it asks nothing that it does not grant. It's a fair request from them for privacy in their territory and a fair understanding of our rights to the same. It accounts of Mospheira as a political entity along with the aishidi'tat, and honors us as a nation. We have *peace*, fellow citizens. We have peace on Earth and now a lasting peace in the heavens!"

Clever Shawn. *Peace* got a cheer. Count on it. So did respect for Mospheira.

And with that, Shawn signaled a farther walk, away from the cameras, and off to the waiting vehicles.

"Good show," Shawn said, his senior, his old boss in State, his ally in the Presidency.

"Good news in that document case, too, for which we're sincerely thankful."

"No surprises in it. Promise me."

There was the sticky part. Tell the truth or not.

Not, he thought. Not at this point. Enough people knew, so

that if something happened to him—critical people knew enough, to pass the word along to another generation.

"No surprises," he said. And that was his decision.

"Take care," Mother said. She had brought Seimei to the foyer, holding her, to see her brother off. Father was there. Father's Guild senior was. And the major domo and a collection of servants that went back and back. Mother had not brought Seimei to see him off when he was leaving the *planet*. And the news services had not been advised then, either. Now they were. It was all to be public, his first solo venture as his father's heir . . . on an official visit to his great-uncle's estate, a holiday as a reward for his bravery in the heavens: that was what they had told the news. There would be news people at the train station, under Guild watch, to show official pictures of him boarding the Red Train, and going off to visit Uncle.

The news people would be down there right now, there getting pictures of Boji, and Eisi and Liedi, while everybody was trying to load baggage . . . and that was embarrassing. Ordinary people did not load on a cage as big as a wardrobe case, with Boji's screeches raising echoes in the station. All through his life, for the rest of time, he thought, whenever the world thought of him, the news would call up their pictures of Boji and the train station.

His new aishid was supposed to meet him down there. That was why they were getting such a late start in the trip—his aishid had had business to finish, whatever it was, and that had taken longer than anybody expected, so with one delay and the other, they were not going to get there for supper. It was all inconvenient. But it also worked out that they would certainly make the evening news, and on this trip, cameras and the most noise possible were precisely what they were after. That was what Father had said. And Father had given him a speech to make: he was horrid at memorization, but he knew, at least, what he had to say.

"Honored Mother, honored Father." He gave a proper bow, and Seimei, disturbed, made a face at him.

"Do not take chances," Mother said.

"Listen to your aishid," Father said.

"Yes," he said to both, bowed again, and headed out into the hall with Antaro and Jegari, with Veijico and Lucasi, and with four of his father's Taibeni bodyguard to be sure he had no difficulty at the train station and linking up with his new bodyguards. That meant a great number of black uniforms about him. He traveled in a red traveling coat with black trim—the brighter side of the Ragi colors, with brown trousers and comfortable riding boots—he had last worn them at Tirnamardi, and they felt good on his feet, the way the light coat felt good on his shoulders. He was out on his own, dressed for the country, headed for days of riding and being free of court dress—and he would have been happy, except for the news, the speech.

And four strangers. Four *adult* strangers about to move into his life.

He had his aishid. They were his very closest associates. *That* relationship was under question today. He had sent Boji ahead, thinking somewhat sadly all the while that this might be the last trip with him, and four complete strangers were waiting for him down at the station, in the lights and cameras, so that any frown on his face was going to be shared with the whole aishidi'tat.

Father's guard had the lift waiting for them, and they all got into it, eleven persons in all, in a drop down all the floors of the Bujavid, below ground and far, far below.

Calm, he told himself, and put on a pleasant expression, his very best, at the last moment, as the car came to a stop in the hollow heart of the hill. The doors opened on an echoing concrete hall, next to the noisier concrete dome that was the train station, a huge space with multiple tracks, and lights mounted on girders.

And a knot of brighter lights, as they came out onto the concrete platform, lights clustered at the nearest of the massive girders. That was the permitted camera position. He had faced it before with his father. With mani. It ordinarily was his job just to walk straight through, and not to talk to them—one rarely did, at this station.

But this was not the ordinary day, or the ordinary time. He stopped and the news people looked hopeful. He gave a little nod in their direction, and they moved in respectfully, with microphones—quietly, as news folk were required to do, who were chosen to be here.

"Nadiin," he said, and immediately the specific words his father had told him to say flew out of his head and left him in a moment of panic. But he had experienced that desertion before. He simply pulled up the gist of it and went ahead.

"One is very glad to be home. There were scary moments up at the station. We met with representatives of the kyo people, and it all turned out very well. My father will have a great deal to say about the treaty—" He remembered that much that he was supposed to say. But the rest went skittering off again. "It was the kyo we met before who was aiji, he brought his son, and we were able to talk to each other and really understand. They just want to be sure we are good neighbors, and we are both happy. I am home now, and I have a few days to go visit my great-uncle and go riding. I have hardly ever gotten a chance to go riding."

"Will more of the kyo come back, young aiji?"

It was an unpermitted question, and his father would have taken it only if it was exactly what he wanted to say—and it was.

"Not soon," he said. And immediately turned and went on his way toward the train, with, he hoped, the finality mani or Father could manage. He probably should have remembered his speech. He probably should not have answered the question. But now he was away, with Guild like a wall all about him, who would not let the news people follow him.

The Red Train was waiting in its ordinary position—freight trains might come up one way and back all the way down the turns, but the Red Train repositioned itself after every run, a little train, with only two cars today. He paused at the steps up to the car, he thanked the senior of Father's security, who had delivered them safely and helped them manage the news people.

He hoped the man did not think him a fool. He hoped he had not answered badly. He wished he had remembered the way his father had said it.

"Tell my father I forgot," he said. He heard Boji scream out from the baggage car, and was mortified. "Tell him—tell him I think it was all right."

This, while Antaro and Jegari climbed up the steps to the Red Car, being sure that all was well inside. He followed, feeling Veijico and Lucasi behind him, and saw that they were not alone inside—that Antaro and Jegari had stopped, facing four older Guild, gray-haired, two of them, and the other two graying.

He stopped, frozen. Veijico and Lucasi stopped. It *was* the new unit: it must be. Antaro and Jegari would have given an alarm, else. That was the first startled thought. The four, indeed, gave a little nod to his arrival, what passed for a bow with Guild, who could not afford to take their eyes off situations. He repaid it with the same courtesy.

"Young aiji," one of the four said.

"Nadiin," he said.

"They are Guild instructors," Veijico said, a hushed voice at his back. "They are *senior* Guild instructors."

"Rieni," the foremost said, introducing himself. "My partner, Haniri. The second team, Janachi, Onami. We have the honor to be assigned to your household, at least for this venture."

Guild instructors. Gray-haired Guild instructors. His father had said Banichi and Cenedi approved them. His aishid knew them. And sounded utterly appalled.

"One is pleased," he said, as the door slid shut, sealing them in. Himself, his aishid. And this unit. "Welcome." It was uncomfortable. He was not prepared for Guild *that* senior. What, he wondered, could *old people* do if they came under attack?

Though they did not at all have a frail look.

"Will you sit?" he asked. "We should have the galley stocked. I have servants, but—" *My servants are in the baggage car attending a badly spoiled parid'ja*—was not what he wanted to say to these people. "They will be in the other car, but we can manage."

"Certainly. Shall we call the engineer, nandi?"

Someone had to call the engineer and tell him they were ready to move.

Or they could have sat there for the rest of the day.

There were a lot of details he and his aishid were not used to handling for themselves.

"Yes," he said, feeling his face warm, and quietly Rieni sent Haniri to make that call. "Shall we take the rear bench, then?"

"Nandi," Rieni said, and made room for them to pass, back to the bench seat, near the little counter-height galley.

They sat down, he and his aishid, while the seniors investigated the galley. "Are we all right?" he whispered to his own upside-down aishid.

There were nods, but with sideward glances, as if they had let something dangerous inside the car.

"Do we have a problem?" he whispered.

"No," Jegari whispered back, still with a wary look, distracted as Haniri rejoined his unit.

Rieni turned and asked, "Shall we have tea, nandi?" as the train began, inexorably, to roll.

"We should serve it," Lucasi said urgently, and got up to do that. So did his aishid, all of them, as Rieni and the other three seniors quietly sat down.

The train proceeded. He sat gazing at four strangers who scared his aishid. His aishidi was not afraid of anything, that he had ever seen. Instructors, they said.

What had his father handed him?

Another aishid. Four men, not youngsters—who expected him to be serious, and not to embarrass them, or to give stupid orders.

And he had been out on the steps apologizing for forgetting every single word his father had told him to say, because he was stupid, and he probably had said something he should not have said to the reporters. He had only remembered to add he was going to Uncle's estate. And riding. They were two separate things. And he did not remember how he had even connected them.

It was going to be, he thought desperately, a long train ride.

Francis House was a place Bren had never seen the inside of—tourists did, in the two thirds of the year the President wasn't in residence, but his own family—himself, his mother, and Toby—had tended to go to quieter places, the heart of the island. In University days, he'd just been too busy.

So here he was, in what had been a private house, before a catastrophic attempt a hundred years ago to colonize Crescent Island had come to shipwreck and financial ruin. The previous owner's taste had been, well, a little floral—a choice which persisted because of a bequest that the house should belong "to the Mospheiran state as a museum to the career of Oliver Q. Francis and the Crescent Island Company." The choice to make it the summer residence of the President was the choice of the Port Jackson city officials, who, presented with the honor, had opted to use Francis House, which spared them building a dedicated residency and likewise upped the tourist appeal of the place, during its months as a museum.

It had one useful grace, high ceilings and tall doorways, which for atevi guests was a good thing. The beds were not oversized. But staff had certainly made heroic efforts since Toby's call, and the Presidential guest suite, an infelicitous four rooms unless one counted the bath, had a stately bedroom and a dining room, with two additional bedrooms. Floral bedspreads, floral curtains—thank God, the wallpaper was only striped.

He saw his aishid look about at furnishings more alien to their eyes than the kyo ship had been. His own just saw it as— a style that had been in vogue before he was born. The current one was a little on the sterile side. "Historic," he said. They had provided plenty of pillows and fans in all the bedrooms. And in the way of things, since Jago would be very happy to share his bedroom, they had rooms enough for Narani and Jeladi to themselves. So it was overall very comfortable, well air-conditioned, given seaside Port Jackson was cooler than the inland cities, and the evening breeze would make it very pleasant.

"Security is not great," Banichi said, looking up at the transom windows of the main room.

"The Presidenta has similar accommodations, one is sure, but do not place wires within the premises: one has nothing so secret as to be worth maiming someone. Threat is far more likely to come on an excursion, or aimed at Toby. And the Navy will prevent that. One is more concerned about these frail historic chairs."

"We shall, with apology, move a few of the larger ones in from the balcony," Banichi said. There was indeed a balcony, which overhung pleasant grounds, behind an iron fence. "It will disturb the arrangement, which we trust will not greatly disturb the staff."

"There are no kabiuteri on the premises," Bren said. "Do it by all means. I should hate to test the joints of that stripewood secretary set even with my weight."

It *was* going to be an issue, in no few instances, chairs, tables— there was a tea service of some antiquity, which his staff would surely treat with respect, but the teapot was quite undersized, and there was no samovar, which posed the problem that *every* call to the kitchens or house staff that Narani might ordinarily make, *he* had to make, and the matter of an electric kettle, the normal arrangement on Mospheira, was his affair.

Well, he thought, there was a phone, and the lines were labeled. He called, asking a flustered first floor housemaid for a teakettle—no, he did not have the number for house services, he was the atevi ambassador, his staff did not speak Mosphei', and would she kindly call services and secure them a fairly large electric kettle?

The kettle arrived, in the hands of a maid who managed to look about, wide-eyed, while delivering it.

Narani and Jeladi, too, remaining with the luggage, had been out of contact with them temporarily, and now did reach them by Guild communications, saying that Toby was away safely, and they were coming up in an elevator, and would be there momentarily.

All that was well, and very soon they were in receipt of the massive cases, which did manage to go through the fairly generous sitting room doors, but not further.

"We shall simply use them as a closet," Bren said, "and consolidate them in the corner: we may move the floor lamp and the chair."

Narani, out of breath, simply gazed at the disarrangement, which, with the help of Jeladi and his aishid, involved a potted plant, a floor lamp, a writing desk and its chair, a much more massive chair, a side table, and a leather hassock—but they managed the cases so that, as designed, they *could* function in that fashion.

The displaced furniture combined inelegantly in a lump in an opposite corner, taking out of service an extensive bookcase and display cabinet.

But they were officially arrived, and in, and they sat down to have a well-earned cup of tea, he, his aishid, and his wind-blown staff.

"We have two showers," Tano reported. "Two accommodations of the predicted sort."

"We shall use whatever is available," Bren said, "sharing everything." It felt less like the arrival in an affair of state than a camping trip—improvisation seemed the order of the day. Shawn would probably view it all in some embarrassment and do all he could to accommodate them, but there was no need: they were in, they were secure, and the last thing he planned to do was entertain in the premises.

They sat, with tea which they had brought—in case: they found chairs substantial enough for all of them, and hot water, and a chance to take their collective breath.

There was a television. Bren turned it on, muted, so that they could watch for coverage and commentary, just to take the temperature of the populace—and find out who was saying what.

The news channel had continual coverage—repeating. And his own image flashed up. He immediately turned the sound up. His aishid disposed themselves, standing about, watching.

"*. . . staying at the Francis House for a visit of indeterminate length. The President's secretary has issued a statement saying that the President is studying the document and will have a statement tomorrow. Legislators who had just left the capital after the kyo event are again flying in from holiday . . .*"

The kyo had arrived during that period when the legislature was on regular rounds in their districts. Their absence from the scene and the subsequent speed with which events moved had helped Shawn push through Gin's appointment to deal with the kyo crisis. It was a little unkind to have surprised them again. But he was not responsible for the timing.

They were in Port Jackson now, definitely—not in session, but stirring about, conferring, gathering information, scheduling hearings.

Now there was a familiar face. One of the Heritage partisans. "*The President has set a questionable precedent, lodging atevi in Francis House. This is just one more dangerous step toward . . .*"

"What are they saying?" Jago wanted to know.

"That is Heritage Party. He wants us to stay in a hotel. Well, actually, he wishes we had drowned on the way over, but his speech is actually fairly moderate."

The scene changed. He was about to mute the sound again, but then the television said something regarding a special report from the mainland, and segued to a very familiar venue for a resident of the Bujavid, but one rarely permitted to be imaged.

The Bujavid train station.

The filigree cage, and a screeching parid'ja, being loaded onto the Red Train baggage car.

"The young gentleman," Tano said instantly.

"The aiji's son . . ." the television said, and went on about his traveling by train, and having made a statement, an unprecedented event.

Indeed, the next edit showed Cajeiri with his aishid, and with four of Tabini's guard, stopping for the cameras.

Jeladi and Narani hovered near. Banichi and the rest sat down. Everybody watched and listened.

There were subtitles.

We met the kyo leader and his son.

The kyo leader. They had no notion at all what rank Prakuyo held, but that was not precisely it.

And Cajeiri's statement that he was going to Tatiseigi's estate to ride came out that he was riding to his uncle's house.

Well, that was a development. They were actually picking up broadcasts from the aishidi'tat and the Linguistics Department was actually permitting the Ragi language to be translated for the Mospheiran public.

It was not the best translation. They had missed the idiom in the first line, correctly gotten the gist of two other statements, if not the wording, left out a great deal, and scrambled the last statement entirely. But *Cajeiri* had just appeared on Mospheiran television—unprecedented, the news was saying, and then the observation that this was Tabini's heir, and then speculation that the powers that moved nations were not resting an instant in selling the treaty to the world—

As if they had a choice, Bren thought.

—and that Cajeiri making a public appearance and their

coming into Port Jackson were a coordinated effort to allay fears of kyo action . . .

Not that coordinated.

Then the reporter stated that it was the boy's first solo trip since he had been designated as Tabini's heir.

Solo trip. To Tatiseigi's estate. Well, that was about the safest place he could visit outside Malguri and Najida. It indicated Tatiseigi was in residence. Maybe that the dowager was there already.

"Where is the dowager? Ordinarily, going to Tatiseigi, she would travel with him."

"She had business pending in Malguri," Banichi said, and added: "The aiji inquired of us and Cenedi about a senior unit, to be assigned, in residence, for the young gentleman. We made a recommendation. It surely must be in place today, if he is traveling alone."

Communications with the Guild were not available as they were on the mainland. They would not be available, while they were here, unless they wanted to route things to Lord Geigi and down, or use code that itself might become an issue in their attempt to soothe uneasy feelings. He had sensed no crisis in the aiji's sending him—no advisement to use a more rapid transport than he had used.

"The aiji said nothing about a crisis," he said. "Maybe it *is* just a holiday."

"Shall we inquire?"

There were signals, there were always signals that could indicate a serious need to be in contact. "We have *received* no signal."

"None," Banichi said.

"Then one supposes that matters are under control. And perhaps the young gentleman is simply out to enjoy a holiday."

"One did understand there were to be two state dinners," Algini said, "one by the dowager, of well-disposed people, one by the aiji, of the mountain clans. One might surmise something arose from there, but one cannot construe what. The dowager's company would be far more important."

"Nothing *threatening* the aiji."

"Nothing," Banichi said, "or we would certainly have had advisement. This does have the aroma of politics in motion, regarding Lord Tatiseigi, and his favor."

"It does," Bren agreed. It was a reasonable conclusion—maybe not the whole answer, or the right answer, but Boji and all, the young gentleman was launched on his first diplomatic mission to a man he could wrap around his finger, no question, so success and a favorable omen was assured. A new heir. And a mission taking advantage of the best news the world could have, that the trouble the ship had stirred up was dealt with and that no harm was going to come from the incident.

It *would* be an auspicious time to have the lad enter public view. A coming-of-age in which his personal participation had meant something, certainly approval from the liberals, and a family visit with his great-uncle, one of the leading conservatives—a homely little visit, in the public spotlight.

And Tabini had very possibly sent that clip to Mospheira for public distribution.

Politics? Undoubtedly. Public relations. No question.

But Cajeiri was the one who'd had to pull it off. And he'd done it well.

Very well, from this perspective.

They had left the city behind by now. Cajeiri knew every switch-point in this route, and he knew when they had set themselves on the line that led north. They had had tea. They had shared sandwiches. There was wine, but his senior aishid did not take any. There was simply more tea. And minimal conversation.

But there was a need to explain where they were going and what they were going to do. It was the second time through for his aishid—Cajeiri had told them, but for them, he had left out some of the things his father had said and concentrated on the happier prospects, like having nothing to do and several days to ride.

They had had *their* theories, in anticipation of others coming in, where his father might have found another aishid, and who he might have asked in, and how they would work sleeping arrangements with the new aishid, who were expected to be older, and who might find more comfortable rooms with his father's bodyguard,—his father's bodyguard were mostly East-erners, from Great-grandmother, except Father's *own* upside-down situation, having four Taibeni as his personal guard . . .

All that depending on this new aishid not being of some in-compatible origin, which *surely* his father would never pick.

But they were not the sort of questions a student would ask of an instructor . . . who they were, where they were from, what clans, what districts—and whether they had ever worked to-gether.

His aishid might hesitate at questions. But he was due the answers.

"Is this," he asked, trying to find a reasonable question to start with, amid the discomfort, "is this the first time you have been assigned together, nadiin?"

"Not at all," Rieni said, amid a little relaxation. "We *are* a unit. Haniri and I are Suradi clan. Janachi is rogue Kadagidi . . ."

"There is *no* man'chi there," Janachi said.

That was good. Kadagidi was appalling news.

"And Onami turned up on the Guild's doorstep one dark night, in a box."

Was that a joke? He let himself show shock, at very least. *Could* these grim people joke?

"So we think he is Shejidani," Haniri said. "But we are not sure."

"I was brought up by a Taibeni hunter," Onami said. "But it is true, I am likely Shejidani."

One hardly knew what to say. Certainly his aishidi had no

help. Unless Antaro and Jegari remembered him. But Onami might have left Taiben before they were even born.

"You know Banichi, of the paidhi-aiji's aishid. And Cenedi, with my great-grandmother."

"Both," Rieni said. "Both."

The silence was extreme, under the thump of the wheels.

"So—did you ask to come, nadiin?"

Rieni seemed to relax a little at that question, too—drew a deep breath and extended his arm along the back of Haniri's seat, Rieni having the corner seat on the bench. "We are provisional in this assignment, nandi—provisional within your discretion, and ours. We are retiring from instruction, whatever the outcome."

That surprised his aishid, he thought. It surprised him. Retiring from instruction. But one never retired from the guilds. The Troubles had proved that saying. He had no idea whether these four had been in the fighting then, or when they had begun teaching. But that was not the question.

"Can you still teach my aishid?"

"Yes," Rieni said. "And while the Guild does *not* teach outsiders, there is a traditional exception made—for aijiin. That, also, we might do."

That was scary. He wanted to learn to protect himself. He had asked his aishid to teach him their lessons, and he could operate equipment he was not supposed to touch . . . a fact which he was not sure he ought to admit.

"It might be good," Antaro said very faintly.

It was not comfortable, even if it might be good. His aishid was far too quiet. The train was far too quiet. For a long, long while.

And it came to him that he was the center of it all. That *he* gave the orders.

So it was his fault, that silence.

"We are permitted to laugh," he said, "and make jokes, even silly ones. My aishid calls me Jeri-ji when we are not official. I have three close human associates, and I greatly favor my great-grandmother and the paidhi-aiji and my great-uncle Tatiseigi, who is very much cleverer than he lets most people know. I speak a little human language and a very little kyo. So can my aishid."

Rieni nodded slowly. "We are not at odds on any of these points. We have, contrary to our reputation among our students, been known to have a sense of humor. Jeri-ji will wait on our permanent assignment."

"Agreed," he said. And wished his aishid would relax. They sat absolutely still.

"So what *is* the normal tenor of your great-uncle's household?" Haniri asked. "What do you do when you visit?"

That did draw a little shift of bodies, an exchange of looks. But no one said what had happened the last time they were there.

"Did not my father tell you?"

"No," Rieni said. "We only received the message, that we were to accompany you. We determined together that this was an assignment to finish our last term in active service—or to extend it, in your service, or your father's."

"Well," Cajeiri said on a deep breath. "What do I do? I *hope* to get a chance to ride. Even just inside the grounds. I would like to. I have never had a routine there. I hope to sleep late and ride a lot. I almost never get to sleep late."

The phone rang in the room in Francis House, an odd jangling sound, an old-fashioned ring that startled his aishid and staff—emanating from a very modern phone. Narani located the instrument on the stripewood desk and picked it up, bringing it to him unanswered.

He thumbed it on. "This is Bren Cameron. Yes?"

"Bren. Shawn. How are you doing?"

"We're all here, my baggage all made it, and we're having tea. We'll be quite comfortable."

"Did you catch the aiji's son on television?"

"I did, by pure chance. Do you have any word on that?"

"We had a notice from the network. I caught the tail of it, and replayed. Quite a surprise."

"Surprise to us, too, but a good time to have the young gentleman make a public show, and I think the aiji is preparing to give him more prominence. The young gentleman's trip is much the same as mine, perhaps, help the world get together on what we need to do."

"Infinitely to be hoped. Well, welcome to Francis House."

"Quite the place. I'm honored."

"One of the more comfortable capital residences. Listen, I'm having staff send a supper up, with choices. I figure you'll want to settle in this evening and rest a bit. Tomorrow, if you will I'd like to have the two of us, just a private session in the executive office upstairs. I can send a guide—no recording, no formality, just a sit down and catch up session. I know your bodyguard has to come, my bodyguard has to come, but relaxed. Is that possible?"

"Perfectly possible. Give me a time."

"Private session at nine, lunch with the cabinet at eleven— they'll want to ask questions. I'll have my own news conference at one. If you want one—"

"I've made my public statement. I'm not happy to go beyond it."

"Understood. Committee meetings, if you're willing. It would help."

"Are you sure it would help?"

"It would win points. And I trust your eloquence."

"I hope. All right. I'll do it. What committees?"

"I can arrange a joint session. State, Science."

"Whatever you think good."

"I'll arrange that. Quiet dinner tonight and tomorrow evening, state dinner, full honors on the third night, same cook, same staff as prepares mine, understand. We're being extremely careful."

"Shawn, I have every confidence."

"We're intercepting a lot of phone calls, some crackpot, some probably people you might want to hear from. Can you give me a list of people you'd take a call from? If you return it with the house staff, I'll get it. Stationery in the desk. Or should be."

"Understood. It's a short list. I'll talk about it tomorrow."

"Good. Good. I'm liking everything I read in the treaty, short as it is. Good job, Bren, God, a good job."

"I'm gratified."

"You've hardly had time to get your feet on the ground. Take tonight, at least. Trust the dinner. Get some rest."

"Thank you."

"Hell with the formality. I'm glad to see you. Personally glad. Get some sleep. We'll talk tomorrow. Old times, Bren."

"Old times," he said, hanging up, but he had no illusions it would be like that. They were neither one what they had been, back at the start.

What they did have was an ability to be utterly frank with one another. Shawn was the best in his office in generations, canny, single—when every prior president had been married—an anomaly in many ways, but efficient. Business loved him because they'd never prospered as well as in the period of cooperation he'd engendered. Regular people loved him because prosperity meant jobs; and he'd led the nation through crises, gotten Mospheira back in space, made peace with the aishidi'tat, and, in the view of many Mospheirans, softened the atevi attitude toward Mospheirans.

The Heritage Party, which wanted to roll back the clock to oppose everything non-human, was not fond of him, vehemently opposed to sharing the space station—never mind that humans in space couldn't fly down and humans on the ground couldn't fly up: it had taken atevi industry to make that possible. First up to deal with *Phoenix*'s return had been atevi. But— the Heritage Party was sure they could have done it *except* for Shawn's leadership.

The electorate, thank God, was not amnesiac, but electorates aged and changed, and they had, themselves, a narrow window to get done the things that needed to be done so that the Heritage Party couldn't revise history and roll back the clock. They had to stop the cycles of upheaval in the aishidi'tat and do something to give an island-bound nation a sense of optimism for their children.

There were tall obstacles to both. But the knowledge of a technologically advanced entity on their border might either scare Mospheirans into arming themselves—or persuade them that that was a fairly dangerous course, given the situation, and given their relationship with atevi, whose policy was to keep heavy armament to a minimum in the world, while humans had been understandably unwilling to release that sort of thing from the Archive—a moot point now, since the ship had arrived with that technology in operation.

But if the world wanted to build a massive defense in space, it had a long run to catch up with the kyo—and if they were not recognizably themselves when they got to the kyo's level, in a non-technician's studied opinion, they would have lost everything they wanted to protect.

"What *is* your thought?" Cajeiri asked Lucasi when he encountered Lucasi and Jegari at the door of the accommodation.

"They are *good,*" Lucasi said, in a low voice, shoulder turned to the group at the end of the car. "The senior pair teach tactics. Janachi teaches demolitions and disarmament and he *has* no nerves. Onomi teaches anything that comes in a black box."

"You would be safer with them, Jeri-ji," Jegari said. "I have no hesitation to say so."

"If only they are not too grim," he said. "They look so serious."

"Some of the seniors are grim," Lucasi said. "But these are the ones who rigged a choke-line in the hall during an attack drill."

"People could have been hurt," Cajeiri exclaimed in dismay.

"We are supposed to be better than that," Lucasi said dryly. "Lives *depend* on us to be better than that."

"Well, they cannot do that in the Bujavid!"

"One would by no means expect they would," Lucasi said with quiet laughter. "But no junior ever takes them for granted."

"Do you *want* them to be with us, nadiin-ji?"

"Do we want to be better?" Jegari said. "If they will teach us—I say yes. I think Antaro will say yes. We have no resentment at all for being second in decisions. How could we, if it protects you and keeps us all alive."

"I say the same," Lucasi said. "I know Veijico will. You will be a target. We have always leaned on Banichi and Cenedi for help until now. On this train, now, are we enough, without them? Sensibly, no, we are not, nandi."

"I will *not* be nandi to my aishid."

"Convince *them* of it," Lucasi said.

"They have to listen to you," Jegari said. "But suggesting lax rules cannot come from us."

Cajeiri drew a deep, long breath. "They still have to get *my* approval," he said, and went back to the rear, to Antaro and Veijico and the new aishid, who gave him a look as if they knew exactly what sort of thing they had been discussing, and said not a word.

Given some Guild equipment, the seniors might know exactly what they had said. He knew about such devices. He was *not* without understanding or experience, and he knew things at a higher level than some who were much older and more experienced.

And *he* did not say a word about what he knew, either.

It was a long, late trip. The Red Train had right of way when it traveled, so they occasioned holds of other trains in their passage, even passenger trains, but there was bridge repair since the summer storms that had come so fiercely. And the need to route all trains around that damaged bridge in the midlands slowed everything on the line and made them still later than they had expected. Delays had only accumulated, and the new seniors at last sent word to Uncle's staff that they would arrive too late for supper, and would manage.

Their supper began to be snacks the Red Car had in store in its galley, and there was at least a good supply of them.

It was well into twilight before they came to the wooded land, the long-disputed boundary between Taiben and Atageini land. Forest closed in about the train at this worrisome and shadowy hour, but his younger aishid had secured contact with Taiben—and Taiben reported their parents had ridden over to Sidonin, to the station, waiting there to meet them. Uncle's estate had promised them a car that could carry them all, and the baggage truck, which also would be waiting at the station, to bring them upland, to Tirnamardi.

"Under any other circumstances," Cajeiri began, addressing Antaro and Jegari quietly, on the other side of the galley, "I would urge you take a day in Taiben."

"But under *these* circumstances," Antaro said, "we cannot. We shall exchange a word or two, by your leave and theirs, but no more than that."

"Tell them," he said, "if all goes well, you *should* manage a day while we are with Uncle."

"Under the circumstances," Jegari began.

"No. I decide, Gari-ji. I do decide. If I order you to go pay respects to your parents and your uncle, you have no choice, do you?"

"They—" With a look toward the seniors, who were carrying on their own conversation a distance up the aisle.

"*They* are to protect us, *not* to approve everything we do or choose not to do. Tell your parents you will very likely have a day and a night to visit while we are here. We are in the heart of Uncle's hospitality, with *his* aishid as well as the seniors, Kadagidi is under Guild management, Uncle has no security threats, and you should not have to be on watch the entire holiday. I am quite sure Uncle would lend two mecheiti, and I have every confidence you can bring them back unscarred."

"If you say," Antaro said, with an anxious glance toward the seniors.

"*Who* gives the orders, nadiin-ji?"

"You, nandi."

"So. Well. So."

The train slowed to a crawl as they reached Sidonin, in the woods, and came to a gentle stop—at which point it was Guild business and staff business to talk to those outside and arrange the matter of baggage.

The seniors took charge. They opened the doors. And the baggage car was surely open, just ahead of them. One could hear Boji's screech above everything else. It was like last time—and not. The last visit he had had his guests with him, and they had seen mecheiti for the first time.

His young aishid exited, and he did, with the seniors following, and indeed the Tirnamardi estate had sent a car, and the truck, which sat on the roadway next to the wood-planked station platform, ready to move. And on the other end of the platform, a number of Taibeni riders were there, on mecheiti that shifted about, tall shadows voicing their low complaints at the train and people moving about. Bronze peace-caps were on the short side-teeth, and riders in green and brown kept them well back from mischief. The two lead riders he recognized immediately as Antaro's and Jegari's parents, and a third might be their younger sister—with four more for company, possibly cousins. They had come to meet the train, a courtesy as well as a chance to see their son and daughter, and Cajeiri personally took his aishid to the edge of the platform, gave a little bow—politely returned, from the saddle, as mecheiti turned and shifted in threat, under absolute control, he was quite confident.

But just then there was a horrid metal bang, an indignant screech from Boji, and mecheiti shied off and surged back under rein . . . one never turned one's back on mecheiti in an upset; but Cajeiri retreated out of range and turned, with a clear view of Boji's cage on the platform, and the perches askew—set down hard with a wheel collapsed under the cage, dishes all spilled, and Boji bounding from one side to the other in wild-eyed upset. Eisi and Liedi were trying to quiet him, Eisi's hand was dripping blood, and Boji's screaming reached new and painful notes as Cajeiri reached the cage.

"Hush!" Cajeiri said sharply—sometimes Boji would listen to him. Boji kept screaming, thoroughly upset.

"Hush, hush," Onomi said, arriving beside him, and made a strange sound that was very like Boji's chattering. "Settle. Settle, settle."

Boji settled.

Right away. The silence was shocking. So was Boji's wide-eyed stare. It was outright daunting, that *Boji* shut up and stared, his whole demeanor changed. He shifted about on his perch to get a look back at Onomi as Eisi and Liedi and two of Uncle's men hefted the cage up on three rollers, moving it toward the edge of the platform, and the truck's own loading bridge.

Wardrobe cases across. Antaro and Jegari went back to the edge of the platform, talking with their parents, among the Taibeni riders, who had settled the mecheiti.

He followed close as Boji's cage was carried onto the truck-bed, asked Eisi about his hand, which was wrapped in a cloth, and not, at least, dripping blood onto the boards.

"It is a cut, nandi, no great consequence."

"You shall have that seen to," he said. "Will you ride in the car, Eisi-ji?"

"No, no, nandi, it hardly hurts. We shall stay with our charge. We shall see the rascal to Tirnamardi."

"You shall definitely have it seen to," he said. "Veijico. Lucasi."

"Yes," Veijico said. One of the items in the black bag that always went with them was a little medical kit. "But—"

"I am not likely to need it, and one is sure the seniors have a kit, Jico-ji."

That was a delay in itself, past the time that they had the wardrobe cases loaded, and Boji's cage secured, and they were now in deep twilight. The Red Train lingered, and Veijico and Lucasi and Janachi together took Eisi back into the car to deal with the wound under the lights, and with a place to sit down. Uncle's men waited. Antaro and Jegari squatted down at the edge of the platform, talking with their parents, in the aftermath of commotion.

Cajeiri found himself standing on the platform alone with Rieni and Haniri and Onomi, with night coming on, in a quiet momentarily deep enough to hear the trees whispering, with the dusty grassland of Atageini land up the road, just beyond the fringe of woodland about Sidonin station.

It wasn't as if the senior Guild were trying to take over. It was just good they were here, or it would have been complete chaos.

Which meant that his father was right, and he should *not* be out on his own, without the seniors. Things that had always just happened in good order with mani's aishid or nand' Bren's—would *not* happen without the seniors. That was how things were. On their own, they had not thought to signal the engineer to move. Without the seniors, they would be later than they were.

Being out on his own was not the freedom he had expected it to be.

And Boji . . . it was not Boji's fault the antique cage had finally had a wheel fail on the rough ramp.

Maybe it was an omen. The thought came to him that maybe he should just open the door and let Boji go, here, in the forest, which was his native habitat.

But if Boji did escape into this woods, the poor fellow would go into the trees and likely starve, helpless without two servants to bring him eggs.

And where would he ever again get boiled ones, which were a treat for him?

No, he had to find a better answer than that.

"Has anyone contacted my uncle," he asked them, "to say we are a little delayed."

"Lord Tatiseigi's staff is aware," Rieni said. "The Taibeni have requested to camp near his grounds. They wish to escort us. He has approved."

All that had passed, no one mentioning it. Things were happening that should reasonably have happened and no one had advised him until he asked.

"One would wish to know it," he said.

"Nandi," Rieni said, acknowledging the instruction.

There were so many, many things he had to learn. So many things mani or nand' Bren knew about their bodyguards' routines. And he was out here in the dark with a broken cage and no proper supper, which he was sure Uncle had intended to be a fine one, welcoming him. He was embarrassed. Deeply embarrassed. He so wanted to make a good impression, and his staff's first request had to be for something to prop up the damaged cage, once they got the thing upstairs.

There were enough seats for them all, with Uncle's estate bus, which seated twelve, so Eisi and Liedi could ride with them, but Liedi insisted on riding in the truckbed with Boji, and Antaro and Jegari said they would ride there, too. They would be within sight of their parents, who would follow them as far as the gate in the tall hedges, and camp outside the grounds—one never wanted to mix two mecheita herds absent supervision, and Uncle's stables were right up next to the house, beside the orchard. Taibeni were much in the open air by choice. They had a grand hall, and lodges here and there, and many small cabins and campsites in the deep woods where they might, in their wandering way, spend a night or two when the mood took them. Other clans had townships, and villages, and one could count the number of their people, but the Taibeni were hunters, much on the move, and did commerce, but never admitted their numbers, their armament, or their births or deaths to official records. They were ghosts, and showed up here and there across a very wide forest, some of which was disputed land . . . it was only last year that Uncle's Atageini had made peace with Taiben.

But Taiben was a solid floor under the north, which had been so sadly disarrayed, and it was a good thing that the Atageini had made that pact, and now took no alarm at Taibeni riders in plain sight—who now guaranteed Atageini security, and kept a watch as far as Ajuri in the north and Kadagidi to the east, just to be sure.

One could at least draw breath, riding in the bus Uncle shared with the near villages, one was quite sure. Everything was in order, though it was full moonless dark by the time the road bent toward the iron gate in the high hedges, the living walls of Uncle's grounds, standing and replenished for three hundred years.

At that turn, the Taibeni fell away from them.

They passed the iron gates in the dark, and gravel sounded under the tires, a long drive even yet before the lights of Tirnamardi showed in the distance, two lights, at first, and then more, a peaceful sight, the windows unshuttered and shining in the dark.

They pulled up on the curving drive, in front of the steps, and Uncle's major domo came out with staff to meet them, to welcome them in, to supervise the offloading of Boji's cage—Boji was already setting up a fuss, disturbing the peace of the night, rousing a bellowed challenge from the stables beyond the house.

"You will have your great-grandmother's suite, young aiji," the major domo said.

One had wondered, among other questions on the train, where one was to *put* the second Guild unit in Great-uncle's house.

House staff had come out to meet them, to meet them, to

direct them and their baggage inside—baggage went one way, past the front doors, and they went up the other, up the stairs to the great hall, where Uncle Tatiseigi waited to greet him. "One so regrets the dinner, Great-uncle." He at least knew how to present himself with proper manners. "One *wished* to be here earlier."

"Well, it would have been happier with your company," Uncle said, "but you will find a good representation of it laid out in your room. Traveling with a full complement, we see, excellent, excellent choice. We are glad to see it. Men of very good repute. Welcome to Tirnamardi. Go up and rest, young gentleman, and safely dispose that creature of yours."

"I swear he will not get out, Uncle! We have had a small accident with the cage, but only to the wheel. The latch is secure."

"We have every confidence," Uncle said, and waved his hand toward the steps. "Come, come. I shall show you up myself."

So upstairs it was with Great-uncle, up and up the grand stairs, and down to the other end of the upper hall, opposite Great-uncle's own suite.

"Enjoy the freedom of the house," Great-uncle said, "and call staff to attend your slightest need. We shall talk at breakfast."

Breakfast, at Tirnamardi, was with the first edge of sunrise. That, he did know.

And through the doors, they entered what was ordinarily mani's suite, a sort of place he had never occupied, not even in the Bujavid. It was a guest quarters that could house an aiji and his guard, grand furnishings, antiques at every hand and underfoot, gilt, gold, silver, and tapestry—porcelains—one winced, even *thinking* how Boji had behaved on his last visit.

In the sitting room of the suite was a buffet laid out. Eisi and Liedi handled the tea service with utmost care, Eisi insisting to serve despite his bandaged hand, while Uncle's staff attended the dishes.

So quiet descended, and they sat and stared at each other, with none of the train noise to soften the silence.

"Do you ride?" Cajeiri asked.

"Yes," Rieni said. Which disposed of that topic.

Silence again.

"You have to talk freely, nadiin," Cajeiri said. "Please. Jegari, Antaro, I am going to talk to Uncle about you visiting your parents."

"There is a problem," Rieni said.

Cajeiri stopped in mid-sip and frowned. "Say," he said. One did not discuss business over tea or during a meal, but information from one's bodyguard was a universal exception.

"Our parents," Antaro said, "say that there has been some difficulty in Ajuri—an Ajuri intrusion into Taiben, ending in an instance of other Ajuri appearing along that area. The intruders left Taiben, and apparently there is still activity along that border, though of what sort we do not know. We have no idea what it is."

"Therefore," Rieni said, "two rode in the rear of the truck tonight, armed."

He was not supposed to swear. But he did think of the words.

"You should have told me, nadiin. Somebody should have told me."

"Lord Tatiseigi should now be aware," Rieni said. "So should Guild Headquarters and Guild units watching Kadagidi. The decision was not to distress you on the drive or shadow your meeting with your great-uncle, but we are indeed informing you."

"Our parents," Antaro said, "advised us. It happened late today. There was no incident between these persons and Taibeni, but considering your presence here, Lord Keimi sent our parents and he is sending others, just to be sure. Our parents will hold a camp within sight of the hedges as long as needful."

"We shall still ride! And you will still visit your parents. Ajuri is probably upset with Uncle over the nomination. They are probably upset with Father. They certainly will have heard the news today, and they know *I* am here. They very likely did this just to upset us."

"Not unlikely," Rieni said. "But it is also not unlikely they would like to be in the news, too, and with no one in charge, there is no one to rein back bad ideas."

"We still shall ride," he said.

"With precautions," Rieni said. "We *ask,* young aiji. Your security *asks* you to observe caution. Your junior security will hesitate to ask you. But do not put their lives at risk."

It *was* polite. It *was* respectful. He could not argue with that.

It was also infuriating.

"We have Taiben on watch now, right at the gate. Uncle will take precautions," he said. He wanted not to be angry. He wanted not to have the urge to swear they would go where they liked and do what they liked and that politics was not his concern. It had to be. He had seen what happened when people were fools and ignored their bodyguards. "Are there not precautions you can take, nadiin, in all respect?"

"There are," Rieni said. "And we also understand that the heir of the aishidi'tat should not retreat from threats. We only wish the heir to understand that little threats turn into disasters, given too much opportunity."

"The heir of the aishidi'tat understands those principles, nadiin. The heir of the aishidi'tat is aware he has a reputation for certain stupid actions, *from which he learned,* nadiin. He is not now a fool."

Silence again.

"Take necessary precautions," he said. And set down the cup. And he reminded himself he was *not* truly here to have a holiday. He was here to be noticed. And the news had left no doubt where he was.

Which meant *anybody* disturbed by Uncle's move was apt to know where he was, and it was not a time, indeed, to be a fool.

Outside, in a stable hardly a stone's throw from the back door, was *his* mecheita, which he had hardly had a chance to appreciate before the ash of Kadagidi had come drifting down from the heavens and nand' Bren's bus had shown up with bullet-holes.

And *they* had all made a run for the capital. But not to retreat and hide.

"So," he said. "Thank you, nadiin-ji. Thank you for the warning. Thank you for your protection. I *shall* listen to advice. But this is what I am thinking: that I have to do as I would do without their threats, if that is what they are up to. If you have to call in more protection—call them."

"May we ask," Rieni said, "that you do not defy them before mid-morning tomorrow. Your father will veto the nomination. That will be done at a certain hour. But a disturbance preceding that event would make it seem your father vetoed it because a threat against you and your great-uncle moved him to do so."

He understood that. He nodded. "After noon," he said. "In the afternoon, we shall go riding. Spread that all about Taiben and Atageini."

"We can spread that report all the way to Shejidan," Rieni said. "With a photo or two, discreetly sent to certain agencies. It will be on the news by noon."

It was a soft bed, sheets light and comfortable, a wealth of pillows. A very little light came from the windows, and Boji slept, over in his cage, quiet, for the time, after an exciting day—for a parid'ja. And the rest of them.

Everybody had rooms, two by two, as the Guild usually slept. There had been food enough, there was comfort enough.

So it was not quite a holiday. He was not sure he had ever *had* a holiday.

But the senior Guild was not so bad as he had feared. They were not stodgy old men. They were, in fact, thinking of things, doing things, and *telling* him things, finally, which was the important part.

He could be scared, if he were out there only with his aishid, and they likely would be more scared than he was, if they had to protect him, with so many details they just were not used to thinking of.

They *had* gotten the information from Taiben, that had run alarms all the way to Guild Headquarters and probably to Father's office before they even got to Tirnamardi. And that was good. They had gotten up on the truckbed where they had a vantage to defend the bus if there had been a problem, and he *should* have suspected something when Antaro's and Jegari's parents had decided to ride up and camp near Tirnamardi's gate . . .

His senior aishid had certainly known what was going on, and given orders, and passed information everywhere it needed to go.

They were not bad, he thought. They were not half as bad as he had thought they would be. He began to think—they might not be bad at all.

The office of the paidhi-aiji
The Bujavid
Shejidan

Currently to be reached at: Francis House, Port Jackson.

Dear Chairman Koman:
I have arrived under the auspices of the aishidi'tat,
representing their interests on this visit. I have recently
operated on a direct commission from the President of
Mospheira conjointly with the one from Tabini-aiji, and
I am pleased to say that I have collected materials

which I shall be happy to provide regarding the recent encounter with the kyo.

These materials are principally in Ragi, the language in which the kyo themselves chose to communicate.

Sincerely,
Bren Cameron,
Paidhi for Tabini-aiji.

He was tempted to add to that last paragraph . . . *in light of which, I recommend that the study constantly crosscheck with Ragi, to avoid multiple layers of interpretation—* but that stepped into Departmental authority to propose and dispose, and it would very surely likely provoke people he had no desire to deal with.

He had sat down, before bed, to write a letter at least explaining his presence, and promising something the Department both wanted and dreaded—professionally speaking: a language they had never dealt with, a language that was going to upset the still-extant rules against voice communication in another language . . .

The rules had made sense, two hundred years ago. They certainly made none now. But they still were producing graduates who read Ragi but who could not write or speak it. Could not pronounce it, in point of fact, let alone handle regional variants.

He could deal with the University. That was the overarching entity that most of the time made sense.

He had far more trouble dealing with the University's Linguistics Department, which had never been at peace with his severance of close supervision, and with his decision, taken in the first week of his assignment, to *speak* Ragi and abandon close to two hundred years of policy . . . because the aiji he served was moved to talk to *him.*

No, he was not greatly favored in the department that had

created him. The retired paidhi, Wilson, had come at logger-heads with Tabini, been told to leave, and it had not been a happy departure from office—which, considering Wilson now sat on the Committee, and considering his replacement had immediately violated a few departmental rules, had led to an attempt at recall and more reprimands than one chose to count.

And the general atmosphere hadn't put relations with the Committee high on Bren's list of things to do since he'd come back from Reunion. He'd thought he *should* do it. He'd several times thought he really *should* clarify his position for the Committee. He'd occasionally thought he should write a paper explaining to them that they never *had* actually understood the office to which they'd appointed him and all his predecessors . . . an atevi office, not a human one, but which the aiji had let them fill. He *shouldn't* be exclusively their representative, as they'd wanted him to be: he *shouldn't* take sides himself, or take instruction from them exclusively, or divulge everything he knew about Tabini. But that wasn't the way they understood it, wasn't the way they wanted it.

Wanted or not, that was the way it had to be, because, among other difficulties of translation, they had never understood the atevi word *paidhi.* He represented the other side—whichever side, equally, fairly, and at whatever risk. He represented *them* to the aiji. He represented the aiji to them, want it or not.

The aiji wanted what he wanted, and meant to have it, and it was the paidhi's job, right now, to explain it in ways Mospheira would not misinterpret.

Including the fact that the aiji was not going to tolerate the situation on the station another year.

Well, duty done. Wilson's closest ally, Koman, was now *head* of the Committee on Linguistics, the Old Guard, who had never trusted Tabini, was heading the committee that advised State on atevi affairs—and under its current structure, he didn't have high hopes for the disposition of the kyo materials he would send over—because they would be re-interpreted through the departmental lens, which viewed the paidhi's office as properly theirs to dispose, and the current paidhi as an inconvenience.

In plain fact, he had notions of a restructuring of the all-powerful department, but that wouldn't come from the bottom up—and bottom of the power structure, indeed, they considered him to be, as their appointee. The restructuring he envisioned would have to come from the State Department, which regulated "foreign contact," and as such, did have a hand in the way Linguistics dealt with situations.

Once he'd *become* paidhi, and once Tabini had accepted him and *refused* any replacement, his attempted removal by the Committee had created a crisis, and in the crisis, he'd begun to be monitored directly not by the Committee but by State, specifically by a deputy officer of the Department of State, Shawn Tyers, before Shawn himself had climbed the ladder in State and then run for President. Shawn had become his contact—and his monitor and rock of sanity during those early days. While his scholarly responses, or lack of them, might infuriate the Committee for Linguistics, once he'd come under State's direct supervision, they'd lost control of him, and couldn't force him to give account to them any more than they could force him out of office. They didn't understand it that way. But that had been the truth since the first attempt to unseat him.

Now it wasn't so much that Shawn was his official contact, but that Mospheira had, in Shawn, a head of state Tabini could work with—and work well with, through him, and even State had ceased to deal with the paidhi-aiji. His communications went straight to Shawn.

The Committee's rulebook had taken another heavy blow during Murini's coup and his takeover of the atevi government. But the linguists, the ordinary translators within the department, that dealt with news and intelligence out of the mainland, had been what Mospheira had to work with in that two-year-long nightmare. State and Defense had overridden rules left and right to get contact with individuals on the mainland, and they had dealt with whomever they had been able to get on the continent. They had worked more or less directly with the Guild itself, on the coast, with whom they *had* to pass messages.

And the translators had done admirably. The Department had every reason to be proud—if only they could see it not as a breach of policy, but as a move to a new age. That two-year period of cooperation had set a new tone—had won the gratitude of many interests on the mainland, and it was what they had to build on, *if* Linguistics could manage to unwind itself from its past, shake off the paralytic fear of another War of the Landing, and set to work on an entirely new basis.

He didn't want to offend them, personally or professionally. He truly didn't want that, which was why he had sat down to write that letter as part of his first day on the island.

He'd be patient, he'd be courteous—but he couldn't go meekly back to fill out forms and deal with their procedural complaints, nor would any successor.

He *needed* the Department to work with three youngsters who knew more colloquial Ragi than anybody on the Committee . . . but he had serious doubts that they were going to cope well with that concept.

And kyo coming *through* Ragi? With the same three youngsters, children under the age of fourteen, knowing more kyo than anybody in the Department?

He really, truly worried how they were going to deal with that.

But he had to work with what existed. And he trusted State, which had fingers in the University, far more than he trusted Linguistics. And he trusted that State could still bring the figurative hammer down on Linguistics where they had to.

He'd made the gesture, stated he had the materials they would expect him to have and intended to send them.

He didn't yet mention the youngsters, or the structure that would have to exist to accommodate them.

He didn't yet mention the advent of five thousand Reunioners, in which the Department also had a role to play.

Most of all he didn't suggest that the rules simply were not going to survive that encounter, assuming the Department did.

6

Dressing in the morning, one gazed into a mirror rimmed with gilt and silver flowers, and took one's collar pin from Eisi on a crystal tray that sparkled more than it did.

Antaro and the juniors had presented themselves in good order. Rieni and the seniors turned up a little later, immaculate, and Cajeiri drew a deep breath, looking at the reflection of black uniforms over his shoulder—at what would be his household for the rest of his life.

It was a lot of people. A crowd of people. And he had not even accumulated a domestic staff. There was really no need of *everybody* attending him, and everybody *could* just trust Uncle's own security and go to the lesser dining room for their own breakfast with no standing about and waiting.

But how did he tell the seniors to go down to the staff breakfast table and leave him to the juniors, or tell his own aishid to leave him to the seniors' care?

And taking two escorts down to Great-uncle's table, even in the large breakfast room—was just excessive, with Great-uncle's own aishid in attendance. It would provide enough Guild in that room to overwhelm a Kadagidi assault—if there were Kadagidi apt to launch one any longer, which there were, apparently—not.

It had been a quiet night. A night without alarms. Somewhere, far along a border Taibeni shared with Ajuri, somebody had trespassed, and the whole world had twitched in alarm—

but that was yesterday. Taibeni were encamped outside the gate. A solid wall of escort was about to stand guard with Uncle's guard during breakfast. It all seemed on a morning untroubled by alarms in the night—a bit excessive, for a breakfast in the heart of Tirnamardi, surrounded by hedges, space, and walls.

He almost said, knowing it was futile—I could go down by myself. They were a crowd on the stairs, not a disorderly one, to be sure—but, walking the steps amid an escort of eight, he was a little embarrassed at the spectacle it presented.

Then he thought—why am I here, but to show Uncle has Father's support? And how shall I show his support but to make as much noise as I can? I *am* Father's heir. I come with Father's intent, and *Father* provided these senior Guild for exactly the reason that I am *not* to be inconspicuous in Uncle's house.

So he squared his shoulders and descended to the bottom of the stairs, preceded by the juniors, followed by the seniors—the simple practicality of the juniors knowing where the breakfast room was, and which way to turn.

So a lot of things might quietly work that way, creating no special fuss, nobody being a fool . . .

If their lord decided not to be one, on this trip.

He walked into Great-uncle's breakfast hall, a place that could seat twenty people easily, and Great-uncle stood up to welcome him this morning, with his own bodyguard along the wall at the head of the room.

"Great-uncle," he said, and bowed as his escort spread themselves about the foot of the room, to stand through breakfast and seek their own after, schedule permitting.

Light was just breaking in the two tall windows. Great-uncle had spread a massive breakfast, and had all the lamps lit, helping the sun. Great-uncle was doing everything as if he had mani in residence . . . as if his guest truly were something other than nine years old. But Uncle knew how to authorize leaks out to the townships.

Of *course* the servants would talk. Guild never did, but

servants would: they would talk to relatives in the Atageini towns and villages, and the news would pick it up, how for the first time the Heir was making an official visit on his own—not just a boy on a visit, but as *Father's* representative, with all his bodyguard—how he had arrived late because of the bridge repair, and how he behaved, every slightest hint of favor or disfavor to Great-uncle. It all would be gossiped, and picked up to be commented on. Father's veto was going to be one piece of news today, but anybody would immediately understand that his presence with Uncle was no accident, and was meant to send signals.

So he bowed again, settled at the other end of a table that could be three times as long, with extra pieces, and said, mani's best tutelage, "I have waked in all sorts of places in the last several weeks, Great-uncle, and this is one of my favorite places in the world to wake up. Not to mention the breakfasts!"

"Well, you are indeed welcome, Great-nephew, and we regret the delay with the bridge. We sympathize, we quite sympathize. It tied us up for an hour on our own trip. How long may you stay?"

"I would not want to inconvenience you, Uncle."

"Oh, you are no inconvenience. You are an exceedingly welcome guest. Three days, four, five. Please take the liberty of the house, whatever you wish. One was greatly disappointed that your great-grandmother had business to attend in the East, so I had only the merest sketch of events in the heavens. She reports your young guests had some little part in it. Are they well?"

"They are quite well. And there are stories to tell. Which I shall."

"I look forward to it."

"And is my mecheita well?"

"She is in excellent form, excellent form. She is making her way up the hierarchy. You may find her a little contentious— but I have every confidence you can manage."

"The Taibeni camp . . . I would like Antaro and Jegari to have a little time with their parents, who escorted us in last night. We might ride out that far, perhaps."

"Well, well, managing your Jeichido among my herd is one thing, but I would have a little anxiousness taking her in among the Taibeni."

There was not a word about Ajuri. And it was a fair caution, about mixing herds. He was a novice rider and Jeichido was a mecheita of high breeding and hot ambition.

"I would not ride even a quiet mecheita into that herd, uncle. I know I am not good enough. But they might, if you would lend two. Or if we could call Taiben and contact them. They will surely have two to lend, if they were assured your permission . . ."

"To come to the gate? Of course. And through it, if they wish. But likely they will prefer the open air. Indeed. I approve, nephew. I approve your good sense."

It would let Antaro and Jegari get whatever news had come in since yesterday. That was in the plan. He did not mention that. But it was part of the plan. Antaro and Jegari would get whatever detail existed. Father would veto the nomination. If there *was* going to be any fuss afterward, Antaro and Jegari would hear whatever Taiben heard.

And he, meanwhile, would still get his ride.

"So may we ride this afternoon? Would you ride, Uncle?"

"Sedately," Uncle Tatiseigi said. "Sedately. We have no wish to stir up that young hellion of yours: she wears peace-caps even in pasture. You will learn to ride on *this* one, young gentleman, you surely will. But all her first lessons should be manners. Manners. Manners. Three times important."

Mani raced. Or had, when she was younger. Raced. And hunted, on the great Babsidi. He wished he had seen it.

But out there in a fair-sized herd, being on his own in every other respect, and with the two who could really ride—Antaro and Jegari—off on their own business, he thought teaching Jeichido manners with Uncle was a very good plan.

*   *   *

"We're secure here," Shawn said. And one had to wonder—how much Shawn knew, or how he knew it.

Bren did know. Algini had come in briefly—into the executive office in Francis House, Shawn's office, with the Presidential seal and all, and set down a little black box, the size of a playing card. It had a green light. That was good. If it turned red, it was not good.

"I take it that thing does not explode if we go off-topic," Shawn said.

"No." Bren gave a quiet smile. "But if that light turns red we turn rapidly to discussing the weather."

"My bodyguards and yours. Perhaps they can organize a card game."

"May the day come."

"Did you sleep last night?"

"Actually, yes. Food was great. Compliments to your chef. And my aishid appreciated the extra pillows. They could pile those up and compensate for the mattress length. May I ask for four extra beds. They can turn them sideways to add a little length and be a bit more comfortable."

"God. The details. I am sorry. If we'd known you were coming over—"

"Honestly, Tabini ordered it. And I think it's a good idea I did come—*as* I came. Shawn, I am always *available* to do just what I did, to represent your interests, and I shall. But the days of applying for Archive items for atevi use are pretty well passing. I won't mediate that any longer, except to say—if there is anything secret left in there, release it to the aishidi'tat and save us all the bother. On a practical level we can get it from the ship. But that function of the Linguistics Department needs to obsolesce. We're building an atevi *starship,* for God's sake. We should be able to get access to whatever's in the record."

"I entirely agree. Explaining that simple reality to certain mindsets is going to be a sales job. But it's only practical."

"It's only practical considering Reunioner science took what's in there and went on developing with access to micro-gravity materials and energy for well over a hundred years. We have people up there, on short rations and a mistake away from injury, who know something about that."

"I've talked to Gin. She wants to land them."

"The aiji agrees and he has a few words on the matter. The aiji will afford them landing on atevi shuttles whenever useful and will bring them to Port Jackson or wherever else you'd like to have them. *You* deal with them, after that. But insofar as these people bring processes and science with them, these items will not be withheld from atevi industry. We have one instance of a man who's brought salvaged manuals from a Reunion research lab. Asgard stationside offered him things it had no right to offer, apparently with Stationmaster Tillington's help, getting his son into a unique program, getting employment which other Reunioners were barred from—not a pleasant situation. Gin's investigating."

"I know a bit about this—from Gin."

"I don't personally fault the Reunioner in question. He saved what would have been destroyed and used it to get his son out of the terrible situation the Reunioners are in. I don't blame him. I do blame the company that took advantage of the situation. The Reunioner is, in my opinion, due compensation. I'm not after Asgard on the ground, understand, but they need to know that their on-station manager was engaged in shady dealings with Tillington, in what was ultimately a deal to get Asgard to try to take atevi materials to launch a station-built Reunioner expedition out to Maudit. You know that proposal."

"Definitely. It's dead. There's not going to be a Maudit effort."

"For the record, atevi mined those resources, atevi have refined them, or lifted them into orbit, and the atevi postponed construction on the starship and held those materials in reserve because of the situation in the aishidi'tat, which is now history.

The resources belong to the aishidi'tat. Human project planning doesn't get to include them. Repair and maintenance of the station is something atevi will support. But Maudit, besides being unworkable, and a dead issue, has one further problem: population balance. Atevi stand by the treaty that set up the station population as equal. And officially calls on the Mospheiran government to stand by the agreement and to repudiate any suggestion that the arrival of the Reunioners changes that requirement."

"Pretty plain," Shawn said without offense. "We accept that we've got an overpopulation of humans up there, and we understand that we have a choice: the station can either build itself larger to accommodate five thousand more atevi—or we bring five thousand people down."

"Five thousand people, I have to say, who never passed screening. Who include some problems."

"So better down here than up there."

"Far better. I have a proposal. An immediate proposal."

"What is it?"

"Get the young aiji's guests down—not to the continent, but here. They're personable. They're smart, they've had an introduction to realities down here, and they don't need the meds, apparently, though their parents may. I have a notion, if you'll hear it."

"I'm anxious to hear it."

"Attach the kids and their parents to the University, the seed of a very small community, to work with the University. Safest environment I can think of, and the Reunioners in general, once we start moving the general population down, *can* contribute to knowledge. If the Mospheiran public gets the idea there is *value* in what the Reunioners know, they can have an introduction to Mospheiran society as people with something to contribute—they can have a much easier start than if they're presented as needing charity. Some do. Some are probably going to be problems. But some are very valuable. Put those valuable ones on University stipend, let the University figure how to use those resources, and the University being the disseminator of the information incidentally spreads out the advantage conveyed by any science they may bring in. Let companies that can take advantage of the information use it freely. There's also history to recover, where records are now lost; there are genetic studies possible. There's work for Linguistics, and Anthro, and Law, and Medicine. I'm sure there are others who'll be interested. Even the Reunioners who aren't in possession of unique knowledge will be a resource. Present them as such."

"Interesting. Interesting. Gin's proposing to start construction on no-return vehicles. She says you discussed it."

"I've presented the aiji with the notion of dedicated drop zones, with atevi transport delivering cargo to the coast, your transport or his, at that point. The shuttles go up with the usual load, and they begin coming down with passengers, about fifty at a time—a full shuttle load, at intervals Mospheira feels comfortable with. Otherwise cargo can go down as ordinarily scheduled. With some passage for station folk needing furlough."

"You have this worked out in specific?"

"Partially. I'm looking for input from you, among others. It's far from set in stone. I've also thought of setting another small community of techs and skilled workers down on Crescent Island."

"Any suggestion of taking Mospheiran technical jobs won't go over well."

"If they bring the knowledge I think they do, there'll be more jobs in the long run. Unfortunately, there will be a period of tension in the short run while things get started, and there are going to be questions—how does it affect me? And inevitably— these are the descendants of old station management, that we hated enough to bail ourselves out of the station in parachutes. Why should they get special treatment? In point of fact, the real station management bailed with us, also with parachutes, but that's not how people think of it. These people are the descendants of people who just opted to go with the ship, and tracing the families may prove that, but the Heritage Party won't care. They'll raise the issue."

"They'll definitely raise the issue," Shawn said.

"So. I've done the talking this far. I'm interested in your view."

Shawn shrugged. "I agree with you. I absolutely agree with you. It's the only thing we *can* do, and your idea of working them into the University community—I don't know if your estimate of value these people bring down with them is overly optimistic, but I do know I don't want a crew of upset people sitting out at Maudit planning how to get back here and get revenge for the way we treated them. Hospitality, a little legal oversight, a firm policy of knitting the Reunioners back into the social fabric— that's smart. They'll change us a little. We'll change them a lot."

"Reunioners don't understand leisurely approaches to things, but they do understand about minimal interference until they understand a system. Stationers and earthborn take similar precautions: they just describe them differently."

"I hope that's true."

"I've a notion who to involve in setting some of this up."

"Kate Shugart?"

"Kate. Tom Lund. Ben Feldman. Kate to handle the University interface, Tom Lund to handle the legalities and corporate interests, employment, the whole legal mess. Ben Feldman to handle the technicals and interpret Kate in a kinder, gentler way."

Shawn gave a wry little laugh. "The old team."

"Together with Gin."

"If we can talk them into it."

"Sonja Podesta."

Shawn's executive secretary. "Sonja's officially retired from State. I miss her." A long deep breath. "This is for your ears only. She spent the mainland upheaval in Intelligence. That's where she still is. And she will do what I ask."

Bren nodded, accepting. "One more I'd like to have, working

directly with the children's parents, first team down. Sandra Johnson."

"Sandra. God."

"Married, two kids."

"Four."

"Four?"

"Last I heard. We do track her. We track everybody who had a close connection to you."

"Sandra's smart, she catches details, she's got typical kids, a husband—John, I think it was, and she's got the best sympathetic ear going. I'd call her at midnight, saying, Sandra, I need a message passed, or I need a permission, and she'd keep after it until she found whoever it was, and got me whatever I needed, if she had to track it down. If I had to pick somebody to keep a watch on the first-down, somebody who'd just be a decent neighbor—Sandra."

"I remember. I couldn't forget. Guess who Sandra called when all else failed."

He nodded. Of course she had.

"So that's your list," Shawn said. "I'll track them down. Never mind Kate. She's been in touch. I'll tell her."

Old names. Old allies. New problem. But if he *could* get the old team assembled—

He'd have to leave them to do the work alone. He'd not be who he had been, back in the old days, when he'd come often to the island, when it was him and Shawn, Sonja and Sandra— or when they'd been cast into a wild rush to space, building on plans from the old Archive, and they'd had to set up the station.

Gin had come to his rescue, up on station.

Now they needed the others. And whoever they could pull in.

For a situation they'd never planned to have.

But Cajeiri's three human guests—were about to pioneer a program that would ground the Reunioners. Give them a world. Take away their access to space, unless they were both determined and qualified.

There were compensations. Sunrises. Sunsets. Mountains. Irene—gazing into an oncoming storm, rapt in wonder.

Some might be terrified. Some might be thrilled. But it was all in their expectations of life on Earth . . . which should be not too extravagant—but not too little, either.

The lamps shed gold light over the sitting room.

And one sat carefully. Quite carefully, despite a long, warm bath.

They had ridden, oh, for much of the afternoon, and Uncle had shown him finesses that Jeichido knew, when she was reminded of them.

She had shed out bronze for the summer. She had eyes like the sun. With long lashes that Uncle said mecheiti had evolved to protect against dust. Her long neck was muscled and strong enough to take the rein away if one lost leverage, and her peace-caps were a good thing, because she was very sly at getting near enough to one of the other mecheiti to swing her head. The peace-caps were blunt, preventing real damage. That had happened once, to his embarrassment—but he had stopped that game.

And in the saddle, he was tall as anybody, well, almost, and he had not done badly, not half. He had ridden before. He had ridden the way most people did, happy to stay on, and on a mecheita mostly content to follow. A young likely herd-leader was another sort of creature, and Jeichido had had time now, living at Uncle's estate, to get another season under her and to form a notion of just how few of the herd dared get in her way.

Not many, in fact. She was bent on getting farther up in the order, and there were only five in Uncle's herd who could bluff her down.

It was scary how fast she could get out of hand; but Uncle, who did not look like a strong person, told him exactly when, and where, to use the quirt—gently, in fact, but distracting; and where to put his balance if she tried certain tricks. He was really surprised at how Uncle had an answer for most every bad behavior, and how to keep the rein gentle, too.

They had talked about the land, talked about the seasons, talked about orchards—which were fruiting now; and the condition of the hedges, and what it took to maintain them—a thousand things about the estate and things Uncle knew.

He wondered if Uncle were as sore as he was, where he was sore, and decided probably not, because Uncle rode more than once a year, and always had, he supposed, from back before there were airplanes or computers, let alone atevi going into space.

"The soreness goes away," Uncle said, "after three days at it. But you will want to have another long bath this evening. If you were here more often, you would not be so inconvenienced. And you *may* be here more often, should you wish. The children, too. One understands the paidhi is arranging for them to come down."

"He is," Cajeiri said, teacup in hand, and hoped that matter did not constitute business, which would be rude, during tea. But Uncle had brought up the topic, so he supposed it was allowed. "And one hopes they will visit often, and they would be very happy to be invited. I would be happy."

"Well, we shall host them here as often as they choose to come. You may tell them so."

"They very much enjoyed Tirnamardi. And your stories about the antiquities. They were very excited by those."

That pleased Uncle, he could tell. Tirnamardi cellars were packed with marvelous objects, all of which had a history, some of which went back to very earliest times. It was a collection like a museum, and Uncle's scary stories and the dark and the artifacts themselves were an experience he himself would never forget.

"And this kyo youngster, this son of the kyo aiji . . . do you anticipate his return? Perhaps a visit to the mainland?"

"One would doubt it. Kyo are very different. I think they

would be very uncomfortable. Cold, always. If *he* were to visit, too, *I* would have to visit him. Nand' Bren calls it *reciprocity*."

"*Re-si-pro-si-ty.*" Uncle tasted the human word. "And is this a kyo idea."

"Nand' Bren says he knows no Ragi word that quite fits. He says the closest would be an echo. The kyo made a signal. We repeat it. At every stage of complexity we repeat it. What they do, we do. What we do, they do. Until we agree. Nand' Bren thinks Prakuyo brought an elder person, perhaps even a relative, and his son, because mani and I were part of the meeting at Reunion Well, I think so, and nand' Bren thought I could be right."

"You are very quick. Astonishingly quick. I told your father this would be an asset someday. And clearly he agrees. Of course your great-grandmother is convinced. So we shall not expect this boy—Hakun?"

"Hakuut, Uncle. Hakuut an Ti."

"Well, well, Hakuut. We shall not expect him to join your association of youngsters, shall we, then?"

"I think not, Uncle. I think he will be as old as Lucasi before he reaches home."

"Such lengthy and inconvenient traveling. One cannot undertake it lightly. But soon we are to have the youngsters *and* their parents at a much more convenient distance."

"Father does not wish the parents to visit, I think, and probably this is how it should be. Mospheira will be strange enough for them. But my associates will learn *both* sides of the strait."

"And visit."

"And visit."

"I will tell you," Uncle said, and set his cup down, in the way of someone who had reached a point that needed discussion. "I am considering a new establishment. A new stable."

"Indeed."

"Jeichido is special. She is the product of Babsidi and Saidaro—very apt to challenge my old lad, possibly even by next year."

"Would you have me move her, Uncle? I might persuade nand' Bren . . ."

"Oh, it need not be far. I have in mind a place over by Diegi . . . a little house, at a half-day's remove. That suffices. I have in mind a plan, if you will hear it."

"Indeed, Uncle."

"Assuming that your young associates will ride, assuming that you will always have an extended guard—it would make sense to establish an outlying herd, often enough associated that we shall not have warfare between the bands, and indeed, the breeding makes sense. Jeichido will lead, and I have a young male, a two-year-old, young enough to be impressed, of, if I may be immodest, a breeding that might bring something special from Babsidi's line as well. A new herd, a new stable, a new establishment, a blending of the Tirnamardi and the Malguri lines. What do you say?"

"I do not think I have a sensible opinion."

"Well, well, let your great-uncle give a gift or two. Your Jeichido will head that herd, you shall own it, you shall favor me with one of that breeding, and in settling a herd at the old summer house I shall pay the mayor of Diegi a favor or two. The old house will suit a small establishment, which Diegi will supply, a stablemaster, which my staff can supply—my own groom has a daughter who could well undertake that enterprise. I shall give her charge of the summer house, and we shall have something of two lines which should produce something extraordinary."

"Uncle, it would be—it would be very fine—I am sure, but— would mani—?"

"It is perfectly appropriate to consult her. We have long said when we found a likely foundation, we should see what results—and when she proposed a daughter of Babsidi to reside here, at your convenience, I knew it was a great trust. Your own stable. *Your* line established of the best of both. I do not think she will be displeased."

"Uncle." Cajeiri hardly trusted himself to speak. It was extravagantly generous. He treasured Jeichido as the most wonderful gift he had ever had. But he had just reasoned it through that Boji was a responsibility he could no longer manage, and that he had been childish and shortsighted to have thought he *could* manage a parid'ja. This was on a far grander scale. He had no idea at all what was involved in taking care of a *herd*, but he could not pay the costs. He had no idea what things cost, or what wages were. Father took care of that. Or Father's major domo did.

"The grass there is excellent," Uncle was saying. "The hills moderate the winter wind. The house itself needs some repair, but a little paint, a few shingles—a modest place, but very quaint. And my groom's daughter is an excellent person, an excellent rider . . ."

"I only worry, Uncle, that *I* would not know what to do."

"That is why you have staff, nephew. The summer house will send that herd over for your use here at Tirnamardi, so there will be no question of security, staff will work out the two herds together, and we shall have that very excellent thing, two separate but compatible breeding herds, and my groom's daughter will have a property and a responsibility to be proud of."

"If Father approves. If mani approves . . . But, Uncle, I have never even managed for myself, let alone—"

"*Staff,*" Uncle said. "Staff, nephew, will manage everything. And you will see. That is the thing you have yet to learn, young gentleman. Your responsibilities lie elsewhere than managing the details. Trust your staff. A good staff will not fail you. Your responsibility lies in knowing who to trust, and when."

That—was a scary thing. Very scary, when he thought about the meeting on the train, and how these four strangers had just—moved in. Older, more experienced, definitely the sort of persons Uncle was talking about. The sort who could turn his younger aishid into—*them.*

Father himself, after poor Eidi and his guard had been killed, had had trouble finding *anybody* of that sort until mani had moved in a handful of her own.

He understood now—what Father had lost, what Father was trying to build back. And Father had sent these four to *him*.

Mani and Uncle Tatiseigi were giving him a stable, not just because riding was one of his favorite things, but because mecheiti were traditional—because the bloodlines went back before there ever was an aishidi'tat. Because these things had to be kept going.

And he could not repay *anybody* he owed so much—except by being what they needed him to be.

That was the scariest thing of all.

7

The morning had gotten off to a quiet start in Francis House, a delivery of flowers with breakfast, and a note about a little rearrangement of an appearance before the Science Committee.

By an hour before the meeting, a second note arrived, from Shawn personally, with a change of venue from Francis House proper to the new wing, and the legislative hearing room. It seemed several committees wanted to join the session—a cascade of committees, in fact, and they were delayed until afternoon so that the head of another committee could fly in.

It turned out to be, in unprecedented joint session, the Science Committee, the Committee on Foreign Affairs, the Committee on Budget, and the Committee on Internal Affairs. Individually, the committees were familiar territory, on one side of the straits or the other—similar concerns, similar problems, similar posturing of one party with its agenda, and the other with its firm convictions that whatever was at issue was all going to go badly for them if it in any way pleased their political opponents.

In some respects it was indeed very like the continent, absent the influence of the clans, but *with* the silent influence of corporations and special interests.

And if they thought the paidhi-aiji had an imperfect understanding of how it all worked, they were mistaken.

Bren knew the questions. He saw, in his mind's eye, the overlay of atevi on human faces. Shawn had said, in the second note,

I hate to do this to you on your second day here, but if you think you can satisfy them, it would keep momentum going. They want this joint session, because they all want to have the first session.

Of course. What could he say, then?

The large hearing was not as intimidating as it had been, years ago, when he'd first confronted Foreign Affairs, at a table in front of a committee panel, under television cameras. He'd been younger, unused to politics, unaccustomed to the spates of formality (when the cameras were present) and a little taken aback by the moments of levity (when the cameras were not). Either could mask nasty agendas.

Now the joint committee itself seemed to have been thrown quite off pace when he arrived in court dress, and with his aishid, visibly armed, stationed in the corridor.

Did he think this show would impress them? The chair of Science was smarter than to ask that, but he overheard it in the recess: not surprising.

"I should state," he said, when the joint committee reconvened, "that I am particularly glad to have this meeting with these key committees. My duties are being reconfigured, not by choice, but by circumstance, to render me an officer of the atevi court—still with strong ties here, but my function as a translator, and my function as an arbiter of technology are both passing into the background. I am here now at the request of the aiji, first to thank the Mospheiran people for their quick response to the emergency situation, and secondly to state that the science we will gain from Reunioner sources, and from observation of the kyo, such as we were able to do—will be equally shared."

"We cannot have the Archive opened up wholesale," an elderly senator objected. He knew the man, Anthony Tosco, not Heritage Party, but sympathetic to many of its aims.

He took a certain quiet pleasure in saying, "I was speaking, sir, of knowledge and science *atevi* possess from the recent contact, which we are offering to share with Mospheira. And certain Reunioner documents which atevi authorities have recovered during the recent difficulties on the station . . . those also, the aiji is willing to hold in trust until ownership has been settled and appropriate agreement has been made with Mospheiran interests."

There was a moment of stark silence, which at least the senator left alone, choosing that moment to summon and confer with an aide.

"Are we to have a list of these documents?" the chair asked.

"I am certain. Yes. Some are in physics, in astronomy, in materials science: Lord Geigi is cooperating with the Mospheiran stationmaster, is taking measures to locate and protect certain additional documents which were hitherto being bartered secretly—a state of affairs Stationmaster Kroger is currently investigating, and pursuing under whatever door seems necessary."

"Why," another senator asked, "is the Mospheiran security force not engaged in this matter?"

"They are, in all operations on the Mospheiran section of the human half of the station. But former stationmaster Tillington created a dangerous situation when he closed the section doors between Mospheirans and Reunioners, and did it so abruptly it caused injury and created great hardship. That incident created a strong Reunioner mistrust of uniformed Mospheiran security. The situation required intervention by atevi and by ship personnel to alleviate the shortages in that area and restore order, a fact not lost on the Reunioners. To date, Reunioners have wished to deal, inside their own sections, with a combination of ship security, atevi, and their own appointed security personnel, though Stationmaster Kroger is making progress in winning back their trust. That is the current situation as I have it.

"But as to your question, sir, atevi acquired some of these sensitive materials on request of a Reunioner who had rescued a store of them. Several other Reunioners, since my departure from the station, have wished atevi to take other materials in safe-keeping, on example of the first instance. We believe others may come forward, if that works well for the first."

"Mr. Cameron," burst forth from several at once, a determined gaveling from the chairman, and a small debate between chairman and committee members with competing and politically positioned questions about the existence of the documents, the location of the documents, and the rumor that three corporations on the station had already laid hands on them.

Bren sipped at a glass of water while that went on. The chairman banged the gavel in final decision and framed his own question, as to what documents were being bartered.

"I understand some materials involved materials science and Asgard Corporation," Bren said, "but as to ownership and propriety, the Mospheiran stationmaster has claimed jurisdiction, since the case involves Mospheiran law and Mospheiran citizens, which the aiji freely accepts, and the aiji does not *wish* to know anything about the Asgard case but the outcome. Though Lord Geigi is still receiving some applications for aid and protection, he is now referring them to Stationmaster Kroger. The aiji is keenly interested in the protection of the physical documents, and in protection of valuable knowledge. *Some* of this information, let me stress to the committee, exists not in written documents, but in the memory and technical expertise of certain Reunioners, people in dire circumstances, lately in physical danger, and still existing in shortages and poor conditions— eighteen people to a bathroom, people with children living in what were original station construction barracks, with no furniture but a bed, and water being provided in *buckets."*

That roused a little stir. And another application of the gavel.

"The question is regarding the safety of the documents."

"Buckets, sir. Those are the conditions in which the technicians and science workers who escaped Reunion with their knowledge have lived for the last year, during which time the only planning for their future consisted in sending them to

build a mining station at Maudit—a plan that had no source of supply, and that clearly violated the spirit of the station's founding treaty."

Gavel. "Mr. Cameron,—"

"The aiji is entirely sensible of the reason for the delay in remedying the population imbalance, and he appreciates the aid of the Mospheiran people in the recent troubles in the aishidi'tat. He will wish me to say that he entirely understands the constraints, including medical issues, that have delayed the resolution of this situation, and that he will cooperate with the Mospheiran people in addressing the matter as soon as possible. He will postpone any increase in the atevi population to current human levels, which would ordinarily mean five thousand atevi going *to* the station, so long as—"

Gavel, as objections burst forth.

"—so long as there is progress toward *reducing* the human population of the station by five thousand individuals . . . counting children. *And* so long as the agreements hold regarding *sharing* new technological developments, where information comes first to human authorities. In effect the paidhi's office will no longer arbitrate the surrender of technology from the Archive to the aishidi'tat. That part of my office is done." He overrode the murmur. "The aiji looks forward to a new era of cooperation, wherein Mospheirans and atevi manage their separate territories in safety and cordiality, neither disturbing the ways and traditions which make us what we are. The world was changing even before the kyo's intervention. With the return of the ship and the technological changes that came on us with the space program, atevi as well as Mospheira adjusted to a new reality. Our recent experience with the kyo has given us a new awareness of our place within the universe and shown us all, kyo as well, what intelligent species should do on meeting— beginning with respect and a willingness to negotiate . . ."

A murmur arose, and drew another rapid-fire gaveling.

"The kyo are out there, ladies and gentlemen, but they are

not our enemies, nor wish to be. They have satisfied themselves that we are not a threat—and they are this moment departing the solar system.

"Our agreement with the kyo is extremely simple. They are, in effect, willing to shield us from their ongoing conflict so long as we do not cross into their territory. We are free to explore all other directions of a sphere as wide as the heavens, but in that narrow path, we are not to set foot until they are done with their war, and until they contact us to say so. If they never contact us again, that is also their prerogative, but another contact is likely. When it may come, there is no predicting."

He finished. There was silence. Lengthy silence, in which scarcely a hand moved.

He had said it. He had delivered the whole message in one packet—ex temp, and not precisely as he would have planned it, but he had had to operate that way far more often than he ever liked, wedging information into minds that really didn't want it—but on which their survival hinged.

"Atevi took it on themselves to make this agreement." That was the chairman of Internal Affairs. Depend on it. That was exactly the argument he expected, from the individual he expected to make it.

He said, with particular satisfaction. "Atevi negotiators were the kyo's specific request—for a reason. The kyo's chief negotiator was held prisoner for six years in a glass cage at Reunion. He was rescued by atevi, with whom he developed a good relationship—and consequently *he* chose to approach this world in a mood of gratitude, not revenge. He was, during this visit, able to meet certain Reunioners who helped him purge that unpleasant memory, but he chose to do all his face-to-face negotiations with atevi and in the Ragi language. We have established that kyo weapons are quite powerful—more so than anything we have. Nothing forced them to come here to make this agreement. They acknowledge a massive error in their attack on Reunion—a mistake on the scale of a war we do not want to see. They deeply regret that error. They wish to establish a firm border with their peaceful neighbors and keep us out of their conflict, so as not to have another Reunion. They wish us well, human and atevi alike, and hope that the Reunioners may recover from that traumatic event—that humans here may find a way to heal the wound they dealt the Reunioners, as they never could. The kyo exit wiser than they were, and more careful. We exit wiser, all of us, and with a certain *pride* in being able to deal with each other, on this planet, in ways that could teach the kyo something. They respect us for the mutually beneficial civilization we have built here. I think we have a right to be proud."

"We exist—we have *always* existed—under atevi domination."

The gavel came down.

"Mr. Woodenhouse."

"We have atevi in possession of important documents, negotiating with these outsiders, negotiating with the aliens, continuing to make private agreements in the assumption they are the authority. What part have they given us in all this arranging of our future?"

He wasn't remotely interested in debating the opposition, whose rhetoric went for charged words and aimed to stir up hate. He had known there was one Heritage Party seat on the Committee for Internal Affairs and he had opted for a joint session purely to have State chairing the meeting, by precedence of committees. He had expected to hear from the gentleman from Hamptonsville, white-haired, wiry, and prone to outshout any reasoned debate, and he had walked into this session absolutely ready for war.

Charged words? *He* owned a few.

And rather than let his own blood pressure get up, he waited for the gavel to establish silence from Mr. Woodenhouse, then said, with the full power of the microphone, low and close, "This the kind of argument that pre-Landing administration used, that humans and atevi could never work together. That administration's overuse of power, its police state tactics, in a situation it could not manage, *drove* our Mospheiran ancestors to risk death and seek an accommodation with the atevi." Woodenhouse shouted his indignation, interspersed with pounding of the chairman's gavel. The racket might affect those nearest, but the microphone was an insurmountable advantage: it fed to the overhead sound system, magnifying even a reasoning, controlled tone to thunder, when he put an impassioned push behind it.

"The administrative mindset of human superiority and no negotiation with aliens was a minority attitude on the pre-Landing station, and it remains a minority attitude now, because Mospheirans willing to risk encounters in an appropriate way remain in the majority. Our ancestors were willing to contact the atevi, and they were open to learning *how* to do it in a way atevi could accept. Fortunately. Because humans and atevi *learned.* In the encounter with the kyo, considering the situation, we would have been mad to consider refusing contact."

"Mad? Who gave you authority to sell us out, Mr. Cameron? A president who takes his orders from Shejidan?"

"My authority, sir, comes from the aiji in Shejidan, but I am *still*, in sentiment of origin, Mospheiran. My ancestors, the same as yours, made the trip down from the station to escape administrators who claimed we could never deal with the people native to this planet. That we were doomed to conflict."

"Sell-out!"

"People willing to risk that encounter left the station in droves, relying on makeshift capsules some of which failed and burned. They left that administration in such numbers that the station began to fail—"

"It was sabotaged."

"Sabotage was not what forced the last to come down. The last-down came down because they had no choice left, Mr. Woodenhouse, because the station had lost so many technicians it was failing, and they couldn't keep it going. Some few stayed, and died there in the last viable sections. The ship, when it came back, did find their remains." It had found other things, too, and God, there were things *not* in the stories they fed to primer-school students, and not the sanitized version they celebrated in Foundation Day. "But the last that did come down, bringing weapons the world had not seen before then, Mr. Woodenhouse, were not the ones who had found a way to communicate with atevi, they were not the ones who made the agreements that let humans settle down and live. Give credit to the first-down, Mr. Woodenhouse. They did not come down here to insist that humans are somehow the universe's wisest and brightest, with rights that trump all agreements. The first-down just wanted a place to live. And bring up families. And here we are, living on land *granted* us by atevi, native to this world. And now when sent a treaty of peace from a neighboring species that could, if it were hostile, turn the surface of this world to volcanic glass in a handful of strikes—with what otherwise are likely its *tools*—who in their right mind now stands up to question the integrity of the negotiations?"

He paused for breath. Woodenhouse was silent for a second. The whole committee room was, for a second, quiet. He took advantage of it, saying quietly: "There is *knowledge* out there in the universe, Mr. Woodenhouse, there is new science which we will be privileged to share with other species."

"Share!" Woodenhouse shouted. "Who determines that?"

"—Righteous lords of the universe, no, Mr. Woodenhouse, we are *not* that, not *nearly*. We are one species of *three* in the immediate vicinity. Mospheirans have just been, in negotiations conducted by an atevi mission, honored by the kyo with a *separate* document agreeing to peace, and the atevi negotiators never questioned Mospheira's interests being important. We are *respected* equally in this document. Yes, as a world, we still have a lot to learn. But we *have* learned to respect intelligence and civility, no matter the physical package in which it comes. With that start, and this relationship with our neighbors, we have a good chance to *become* wise—if we learn what the other two species know and let them know us. And once we *are* wise, I doubt very much if we will ever despise good quiet neighbors. I am an optimist, Mr. Woodenhouse. I insist humans can not only survive, they can become a relevant *participant* in a multispecies universe, and that calling each other foreigners on the same planet will lead nowhere good."

Woodenhouse was still shouting, the gavel was still banging as he finished, and Woodenhouse finished with, *"Damned traitor!"*

"Mr. Woodenhouse," Chair said. "Mr. Woodenhouse, you are warned." And when Woodenhouse continued to pound his desk with his fists: "Sergeant-at-arms, remove the delegate from Hamptonsville."

"Our liberty is done for!" Woodenhouse screamed. "We are delivered over to aliens and foreigners! Tyers has sold us out! We are selling out the human dream!"

Bren stood up, abandoning the advantage of the microphone, but claiming his own share of visual attention, and showed a calm face to the committee members as the sergeant-at-arms took charge of Woodenhouse and escorted him toward the door. He had not gained place in the aiji's court by engaging in parting arguments, figurative or literal. He simply put on a slightly regretful expression, folded his arms, and watched, as no few watched from their seats, until the irate representative was set outside the door and the door was shut.

His own aishid was outside, under strict orders to defer to the sergeant-at-arms and to disregard any uproar short of bloodletting. They understood. They had stood by him in meetings of the atevi legislature.

He sat down—speaking no word until he had control of the microphone again. "Mr. Chairman," he said equably, "thank you. Should the delegate from Hamptonsville wish to revise and amend his remarks, I shall ask the same privilege."

"The gentleman from Hamptonsville was not accorded the

floor," Chair said, a member of State. Bang went the gavel. "Recorder will strike his remarks."

"Mr. Chairman," Bren said quietly, reasonably—and immensely satisfied to have linked the words *station administrators* to the Heritage Party program, publicly and on record. "I ask that the remarks of the gentleman from Hamptonsville be appended into the record as preceding my own, so as not to lose the context of my reply, which I would ask be included."

"Granted."

"I conclude my remarks and rest, open to questions of whatever nature."

Getting back into the saddle—required a strong, quick move. Which, predictably, hurt, as rump met leather, and hurt again as Jeichido straightened from her mounting stance, and rose up the height of a tall man at the shoulders, not counting the neck and head, peace-caps glinting as she turned a bright gold eye to look askance at Uncle's herd-leader.

Herd-leader was having none of it. He snorted and sauntered past, daring a young fool to rake a tusk across *his* rump.

Cajeiri took in the single rein and tapped Jeichido's rump gently to swing her about and follow, as his aishid, the four seniors and Veijico and Lucasi, with two of Uncle's own, single-filed out of the stableyard—the latter two riding the mecheiti from *their* last visit, and the seniors riding the ones from their own first day, which might become a permanent selection. They took two with them, since they were picking Antaro and Jegari up at the gate. *They* would change mounts, so those two went under saddle. Others including the pushy two-year-old male Uncle proposed to send off to Diegi with Jeichido, went bareback and without restraint, attached to the herd-leader in fairly reasonable order. When the herd went out, everybody went, and the more of them that were ridden, the better, so three of the grooms went along, including the young woman Uncle proposed to run the Diegi stables . . .

It was a plot Uncle had put together during his last visit. He began to be sure of it. Uncle had a lot of yearlings and two-year-olds, and it probably *was* a good idea to split the herd . . . but if the other herd-leader was going to be Jeichido, *he* had to learn a good deal more than just how to stay on and stay out of trouble. He had to do a *lot* more practicing, and Uncle and mani could teach him, but *he* had to learn, given Uncle thought they were going to shift another herd-leader in periodically and not have a fight.

Politics. Even among the mecheiti. Habituation. Respect. He saw that one thing was not the other, but neither were they entirely separate. Like people. Like mecheiti.

Like his aishid, and the new one. It was *his* fault if things went wrong, because he could find no ill will in any of them, none at all. The seniors could still leave if they wished—but he had begun, as of yesterday, to hope that they would not. That would mean, for one thing, that *he* had failed, and he would not do that.

He paid attention to Uncle's lessons, very tiny lessons, just the most minute things about where his feet were, and where his hands were, and how he sat—the most minute twitches of the rein, and the smallest twitch of the foot resting in the bow of Jeichido's neck. It occupied her attention, for one thing, so completely that she moved easily within reach of Uncle's herd-leader, not fighting, not trying to nip or slash.

"You know so much," he said to Uncle. "One hardly knows how many things you know."

Uncle laughed—one almost never heard Uncle laugh. "This thing I know, and your great-grandmother knows. Mecheiti detest boredom. Your touch, your voice, your balance is a conversation that engages them. Mospheira can teach your human companions to be Mospheiran. The mecheiti have lessons for us, many, many lessons."

It was true, he thought. He *was* learning. He had never been so conscious of his own self as giving signals, constantly, or withholding them. It was a deep thing, an important thing, he felt it—something mani practiced better than anyone. One could read her displeasure—yet again, read *nothing*, or read just what mani wanted read. One could be scared, but Jeichido should never know it—one could be interested in a thing, and Jeichido's head would turn, and she would look, and estimate it for herself, but he could *feel* her mood—interested, but not excited enough to go there.

There was so, so much to learn before he could have a seat like mani, or Uncle. He could still be caught by surprise, and earnestly hoped not to be made a fool in front of everybody.

They were on their way to meet Antaro and Jegari at the gate. He had thought yesterday he would like to go all the way to the Taibeni camp to meet them, but this morning, sore as he was, yielding to his senior aishid's request to meet at the gate had great merit.

So they had agreed.

It was still a long roundabout ride, coming around again to the tall iron gates and their deep stone pillars, overgrown until the hedges had to be pruned to clear the hinges.

There they stopped, and there Rieni said, quietly, "Be aware, nandiin, the caution from yesterday persists."

"They have not dismissed it," Uncle asked.

"No, nandi. They have not seen a repetition, but they have not discovered the cause. They have filed a report with the Guild, not a complaint, but a request for an explanation of the intrusion, and thus far Ajuri has not answered."

"No one there," Uncle said, "is able to take responsibility. Nor can." By now it was sure Ajuri still had no lord. Father would have vetoed the nomination, Uncle's associates were likely unhappy, and the situation in Ajuri continued unsettled. It was not, Cajeiri thought, a good time for Ajuri to be making incursions well into another Clan's area. They might be a *little* over their limits, in the borders, among settlements and villages and farms that were a little of this clan, a little of the other, a status respected by both, but to go beyond that—if the one region was unsettled, with nobody in charge—that was enough to upset Taiben.

But Rieni and Antaro began using communications halfway through the ride, and affirmed that there was no problem, nothing further, just nothing explained. And when they did come near the gate, and opened it, it was no long wait at all before Antaro and Jegari turned up, having come some little distance afoot.

"Up, up," Uncle said, and with Uncle and his aishid making a living screen, keeping order, Uncle's aishid quickly moved the two reserve mecheiti into position for Antaro and Jegari, who were into the saddles with no fuss. Cajeiri felt Jeichido's unease, right through her body into his, and he administered the lightest little touch of the quirt, just a distraction from her fixation on the unusual activity. Jeichido swayed her tall neck and swung her hindquarters still to have a look at the two, and she sucked in wind to utter an opinion: another tap, two more, and she let the breath go with a grunt.

Manners. Not just staying on. Manners, and listening to each other. That was what Uncle said. He was just mildly proud that two of his aishid could manage that slightly dangerous move that smoothly.

"Was it a good visit?" he asked, as Antaro and Jegari rode near.

"Very good, nandi," Antaro said. "Everyone is well. Everyone is very well." The gate was shutting, controlled from the house, and Uncle was turning the herd back the way they had come, sedately, no matter the mecheiti were anxious to go. "We have been in contact with Lord Keimi at Taiben. There has been no further trouble."

Uncle was near them, in a position to hear it, too. "Excellent," Uncle said, and they rode on their way.

Uncle gave another exercise, which was having the herd quicken pace—and then slow down, not what they wanted to do, with the prospect of stable and food in their heads. Speed up. Slow down to a walk, all disciplined.

He was amazed at himself. Not a year ago he would have let Jeichido go as fast as she could, just for the joy of it. But the notion that he could get control with just so very little a touch—*that*, he thought, that was how Uncle sat that way, and managed the herd-leader, whose behavior dictated all the rest. If Uncle were not keeping the leader in hand, *he* would not have such an easy time with Jeichido, and what Uncle did with the herd-leader—that was a kind of communication that had not happened all in one try. *He* wanted that kind of control. *His* herd, his stable, with Jeichido . . . he understood, finally, it was not just a building and a handful of mecheiti Uncle and mani picked. It shaped the people who rode in a company. It *taught* them things. Even the seniors were paying attention to Uncle, even Antaro and Jegari were, right along with Lucasi and Veijico, because there were a thousand ways to do a thing wrong, mani would say, but there were many fewer to do it right.

He was *glad* he had come here. He was *glad* to have taken Uncle's mind off the veto and *glad* he had finally had this chance with Uncle, just the two of them—well, officially just the two of them, with Uncle's full attention, after all the association in his nine years. Finally he began to *know* his great-uncle, and to feel a connection of his own, not through anybody else.

Hardest, when they had gotten very near the stable. *Then* he made a mistake in attention, or twitched a foot, or something. Jeichido made a move forward, which, if she broke past Uncle and the herd-leader, would bring the herd-leader onto the move, a danger to Uncle and him if a fight broke out.

Quirt, gently; rein, gentle, body-shift, slight—his heart was pounding, but he applied pressure to turn, just matter-of-factly, the same as he had in other orders, and Jeichido turned, quite easily, shaking her head and taking a swipe at Antaro's mecheita as she circled back. He had her listening, however: he gave a little tap, a little pressure, and kept Jeichido moving, long strides, spring-loaded as if she could explode at any instant. Move, move, move, and turn, as he reached the stragglers— their passage crosswise disorganized them, and one confused youngster followed Jeichido a moment, but fell back.

Another turn, to make a small circle, to give Jeichido another focus beyond the stable, and as he swung about he felt her every muscle tense, neck no longer lax, head forward, sharp focus, not on the herd-leader or the stable, but the orchard a good distance beyond the stableyard rails.

Movement. His eye caught it. For a cold, clear moment he saw a man *in* the orchard, moving among the trees, and he felt Jeichido move.

No. He reined in, settled her, thinking, *Fool,* and rode Jeichido back toward the fore, with a little space to make it back in the order. The gate was opening. Herd-leader was going in. Jeichido was not far behind, scraping the gate-post with her shoulder, still on the alert. She made a sound that the herd-leader echoed, a low moan, and Cajeiri was, for the moment, glad to settle her down, glad that the herd-leader was making his bow to let Uncle dismount, and glad to be safe in the yard.

He could dismount with a swing on the mounting-straps, and just get down, but today was for care and training, and making rules. He made Jeichido extend a leg and lower a shoulder, so he could swing down and set his feet on the earth. He began to work at her harness strap himself, but Jegari came over to help him, and took over.

"I saw someone," he said. "Someone was in the orchard. Jeichido saw him."

"Where did he go?"

"He vanished. He may have climbed a tree."

"I would, if I were out and saw the herd coming in."

That was a thought, if it was staff taking a chance despite the warning that always went out when the herd was abroad. On the one hand somebody could get killed, but on the other, it was bad for the herd, too, to kill someone who smelled like the household, and Uncle would be twice upset, really upset.

Granted that was what the person was.

"Tell the seniors," Cajeiri said. "Uncle might fire whoever it was. But we had better ask who it was."

Jegari moved. Fast.

Cajeiri finished the job, a little anxious taking the bridle off, and hoping Jeichido did not pick up his nervousness. He managed to get her head down—and she tried to rake the bridle off, but when he did drag it free, she moved away, not toward the grain, as the inner doors opened, but out into the yard. There she stood staring toward the orchard, nostrils wide and sides heaving with deep breaths.

Uncle was looking in that direction, too, for a moment, before they all, Guild and himself and Uncle, went out the gate a groom opened for them.

"She smells something," Uncle said.

"I saw something," Cajeiri said quietly. "I saw some*one*, Uncle."

By then the seniors had headed through the rails and over toward the orchard. Jegari came and joined them.

"The seniors want us to go inside, nandiin," Jegari said.

"Go. Assist them," Uncle said, and his two Guild headed off to join the seniors, who were headed toward the orchard.

They went inside, into the lower sitting room, a place with leather chairs, and dim lighting, old, and rough enough for people who had come in from riding. Uncle ordered tea, and they waited, while Cajeiri sat and recalled that once before that orchard had been a route for assassins.

"You rode very well today," Uncle said to him. "Very well. One noted Jeichido's little move."

"Do you suppose she *saw* something, Uncle? I know she did, when we moved to rejoin the herd."

"She might have," Uncle said. "The wind was blowing from

us to the orchard, so it was not scent. If it was one of my staff out there to pick a little fresh fruit, I will not be pleased."

"One understands," Cajeiri said quietly, and took his tea in hands still grimy enough to leave a fingerprint, a scandal, upstairs, but here—in this place full of riding gear and competition mementoes, it was of no consequence.

Two cups of tea.

The senior of Uncle's aishid came in. "We do have an intruder, nandi. He did surrender to a verbal request. He claims kinship with the young gentleman."

"With *me*? I have remote cousins in Taiben . . . and in Ajuri."

"Ajuri would be the case, young aiji. He identifies himself as Nomari, of Ajuri. He claims a relationship to you through your grandfather."

"That is no recommendation," he said. He was embarrassed, upset—he was not sure what he felt, except that they had a problem that had upset a perfect day, upset Uncle Tatiseigi, upset the whole household, and scared him, which was a feeling that deeply embarrassed him—not, mani had pointed out, his finest point, because the next thing he became was angry. And stupid. "What does he want?"

"He says he wants to talk about the nomination."

"I dare say," Uncle said dryly. "Was he sent?"

"He says no, nandi. He says that he is not one person, but represents others, that he wishes to talk to you, and that he is not here for any illicit purpose."

"That covers a broad front," Uncle said. "And most every dealing we have had from Ajuri this year. We are tired, we have ridden a fair distance, we want a bath and we want a dinner, which cook has again prepared in the hope this time of serving our guest in proper style, unhurried and uninterrupted. Unless this visitor is bleeding to death this moment—is he in good health?"

"One would say, perhaps in want of a meal or two, and he has been living rough."

"Then we should feed him and shelter him, but his mode of introduction does not warrant an immediate hearing, or we shall be inundated by visitors. I fear the gap in our hedge is at issue, and if this person has broken the saplings we have just planted in that gap I shall consider damages."

"We shall inspect it, nandi, and set a device there."

"Advise the Guild over at the Kadagidi estate, too. Tell them to look sharp, and advise them and Taiben that this person claims to have companions."

"We shall."

"As for this person, advise him, if politics has prompted him, that the nomination for Ajuri has been safely vetoed and that issue is done. If he still wishes to speak to us, tell him I will hear him sometime tomorrow, at my convenience, and he may use the time to put his thoughts in order. Whether the young gentleman will speak to him, the young gentleman and his aishid will judge. And I am sure the aiji will have some interest in our visitor's actions and his provenance."

"Do you think he is Shadow Guild, Uncle?"

"It will be a very long time before we can assume we are free of *that* plague. We have him, we shall *not* lose him, and I shall be entirely vexed if he has ruined those new plantings. Come, baths are in order. Then dinner. Without disturbance, let us hope."

Would there, Bren mused, back in his own guest quarters, with his aishid about him—would there, once the Reunioner landing became public expectation, be a refocus of the Heritage argument, on *Reunioners* as the new villains in the world? The Heritage Party needed something to point at with alarm.

Even if it was the origin of one's ancestors, no matter the experiences that, in either population, lay between.

The Heritage Party line was that the Reunioners were descended from the population that had deserted Alpha, left it to fend for itself, stripped of the means to do so—with half its population gone and no ship to assist them in mining the system for resources. The Heritage Party held that the desertion had *forced* their Mospheiran ancestors to desert Alpha and fall to Earth in petal sails, giving up space flight for the foreseeable future. In Heritage Party doctrine, the Reunioners had gone off to serve the ship, and the ship had either come to grief or deserted them, leaving *them* the sole bearers of the human legacy, possibly the *only* humans, with a tradition to uphold and a legacy to reclaim. Someday. That had been the line—until the ship *had* come back, two hundred years or so late . . . and Mospheirans and atevi had joined the ship to rescue the stranded survivors of Reunion Station, in a situation that had gone very wrong.

Had the Reunioners ever regretted their leaving and longed to be back at Alpha? Had the mission to find the ship's home-world ever become a burden to them? The ship searched and observed. Reunion had mined and built and supplied the ship's missions. As a purpose and a collective goal, that had served. But for the last decade, Reunioners sitting abandoned in the wreckage of the station, with no sign that *Phoenix* still existed, with no ship in their future but the kyo that had attacked them—the survivors at Reunion had been through their own War of the Landing, their own ten-year hell. They were *not* all virtuous. They were the same as the survivors when *Phoenix* had met its original catastrophe, the same as the Mospheirans who had gotten safely down to Earth. Every incident had sifted them down and down to individuals with the courage, luck, and sometimes the ruthlessness to stay alive.

And while Mospheirans now enjoyed life, celebrating a past that had never quite existed, enjoying their television and their vacations at the beach—Reunioners were not merely the de-scendants of survivors, but the survivors themselves—not all of whom were nice.

Some were. Like Artur's parents. Like Gene's mother. But like Gene's mother, they were fragile. Braver than they looked. More fragile than one expected.

Then there were those like Irene's mother—who hadn't even asked what had happened to her daughter. Nor seemed to care. Resilient . . . but very self-focused.

"Is it a problem, Bren-ji?" Jago asked.

Did he have a theory on things fairly vital that the Linguistics Department didn't know and probably should?

Oh, several. One thing was fairly certain—that the Heritage Party preaching fear of aliens and the special rights of humans might find fertile ground in the Reunioner experience . . . and in the ragged edges of the survivor psyche.

Did he want to go over to the University now and explain the Reunioner experience, just as he was preparing to sell the proposed Reunioner landing to the Mospheiran legislature?

No. The landing had to happen, for the sake of the station, which could not support them. There was no choice.

"Is there a problem?" Jago asked him.

"One was merely recalling a set of notes."

"That man . . ."

"Woodenhouse."

"Woodenhouse. Will he have any power to trouble us?"

"Not at present. He was a comparatively easy target. Internal Affairs is a committee of legislators more locally focused—and Mr. Woodenhouse is from a very, very small town, almost a village, and he likely gained his seniority through being the only candidate on the ballot. His seniority put him on the only committee for which he has any qualifications, and the Heritage Party, one is sure, was particularly glad to have a seat on Internal Affairs. Think of him as a human Lord Topari—willing to demand war with the continent, since there is absolutely no chance that atevi will ever descend on his village. His people live comfortably enough, absolutely certain that they are in constant danger from atevi, and Woodenhouse is their voice *and* their source of information, because he tells them what they already believe: that outsiders lie to them. I do not know him, but I know the sort. I know, from Gin, that the Heritage

Party has nineteen legislative seats out of two hundred, but only one committee post, and Woodenhouse is in it. If all the Heritage Party were the same degree of threat as Woodenhouse, they would not worry us. What is worrisome is certain interests, including corporations, who want a far freer rein to run as they like, still fund the Heritage folk as the *only* check on the Presidenta, who has only once fallen behind in the popular vote. There is no opposition party except the Heritage folk, though attempts have been made to found one. It is not, in our culture, an entirely healthy situation, but unless the Presidenta forms a party to oppose himself, the only opposition the corporations can throw up is the Heritage Party, which is constantly looking for ways to gain membership."

"The Reunioners when they land—what side will they take?"

"I think the Heritage Party will confuse the Reunioners— though possibly it may divide them. Some of the Reunioners will greatly interest certain corporations, the very people who fund the Heritage Party—but the Heritage Party has always maintained that the people who went with the ship to found Reunion—had betrayed them. Meanwhile the Reunioners have yet another version of history, namely that the Reunioners are all descended from people who remained loyal to the ship and believed in its leadership, and that the station was left with people who gave up, too tired, too mistrustful or too afraid to go on and find another place in the heavens. Now, for practical reasons, the Heritage Party, which likes to think of itself as pro-space, may even decide to change its story, find virtue in the Reunioners, and find in the Reunioners a source of new recruits. Is it not the same with atevi? Politicians end up facing a direction opposite to their original position. Lord Topari now considers me an excellent creature."

Jago had not laughed when Topari had said it. She did manage a flash of humor now.

"One does not believe, Bren-ji, that this Woodenhouse will ever become your ally, in any turn of politics."

"I much doubt it. I do not think Woodenhouse has greatly helped his party in that outburst, and very fortunately I did not say all that I thought at the moment. He was not entitled to speak, he violated committee rules of precedence, and while his partisans may feel he was unjustly silenced, many Mospheirans will be mortally embarrassed, even anxious, about the angry show he made, at a time when their prosperity is directly related to the resumption of good relations with the aishidi'tat. We were televised. And while it may please his town, it will not appeal to the cities, where the votes lie."

"Your aishid," Banichi remarked, working at gun-cleaning in another substantial chair, "would be interested to hear the translation of the session."

He reached for the television remote. "Let us see what the news channel has of it. I truly wish it had not happened. But there was bound to be such sentiment in certain places in secret. I am glad it surfaced as it did. I am glad it was so ineloquently presented. And glad that the matter has been laid out before the Presidenta's state dinner. If any opinion surfaces favoring Woodenhouse, or taking umbrage at my remarks, that may let me know it."

Last night had been good, but tonight Uncle's cooking staff had especially outdone themselves, making all his very favorite dishes. Uncle *liked* his food, and Cajeiri was glad that Uncle liked his food. Bindanda, nand' Bren's excellent chef who had made the teacakes which had convinced Prakuyo an Tep that they were civilized . . . had once been Uncle's—and Uncle's kitchen had coped with human guests, and mani . . . and they truly could turn out food of every sort. *Uncle* was adventurous, when it came to dinners—in a good way.

Dinner for the mountain clan guests had been—well, an *adventure*, but not one he wanted to repeat. He had eaten things off a spit at a cookfire that were good. For Father's fine kitchen to turn out something that tasted that way—

But Father's guests had liked it.

He ladled on a generous amount of sauce and wondered if perhaps a few mountain cooks could learn to appreciate salt. And flavors. Savory things, and sharp things, and sweet and peppery hot. Nand' Bren, who had to be careful, was not so averse to flavors as that lot.

He did wonder how their guest was faring right now, and whether he had gotten this good dinner. Probably he had: staff was only waiting their turn, and Uncle was never stingy with good things for staff, be they house staff or stables, so there was always plenty, and always pastries left over for snacks at any hour.

Uncle had scared him once, but that had been a long time ago. Uncle was conservative, but Uncle hadn't *stayed* foolish and old-fashioned. Uncle did not quite understand traveling in space, but he had accepted it as a good thing if it led to better medicine and better management of the land, and kept the world safe. He did know about the old ways and the important events before *he* was born. Uncle was someone who had had no respect for nand' Bren's predecessor, but he had become quite happy with nand' Bren, and happy, too, with Irene and Gene and Artur, who had been equally delighted by his collection of artifacts, even the old pots, who had admired his fine porcelains and been brave enough to ride.

So Uncle and he got along *very* well. He trusted Uncle—who had been his father's staunch supporter and his great-grandmother's closest ally through everything, and who now treated him as a person in his own right, who talked to him, who *saw* him, and *listened* to him as if everything he said mattered.

He had come to help Uncle, because Uncle deserved help.

He had met a welcome for his own sake, not for mani's, not for father's, not for mother's. And that mattered. Uncle might not be right about everything, but Uncle cared to tell him, personally, the truth of things as Uncle saw them.

So when, after dinner, they had adjourned to the sitting room for Uncle's brandy and his fruit juice, he asked:

"Uncle, *what* would happen if Ajuri and Kadagidi were broken up?"

"Have you heard such a plan?"

"I have heard that *could* happen. But no one I know thinks it a good idea."

"What does your mother think?"

Like that, Uncle had known who had said it. "Mother does not want that for Ajuri. Neither does Father. He says not. But he will not let Mother be lord of Ajuri, because everybody dies."

"That is an unfortunate truth."

"Did you think this person you nominated would die?"

"I was sure your father would veto the nomination, or I would not have made it. I promised it to conclude a conversation, and I am certain the person to whom I promised it knew it would never be approved, but saw it as a way to keep the issue active before your father. He will be glad to be rejected— but with your father's favor for it. Practicality. And paradox. Was it your father who sent you? Or was it your mother?"

"Father said I should go. But I think Mother approved. She brought my sister out to see me off. She never did that when I went to deal with the kyo."

Uncle nodded slowly.

"Your father arranged the news coverage," Uncle said. "They are camped out in every hotel in Heigian and Diegi." Those were two of the Atageini townships closest to Tirnamardi. "And I do send staff with small bits of gossip—selected bits of gossip, to be sure." Uncle took a sip of brandy. "Your coming, nephew, was very welcome."

"I was glad to come. And I know mani would have."

"She could not. Changing her plans would have unsettled Malguri, and the proposal had been under her roof, so to speak. She could not then associate herself here, with a candidate our party forced, with the veto very surely coming. But my nephew could come to visit, and quite occupy the news."

"I tried," he said.

"You did very well, nephew."

If Uncle had heard it, it would have been on radio, likeliest. Television was not to Uncle's liking. He was, in some ways, still extremely old-fashioned.

But sharp. Very sharp.

"I want to understand the succession, Uncle. I want really to understand. I want to know what can happen. I talk to Father. But Father gives me short answers. And if I ask Mother—I never know how to make her happy. I sometimes think *I* upset her, just being there."

Uncle was silent a moment, turning the glass in his hand, slowly, slowly, and maybe not going to answer at all. Maybe he had upset Uncle, even asking.

"I have asked myself the same question," Uncle said then, "what could be done to make your mother happy, in Ajuri's sad condition. Let me explain to you *my* situation."

"Uncle?" he asked in the ensuing silence.

"I am well along in years, I govern a keystone in the structure that is the Padi Valley Association, which is the oldest association in the aishidi'tat—the *center* of the aishidi'tat. I have made peace with Taiben. That *had* to be. It was the time to do it. So that has bolstered the floor of our association, but the two wings—Kadagidi and Ajuri—have fallen down in ruin. Kadagidi was always a problem, from a hundred fifty years ago, when the Kadagidi lord took a wife out of the Dojisigin Marid— that began an association of ambition, a constant working at the fabric of the association that was never a great advantage to the Padi Valley Association. It harmed us. It more than once brought Marid unrest into our midst. We thought it had stopped with the death of certain individuals, but we did *not* know it had set roots into Ajuri. You know about Shishogi."

He did know. Shishogi was a relative in Ajuri. He had been an officer in the Assassins' Guild, the officer in charge of Assignments, for years and years and years, as long as anybody could remember. And nand' Bren and mani had had to take him down—they had meant to arrest him, because his moving people about here and there and completely controlling Guild assignments, had put the Shadow Guild in place to try to assassinate him and his father and mother and everybody. But Shishogi had blown himself up and completely disarranged Assignments in the explosion, so that they were still trying to reconstitute some of the records. That was what he had heard, in bits and pieces.

"I know," he said, "what Shishogi did. And that he was my grandfather's cousin or uncle."

"Both, actually," Uncle said dryly, "though do not ask your mother how that relationship ran. Ajuri is a little clan, even if you add in its subclans. It has had very little distinction *since* the War of the Landing, except in the last six decades, through Shishogi, who was very well-reputed, once. Then he slipped into the shadows, so to speak, as Guild do who rise into administration. He never came back to Ajuri, but he never left them, either. He exerted a control over that clan tighter than any clan lord, and without check. He proposed, and the lords of Ajuri were *told* what they should do, where they should send funds, who they should contract with, and who they should not, all quietly—and those of any rank who moved contrary to Shishogi's wishes—died."

"My grandfather, too?"

"Very probably your grandfather. I am not certain that your grandfather even knew who in the Guild gave orders, or what reason they had. He did know, surely, from a young age, that he would live his life under orders. He was in good repute when he met my sister, your grandmother . . . and our father, then lord in this house, was reluctant to countenance the flirtation. It went on for five years and more. Our father died, I became lord here, and my sister refused other contracts, no, she affianced herself to your grandfather and asked my consent only when I flatly refused to let him continue his visits without formalities. I was certain old Benedi, in Ajuri, would oppose it—the contract granted no land-use, any rights of inheritance requiring my seal, and any offspring to be resident here at Tirnamardi—but he agreed, young Komaji and my sister were contracted, signed and agreed. They had their quarrels, but they did seem to get along, and my sister—her name, your grandmother's name—was Mureino. There were many years I did not speak that name."

What did one say? One simply sat still. Listening. And Uncle took a sip of brandy. "I had not spoken Komaji's name, either, except after his return to assist your father. And his entry into your house. I had chosen not to speak it. But we try to be modern, where possible. Your grandmother and grandfather occupied the suite you have taken, that your great-grandmother usually takes."

That was a spooky thought.

"For the last year of her life they seemed happy. But he . . ." Another sip of brandy and a moment of reflection. "You met your grandfather. You may have noticed he had strong opinions."

"He did."

"And when he wanted his way, he was very determined."

"Yes."

"So—especially considering our uninvited guest downstairs, who claims some kinship with you, you should understand the descent. Before your mother was born, a man called Areito was lord of Ajuri, having inherited the lordship from his brother Benedi, whose demise may also be linked to Shishogi—who was Benedi's cousin. Benedi had four children, your grandfather Komaji, a daughter, Geidaro, and by his first wife, two other sons, Kadiyi, who became lord, and Basari, of no current consequence. During Areito's lordship, young Komaji was quite the fellow, handsome, with many followers. That was the sort he was.

"While he lived here, he was constantly informing staff how to proceed, constantly interfering in the stables. And he and my sister were often enough at odds, especially as regarded her mecheita and her management of her staff. There was one loud three-day quarrel for which I cannot even recall the reason, but it upset the staff.

"There were constant other quarrels, even when your grandmother was pregnant with your mother. Komaji wanted her company out and about the roads. He was an adequate rider. That she was better he would never accept, and he was constantly telling her how to manage. He was constantly about the stable. His notions led to two infelicitous breedings—one of my sister's mecheita. He and I certainly did not get on well. And we particularly did not get on well when, during the month prior to your mother's birth, he kept wanting my sister to be out at the stables at risk of her safety. I flatly forbade it, we quarreled, and my sister and I quarreled. She absolutely insisted to be out there, involved whenever he was. I only later learned that your grandfather had entered into a flirtation with one of the groundskeepers, and I think she drove herself to be out there, and to be involved with the mecheiti, to keep watch on *him.*

"Komaji had also, in the last month, decided that despite the contract, your mother should be born in Ajuri, and he wanted my sister to press for it—for reasons which I now suspect may not have been Komaji's own. His family may have been pressured . . . even threatened. That was how Shishogi worked. The motive seemed then and now to get a potential Atageini heir under their roof, brought up Ajuri or with special ties to them. Taking advantage of that would take getting rid of me . . . but that might have seemed easier then than now. Your great-grandmother was aiji-regent at the time. We were not, at that time, close. I had little protection. The scheme had possibilities.

"Not being smitten with Komaji, however, far from it, I had

seen a threat in Komaji, one I wanted to deal with. So I had my sister, though not without a bitter quarrel and words I to this day regret, specifically renounce any inheritance in Atageini lands without my written and sealed grant—not my successor's—mine.

"We were not speaking at the hour your mother was born. Komaji attended and I did not. The birth went well. My sister seemed well. She insisted she was well, and she insisted on being out and about with Komaji, whenever he was down at the pens. Five days after giving birth to your mother, my sister got up on a nicely mannered last-tier mecheita and accompanied Komaji about the grounds. Beyond that, no one but Komaji witnessed. I was in my office when staff came running, reporting that Komaji had come riding back, that my sister had taken a fall out on the west grounds.

"I did not see Komaji. I ran out the front door, nearest, with a quirt I kept by the front entry—I saw three of the herd out there. I found her dead—untouched by the mecheiti. It was a skull fracture. And then the servants reported Komaji, with most of the herd, had gone out the gate, which, no, we had not secured. Servants inside the house were injured. Komaji had knocked them down the stairs close by the room—one an elderly woman. And your mother was gone. Komaji had taken her, taken his mecheita, and loosed the herd from the pens.

"My bodyguard took the estate truck and went in pursuit, but they found the mecheiti coming back, including the one Komaji had taken. Of him and of your mother there was no trace, but vehicle tracks on a little-used road near Taibeni lands. *Someone* had met them with a car, or truck, someone who knew to meet them.

"Clearly we were meant to blame Taibeni, with whom we were known to be in a state of war. *I* did not blame the Taibeni. All the evidence blamed Komaji." Uncle's face was frighteningly grim. He had never thought Uncle could be scary. But he was. "Over the years, things changed. One year—at Winter Festival—

your mother, a young woman, left Ajuri, and came to our banner, asking to be Atageini. I fear I bear some responsibility for
her going back again. I did blame her father for her mother's
death. I *was* intemperate in my remarks. I fear I disappointed
her hopes of an easy cure for the matters between our clans. I
could not stand with her and reason with her regarding her father; least of all could I reconcile with her father—all those
things a young woman might ask of her uncle. I wanted her to
stay with us, I would not hear her arguments. And she wanted
not to be trapped between her father and me."

"I do not think Mother feels that way. I think she has great
regard for you, and far less for her father."

"I would hesitate to say your mother fears anything. But I
may have been too forceful. I may have set her at a distance
neither of us can ever quite cross. Which is more than unfortunate. I have no heir. You, young nephew, would have been my
first choice."

"I am honored, Uncle, I am very honored. But—"

"But you are your father's, and I would not wish otherwise.
So someone must manage Atageini someday. And for reasons of
that close Ajuri tie, your mother has divided loyalties that
might put her in doubt. I would hope—I am saying this for the
first time—that your *sister* might inherit."

"Seimei."

"Is that what you call her?"

"For short." Her name was Seimiro. "But Seimei is Mother's.
Mother lost me. Father promised her—"

"And so she should ever be. But your mother as lord-regent—
would be of a different character. Your mother as lord would be
half Ajuri. But your mother as regent for your sister—*that*
Damiri would look out for Atageini interests, as fiercely as she
would defend her daughter."

That was a thought. He could see it. He truly could.

"I would defend her, too," he said, and meant it. "But, Uncle,
you will be lord of Atageini for years and years to come."

"One hopes to be. And I shall be a less lonely old man, if I have a nephew and a niece to brighten up the halls. I trust your parents, you know that I trust your great-grandmother, and I trust you. I think one day I shall trust your sister, too."

"I shall see that she knows," he said. "I shall whisper it to her, so she grows up knowing it. I shall tell my mother, if ever I find the chance. But I shall watch out for my sister."

A momentary silence. "I should like that. We are in ruins here in the north. We have had a long, long run, but we have become like a mecheiti herd too long isolated. We need new blood. We need new ideas. One wishes an exceedingly uncomfortable afterlife for Shishogi. His actions poisoned three generations, and Kadagidi's flirtations with the south nearly ruined us all. We *have* to repair Ajuri. We have to bring Kadagidi back under sane leadership. We cannot, with the dangers in the heavens, act like brawling youths.

"I fear too many of strong will have done the same, sensing an impossible situation brewing underneath it all, thanks to the Kadagidi influence. Your own relatives, lad, are questionable. Komaji's sister, Geidaro, married the traitor Murini's cousin, Ajechi. They had a daughter, Caradi. After he was made lord of Ajuri, Komaji contracted with another woman, producing Meisi . . . your mother's half-sister, and *she*, Meisi, contracted a marriage with another Kadagidi, Muso, and produced Dejaja, who is a sweet child, with the sense of a—well, but at least *she* is not ambitious. Geidaro is. Be wary of that woman or anything she has touched. If there is another Ajuri as venomous as Shishogi, it would be Geidaro. You should know these things."

"What about that person downstairs? Do you have any idea, Uncle?"

"I have *no* idea. But I find it interesting someone has been so stirred up as to try to penetrate our defenses—*while* upsetting Taiben, which either says that he has operated along that border, or that he wishes us to think he has. I have not had the most cordial relations with the Dur sub-clans or their allies in the north, but I cannot think they would make such a move, offending *you*, nephew."

"I cannot think it either. Dur has been our ally forever."

"So we are led to think mid-coastal, or southern—not to forget our two acquaintances of this spring, who arrived from the Marid under Kadagidi auspices. They, however, declared man'chi to this house. Their missing partner is a possibility—I have not heard they have found him—but I cannot connect that so closely to the Ajuri nomination. And this young man gives us a name, Nomari, and claims kinship to you. Convenient. It at least obliges me to dig deeper."

It was scary, what a clan lord was within his rights to do, if someone threatened the house. He could not foresee Uncle just letting this Nomari go with a promise not to come back. Involving the Guild was likeliest, and his own aishid and mani's and Father's was likeliest to take this person back to the city, to answer all sorts of questions, until *some* clan lord stepped in to take responsibility for him.

But this man, if he was Ajuri, *had* no clan lord to step in for him. No clan lord and no guildmaster to speak for him and get him out of his predicament.

"So what will happen to this person, Uncle? He has no lord but maybe Mother."

"That would be true," Uncle said. "In fact, considering the circumstances and the manner of his visit, I am quite curious about him. I am curious about names and relationships. Does he frighten you?"

"Not as things are," he said. "I would not like to have met him in the hallway. But I am not afraid of him being downstairs."

"Suppose that you were to talk to him."

"I would," he said. He was as curious as Uncle, who this person was claiming relation to his mother and to him. "I would, with my bodyguard."

"Definitely with your guard. All your guard. I would like to know what he might tell someone he calls cousin. But let him simmer a little. Let him be comfortable, and cared for, and let him rest a bit with no one to talk to, tonight, possibly all day tomorrow. Let us see what he attempts to ask, say, the servants. Or my bodyguard. *Then* you shall see what he has to say."

"I heard about Woodenhouse," Shawn said quietly, in the hall near the Francis House dining room, a little gathering of fortitude, before walking in to the official state dinner, in the official Francis House dining room. They lingered in the drawing room, waiting for the last individuals to arrive.

"It was unfortunate," Bren said. "But the man simply would not stop."

"He has that reputation. Let me say Dean Caputo, as Chair, was not wholly your friend when the session started. He was more than a little put off when you came over as atevi, not a Mospheiran, but you won him over entirely when you set Woodenhouse down. So he says. In point of fact, he understands now what you came here saying, that the job *has* changed while we weren't looking—or at least, we weren't expecting it ever could change from our end. The slow surrender of the Archive was always a messy, frankly embarrassing business—and that the atevi feel they don't *need* it in the old sense. . . ."

"It was an embarrassing process on the atevi side, too. They won the War, but the idea that they couldn't cope with the tech . . . that concept worked so long as atevi connected human tech with human strangeness. That atevi have managed to swallow as much as they have, and keep their own ways—more, find new validity in their ways—has been one change *atevi* didn't see coming. At a certain point, in the coup, old ways rose up, but the leaders of the coup found the people weren't in agreement. People *wanted* their televisions and their space program and they saw themselves as *embarrassed* by the rebels, in a way. And angered by the rebels' reprisals against political enemies. Tabini was reported dead, his family missing on a ship that might never return, and the rebels said that space only served humans, and that the whole program had been Tabini's imposition on the people—but when Tabini's family came back with the ship, safe, in partnership with humans, and Tabini turned up alive, and saying there *had been* a good outcome, and there *was* a future, and a universe out there atevi should participate in—then the old ideas began not just shifting: the walls came crashing down. People used to ask if the air would leak out of the world because of the shuttles piercing the atmosphere. Now—they know there's something beyond the Earth. They know about other worlds. They know this is an atevi world, and, post-Murini, hearing how Mospheira had actively helped them during the takeover, they choose to share the world with humans. Humans didn't attack them in their moment of overthrow. Humans actively helped the Guild resist. Geigi, on the space station, had at least enough cooperation with humans—even Tillington—to do what he did. Maybe it was because Tillington wanted the shuttles out of the hands of the rebels, and to get them flying again, but it was at least cooperation, which, honestly, should be a plus on Tillington's side of the balances, whatever he did later, with the Reunioners . . ."

"He'll get credit for that," Shawn said. "Not for the rest, but for that, at least—at my direct orders."

"You're another reason for the atevi's change of attitude— now and again humans may elect a George Barrulin—and promote a Deana Hanks; but atevi understand those types. They watched those go down, and watched your administration reassert itself. They're happy with that. Tabini is perfectly content to trust you with the Reunioners' science, whatever it turns out to be, with the simple understanding that *my* old job is finished, that you're not agonizing over what tech to trust atevi with next, and that atevi aren't embarrassed by your having to reckon whether or not they're advanced enough not to blow the planet up. We both admit blowing the planet up isn't a good idea, we put on a great show of unity for the kyo, and, God, if one of us conquered the other, we now understand that we just can't biologically live with one of us adapting to the other's emotional structure, so we sensibly don't try to convert each other. You and I won't feel man'chi, but we can be pretty decent human beings, and we won't have to cope with atevi trying to make associations with human beings that push them too far, emotionally, either. How much we'll ever live together at close quarters, I don't know. I think we'll always want places that are purely human, and purely atevi, for our own mental health. But after all that's changed in our lifetimes, I won't say some may not find a way. I know—if I had to make a choice—well, I suppose I *have* made the choice, haven't I?"

There was quiet for a moment, quiet, with the distant sounds of a gathering entering the dining room. They needed to go there. They had politicians to meet, industrialists to meet, representatives of this and that organization, a quiet dinner for about fifty, so that even distinguishing faces at the end of the table would be difficult.

He had a speech to make, explaining what he'd learned from the kyo, and what had happened on the station . . . and it had to be attuned to the mood in there, develop with it, and bring that varied group along with it.

"I've never asked you," Shawn said. "Are you happy? Are you happy, where you are, as cut off from the island as you've become?"

"Yes," he said without hesitation.

"Speaking of whether that choice *can* work."

"I have reasons that wouldn't be common."

"But you can make that transition. You have made it. That's a question."

His mind leapt to recent memory, a cell, a human face. Guy Cullen. A man he'd outright lied to, and cast into precisely that situation, aboard a kyo ship still in the solar system. The kyo might have more in common emotionally with humans than atevi did. Were less like humans biologically.

"Make the transition?" he said, recovering the thread of Shawn's question to him. "Yes. I could. But I don't have to, totally. I have Toby. I have Barb. You. The people I've called on. Jase, on the station. A lot of people that can pull me back." He drew a deep breath, attempted a laugh. "But it doesn't stick, these days. I dream in Ragi."

"Do you fill out Department forms for that?" Shawn said, in levity. The Linguistics Department had used to demand an accounting of every new word, every unapproved word used, back in Wilson's time. Paperwork. Paperwork. Paperwork. You recorded every encounter. Your journal went back to the Department, every move and every new word written down to be analyzed and recorded.

"Our own rise from the ashes," Shawn said then, soberly, "was slower, you know, because we didn't *want* really advanced tech getting across the strait, and if we had it, the aishidi'tat would find a way to get it. Now—we're worried about space tech disrupting our *own* way of life, coming down on *us* too fast. Pacing still is an issue. It's been a question, in the last two years—do we take everything the ship can offer? And now we've got Reunioner science coming down on us. There's excitement about that in some quarters. But there *will* be resistance, too, of a sort that the paidhi-aiji is uniquely fitted to understand."

"Cell phones," he said. "And sat phones. Very serious question. I'm not allowing them. I've thought about it, and, functioning *in* my old capacity, I've advised Tabini not to allow them for the public. It won't be the paidhi's decree. It'll be his."

"They're a damned nuisance. People walking into traffic—"

"They'll exist on the mainland, but they'll be restricted to the Assassins' Guild, who already have a similar technology. Clan lords, maybe: that's still under consideration, but that's a decision the Guild may make, with their own technology. I've said no. So I'm not *totally* done with saying no. And here I am, recommending Reunioner tech to the whole world."

"Most of which is in energy and materials, as I understand it."

"Which will change us both economically. You have to worry about the corporations, who's to be blessed and who's going to lose. Tabini-aiji has to worry about clans and regions. It's the same, but it's different. We get along much better as individuals than we do in groups."

"That's not a uniquely atevi attribute," Shawn said.

"The difference will be," Bren said, "is *beginning* to be— that the aiji is the one who'll make the take-it or reject-it decisions. He'll have access to everything. I'll interpret it, and he'll consider the impact, with my advice, but it's his decision, moderated by other advisors. And his son, his heir, is not going head over heels for his experience on the ship, which pleases us all. He'll have these youngsters, very likely, as advisors in one capacity and another. They need education *as* paidhiin. Linguistics, economics, geography, history, biological sciences, physical sciences. They're the future. And they have to be human. The way the heir has to be atevi. That's why Tabini is protecting them—but he's sending them to you. *Entrusting* them to you."

"*And* the University."

"And the University. Let me be honest, Shawn. If it weren't for you, I wouldn't have survived the University. They'd have put me at a desk and kept me in residency, knowing too much to be let loose, and too free with the rules to get the appointment when Wilson retired—too reckless to stay appointed without your intervention . . ."

"And Tabini's."

"Without his support, I wouldn't have lasted a week. But without yours—it would have been a far rougher road."

"You're asking me to look out for those kids."

"Definitely." He hesitated, then: "I'll have Sandra on it. And you *will* get reports."

"They'll get to my desk," Shawn said. "I'll make a point of it. If I *don't* hear, I'll ask."

"Mr. President." One of Shawn's aides had stepped into the room, with an accompanying increase in noise from the opened door.

"Well, Mr. Cameron," Shawn said. "Shall we do our best?"

House security had a camera in the staff washroom, where Uncle had confined the intruder. Uncle's aishid had questioned him, and Rieni and Cajeiri's aishid had questioned him on the same points, over and over, and received the same limited information. The intruder refused to say more until he met with, as he put it, his cousin.

Cousin was an odd way to think of somebody who had sneaked onto the grounds. He had come in the same way the last intruders had come in—but it was possible, Rieni said, that, it being known in the neighborhood that there had been an intrusion from the Kadagidi estate, he had simply looked for a breach on that side and found it.

Indeed, he had damaged the new plantings, but not fatally, and a search had not turned up evidence of multiple intruders. That was good, Cajeiri thought. And that the path had led through the orchard was a good route: at least there were trees to climb, if the mecheiti had gotten wind of him. He had also not been there long, since the wind had been out of the south, and the day before, it had been out of the north, which would have betrayed his presence to the herd.

So they had a good idea how long he had been there, and they had an idea what had prompted him to try—Uncle's nomination and *his* presence, his younger and his senior bodyguards agreed on that . . . if he truly was Ajuri.

He had maintained consistently that he was Ajuri. And he generally had done absolutely nothing to try to escape or to quarrel with anyone. He was waiting—waiting for a meeting or a resolution that had, in a proper house, eventually to come, whether in a case laid before the Guild, or in this case, before Father—or the meeting he asked to have.

Uncle had afforded him proper food, proper care. He had wanted a bath last night. Uncle had allowed it.

Had Uncle notified Father they had a problem? Cajeiri somewhat doubted he had, but it was possible the Guild had. Certainly very high-up Guild, as high as Father himself could send, was already on the premises, doing their investigation, and possibly asking questions elsewhere.

But came breakfast, and everybody adult was still planning on him talking to this person, which—he had no desire to say—was scary, in the way the unknown was scary.

He was absolutely certain nothing would happen to him. He thought about that, and thought that was not the reason he was afraid. It just would not happen, not while his aishid was with him.

No, it was something more in his imagination than in anything physical—and maybe, he thought, maybe it was because this person might know something about Mother.

He wanted to know—if there was something bad or something good. But he did not want to get something bad from an enemy. He wanted to be strong enough an enemy could not see whether he was upset.

Mani was that strong. Father was. And if there was something he ought to know—then he had to go find out.

"I shall talk to him," he said to his aishid, older and younger. "I think maybe two of Uncle's should hear. This is his neighbor."

"A good idea," Rieni said, and sent Lucasi to bring them in.

So it was with a lot of Guild attendance that he went down the stairs, and down to the lower level of the house.

Servants attended, too, two men from the general staff, and with such a large group, he let Uncle's men suggest they meet in the servants' dining room, which was a comfortable place, with a long table. He sat at one end of it, proper and patient, dressed in soft country clothes, nothing remarkable, but he thought this self-claimed cousin should know who he was without so much a gold pin in evidence.

Uncle's men brought their intruder from his room down the hall. He was likewise in country dress, as he had arrived, but a good deal rougher, with a split seam in his coat and splashes of mud on his trousers and coat alike—old splashes, or he had made shift to try to rub them off this morning and look as presentable as possible. He had a hard face that could go much younger. It was not easy, Cajeiri thought, to be sure about his age, but it might be somewhere near his father's. Wind and weather figured in it. And hard labor. The hands showed it.

He was very conscious of his own age, but also conscious of as much force about him as his father would generally muster in a chancy meeting. He offered this intruder no expression, nothing so telling as a frown. Nothing. He made himself as calm as mani could be. At least he hoped so.

"Sit, please," he said. There was only one chair set at the table, and that at the other end, so it was a long, safe expanse of wood between them.

Nomari gave a polite bow and sat down. "Thank you, nandi," Nomari said, "for the meeting."

"Thank my great-uncle, nadi," he said. "You really might have come to the front door."

A sharp look, measuring him, not the guard around him. *"You* are my cousin. Third cousin, it may be, but you are kin. Your uncle owes me nothing."

"Third cousin is not very close. I have a lot of third cousins. But I am here to listen."

"Then," Nomari said, opening his hands. "I make a request. Your uncle's nomination for Ajuri is not one Ajuri will ever accept."

It was a firm voice. An absolute one. It was odd, how much assurance was in it. And he threw it right back again.

"I am sure my father did veto it. It is already done."

"Then there needs to be a new one. Young aiji, I have a thing to say. Let me say it."

"Say it, then."

"The lordship of Ajuri has been a death sentence. Two of your great-uncles, your grandfather, all dead. *You* would be qualified. I cannot think you would want it."

"I am *not* qualified in the first place. I am my *father's* heir."

"Your mother could well take it."

"My father is not willing to confirm her."

"So no one in that line can hold the lordship—the one who would, your father will never approve. The one who could, your father has blocked from taking it. Lord Tatiseigi has nominated an old man, an associate of his with the blood—but he has only resentment within the clan. He would very likely die before the year is out, to no one's advantage. But I would take the lordship. I could do it. I *have* support. I *am* your third cousin, through your grandfather."

"So why come here, and not there?"

"If I should go in alone and raise a claim *inside* Ajuri, the ones in charge now will not back it and I probably would be dead in days, of some accident never even reported in Shejidan. I would vanish without a trace. That is why I came here. Now I cannot vanish. *You* have seen me. You are my witness. I *am* an answer that could raise Ajuri out of the pit it has fallen into. I *am* out of the cadet line, out of Nichono. I have served outside the clan, in the guilds, I have no ongoing quarrel inside the house, and hearing that Lord Tatiseigi had entered the question, and that *you* were guesting here—I came to present my case. Give me the appointment. Give us all the chance. Ajuri is too important, too old a clan to see it broken. And it *is* your heritage, the same as mine."

It was a lot to take in. Nichono. He could not even remember where that fit, or how that was related.

A lot of twists and turns. He thought of his map, with all the holes in it, the wreckage of two clans that were, with Uncle's clan and four others, the heart of the aishidi'tat. Ajuri might be a little clan, but it had wielded influence, and real power—power that had helped the aishidi'tat be born. It had never produced aijiin—but it *had* produced his mother, aiji-consort, lastingly married to his father. And through her, him, and Seimei.

Should they destroy it once and for all, so that nothing else wicked ever came of its stealth and planning?

"It was Ajuri itself that killed everybody," he said. "It killed my grandfather for trying to talk with my uncle . . . because of what he might say about Ajuri and Kadagidi. I think so. Do you?"

"I think you are probably more right than you know, young aiji."

"I think my uncle is right. *He* thinks so. Were you responsible?"

"No." The expression was even a little surprised. It looked like the truth.

"Do you know who was?"

A little hesitation on that answer. "I might. I have my suspicion."

"Who?"

"I think it was my great-uncle. Shishogi."

They shared that relation, then, one he had rather not own. But so did his mother. One could hardly condemn him for that.

"Probably you do need to talk with my uncle," he said. "Shishogi is not a good name in this house. You should know that."

"It is not a name I favor—not now. And I am not alone in feeling betrayed. We had hope when your father came back. We had some hope. But people died. People who tried to do something—always died. My father, my mother, and my brother of another wife—they died years ago. I owe *nothing* good to his memory. You think Ajuri gained advantage from him—no. For most of us it gained *nothing* good. Families have set themselves against each other, families killed families to protect their own, because man'chi is broken, trust is broken, and it has been for years. There are those Shishogi favored—but it was not *our* family. We knew Shishogi—at least we thought we did. But Shishogi wanted *no one* to know him. He was a modest man. He never wanted to have his name on an order. He *never* sent anyone to do anything. But people *died*, who questioned things they should not. Some of us went into the guilds. Some of us just went away and nobody knows now whether they went on Shishogi's business, or whether they are dead, or just living in hiding. That is how it has been. Lord after lord after lord has gone down, and now there is no one inside the walls who either can or will claim the lordship—a lifespan measured in days does no one any good."

It was a lot of information. He knew he did not know everything about Shishogi, who had sat in the heart of the Guild for years and years and years, in a cramped little office stuffed with paper records. Shishogi had been the Office of Assignments for the Assassins' Guild. He had determined how teams were put together, and what teams were sent to what district, in the Guild's insistence that the guilds should all be free of clans, and not go to areas where they had family. Assignments had let Shishogi move certain people about the aishidi'tat, give good protection to some lords, and not to others, arranging some to die, even within the Guild.

Assignments had arranged the accession of certain lords and the fall of others, and set a collection of conspirators into position to kill people—including his father and his mother, all to set an association of very bad people in power.

He knew those things, and nothing Nomari said was out of agreement with what he knew, but it did not prove that Nomari himself was not one of Shishogi's people looking for a way to move back in.

It was not a question he could decide.

But his senior aishid, who had been deep in the Guild's workings, and come back when mani and nand' Bren had moved to take Shishogi down—*they* were listening, too, and so was Uncle's senior aishid, who had lived right between Ajuri and the Kadagidi who had conspired with Shishogi; and even Antaro and Jegari, who had grown up in Taiben, sharing another border with Ajuri: the attack on Father had happened in Taiben, and Taibeni had been killed.

Facts could be checked. Rieni could do it without appearing to do anything, in much less than an hour.

"Is Nomari your name, nadi?" It was Haniri who asked that question, from Nomari's left, along the wall.

"Yes. It is. My father was Senarii. My father's father was Anoji. Anoji's mother was Nichono, Ajuno's daughter by Haro."

Ajuno was a name he knew. But Ajuno's legal wife had been Seniro. Dry as dust memorizations on a summer afternoon became vivid, scarily vivid. Who was Haro? Someone his tutor would hesitate to mention?

"Your guild," Rieni asked.

"Transport," Nomari said. "Ninth tier, third rank, line maintenance, in Shejidan and Asho."

Again, the Assassins' Guild would contact Transportation and check it—fast.

"I shall talk to my great-uncle," Cajeiri said. "And tell my father . . . which is what you want, is it not?"

A respectful nod. "Yes, nandi. It is. May I ask—there will be a number of people concerned for my whereabouts. One does not believe they would follow me onto these grounds—I asked them to wait for word. But would you—hang a white cloth on the main gate? It need not be conspicuous."

Set up *his* signal on Uncle's gate?

He wondered whether there was any chance Antaro's and Jegari's parents were still in camp, or whether they had pulled back. And who had intruded into Taibeni land.

"What direction did you come?" he asked. "Did you cross Kadagidi land?" There was a Guild watch there, not lightly to be transgressed.

"Only along the hedge. I came up from Sidonin."

"Not from Ajuri?"

"No."

"Have any of your associates come *out* from Ajuri?" Rieni asked.

"No. None of us have been *in* Ajuri for years."

That was one place where stories did not match. And Rieni had gone right to it.

"I think you should go back to your room now," Cajeiri said. "And wait. If you need anything, let someone know. Uncle has no wish for you to be uncomfortable."

"I should like a book, if it becomes convenient. I should like pen and paper."

It was an educated sort of request. Someone else might have asked for dice.

"I shall tell Uncle. Please be patient."

"Yes," Nomari said, and got up carefully and gave a little bow. "Thank you."

Cajeiri sat still, thinking about the dice. And the front gate and a signal that could mean anything.

"What do you think?" Antaro asked.

"I think he is a very superior class of burglar." He rose from the table and looked at his younger aishid, the ones who knew him. "And I think we are not going to go riding this afternoon. Or maybe for the rest of this trip. Damn." He swore in Mosphei', which nobody else might understand. There was going to be some kind of mess, whether it was political, and a fuss in the legislature, or something a little scarier, involving guns, and the Guild.

8

Cabinet meeting. God. Shawn's nine advisors, that met with him regularly, and that generally had compatible opinions—but no scarcity of concerns.

There had been perhaps a few too many glasses of wine at the dinner last night. Not on Bren's part, but on the part of several of the North Shore political elite. There had been far too many pointed questions. He had felt he was constantly parrying attacks, or fending off people trying to score points.

This meeting had the potential to go the same direction, since it included several of the Secretaries present last night. Atevi legislators were generally a little more careful with the alcohol, and atevi dinners did not *allow* serious discussion at table.

Not so, on the Mospheiran side of the strait. Mospheirans were a little rougher on their President. And his guests.

He straightened his cuff lace, asking himself whether the bulletproof vest—brocade as it was—was entirely the thing for a gathering of the Mospheiran cabinet, with Shawn's own security and his in the hall outside. It did make him a little stiff and less natural. But Narani had recalled to him a certain promise, that he *would* wear the thing if for no other reason than because his best coats accommodated it, and Narani and Jeladi were the arbiters of wardrobe. The coat did not fit as it should without it, he needed to look his best for a meeting with Shawn's advisors, and that was that, from the elderly gentleman who had crossed the strait to keep him in good order.

Banichi and the others were not unhappy about the decision. They had been a little uneasy with the questions last night from less than sober sources. Bren, on the other hand, had no apprehension at all that the elderly Secretary of Education was going to produce firearms. No. The man was a different kind of problem, a tenacious fellow, not from Linguistics, but a former professor of Business Administration, whose chief weapon was a slightly inflexible mind.

At least they were not stinting with the air conditioning this afternoon, which made the vest slightly less uncomfortable. Port Jackson was just a shade warmer, compared to Shejidan. It had no mountains within view, and its sea breeze could be muggy.

The door opened. One of Shawn's aides held it open for his entry into the meeting room, Shawn and the rest had risen in courtesy, and he walked to Shawn's side, attentive to the introductions for those who had not met him last evening. He was appointed a courtesy seat endmost, at a table that, being only for twelve people at max, didn't use microphones. They served tea—that was welcome. Even more welcome, Shawn had promised him that he would be first on the agenda and that he wouldn't have to stay for the discussion on the Port Jackson harbor dredging issue.

He sat through his introduction, nodded pleasantly to the cabinet officers, and thanked Shawn for the invitation.

"I'll start with the good news. The treaty. I'm sure you've all read it by now, and know the gist of the agreement. Behind the agreement, there's no denying we dodged a real danger up there. Very, very fortunately, the kyo don't want to fight us. It's my impression they had rather not fight anybody—which makes them good neighbors. They don't want to trade. They don't want to deal with us at all, at least for now. They have problems in another direction, and I gather we're fairly well on the shelf until they can settle their other border. Will they then become aggressive toward us? I hope not, because our science is far, far short of theirs. Their speed, their weapons, all are far, far more than we can deal with. *Phoenix* did create a pile of data and observations from the contact, and has been working on it. They're willing to release what they do know to scientists in various fields, atevi and human. That study is likely to bring us new discoveries in propulsion, among other things. But it doesn't say that kyo science won't advance, too, while we're trying to catch up. Our best goal, in the atevi government's official opinion, is to believe they *may* return, in some number of years we cannot predict, and to be prepared to deal fairly with them if they do. I'll take questions. I'm not sure I can answer *any* of them."

"They came once, unannounced. What's to stop them from doing it again? How are we *sure* they're not going to be back next year, and maybe in force?"

That was a fairly reasonable start on the unanswerable, from Commerce.

"It *is* a situation we can't predict, because we don't know everything about them. But their reason to do that, based on their statements, and based on the enormous distance, travel time, and expense, seems lacking—for any reward unique to this world. They were interested primarily, I think, to see what we were, whether the tip of a large iceberg, some massive civilization that might involve several solar systems—or just what we told them, two species sharing the same planet, who live fairly quietly. Their optics could easily see, from orbit, any group of people waiting for a bus, farming a field, boarding a train—some of which, mind, are still steam engines. The pattern we showed them can't be faked. We're not a vast interstellar empire, we don't have much in the way of defenses, let alone weapons of any sort to make us a threat to them, and they're satisfied that what we represented to them at Reunion was the truth. We're no threat and we don't bother them. Metals, water, rock—there are abundant sources much closer to them and foodstuffs can be produced in orbit. What we do have—is a peaceful community. They wanted to know how we manage that with two species. We explained. They saw. And they left."

"Why wouldn't they meet with humans?" Education asked.

"Well, despite the clothes," he said, and generated a little laughter, but not from the questioner. "I am human. So is Captain Jason Graham. Various operations people. And a handful of Reunioners—the young aiji's associates, and their parents—all meetings that weren't quite planned, but that the kyo requested for their own reasons, as they asked specifically for me, for the aiji-dowager, and the young aiji, to start with. Ragi is, for one thing, the language they find easiest to speak, the language we dealt in at Reunion. That was why we began negotiations in Ragi. We were simply the contact they knew, from Reunion, and whose word on how things are here, was, if I read them correctly, their primary reason for coming. There is also another reason for them to request to speak to us first. If we three were appointed by this world to deal with their fairly dramatic arrival—they could at least have some confidence we had had some authority behind us at Reunion, and still had it in order to come up and meet with them. *Your* support was also there, and we felt it at every moment, in Dr. Kroger's support and that of the ship. We were not negotiating just for the aishidi'tat. We were—at all times, here and at Reunion—negotiating for *all* of us."

"I have a question." That was Industry. "How do we have any certainty *what* the top of that document says?"

"Good question. I worked with a kyo counterpart to understand their alphabet. I can't say I'm literate in that language, but I can actually make out key words that correspond to the Ragi and the Mosphei' versions, and I'm attempting—in my spare time—to work out the grammar and vocabulary. The document is a sort of Rosetta Stone."

"A what?" From Transportation.

"A document which can provide keys to understanding the kyo language, by its close correspondence to the other two. I have a fairly extensive vocabulary besides that . . ."

"From the prior meeting."

"And this one. Principally from this one."

"Your office," Education said, "requires you to turn over materials of this nature to the University Linguistics Department, in conjunction with the State Department. Withholding them is a violation of the terms of your appointment."

Well, it was clear the Linguistics chairman had made a phone call and had an opinion.

And, damn it, it would be so much easier to have the University system helping ease Linguistics into the current century . . . not to mention the roadblocks it could throw down.

Funding was always a matter of taking wealth from somewhere and putting it somewhere else.

Crockett, the man's name was. From last night's dinner party—one of the less happy individuals last night.

"I have supplied Linguistics with materials for many years, sir, but first, materials have to be created and organized. Right now many of them are still here." He tapped his forehead. "They *will* be presented, in due course, as a gesture of cooperation from the aiji in Shejidan, but—there is a great deal more to the kyo language than a vocabulary list; and as to that matter, I will get to that with Linguistics, as soon as I can. I have only just landed, and I have come here, on a priority—as a gesture of good will from the aiji in Shejidan, to present the treaty, and to raise matters of mutual concern. There *will* be atevi working on the kyo language; but the Department of Linguistics also has useful resources, given some adjustments in priority."

"That is a University matter."

"Not wholly, sir, given the global importance of the outcome. As I'm sure you know, but for a statement of the current situation, the University of Mospheira has had the sole responsibility for linguistic studies, and for the training of the paidhiin, unique on the planet. The aishidi'tat has hitherto maintained no such study, and has relied on the University of Mospheira to train its representatives. Bear with me, sir." Crockett was looking decidedly restless and out of sorts. "And bear with me for one further point. The University Department of Linguistics itself has two divisions, Historical Human Languages, which is further subdivided into several specialties; and Ragi Studies, which is also subdivided into Historical and Current Ragi. *Neither* of these divisions is currently appropriate for kyo studies."

"You are hardly charged with recommending the allocation of University resources, sir."

"On the contrary, sir, I am *uniquely* qualified to recommend a new division, as you are qualified, sir, among your fellow Cabinet members, to recommend allocations of resources—for national security and for new global interests. We never foresaw that Mospheira and the aishidi'tat *would have* such vitally unified interests. But we live in one house, on this world, and it has been visited. The aiji is asking for a new era of cooperation, us together, the station with the world, and the ship with the station, and the Department of Linguistics can transition into an invaluable resource. It has in the past linked closely with State and with Commerce. Its stability has proven valuable—but now its flexibility can help bridge gaps even within the University tradition, so that the University can bring all its resources to bear. The kyo language has characteristics not found in the verbal aspects of human language or Ragi, questions in which the life sciences will be very helpful. In point of fact, sir—and bear with me again, I have a limited time on the island, so I beg the cabinet extend the courtesy of hearing me out on several issues."

"Go on," Shawn said, from the head of the table. "These *are* matters of national interest."

"Thank you, Mr. President. I recommend not only that Linguistic Studies extend itself to kyo, but also to ship-speak, *not* as a bastard relative of Mosphei', but as a foundation for the Reunioner dialect, which probably deserves its own distinct professorship. There is a *lot* of unique vocabulary and a richness of expression—one will *not* always understand some Reunioners—

that also involves the Reunioner experience. That dialect is on its way to a separate form, which should be preserved for study, and not allowed to become extinct without record, as one language blends into another. In fact, I would make another proposal. In the same way Linguistics has had supervision from within State—" He gave a slight nod to State, Caputo, who had chaired the joint committee meeting. "—State should also develop a cadre of scholars with special interest in kyo studies *and* in variations of our own several dialects, for future reference. We now have three active human dialects, each with its own unique knowledge: Anthropology should be interested. History should be interested. For that matter, considering the situation, Science should be interested. Academic walls that compartmentalize these studies should be extremely permeable. We cannot know at what point in our future it will be necessary for State to call on Linguistics to interpret a kyo message, or deal with the arrival of a ship from places entirely unknown to us or even to the kyo, for that matter. Linguistics has the potential to embrace history and anthropology, and specializations in a changing world need the flexibility to cross academic divisions. There are those who will spend their whole *lives* puzzling out the fine details of what we've just met, and there are urgent studies and records that should be made soon, while living persons can be interviewed. I propose to give the University access to people with this knowledge. I am one person. I cannot both serve as I serve, *and* write the textbooks and teach. I say this here, because this issue must *not* be swallowed up in a cloistered community detached from what has just happened to us. You, ladies and gentlemen, have the power to support change, and fund it, and to move this world in a way that will make us all safer."

"I'm sure you have your concerns, Mr. Cameron, but one issue is not grounds for restructuring the entire University."

"Mr. Crockett, a few days ago the existence of the *planet* hinged on the existence of the Linguistics Department."

"Which adequately produced *you*, Mr. Cameron, with no trouble at all."

"Mr. Crockett, the program taught me the techniques, gave me vocabulary and structure, as it was before we began to *speak* Ragi, participate in Ragi culture, or venture into space. I took the step of verbal communication *in* Ragi at the specific request of the aiji, on my arrival, and I nearly lost my position because of it. But it was my experience actively speaking the language that gave me the expertise to break through the language barrier with a completely unknown people. The rules in the Department have not changed. But the world has changed. The requirements of the office have changed. What the Linguistics Department needs to do now is plan for my successors, who will have to be adept—and fluent—in Ragi, in Ship, and in kyo. And most important of all—they will have to have the ability to work with anything *else* that comes to us from outside."

Crockett had an objection. He gave it no window and plowed ahead:

"We are giving off, sir, by our very existence on this planet, a remotely detectible signature of *life,* which guided *Phoenix* here in the first place—it was no accidental find—and we are now emitting a signature of space-age civilization, unmistakable to remote instruments of sufficient sophistication."

"The kyo have such things," Defense said in alarm.

"I am absolutely certain they do, sir, since *Phoenix* has such things, which is how they fell afoul of the kyo in the first place."

There was a decided stir. Defense asked: "They were probing for civilization?"

"*Phoenix* was doing what it had always said it was doing— looking for the motherworld. We simply did not understand their word *looking.* They *found* a civilization that breathes the same air, circles a sun of somewhat the same sort, has a gravity a little off from what we enjoy—our brighter sun and our gravity are a little less than comfortable for them, so the kyo had absolutely no desire to land on this planet—but yes, *Phoenix* visiting kyo space was precisely what brought us into contact, a decision we are fortunate enough to have survived, even more fortunate to have exited with a somewhat distant ally. Our next job is to increase our knowledge, improve our science, and try to come up to par with our visitors' science in a non-threatening way. We can't afford to offend the good neighbor we think we have, but we should also consider that someone who comes at us from some other direction may *not* be a good neighbor. Should that happen now, we would have to voyage, as the treaty provides, to Reunion, which is now in kyo hands, and ask the kyo very politely to come help us, as they have *every* motive to keep a buffer of well-intentioned species between themselves and any other."

He left a silence, and let it continue, while Defense thought that over without much trouble. He had made no rash promise that they should never fear the kyo, but he *had* pointed out that there was a reason for Defense to exist *and*, that most important word in this room, to be funded.

"*Phoenix* possesses the technology to search for lifebearing worlds," Defense said.

"I have a confirmation from *Phoenix* command that this has always been the case. They have not shared the technology with us, nor with Reunion, so far as I am aware. A captain now deceased took a chance. This decision is not well-regarded by the crew or by current command."

"*Phoenix* should give us that data," Defense said. "And we should have that technology."

"I would agree, sir. We can ask. But I urge that we should also accept the ship's decision, whatever it is, and work with them, and trust them. This planet, wrapped in atmosphere, cannot do as efficiently what they can do, or see as far. This generation of captains, having experienced what they have experienced, may be willing to share information and possibly the technology. I would definitely urge we ask in the most constructive way possible, and prepare ourselves to deal with what turns up. Convincing the ship to take a cautious course and keep us fully informed will be far easier if we are working together on the same projects and sharing our discoveries. We suspect the kyo ships have a range far greater than *Phoenix* has. Range and speed. *Phoenix* has observational data, and if we can bring science to bear, here on Mospheira and in the aishidi'tat, we may find clues to something useful. Likewise Reunion collected data, some of which the ship has, and some of which living Reunioners have. The plan to send them out to Maudit and lose that potential—would have lost us all they have developed. There is the potential for us to advance on multiple fronts if we handle this well. We can become more prosperous *and* more prepared."

"We cannot," Crockett said, "in the process, *destroy* the University."

"I am in absolute agreement with you, sir. It is vitally important. The University must, for one of its functions, keep up a constant exchange of information with the ship and the station, and it must, in a modern context, prepare other paidhiin, or it ceases to perform a function which, in past and present, has protected Mospheira. We need its records, we need its expertise. We desperately need Linguistics willing and able to go on preparing paidhiin beyond my lifetime, and for situations we have never met. We need one now ready to deal with the kyo."

"State concurs with the paidhi," Caputo said somberly.

"Defense concurs."

That was major.

"It means money," Economics said.

"More science," Science said, "means more money."

"Debatable," Interior said.

"I recall," Shawn said quietly, the agreed-upon safe exit, "that Mr. Cameron has an appointment that will call him away at this point. But he has certainly given us a great deal to consider."

"May Mr. Cameron delay long enough," Justice said, and one

knew where *this* was going, "to give us his opinion on the Asgard matter?"

"I can give *opinion,* sir, that it would not be in Mospheira's program's best interest to jeopardize a major aerospace company for the sake of one officer's actions. Stationmaster Kroger is attempting to broker a deal that relies on precedent, and she believes she is on the verge of a solution."

"Thank you, Mr. Cameron." Justice looked satisfied with that.

And it was a good time for an exit.

"Thank you, sir. Mr. President." Bren rose. Bowed, once to the cabinet, once, slightly more deeply, to Shawn. And headed for the door.

Out. Clear. He'd mortally dreaded that one. They had not asked a single question about the Reunioner landing . . . possibly Shawn had asked them to hold that one, which was bound to become an issue, but not one that needed to interfere with the initial landing—the several children who, without support from the University, were going to have to rely heavily on State to order elements of the University to provide services . . .

That, or Tabini was very likely to take them into *his* hands, which was not what Tabini wanted. Not in the least.

It was tomorrow's problem. Tomorrow's issue. Mospheira understood the children landing. Mospheira would understand the children's parents landing. Mospheira had not liked the idea of the children landing on the mainland, and it would welcome them . . . adopt them, one hoped. Learn their story and get an understanding, through them, that the Reunioners were *not* the hated administrators of the old station.

Just—God, imminent as the first landing now was—the rest seemed a very distant hope.

He was very glad to be back with his aishid, in the hall— people whose minds he knew, whose objectives he knew top to bottom, with no complications.

He'd had his briefing from Shawn before he'd gone in. He'd suspected Crockett was under pressure from the University, and he knew where in the University that pressure came from, the private kingdom of Linguistics, who was not happy with the current paidhi, no.

"It went fairly well," he said to his aishid as they walked toward the stairs. "And they did not ask questions into the station business, except about the Asgard matter. Not even about Tillington, for which I am also grateful. We are free, we are at liberty to go back to the room, where for several blessed hours I shall sit and think of as little as possible. We shall send to the kitchens, we shall have two bottles of wine, and we shall all eat together. Is this acceptable?"

"Deep-fried fish," Tano said cheerfully. They had had that Mospheiran dish twice in their time here.

"I actually know how to cook that," Bren said. "My mother used to do it. Actually Toby knows how." His mind sped off to Toby and Barb, out at sea, out of touch, and hoping they were resting safely. They had to be—given two navy ships riding their horizon.

He so wished he were there.

"Nandi," Algini said quietly. "Narani reports a call from Jase. The kyo ship left the system about an hour ago."

He stopped when he heard that.

He thought of a corridor aboard that ship, in dimmer light and warmer, moister air. Prakuyo an Tep. And Guy Cullen, whose name only a handful of atevi and three other humans knew—was on his own voyage. Things he'd set in motion were launched now, beyond recovery, for good or for ill, things that might have effects wider than he could possibly imagine.

Or come to nothing.

Not within his power to change, now. There would have been an effect, for good or for ill, whatever he did.

And he couldn't stand in this hallway looking perturbed. He

didn't, he hoped. Experience in the atevi court had taught him to keep his face tranquil, and he recovered with a slight shrug and continued onto the steps with his aishid.

"One hears," he said. "One wishes them all a long life and a good outcome."

9

There was, indeed, to be no riding today.

And the white cloth on the gate was an issue that had had discussion, with Uncle Tatiseigi as well as the senior Guild.

"If we do not signal," Uncle said, "we shall possibly cause a misunderstanding with people who might become allies. If we do place such a signal, and they make a hostile move, we can deal with that, and we shall know the character of this would-be heir of Ajuri."

Everybody thought that made sense. Cajeiri thought so, but it worried him that somebody was going to have to go out to the gate, which was exposed to the road, and place that signal.

And they had to get messages to the Guild and to Father and to Taiben, which would have to get contact with Antaro's and Jegari's family, which they said had moved down to the Sidonin train station, at forest edge, because of the summer heat.

Which was exactly where Nomari, who was Transportation, said he had come from.

And they also had to tell Taiben that their visitor said he and his associates had not disturbed their border with Ajuri—which left Ajuri itself as a possible problem.

So before noon one of Uncle Tatiseigi's aishid, dressed in country clothes, like a groom, mounted up on the herd-leader and took the herd on an exercise lap of the grounds. Cajeiri watched from the windows of the breakfast room as they came along the side of the yard—on their way to the gate.

Nobody would want to be on the grounds afoot with the herd abroad, and one whiff of a foreign scent, even hours old, would have the herd on the alert. No ambush could conceal itself at the gate without the herd knowing, and Uncle's bodyguard was not unarmed.

Still, everybody was relieved when that man was back safely, and when grooms had gotten the herd settled again in the stables.

Uncle had had, meanwhile, a talk with staff in the lower hall, saying that while they had wanted to keep the news services generally informed, any trips of staff to town were canceled. It would not be good to lie to the news services, but it would not be helpful to have the whole country involved in the situation, either.

"We will all benefit," Uncle said, "if we can resolve this incident quietly, but likewise there will be adjustments until we have a resolution. Sio and Dylani, you had an excursion planned."

"For supplies, nandi," a man said, from midway in the gathering. "And fresh vegetables."

"We shall postpone that a few days," Uncle said, "by which time it will either be fully clear that we have a difficulty or we shall be relatively certain we do not."

There was a little murmuring about it, a suggestion they might ask the grocer to deliver, but Uncle said no, that if there were trouble, they should not be inviting the grocer's employees into it.

Right now messages were flying back and forth. Uncle was not enthusiastic about phones, for himself, but he insisted on hearing every scrap of information that came in. Guild was talking to Headquarters in their own way, and maybe to Guild in the townships and over on Kadagidi land, and they reported what they had been able to learn, which was detail from Transportation, which gave Nomari's previous assignments and the fact that he was currently on a seven-day leave from the Shejidan repair station.

Then Father called, himself, to talk to Uncle and Uncle definitely accepted that phone call. They were by then in the sitting room, which was the place where everybody came to report and exchange information, and Cajeiri sat quietly in an adjacent chair, listening as Uncle told Father about Nomari, and gave the names Nomari had given, with some discussion of which Cajeiri could only hear one side. Then Uncle assured Father they were safe, and that, yes, he had heard the nomination was vetoed, and yes, they were well set and supplied.

Then Uncle passed the phone to Cajeiri. Cajeiri had hardly ever in his life had a phone call, even a borrowed one.

"Yes, honored Father?" he began it.

"How are you getting along with your bodyguard? Are you listening to them? Are you comfortable with them?"

"Yes, honored Father. I truly am. So is my aishid. So is everybody. And I am not being a fool."

"I would trust not," Father said. *"Riding can wait. Do you hear?"*

"Yes, honored Father. I do. Uncle says so, too, and I understand."

"Good. Good. Take care. Listen to your bodyguards."

"Yes," he said, and gave the phone back to Uncle, who handed it to his major domo, who unplugged it and took it away.

"Your great-grandmother is aware," Uncle said, "and is threatening to fly back to the city and take the train from there, but we are all trying to dissuade her, since this problem does seem to involve the train station, and it would only draw attention, possibly from some random individuals, only to complicate the situation. We also have an advisement from Lord Geigi that he is observing an uncommon amount of activity of vehicles and mecheiti around Ajiden. Can he look down see such things?"

It was something, when one had to say to Great-uncle, "Yes, Uncle. I think he can. They use very strong lenses."

"One is tempted to draw the curtains," Uncle said uneasily.

"They do not observe people, generally, Uncle. They have to set up to see a specific place. One asked, once. It is fairly complicated to do, and they do it only for business."

"Well, well, this modern notion complicates matters. And makes them simpler. So our neighbors are stirring about. One would have thought news that your father has vetoed the nomination would have settled them somewhat. Perhaps they have caught wind of our visitor's people, whoever they are."

"We are safe where we are, surely."

"We certainly should be. If our signal at the gate does not bring down attack, then we may simply sit snug and hope not to involve the news, though our postponing our ordinary grocery trip may bring gossip on its own—and deprive us of what news our people ordinarily pick up on such trips. It *is* remarkable that we have had no calls from the townships—so they have spotted nothing conspicuously questionable. Word of the situation has gone to Taiben, and they are doubtless watching both within Taiben and the Sidonin train station. Still there is no report. It does seem that if our visitor has asked us to put a signal at the gate, there *will* be someone out there in a position to see it, so are we to believe that approach will now be made at the gate, and not through our abused western hedge? We have advised the Guild unit keeping watch over Kadagidi that our visitor used the gap in the hedge, but truthfully, our intruder only skirted the very edge of their land, so one cannot fault them. They are on the alert for anything crossing their area. My aishid has taken measures at that gap, so we shall not, at least, be surprised."

The very size of the grounds made it difficult to watch all the approaches, but likewise that great open expanse posed a problem to enemies. That was the notion that had defended Tirnamardi back in the days of cannon, and it still worked, but now there were modern safeguards like a camera at the gate, which they hoped might catch anyone taking interest in the signal set there; and there were an array of perimeter alarms which could be set, except wildlife was always setting them off and Guild had any number of ways to get past them. So the small alarms were not that reliable, if it was someone trained in the Guild, who were the ones most to fear.

Guild Headquarters and everybody proper was on *their* side. But Haniri had said it: the old man in the Guild, Shishogi, had ruled the Office of Assignments there for a long, long time, and while they had taken out the Shadow Guild wherever they had found it, they were never sure they had gotten every last hidden problem—and if there was any place where Shishogi's people might still be holding out, Ajuri itself was high on the list. Individual Guild might retire, but they never, ever resigned, because there was nothing but death that could take away all they knew, and the skills they had—so if a person tried to leave field work, they either took a job at a desk inside the Guild, or remained on call and available for the rest of their lives. If they went rogue, the whole Guild hunted them down.

The problem was—Shishogi had kept only paper records in his office, and he had blown up his office around him, so that the records that had not burned had literally to be pieced together, so they might have missed some placements that they would want to know about.

Ajuri land was just a good ride across the hunting range outside the gate, and Atageini and Ajuri shared that range, a rolling expanse of grass and small brush, occasional copses of trees, but nothing like the deep forest that was Taiben . . . which had poached that hunting land for generations, and now itself had an agreement with Atageini to use it—but none yet with Ajuri.

Politics, politics. Dull, until one looked out the second-story windows toward the hedges and wondered what was going on out there on the part of one's mother's own family.

"We are watching the gate," Veijico said, *we* being the Guild. "And the perimeter system is now on. We may have false alarms. Fruit is ripening, and a variety of orchard pests will set it off now and again."

"Taiben is moving other groups in to watch Sidonin station," Jegari said, "and our parents are advised of the situation. They are ready to move back to their camp near the gate, but they are trying to observe without confronting our intruder's people— assuming they are somewhere within view of the gate. Guild occupying the Kadagidi estate are likewise on alert."

"Do you think the news is aware?" he asked.

"Likely they will be watching." The law forbade the news from giving any notice of Guild maneuvers. They could only report what had happened once a licensed action ended, and they could not intrude into the area of dispute unless the incident broke around them.

But once the news started looking interested, it was sure the townships would.

And if that piece of white cloth was Nomari's signal to his associates that he was in Tirnamardi and safe, it was meant to be seen by somebody on the road—so if they were out there, they were likely trying to look like ordinary people on business or holiday, or any reason one could imagine for somebody to be hiking a road in the middle of a vast grassland, north of a very large woods and a train station that almost nobody stopped at. The two estates, Atageini and Kadagidi, formed a sort of island, restricted land almost back to back, in the heart of the region's largest hunting ranges, and Sidonin, one of the oldest train stations that still existed, and overgrown by forest, nowadays served just Uncle's estate and the Kadagidi estate, but the public stations northward, in the townships that sat on the river, and east and west of those, were busy with freight and ordinary passengers, so it seemed likely *anybody* could slip in there, among the crowds.

He imagined so, at least. He imagined all sorts of problems just walking down the platforms, in ordinary clothes, carrying tools or goods or such, looking just like anybody. It was very hard even for Guild to tell that a certain person was Ajuri, just that he was headed somewhere peacefully, and catching a bus for, say, Diegi, after which it was possible to walk down to Tir-namardi's hedges, even with Geigi watching from the heavens and news people watching everything in Diegi. Regular people were entitled to do that, and sometimes regular people did things just on a whim, so one could not say *anybody* walking along the road was a problem. Regular people routinely went places and did things they thought of, unless there definitely *was* a problem in the area.

His bodyguard would never let *him* put on town clothes and go for a walk in Shejidan. Or in Diegi. Or wherever. He thought he should, sometime, do that, so he should have some better idea what it was possible to do out there, or what people actually did do.

Leave Guild business to the Guild, Father would say.

But Father himself had taken the field in the south, when they had fought the Shadow Guild. Father and Mother both had hidden out in this very district, sleeping in hedges and getting food somehow.

And he had never even walked a regular street in Shejidan.

Could he live the way his father had? Could he even walk up the road to Diegi and even find food or a cup of tea? He knew it cost money. But he had never even held a handful of coins.

His father, right now, could say a handful of words and give Ajuri another lord, just like that. But was it the right lord for people who had trades and businesses and sold tea in shops?

It was something, to know that there had been an outside reason Ajuri kept losing lords. He understood *that* now, if Nomari had not made it all up.

But nobody had made up Shishogi, who really had set up terrible things, and killed a lot of people. That people in Shisho-gi's own clan had had most to fear—enough to leave and go into the guilds—he could believe that. But Shishogi had done all his harm just by putting people in positions to do very bad things. He'd been in charge of Assassins' Guild assignments, but that didn't mean he hadn't ordered certain people to go into other guilds, to position them to do things useful to him. So how many Ajuri who were scattered out in the guilds were honest folk, and how many were there because Shishogi had put them there, and knew where they were, and where their relatives were, and knew how to threaten them into doing things?

How did they straighten all that out? How did they find the bad ones, and save the good ones?

And there they were, with a white rag on the gate, Guild on alert, and Tirnamardi settling in to defend itself, the same as when riders with swords and lances had fought outside the hedges.

He had just been in space, where they could see the whole world without borders of any sort, and where light webbed the civilized areas at night, so that Mospheira glowed bright all about its coasts and the aishidi'tat had just scattered bright stars across the land.

He had seen that. And he would never, ever forget it.

Now he stood at windows that still could close defensive iron shutters, thinking about people creeping through the hedges and attacking the house. They should have gotten beyond that. They *should* get beyond it.

That was the world he wanted to make. A fair one. Fair for the towns and the people and the guilds.

Was that too much to expect?

10

There was a visitor wishing to come up, the phone call said, one Dr. Shugart, who claimed to have an appointment.

Absolutely, Bren said, to front door security, and asked Narani to stand by with hospitality at the ready, which put Jeladi to arranging tea and Narani waiting by the door for Kate's arrival.

One knock, and that door whisked open, admitting an old ally, leg cast, crutches and all. Ponytail style with a black bow. Gray going over to streaks of pure white. White tee, ample pink skirt over the cast, with an odd space-age unit attached to the casted ankle. Thong sandal on the other foot. Tanned. With a fitness a twenty-year-old could envy. All Kate lacked of the Port Jackson tourist was the straw bonnet and the sunglasses. Small wonder the front door had called to ask.

"I didn't dress," was Kate's opener. "Can't find a pair of pants that I can get on. Two more weeks in this damned cast. How are you?"

"I love you," he said, laughing. "Come in, sit down, trust Narani with the crutches. I thought it was just the ribs?"

"Would you believe the hospital steps?" she said. "Stupidity which cost me the chance of a lifetime. Gin's gotten close to them twice."

The kyo, Kate meant.

"I come bearing compensation. I've got an interesting job for you. If you can be pried loose from company work."

"Street sweeping could pry me loose from the damned company. The president's a fool. Not Shawn. The *company* president."

"Would you take on the *University* president?"

"University. You're not going to stick me in a classroom."

"No. Absolutely not. I want you to run a village that the University, particularly Linguistics and State, are both going to want to take under their own wing—and shouldn't. A village that may grow a bit, connect to Crescent Island, occasionally raise a few eyebrows, and attract the interest of the Heritage Party in a major way."

"You're bringing down the Reunioners."

"God, am I that transparent?"

"What do you want me to do for them?"

"Everything. I'm calling in Tom Lund and Ben Feldman. These people are coming down with the knowledge two hundred years of independent science and the experience of another solar system could give them. Not mentioning a decade of stubborn survival after the kyo strike. Some of them have access to science; more have awareness of materials and processes they may have used at an operational level, as techs and maintenance. Some are outright thieves. Some have mental problems. Some are children. Families and friendships among these people were broken by a terrible loss of life. And all of them were exposed to an event that ought to go into the University's memory as accurately as the record can be assembled—because *our* knowledge of the kyo is locked up in those memories. Not anything we're going to see again soon, we hope . . . because the kyo have their own problems to work out. They regret the attack. That's the bottom line. But we've potentially engaged with all that's out there. Anybody out there with sufficiently high tech can see us, in ways probably no news to you, but a revelation to me. And whatever's out there may one day come here. We have one population who's lived through it and made some serious mistakes. We can learn from them. We can learn about them. And meanwhile we can't confine them as a laboratory experiment. Three of the kids may become *my* replacement, in due time."

Kate listened, with that intensity that could make techs fear for their lives, while Kate was thinking. Curiosity was an intoxicant to Kate. Boredom and routine was hell.

Kate gave him that underbrow look that said she had a target in view, a program, an objective.

"Funding."

"Shawn's backing it. So is his Cabinet. You'll have total control. You *won't* be under the University. You'll be the Reunioners' defender—you'll appoint people, you'll fire people, you'll work them into Mospheiran life and you'll extract every piece of information they don't know they have. Plus protect them from the unscrupulous—cushion their entry, help them fit into Mospheiran society."

Kate laughed. *"I* don't fit into Mospheiran society."

"That makes you perfect for the job. You'll be dealing with every type, every level."

"You mentioned kids. I *hate* kids."

"These kids have met the kyo."

Instant focus.

"Three kids," he said. "One of whom effectively has no parents. Bright. Incredibly bright. Tabini-aiji wants them educated as paidhiin, but allowed to be human. You can imagine the number of people who'd like to direct *their* education."

"I'm not the motherly type."

"You're the type that can keep them safe."

"God."

"Tea," Bren said, and signaled Jeladi.

Jeladi and Narani served, quickly and with economy. And Kate sipped tea, staring off at the balcony, at potted plants, rooftops, and a sliver of ocean. He knew what was out there, but it was not, he was sure, what Kate was seeing.

He drank his own cup, waiting.

"You want me to play god for them. Five thousand people. And three kids."

"You won't be the only one. Ben Feldman to deal with specifics, Tom Lund to be sure where the Reunioners do interface with the corporate powerful, they don't get robbed. You, to define the boundaries and make sure who gets in contact and deals, in either direction. Parents of two of the kids are coming down with them—good people. I have somebody in mind to teach them how to cope with day-to-day living and get some sense of normalcy in their lives. The main establishment, the seed of my idea, is a simple apartment building within University housing. Initial community of three households, maybe a few more each month, progressing toward independent living— you'll arrange that too. I neglected to mention a fourth youngster under the aiji's protection, whose father is tied up in an investigation of improper dealings with Asgard on station, something Tillington had his fingers into."

Mikas Tillington, ex-stationmaster, was the person Kate herself had been intended to replace, if Kate hadn't fallen off a mountain and then broken her leg. Gin Kroger had stepped into that position, another of the old team, the team that had gotten the space program flying, supplied the station, gotten it populated in the current arrangement.

"I personally," Bren said, "don't particularly get along with the boy's father—he's got a temper and a number of issues—but I don't think he's a criminal. He had the foresight to salvage Reunioner company processes, and offered them to Asgard in return for jobs for him and his wife and an education for his son, and in the atmosphere Tillington created, I don't blame him for the way he went about it. He had the resource, and he used it, and a Mospheiran company's got a process Reunion developed. It'll be under litigation, but I'm hoping they'll settle it and straighten it out. I'm getting Tom and Ben involved in that issue. You won't have to touch it. And I'm not that sure that family will be one of the ones coming down. They might. But likely there'll be others in industry or technology, people who *will* be screened for problems."

Kate heaved a sigh. "You *know* Gin and I were already campaigning to get the Reunioners down here. The Maudit deal never was going to work. Everybody who knew anything knew it was politics, not a program."

"I know. I hate it about your leg, but honestly, it may have put the best woman for the job right where she can do what others wouldn't have the fortitude to try. And I mean you, Kate."

"Bren, you are a golden-tongued bastard."

He shrugged, smiled, reacting, after days of exposure, in human modes of expression—which he would have to shed, going back to the continent. *Soon,* he devoutly hoped. "Kate, you know you want it. When Gin wants a year or so on the planet, who knows? You'd slip right into place up there. And vice versa."

"I've been so damned frustrated. Bored. Bored of meetings. Bored of board meetings. I'd cheerfully just not show up in my nice river-view office tomorrow. Or ever. I at least have to advise the board I'm leaving. Two weeks."

"Deal?"

"What do I answer to? Not the University, you say."

"State, most likely. Shawn, in effect. They're not officially citizens, except in Shawn's declaration that they are. Their citizenship has to be made official. But we have to move faster, get them down here for security reasons while the legislature's still arguing. And those three kids are under the aiji's personal protection. So State is who *should* be involved, and if I have my way, because it *is* a matter of working new citizens in, that's who'll manage to *stay* involved."

"Deal. I'll do it. You knew I would."

"Of course I knew. Absolutely I knew. I'm *sorry* to approach you like this . . ."

"No, you're not. I pick my own staff?"

"Absolutely."

"Held to civil service qualifications?"

"Absolutely not. No civil service, no education certifications required. I'm also available if you need me. I'll come over for you, if ever you need me."

"Do I get a trip to Najida?"

He had no authority to promise that. But he also knew Tabini wouldn't choose to notice it.

"Research," she said blithely. "I need to know what conditions those kids experienced on the mainland. Don't I?"

He smiled, automatic and unthought. "There's a *reason* I put you in charge. Of course you need that experience. As you say—informational."

"A substitute for meeting the kyo," Kate said. "Probably with much more freedom."

"I can promise you that's true. Guest treatment. Trip to a neighboring estate. Meeting the original inhabitants of Mospheira. Local food. Good wine. Give or take the alkaloids. What else can I offer?"

"A ride on a mecheita."

"I'll work on it."

"Sold," Kate said. "I'll call people I have to call."

"Don't quit until I get the absolute go-ahead. I have the plan drawn up. I've got to talk to Gin about the schedule, shuttle space, who else might go—if the kids have relatives or close friends, they'd be a potential first-down. After that, Gin's using the lure of a lottery."

"Lottery."

"For free housing and goods, possibility of jobs. People-moving, housing and supervision is your problem. Free transport, help settling. We anticipate a few at first. Good reports will draw the others. The happiness of the experience is yours to arrange."

"Thieves, you said."

"You'll have a few problems. We'll try not to send those unidentified. And definitely not in the first few waves."

"I'd so appreciate that."

"I do love you, Kate."

"Flattery to boot. How could I refuse?" Kate accepted an-other cup of tea. "Seriously, I can't wait."

"They have found confirmation of major things this visitor has said, nandi," Jegari said, in their suite, where Cajeiri had gone to change clothes and put on a cooler coat. Only Antaro and Jegari had come up with him—considering that just going up to the suite, with Eisi and Liedi in attendance there, did not require his whole aishid. "The accounts the Guild has are good so far as they go. And Rieni has asked us to make a particular request. He believes this person would give *you* certain infor-mation . . . if you would ask him. I have a list."

"Give it to me."

Jegari drew a folded paper from inside his coat and handed it to him. Cajeiri stood in shirt sleeves, beside Boji's cage, as he read the missive, paper tilted to use the window light. Rieni's hand was old-fashioned, and not easy to read. Boji reached out a little paw to try for the sheet, and chittered at him. "Hush," he said, moving the paper slightly out of reach—and Boji made a try for his shirt cuff instead. "Little pest. Did we bring his toys?"

"I am sure," Antaro said, and went to look, while Eisi arrived with the requested change of coats. Cajeiri offered an arm for the coat, still reading the list, then traded arms.

"Do we have his toys?" he asked Eisi, the person who should know most. "He sees a hundred things he would like to get his hands on, and none of which he can have." The ornate furnish-ings and vases, the high ceiling, the hanging lamps . . . one could only contemplate the disaster. "We cannot have left that box."

"I have it," Antaro said, bringing the box over. They let Boji choose, offering his treasures close to the cage. Boji put out a hand and took a rope ring he liked, which would not fit through the bars. Eisi took it and delivered it through the feeding gate, and Boji immediately flung it onto the floor, bounded onto the bars and put out his arm for another.

"Spoiled creature," Eisi said, who had done the spoiling. "Here." Eisi delved into the box for an old sock with a knot in it, which he also delivered through the feeding gate. Boji picked it up, and began to run the knot over the cage grillwork, making a soft music, chittering the while, amused for the moment.

Cajeiri went back to his reading, standing in the light of the tall window, trying to memorize the list. He could hardly interview his so-named cousin with a paper of questions in hand. Thirteen questions. He could remember them as fives and a three, and he understood the gist of them. Several were to test Nomari's knowledge inside Ajuri, several were to gain names of his contacts, and others were specific as to the whereabouts and routes of those associated with him.

Boji threw the sock down and bounced on the perch, screeching at the top of his lungs. Uncle, fortunately, was not upstairs at the moment.

Eisi slipped him something small, which Boji took and popped into his mouth.

"Are you giving him fruit drops?" he asked.

"Nandi, it keeps him quiet."

There was that to say for it. But sweets often sent Boji bouncing about for hours.

"None of those too late in the day."

"The house is short of eggs," Eisi said. "They were to go to town today. And did not. We have enough for today and tomorrow, but nothing to spare."

Inconvenience shed its problems in unexpected places. If they had to ration Boji's eggs, there would be complaints. "See what the house can manage," he said, and pocketed the list. "Fruit. Fresh fruit." Of that, with the orchard, Tirnamardi had no scarcity. "He may have that. He likes it over-ripe."

He could remember the list, he was sure. He understood

what the Guild wanted: names, places, times, and they would probably welcome anything extra he could get.

Boji wanted out of his cage, a privilege denied him in this fragile and beautiful suite, and by now, in a very boring little room, certainly his cousin did.

Front door security called with another query. A woman with a package who, yes, was on the list, but she didn't want to open the package. Was she permitted to bring it?

"Yes," Bren said. "Absolutely."

Sandra Johnson. With a package. One couldn't imagine. Well, one could—Sandra had been responsible for the spider plant that had festooned his cabin on *Phoenix* and grown during ship-moves to an amazing swaying curtain.

"Nadiin-ji," he said, "Sandra-nadi is coming."

The teakettle went into service, Narani took his position by the door, and Banichi and Jago, Tano and Algini, all waited for a woman who had been his sole staff when he had had an office on Mospheira.

The door opened. Sandra entered, a blonde, neat woman in a dotted blouse and dark trousers, carrying a fair-sized package done up in blue paper and a vivid pink bow. Sandra had never seen atevi at close range: she did stare just a second or two, taking in everybody, and then the gaze swept to him.

"Sandra," he said warmly. "Is that for us?"

She held it out. He took it and handed it to Narani, who had never received such a festive article, and hardly knew what was expected to be done with it.

"Can I still call you Bren?"

"Of course you can. So glad you could come. Shall we open the package?"

"Yes," Sandra said definitely. "And I wasn't sure you had a knife, so I brought one, but Security wasn't happy with it."

He had to smile, and had a good idea what the present was. "We have a little silverware and such, with the buffet." He changed to Ragi: "We should open it, Narani. Just set it on the buffet, and open it. Pull the ribbon off: it's to be thrown away."

"It is quite handsomely done, nandi," Narani said, setting the package down. He began to work at the ribbon, discovering the tape, and in a moment had the wrapping unfolding on a plain cardboard box, the lid of which opened to show, yes, a cake, Mospheiran-style.

He guessed the sort. "Sandra, that's *very* kind of you. Rani-ji." He changed languages again. "One slices it radially, in finger-widths, and it will be very fine with tea. Please, will you serve it?"

Staff would, indeed. It was a problem in geometry which he trusted Narani to solve. They did have saucers with the teacups.

"Do sit down," Bren said, taking one chair, and Sandra picked the one opposite, a little prim, anxious, while Narani sliced the cake and Jeladi provided tea. "Did you have a good trip?"

"I did. I heard everything on the news. I couldn't imagine you'd send for me."

"I'm delighted to see you. John's fine?"

"He is." Sandra accepted a cup of tea. Bren took the other.

"And the kids? I understand there's been one more."

"Two," Sandra said after a sip. "I have four."

"Amazing."

"The youngest is three."

"I am so out of touch."

"You've been a little busy. We were so worried. But we knew you'd solve it. I told my kids you would."

"I wish I'd had your confidence. But we did it."

"They really are gone."

"And will stay gone."

"Were they scary?"

"Oh, they could be. But they're emotional folk, a lot like humans, though you wouldn't think it to look at them. They thump." He laid a hand on his chest. "From somewhere in here.

And make other sounds. That's their equivalent of having facial expressions, which they don't have—their faces are bony, fairly rigid. A group of them thumping away—they're rather noisy. But some of it's laughter, or just surprise. A lot less threatening when you understand what the noises are."

"Do they talk besides that?"

"Absolutely. And at the same time, which when you think about it, is what we do with our faces. It's really quite remarkable."

"But they won't be back."

"Not likely soon." But he was talking to a woman who had children. "And when they do, they'll come speaking a little Ragi, and a little Mosphei', and in expectation of a good meeting." Cake arrived, with small silver forks. Bren had a bite, and a sip of tea. "Sandra, you haven't lost your touch."

"Thank you."

"You're living up in Bretano."

"Yes."

"House?"

"Yes."

Over several bites of cake.

"I understand you're living in the capital, mostly," Sandra said.

"Most of the time. I do have a place on the west coast. I'm there when I get the chance."

"Are you—" Sandra started to ask and blushed, and he could almost guess what that question was. They'd dated briefly, in the time before John, before kids. And he didn't quite want to explain his relationship with Jago, God, no, not to Sandra, though he was sure she'd find a way not to be shocked. "Are you happy there?"

Second person to ask him that question.

"I really am. Very happy." But they couldn't go too far into old times and present relationships, with his aishid towering over the conversation and Jeladi pouring tea. He set his cake aside, half finished, had a final sip of tea and set down the cup, habit he didn't even think about until he'd done it.

"But it's not just a visit I called you for."

"For what?" Sandra swallowed, took a sip of tea and quietly set her plate aside, holding the cup in both hands.

"A job offer. I don't know if you'll be interested. But you'd be ideal."

"Are you coming back to the island?"

"No. But it's a job on the island. John's a landscaper, isn't he?"

"Landscape architect. He works for a construction firm. In Bretano."

Bretano was a distance away. A long move, as Mospheirans saw things. "I know. I know what I'm asking. Your husband's business. Kids. Schools. Friends. A major move. But I have a good offer, Sandra. It'd pay for your kids' education. All four of them, all the way through University if they want that. It'd offer you a salary; and a retirement. John, being in the work he does, could easily work into a job somewhere in the situation, a good living. And you'd be doing something I think you'd do very well—with kids. With families. Do you want to hear it?"

"I—I'll *hear* it."

"The last thing I want is to cause a disruption in the life you've made for yourself, for your husband, for the kids. But that seems to be what I'm good for. Here's the heart of the matter. The three Reunioner children, who've been in the news."

"Are they coming down again? Here?"

"Yes. With their families. They're going to be settled in an apartment, near the University. The kids will be taught by University personnel. Because of the level of attention they'll have, and because they're under the aiji's protection *and* the President's, they won't be able to go out and about without security in attendance, they won't be able to do many of the things ordinary kids do. Their parents—there are three, among them one girl with, effectively, none—they're complete strangers to the world. The parents have never seen a storm, never looked at a flat horizon, never seen the seacoast, never seen the sun, for that matter, as a sun in the sky. Absolutely everything is new to them. What I would wish—*if* you want to take it on, you and John *and* your kids—is to move in, and be their neighbors. Your kids—could be in contact if *you* choose. John, the same. But you—living there, just helping the Reunioners adapt, teaching them to cook for themselves, teaching them what a grocery is, what to do under a thousand circumstances—you'd be their tutor. And their social contact. They're good people, these first down. They'll help the ones who come after, some of whom may be cousins or some degree of relatives. But there were a huge number of deaths on Reunion, so families were not just broken, they were shattered. There are problems that Reunioners and probably specialists are going to have to work out—that's not *your* job. You're just to work with those first few, and be their teacher—their mentor—just in how things work, and what to do. That's what's needed. And you have skills you might not think of as skills, but they're vitally important, for people who've never stood under a blue sky or—" He smiled. "—Baked a cake."

"God."

"Financially—you and your family would have a good solid living, education for your kids, not fabulous wealth—that's not what we want to provide the Reunioners—but enough to be comfortable. You'll work out—with your own considerable good sense—how much affluence you want that to be, to teach them how to live as regular people."

She frowned. "You say they'll be under heavy security. That we'll be living in this facility—"

He saw where that was going. "You won't be under the restrictions the Reunioners will be. Just don't advertise who you are or what you do. Take a vacation, visit relatives, visit friends, no problem. But your job, a small office in the building, will entail exactly what you did for me—solving problems. Only you also get to teach these people how to fend for themselves.

The Reunioner kids—by the way—the first you'd meet—are nice kids. Polite. Sensible. Way older than their years, by what they've been through. But very good hearts."

"I can't decide this alone, Bren."

"You're thinking about it. That's all anybody can ask. It will be a fishbowl. There will be frustrations. But the first-down will be these kids, possible relatives, and some science and engineering types. There's to *be* no disruptive personalities in this first residency. If you can't work with somebody, or they're having psychological or medical issues, you make a phone call, and they'll move somewhere, but you won't have to cope with them. Your job is solely to enable these people to live a normal life, and cook a meal, and ultimately, to form friendships, get jobs, and know how to catch a bus. The original three kids—and their families—will pretty much stay in the bubble, restricted because of security. The kids will travel to the mainland now and again. Their parents won't. These kids—are going into the Foreign Office track, educationally speaking; and if ultimately they don't want to be there, that'll be their free choice, but for right now, and until the world gets used to them, they need protection."

"I understand. I understand what you want, I think. God. It's enormous."

"Staff would be no problem, if you turn out to need it. But these people themselves may be able to handle some of the incoming."

"I can't say yes. I have to explain this to John. And the kids. My oldest. It'd be everything. But—"

"It's tremendous freedom, economically; and considerable restriction, socially. Yes. You've worked with me. You know exactly what it is."

"I do." She looked at the teacup, in which the liquid had to have gone tepid. "It's huge."

"It really is. And now I suspect you can't enjoy being in Port Jackson. You need to fly back home and talk to John. If you do say no, I'll know it's for very good reasons. You're just the best answer I could think of. Things can get handled if you say no. But I hope for a yes."

She set the teacup down, to the side. "I'd better get a flight."

"You just get to the airport. This time we'll get one for you. Ticket will be waiting at the counter when you get there."

She got up. "Thank you so much. It's good to see you, Bren."

"Good to see you." He got up, came and took her by both hands. "You do what your good sense tells you. All right?"

"Right," she said. And left, not without a backward look, and a nervous little nod to Narani, who opened the door for her.

He had immediately to arrange the ticket. He thought, ridiculously, that he also ought to call down to security and tell them give her back the knife, which was probably part of a set.

"Will she agree to do it?" Jago asked.

"I have no idea," he said. "I hope I haven't just upset her life. But I don't think so. She's stronger than she looks. A lot stronger. Very sensible. And a very good cook. I heartily recommend the cake, nadiin-ji."

11

Nomari arrived in the staff room in better appearance than the day previous—his clothes cleaned, the ripped coat sleeve repaired, a courtesy Uncle had ordered—but Uncle was not present. Guild was, Uncle's, Cajeiri's own—and two of Uncle's senior staff, who stood by, there if needed.

Cajeiri sat down. Tea might have been appropriate, if the occasion were in any wise social. It was, Cajeiri instantly felt, a Guild affair, top to bottom, with Uncle officially absent, but with Uncle's own people there.

He was there to help, he instantly felt. He was not in charge, but he was the polite presence in the situation, there to ask the Guild's questions. But not only the Guild's questions.

He was also there to represent Father, who, if he were present, would not take second place to the Guild. He could not *take* charge, no, nor interfere, but he could at least ask his own questions, and not be a fool, either.

"Nadi," he said with a little nod.

"Nandi," was the respectful answer, the proper answer.

"The Guild has been checking things. And they would like me to ask, courteously, certain things. I have talked with my father. I have talked with my great-uncle. I have not spoken with my mother, but probably my father will tell her. My aishid says you may be my third cousin. And that you are Transportation Guild. And you say you came here to talk to me, and I suppose to my great-uncle. The Guild asks—why now?"

"Because," Nomari said, "because something has to be done about Ajuri and Kadagidi, and done fairly soon. Lord Tatiseigi's party is pushing for a solution. And there are not many solutions to be had. Lord Tatiseigi might not have welcomed me showing up at his door uninvited. I doubt I could pass his gate. I have no claim on his consideration, myself, and if he inquired with the Guild—and it reached the wrong ears, it might mean my life."

"Do you think it will?"

"I have lost my cover. I *will* be in danger—whatever happens from here."

"Nandi," Rieni said, from the side of the room. "Ask him why he chose this place, this time."

"Nadi," Nomari said quietly, in direct answer to Rieni, "I am not high-ranking in my guild. I could not reach Lord Tatiseigi in the Bujavid. I certainly could not reach your father, except at fall audience, and that might be far too late. The pressure is mounting to do something about Ajuri, even to break it—and if I spoke out in Shejidan I would be without protection. Here—I certainly have protection."

It might be a grim joke he was making. But it was also, in a way, true.

"Was it safer to risk the mecheiti, coming through the hedge?" Cajeiri asked. "Where were you trying to go?"

"To the house, nandi. Precisely to the house. And with all respect, nandi, I did not finish the first question. You asked why now? And the answer is—I was already asking myself what to do about the nomination, whether to send a letter to your father, whether to send a letter to Lord Tatiseigi, when I heard you were coming to visit Lord Tatiseigi. I have my guild pass—I could quietly, with no permission, go as a worker between districts. So I reached Diegi, and I walked."

"Alone?" Haniri asked.

"Yes."

"*Are* you alone in this undertaking?"

"No. I am not. But it was *my* part to come here, and reach the house, and beyond that—to rely on the young gentleman, as a relative, and on his guard, to ask who I am, so I can prove at least that much."

"Did you intend to break in?"

"I hoped to get to the stables, at least, and to contact the staff. I hoped, as happened, that with a claim of being your cousin—"

"Third cousin. *Half* third cousin."

"Your third cousin, nandi, to be sure—that Lord Tatiseigi would at least inform your aishid of my existence. He owes me nothing else, though I owe him for clean clothes and better food than I have ever had . . ."

"I shall tell him you said so," Cajeiri said. "But what do you want?"

Nomari drew a deep breath. "Ajuri. Nothing less. But I do not expect it without answering a good many questions."

"You claim support," Rieni said.

"I have it."

"Within the clan."

"Within the clan, nadi. I do not say—within the hall at the moment. Ajiden is far from safe, for anyone who lives there."

Ajiden was the Ajuri house, where Mother had grown up. And Cajeiri had no concept what it was inside, because Mother never discussed those years. But outside, he knew, it was a long, sprawling place with seven residencies connected together by a wall, and with a natural spring and a garden at the center. And it had no rail station of its own, but its town did—a town mostly built in the style of a hundred years ago, with streets that wound around the natural halls. There were public gardens, there was a museum and a number of galleries. There was a big electronics maker, and a number of furniture makers, and a number of big orchards and egg farms with a network of other towns, all tied by rail. There was a lake, too, with fishing. There was irrigation in two of the sub-clan holdings, and a dam that had been controversial with Dur's claim on the water. Everything he knew about his mother's clan was through pictures and geography lessons and his tutor. Mostly he thought of that curious clan house, and a lot of fields a lot like the view around Tirnamardi.

Ajiden is far from safe.

That described the situation of Nomari's entire family, apparently. And Shishogi being from Ajiden . . . and still having living relatives . . . that probably was true.

"So tell us," he said to Nomari, "how are you going to go in and be safer than anybody else?"

"It would not be that simple," Nomari said.

"Then say," Rieni said, "how you *will* survive. By illegal assassinations? That has been the pattern."

"And how," Uncle's Guild senior asked, "were you educated, and where?"

Nomari said, "I was not, nadi. I was not educated in any higher way. I am Transportation Guild. I have learned where I could, what I could. I have read. I have most of all . . . moved about. I have seen most of the aishidi'tat. I have talked to people. I have talked to other Ajuri who cannot go home. I carry a name my great-uncle could track and trace, and I know now he likely did, but I kept myself as far as I could be from raising any claim or being in any way remarkable, since I did not know who my enemies were. I played the coward. And I was lucky. Some of my sort did disappear—just vanished entirely. I know quite a few who go under other names, but changing one's name triggers suspicion from the start. So long as I stayed visible but harmless, and careful, the watching stayed quiet. I never was sure who might be behind the watching. There was a time we all believed our uncle Shishogi protected us, and that someday we would find the one thread that would make sense and protect us from our enemies—from the ones responsible. We just did not know who we were guarding ourselves against, but the thought was, through all the confusion, that the problem was in our lords, that maybe the lordship would settle on someone who could keep the peace among the houses and let them come home. But for myself, I feared our troubles were irreparable—because of our being who we were, and because of my father's speaking his mind. When my father and brother died, my mother told me go, get out, get away. And then she died. I learned that later. I thought it might be Kadiyi's order. And I was not the only one, or the only generation who were left in the dark, without kin, with no clear reason. I found some of the displaced had fled Benedi, before Kadiyi took him down. And we all had somebody we blamed. There was, among us, distrust. So much distrust. And when Murini took the aijinate and replaced your father, nandi, then—then finally some of us began to get together and wonder—first about Kadiyi, then about your grandfather, and all those threads of relation and marriage . . . but we were puzzled. Why, we asked, would Murini aim at your mother along with your father?"

"She is loyal to my father!"

"Certainly she has proved that. But at the time, young aiji, we asked that question. We thought perhaps the assassins aimed to rescue her. But some thought not. Several of us who had never trusted each other got together and asked that question—asked, again, why Lord Tatiseigi had stayed in power, when other lords supporting your father had fallen. And we began to look for answers in the lines of inheritance, in the favored, and the unfavored, and the deaths that had led, one after the other, to Kadiyi, and to Geidaro."

"My aunt?"

"Great-aunt, yes. She had a contract marriage with one Aiechi, whose line has roots in the Marid. Aiechi's cousin was Murini, and their son was being groomed to high office. Caradi. Perhaps you have met him."

"Once. I think." The days after his father's return to Shejidan were a haze. Ajuri relatives had come and gone in a blur, and only his grandfather had stayed long, his grandfather, his aunt Meisi, and his cousin Dejaja, who had actually been nice.

He could not say that of his grandfather Komaji, his mother's father, who had become lord of Ajuri, and who had tried to put himself closer and closer to them, the more his mother tried to push him out. It had not been pleasant. It had gotten downright scary, before his father had banished Grandfather Komaji from court. His mother had been upset over it and glad of it at the same time . . . his mother, he had to remember, having been stolen away by her father once.

She had left Ajuri when she found a chance—she had lived with Uncle Tatiseigi and then run back to her father again when she had quarreled with Uncle. Ajuri was like that, so far as he had observed: people changed sides. Nobody trusted anybody. Years and years ago Shishogi moved into that little office in Assassins' Guild Headquarters and started managing things not just to favor his little clan—but to use it on a path leading to power.

And that was before his mother was born.

"When several of us sat down together to try to understand," Nomari said, "we put all those names together and nothing made sense. Murini ought not to have risen—he could not have risen—without backing. It was a puzzle to us, how certain pieces remained in place on the board, and others did not. It was as if the world had turned as confusing to our view as Ajuri had been—as it should not have been if things operated the way we had always believed. Then, though Murini had gone down, though your father was back—word filtered through the guilds that the first of guilds had splintered, that the part that supported Murini was refusing to stand down, and undermining all the peace and reform was this moving cluster of problems, east, and south, and west and north again. Your great-grandfather Kadiyi died and your grandfather took the lordship, and then bolted from the house. He wanted to be anywhere but Ajuri. He feared for his life . . . and he feared Ajuri more than anybody."

"Do you *know* that?" Cajeiri asked sharply. "*How* do you know that?"

"Because we have contacts—many contacts—inside Ajuri. And from the moment Shishogi himself went down—we have begun hearing from them. Secrets long held have begun to slip out. Ajuri secrets are finally making sense—how the lords of Ajuri either found ways to move as Shishogi wished—or they died. Your grandfather was only the latest." Nomari folded his arms and looked toward Rieni and Uncle's bodyguards. "So I know deep secrets of your guild, nadiin, and if you do not know them I will tell them to you, but I think you know—that there was a faction, and may be a faction, so convinced that humans will change us, that *they* changed us. Shishogi may not have been the only one, or even the main one at the start of everything, but he was in a place to move all the pieces, and he made a nightmare of Ajuri and Kadagidi. I know very little about humans, but I care very little about them, too. They are not the monsters. The monsters were the ones who killed their own brothers and sisters so we could then go kill the humans. And the monsters may have failed to move the aishidi'tat, or to replace the aiji, but they are still alive in Ajuri."

"Have you names?" Rieni asked, in such a tone it sent chills down Cajeiri's arms.

"I will not damn anyone without knowing more than I do, more surely than I know," Nomari said. "I was not educated to be a lord, I am not trained in economy and philosophy, I have nothing to recommend me, except I know names, I know contacts, I have a network of individuals who can fish information out of that well, and move other individuals on nothing more than kinship. That is all I have. But I believe in Ajuri. I believe in what it was, and what it could be, if enough people got together to say we cannot go on killing each other, and that we owe the merchants and the trades and people trying to bring up children something better than the lords of Ajuri have been dealing out. I do not know that I can do this. But I have a claim on the lordship. I may *not* be educated to be a lord. But the people who are scattered out across the aishidi'tat, that want to go home—we do not want to see Ajuri broken. And we know the trades, and we know the merchants and we have people in those guilds. If I become a target and then back down to save my life—well, then I will be an old man knowing I could have done something, and despising myself."

Not trained for a lordship, but he could talk. He could argue. One could only wish to argue as well as that.

"You will not trust us with the names of your enemies," Rieni said. "Will you give us the names of your allies?"

There was a long silence. Then Nomari said, "I will give you those. At least a few. If I cannot trust the Guild now, if I cannot trust the young gentleman's guards, then we are out of hope. Check the names out. I only ask you to tell me if you find anything in them—that I should have known. That those in authority need to know."

"Do you have associates inside Kadagidi?" Janachi asked.

"I do not," Nomari said. "I have avoided Kadagidi associations—of any nature. The troubles there—one has no idea. I have met individuals in Transportation. I know one in the Physicians. But any personal entanglement—no. I have not had any but working relationships, nothing beyond it."

"Personal attachments?" Haniri asked bluntly, which meant, well, sex. Cajeiri felt his face go warm.

"None at all," Nomari said, and added: "The risk—to either—no. Not even inside our circle."

It seemed very lonely. One knew a little something about associations—and being aiji. And everything Nomari said added up to that. His own father and his mother had made a permanent contract, and when he looked at his father's father, and a string of relationships all of which had been simple contracts, and not even that—he knew why Father had insisted on a life marriage. Being aiji was complicated enough.

He listened while Nomari provided seven names, a fortunate number, and the guilds they belonged to, two within Transportation, two within the Merchants, one in the Physicians, one in the Messengers and one in the Treasurers. And Rieni said that was enough for now, and they would take Nomari back to his room, and see that he had a good lunch.

Nomari stood up, and bowed. Cajeiri stood up and returned the courtesy, and watched as his senior aishid took Nomari back to be locked up and guarded again.

Uncle's bodyguard had a recorder going. So did Rieni. He knew that. He knew that Uncle would want to hear it, and Father would.

He really hoped Nomari was what he said he was. Nomari looked weary, and sometimes sad, and could go hard as ice for a moment, but it was Rieni and Janachi who had been scary—Rieni when he had asked for names of enemies, and Janachi when he had asked about Kadagidi. Which Janachi was, if he could believe what his senior aishid had told him.

He looked across the room at his younger aishid, who had not left him. The servants had left. Uncle's bodyguards had gone out with the seniors. "Do you believe him?" he asked.

"He had answers," Jegari said. "I think the seniors are going to dig deeper than the seven names he gave. And there was one guild where he named no associates."

"The Assassins," he said. He had marked that, too.

"I doubt he should trust Ajuri in our Guild," Lucasi said, "and there are some, but none in Headquarters. They have all been assigned out." Lucasi clamped his lips together. It was probably information regulations said he was not supposed to give out, but it did matter, now, to what Nomari had said. "There were some juniors, too," Lucasi added, "but they have all been put back into training, until the new Guild Council decides they should go into assignment. And that probably will not happen until Ajuri has a clan lord and he has their man'chi. Until then, no one trusts them."

Down the hall a door closed. And his younger bodyguards said nothing further.

12

Tom Lund and Ben Feldman came thorough front door security with no advance warning but a phoned, *"Mr. Lund and Mr. Feldman are on their way up, Mr. Cameron."*

Depend on it, neither of them came in a cast or carried a cake and a knife. Business suits—in which Tom Lund, stout and graying, looked like a banker on business—he always did; and Ben Feldman, slender to the point of gauntness, looked like an accountant on deadline. He was much happier in tees and short pants.

They worked, if not together, at least in harmony. Tom, whose only request was never to have to fly in the shuttle again, was thoroughly familiar with the station's architecture, inside and out, familiar with the power structure of every company that had worked on it, depended on it, or hoped to profit from it, and knew who dealt with whom in the legislature. Ben Feldman was the man to go after data, find it out, and find out the secrets or open the most stubborn doors—figuratively, of course. Ben had logistical skills, figuring out what had to be done and lining up the materials and companies to do it by hook, crook, or Tom's persuasion.

They hadn't been up to the station since they'd come down in Tillington's restructuring of Mospheiran admin up there. They'd been *glad* to come down, excepting the shuttle ride in Tom's case, so Gin had said. Tom had drunk way too much on the way down and it was not an experience Tom wanted to repeat.

"I don't have to go up to the station," had been one of Tom's first questions when Bren had called him, and "You absolutely promise me no shuttle flight," had been his last.

No shuttle flight, Bren had assured Tom, and meant to hold to that. Tom having a heart attack was not in the program.

Tom using his considerable pull with certain contacts in the legislature and industry would be a major asset in getting the Asgard roadblock out of the way and dealt with—fairly, reasonably, and to the good of innocent parties.

And Ben—doing the groundwork on the Reunioner flights and the cargo drops—was a second major asset. Ben would make things work, down to the fine numbers.

"So," Bren said, with the two of them in his sitting room, "you think you've got the thing tied down."

"This is the essence of it," Tom said. "I've talked to Asgard. They have two major concerns: their company's reputation, and the financial commitment they've already made to that materials project. They'd like to recover their reputation regarding the deal. Their on-station manager is expendable in that context, but they think he offered fairly what the Reunioner asked for, in a hostile legal environment—namely Tillington's administration—and if they'd done more than that, their manager believed it would have drawn attention to the man, put the papers in Tillington's hands, and gotten the Reunioner nothing."

"They do have an argument. In that light, are they willing to give a deposition against Tillington?"

"They might be persuaded. And it might not take much. They could work with Tillington, in the sense of getting rules bent. They're going to miss that freedom but they're not going to miss entertaining Tillington, and do they have information they'd be willing to impart? Yes. They'd like to keep that program, they'd like to keep their manager, and they'll keep their commitment to the Reunioner they dealt with. They'll give him a small research division to pursue what he was pursuing on Reunion and provide a scholarship for his son. The boy's extremely bright, and deserving, and his field of study is right along their track. What they want is legitimization of the patent they dealt for."

"Having the patents tied up in litigation doesn't benefit anybody but the lawyers."

"That's my view. And there is a precedent for this: the Brightwater decision, back at the founding of Mospheira. Then it regarded ownership of certain knowledge brought down from Alpha. In the absence of ownership or patent, unique processes emanating from the original are patentable. If there are living owners, their rights are considered to be creator rights and must be compensated. But so must the rescuer of said knowledge. We can handle this. The companies will be very happy we're settling this fast. And one judicial decree will legitimize the Reunioners' claims with a minimum of litigation. With the Reunioner and Asgard in essential agreement, we can invoke Brightwater and legitimize any agreements regarding other properties."

"Excellent," Bren said.

"Tillington, however," Ben said, "has proved a very slippery character. Gin can easily get him off the station, but she's keeping pressure on him and his staff. They're starting to tell tales on each other. And if we *can* get Asgard's cooperation, we have him. Once we have him, we have the others."

"He started out well," Bren said regretfully. Which was true. Tillington had been a good administrator . . . until the meltdown.

He'd started with monumental ambition, wanted to refurbish the residency areas of the station—he'd tried to negotiate a larger share of materials from Lord Geigi's mining operation, and with Geigi's cooperation he'd managed to do some major restructuring and building.

But he'd had still bigger plans, among them that there'd be a human shuttle built in orbit, though the original treaty with the aishidi'tat had emphasized that atevi would provide the shuttles until essential goals were met.

They hadn't gotten to that, when the ship had left on its mission to Reunion.

And when the crisis had come in the aishidi'tat, while the ship was absent, when Tabini had been temporarily overthrown and the shuttles had been grounded, depriving the station of supply—Tillington demanded the one atevi shuttle that was still aloft go into service to Mospheira.

Geigi had refused on the grounds Mospheira had no ability to service it, and that refusal had been a breaking point of the cooperation. Lord Geigi refused to cede critical materials, being set on his own plan to rescue the aishidi'tat, restore the atevi shuttle flights in the process—and letting Mospheira build its own shuttle on the ground . . . while Tillington had wanted to build his in orbit.

In the midst of that, the ship, feared lost, had come back— with Reunioners. Lots of Reunioners. Unloading them to Mr. Tillington's side of the station had doubled the human population overnight, stressed supply, and overcrowded Mr. Tillington's new facilities.

Atevi on the ground, meanwhile, had taken back their government. Tabini-aiji had come back into power and sent shuttles up with goods to relieve the station, and Mospheira had pushed ahead with their plans to launch a ground-built shuttle, a move that would make Mr. Tillington again just an appointed official.

Tillington's half of the station meanwhile had had to be re-configured for the new residents. Atevi had been too busy with their own recovery to assist anybody beyond sending up food and needed parts—and that, unfortunately, had been the tipping point for all manner of ills. Tillington's under-the-table deals with the companies continued, and to keep Mospheirans from complaining, he'd shorted the Reunioners on services, backing an ill-conceived plan to move the Reunioners off to a new station construction, about the barren rock called Maudit.

He'd kept the Mospheirans happy, at the cost of serious hardship for the Reunioners and increasingly bad feelings on the station.

And then the kyo had shown up.

But the meltdown Tillington had had then was not the fracture of an otherwise good administrator faced with crisis. No, the dealings Gin had begun to uncover—coercion, favor-trading, and outright bribery—traced not to the arrival of the refugees, but back to the beginning of the supply crises.

"He *started* as a good manager," Tom said. "But that wasn't how he finished."

"My fear is the Heritage Party will be campaigning on his side the minute he sets foot on the ground. I don't know his mental state, but they might find use for him."

"Maybe not," Ben said. "Gin's got five people in detention, and one staffer doing nothing but taking truth-readers on complaints and building a case, bribery, coercion, physical threats and intimidation, improper grant of licenses and payoffs in material goods, not just with one company and not just in the last few months. He may become far too hot to be useful to the Heritage Party."

"Devoutly to be wished," Bren said. Filing Intent? Among atevi, human biology didn't qualify him to make that call. But he had had that dark thought. He had indeed had it, in Tillington's case, and, however briefly, up there, he'd been a position to do it. He hadn't, for which he was glad—now.

As for the specific Reunioner involved in the Asgard case, that was one Karl Andressen, father of Bjorn Andressen, the fourth youngster of Cajeiri's acquaintance. Cajeiri hadn't entirely dismissed Bjorn from his concerns, and by Cajeiri's intent, Bjorn had come under Tabini's protection, right along with the three youngsters who'd gained court status. Bjorn's parents wanted him to have what they'd traded secrets to get. And that was their choice, to keep him apart. And Bjorn's choice, to stay with them. But that could change.

"So we may have the Tillington matter handled," Tom said. "Right along with Asgard."

"As for the robot landers," Ben said, setting up his briefcase, and taking out a set of papers. "This is the schedule of production we'd like, if we can get Lord Geigi to cooperate. We just need a translation for Geigi, to be precise."

"Absolutely."

"Once we have an actual schedule," Ben said, "Tom can present it to the legislature, and we can move on it. The fact atevi land is going to be the drop zone raised a few eyebrows in preliminary discussion, but when we mentioned the degree of imprecision in the drop zones, there was a quick shift in opinion. We don't have that much flat land that isn't lived on."

"I'll get you a translation, I'll talk to Lord Geigi, and get a firm proposal with dates before I clear the island," Bren said.

"Fifty down per shuttle?"

"We could manage more, but fifty is a reasonable load—at the assimilation end of things as well."

"A hundred shuttle landings."

"Five shuttles, six with yours . . . one landing to start, and a few months to work out the human problems with the first-down. Then fifty come down. If that works, maybe a hundred in the next cycle. At every stage—we'll have to make adjustments."

"On University grounds. You want the University to work with those three kids. And then the rest."

"In very different ways. The three kids, first-down, need private tutoring, leading to Linguistics, ultimately to the Foreign Office—*my* track. And special protection. I'm not saying there's any resentment aimed at them. But as politics evolve—or some random lunatic gets a notion—they have to be protected. Their entire lives—they have to be protected."

"I've got an appointment with the University President to talk about that," Tom said. "I'm assuming *funds* will be there. They're around ten years of age, right?"

"About that, with an education pretty well as a caretaking operation, what I hear, to keep the kids out of the hazard areas. But they're bright. And what they need to know, they can learn. They speak and understand Ragi, court and a little colloquial. We don't give a damn about the academic scores. They need to learn Mospheiran history, Mospheiran customs, math, science, and anything else they want."

"You're talking about tutoring. Special materials, special staff. I imagine special everything for that initial group. Not to mention the constant security."

"The aiji will fund their program. In a sense, he's already chosen the next paidhiin. He wants them to represent Mospheira to him and to his heir . . . always presupposing that's what they choose for themselves. But there's every indication that's what they *will* want. The President supports the plan, and logically it should come under Linguistics, which already has close ties with the State Department, but it might require a new entity handling it, should Linguistics prove intractable. The question remains whether Mospheira will view these three, if they become paidhiin, as representing Mospheira . . . or Reunion. I hope by the time these youngsters stand on their own—that will not be an issue, because I do *not* foresee Tabini-aiji being willing to make that distinction. I think it very valuable for Mospheira to feel it has a traditional Mospheiran representation, and I think it valuable for those kids to feel a strong indebtedness and grounding on this side of the strait. In the whole process, they need their parents, such as they have. Bottom line, the aiji wants them to have their parents, and wants them to grow up human, to represent Mospheira to him and to his heir, which I think is a very good decision."

"Thank you for that argument," Tom said. "I'll use it."

"There's an apartment building I'm thinking off—Heyden Court, they used to call it—it was a bequest to the University with the grounds and garden. They've never been able to convert it to dorms, because of the restrictions on the will, as I understand it. They've used it as storage, they've used it as a display hall for the Art Department, they've used the upper floor as a guest house. The sports field next to it—Heyden Field—is also part of University grounds, but they can't build a stadium, and best I can figure it's been a problem to them for fifty years. I've stayed there, on occasion, and it was nice, old-fashioned, full of history. Move the art to another building, if the program has to build them one, and it could take the kids and families next week. With resident security. And offices for the staff that's going to set up to work with the other refugees as they arrive."

"What *is* your timetable?"

"Next shuttle flight, or the one after, for the kids and parents."

"Fast," Tom said.

"There's something to be said for not shocking people with our speed, but there's also something to be said for not letting opposition get organized. I'm not set on Heyden. Ames Complex, which is right next to campus, could be ideal if they closed it down before next trimester and moved the students out, but it's larger than we need now. Mospheiran security may have their own notions. I'm only interested in the quality of security and the notion of a comfortable residence, ideally *with* a garden. The parents have never seen a tree. Just the freedom to walk in a natural environment, safely, would be good for them. The Heyden gardens would be ideal."

"I'll talk to the University," Ben said.

"I'd like to get a second building, ultimately," Bren said, "for others, when they come. Teach people the basics, let them form community, move them out together to settle here and there around the country in small groups, no more than ten families per community, with continued oversight. It's not a case of dumping them down here in one cohesive mass and letting them struggle. We do what we can to socialize them as Mospheiran. Find them jobs, though there's a whole generation in which certifications and licenses and anything like formal education is a little iffy. Our license-loving Mospheiran authorities are going to have to deal creatively and swallow their objections."

"Culture shock on both sides," Ben said.

"Absolutely. Medical care. Psychological support. Psychiatric care in some instances. But we can do this. Five thousand people are a huge matter, on the station side of the operation, but in the general population—very minor. We want them to blend in. But we can't let them get lost, in the bad sense, either."

"It'll still change us," Ben said.

"Both populations are from islands," Bren said, "one stone, one steel. We have that in common. I have every confidence in you two. You can set this up. You've got Kate Shugart. You've got Gin, upstairs. I'm also bringing in Sandra Johnson—my secretary, from back when I had an office. At least I hope to have her. She'd be an on-site counselor and instructor in basic living."

Tom sat, chin against chest, arms folded. "I have a few contacts in mind. If Ben can't liberate Heyden Court, I know the current Heyden executor from another deal. I think it could be finagled. Turning Heyden Court into a Linguistics center, so long as the gardens are preserved—that might have real appeal, if it comes with finance."

"Next shuttle cycle?" Ben said. "Give us a few more weeks. Give us the next Mospheiran shuttle cycle, and we can do this."

Four weeks? "I'll take it," Bren said.

He'd like to be on site for the children's landing, he'd like to escort them over the same way he'd come, a leisurely trip on the boat, a chance to adjust.

But if Tom and Ben, Kate and Sandra were on the case, speaking ship as readily as Mosphei', and taking care of the kids and their families?

He'd trust that. He'd trust that as the best situation he could arrange on the island.

13

It was another conference in Uncle's sitting room. Cajeiri was there, not just to listen, and Uncle was there, in his afternoon coat, and everybody else was in Guild black, with sidearms, and being very careful of the beautiful gilt furniture.

Everything going on here had sent disturbance all the way to the Guild in Shejidan, all the way to mani out in Malguri, and certainly to Father's office and probably, by now, to Mother—who might want him home. But going down to Sidonin, to the train station in the woods, was a real risk. So was, even more so, going up to the township to *that* train station. There was nothing Ajuri could muster that was going to threaten Tirnamardi, inside its hedges. So he was safer staying where he was.

More than that, he was what the Guild called a principal in what was going on—which was to say, *he* was involved as much as Uncle was, and he had an opinion, *he* was the main person their visitor wanted to talk to—

It was the second time in not very long that his opinion had mattered, and all he could hear at the back of his mind was mani cautioning him not to be forward, that his having an opinion might be exciting for him, but not necessarily to the room at large. He did not want to embarrass himself, or annoy Uncle.

Still—he was part of deliberations. And he was forming his own opinion about Nomari, slowly, as mani counseled. On one side of it was the chance Nomari was up to no good, and on the other was the chance that he was telling mostly the truth.

On the side of the first opinion was the simple fact that Ajuri in general had been up to no good for quite a long time.

On the other side was the fact his own mother was Ajuri, and *she* had done her best all her life to navigate between Ajuri and Atageini and to do right in spite of what was going on.

On the side of the first opinion was the possibility that Nomari was no different than Shishogi, up to the worst sort of mischief, trying to launch another War of the Landing.

So there was some possibility that Nomari had done what Mother had, and simply ricocheted from one place to another, trying to keep out of trouble until Shishogi was dead and he was in a position to do something.

It would be very nice to believe all that Nomari said, that there was a whole association of Ajuri, mostly young people who had gone into the guilds for a refuge . . . but there was also the possibility the person who had carefully placed his people in key spots in the Assassins' Guild had just as carefully arranged spots for people in other guilds.

If there was a network of honest people who despised Shishogi—and they had the possibility of Nomari telling the truth, and being such a person—then Nomari was somebody they needed to protect—somebody Uncle needed, because of being Ajuri's close neighbor. He was somebody *Father* needed, not just because Ajuri was an ancient and important clan—but because of all the years that Shishogi had been sitting in that little office in the Assassins' Guild trying to corrupt *that* Guild, and maybe placing people into *other* guilds, like Transportation and Treasurers, Merchants and Messengers, and *everything!*

If there was a way to unravel all of that harm—Ajuri might know names, might know places. Ajuri might remember.

If—and it was an if worth considering—Nomari might be Shadow Guild himself.

If he were, surely he would seem—more wicked.

Would he not?

He had told lies in his life. When he was younger and up to

no good he had thought himself quite good at tricking people, and he had made up some very good lies. But to come into a place and make up absolutely everything with all those credible names of people with man'chi that fitted together like puzzle-pieces, that would not be so easy, if it were a lie.

He wished mani were here. He was sure mani could tell. Mani could look at somebody and know things.

But he saw what the Guild had been doing, repeating the same question in different ways, and getting names, and calling people. He listened to what they reported, and in every case, there was such an individual, and they all happened to be on emergency leave with sick relatives or just on personal leave, and they all had turned in a request for that leave on the same day, which was the day after Uncle had nominated a lord for Ajuri.

That showed, not surprisingly, that Uncle's nomination had started something in motion. All these people were Ajuri, they were in different guilds, and they all were connected to Nomari.

Rieni said, too, that the Assassins were investigating their own records, but that they were relatively sure they could account for the whereabouts of all units.

Then a servant came in and handed Uncle a note. Uncle read it with no change of expression, then passed it to his Guild senior, who passed it to Rieni, who then passed it to Antaro. Cajeiri wondered just what, and why.

He also saw hand-signs pass, and the one that passed from Antaro to Jegari said, just, Father.

His father? Was Father doing something? Sending someone?

But a second hand-sign said trouble and *from the north and west.*

Then he realized there was one other father involved in the current situation: Antaro and Jegari's father.

North and west . . . of Taiben.

That was *Ajuri.*

14

Office of the Chairman
Department of Linguistics
University of Mospheira
1 University Street
Port Jackson SE

Dear Mr. Cameron:
*   You are requested and required by the terms of your*
office to report and give account. A hearing will be held
in a special meeting of the Committee on Linguistics on
the 15th, at 1300 hours promptly, in room 33 of Obert
Hall. Please bring a copy of your written documents and
materials.

*   Sincerely,*
*   Albert Salin*
*   Secretary to the Chair*

It was the same wording as he'd gotten the last time he'd been in trouble with the Committee.

A letter from the chairman's secretary. Nice.

"Will there be a reply, nandi?" Narani had brought the letter, couriered in. "One understands the courier did not wait."

"Well, I shall request a courier from Francis House," Bren said. "I am, as of about a year ago, not receiving pay from the

Department. One rather thought they considered me no longer under their supervision. But I shall answer them. They want my attendance at a disciplinary hearing—so to say."

"Is this worrisome, nandi?"

"As a response to my message to them, it is frustrating."

He took Francis House stationery. The executive secretary wrote. The executive secretary was due the reply.

Bren Cameron
The Bujavid
Shejidan

Currently to be reached in care of: The Francis House,
Port Jackson.

Dear Mr. Salin:
I regret to decline your invitation to address the Committee on the 15th, at 1300 hours, as I am otherwise engaged at that hour. I have not yet had time to prepare the materials which I mentioned in my last communication, but I shall find that time in the near future. Please convey my regrets to the Chairman.

> *Sincerely,*
> *Bren Cameron,*
> *Paidhi-aiji*

That . . . was not going to sit well with certain people . . . certain people, most of whom would be on the Committee. There had been a time he would have worried. And he had a strong feeling that Wilson would be there.

He had *some* faith in his predecessor's professionalism, that Wilson still maintained his loyalty to principles—the breach of which Wilson so decried in him. In the rules of Wilson's day, Wilson had never spoken the language. He'd communicated with the aijiin he served only in written memos, and over the decades of his service had become a very strange, withdrawn man. One could respect Wilson's steadfastness, one could feel sorry for what he'd been through—but Wilson had tried, early on, to get him dismissed from office, had tried to alert the State Department to his dealings with Tabini, and gone fairly well off the rails when the ship-folk had decided to deal with atevi rather than Mospheirans, with one Bren Cameron deeply involved in the entire process.

That had been the last straw, with Wilson. The Heritage Party had published no few of Wilson's observations, and Wilson had been a darling of the Heritage faction during their brief time in power.

Since the Heritage Party's decline, Wilson had been much more on the sidelines, and once Bren had come back from deep space with the Reunioners in tow, he honestly wasn't too sure what Wilson thought—a rare situation in prior years.

But there was a reason he'd set up his own staff to deal with the first-down Reunioners, including the children, with Kate Shugart and Sandra Johnson, and set Tom to pull strings with the University Administration, and to be sure there was no nonsense from Linguistics, which was probably highly upset that he had not consulted regarding the kyo approach, and doubly upset about his suggestions to the Cabinet regarding changes in the Department.

Wilson would likely take it all personally. Which was probably justified. Were Wilson *not* involved, he might well have gone directly to the Department with certain of his requests, but it was impossible to deal with the man. There was no denying Wilson was absolutely expert in some aspects of classical Ragi. As a scholar, he was brilliant, producing a grammar that was absolutely invaluable for courtly nuance, including the ins and outs of numerology. Wilson had done a *lot* of reading, and made a good many useful additions to the dictionary and the grammar.

Brilliant scholarship. But deal in the day to day language—

no. Wilson had made a virtue of refusing that step—which, ironically somewhat thanks to Wilson, had become increasingly likely in the next paidhi's tenure.

He would say so to Wilson—he would give him full credit. But the number of times they had clashed personally in the past made it a good guess that somewhere—somewhere in the Chairman's decision to have his *secretary* communicate with the current paidhi, was Wilson, and at the most inconvenient moment in relations with the aishidi'tat.

Damn, should he send that letter? Should he mend his manners and address himself instead to Chairman Koman? Should he be conciliatory to Wilson?

He could.

He should.

But Wilson would persist in a feud now too deep and too long to resolve, not with so much at stake.

Worse, these people would expect have some power over the children—until they ran head-on into Kate Shugart.

No, damn it all. It should never get that far. There was ample reason to put the children now, by virtue of Tabini's protective order, into the hands of the State Department, where the Committee on Linguistics could not prevail.

And to do that . . .

He picked up the phone and called Shawn, this time without a lengthy delay getting through.

"Trouble?" Shawn asked.

"A little organizational question," he said. "I have a recommendation. To put the kids directly under State *now*, same status as a paidhi during service. The aiji's protective order is not contingent: it's current and ongoing. That takes it out of Linguistics in that regard. But here's the problem. The Linguistics Department does need to deal with the kyo materials—and the kids *have* interacted with the kyo, and need to maintain their memory of the language . . . but they will *not* be under my predecessor's supervision in any sense. I'm sorry to bring a personal grudge into it, but I'm afraid it's headed there. The children are one problem I can set a fence about. The kyo materials, on the other hand, have to go into the hands of this department, and two-hundred-year-old rules cannot apply with that study."

A little silence on the other end.

"Academic details," Shawn said. "With security implications."

"Exactly. I can talk to Tabini-aiji and *get* a Guild unit or two specialized in the kyo material, and they will create a response. Over here, the nature of the response tilts naturally toward Linguistics. The Committee has its procedures, and right now we have half the department focused on historic human languages and the dominant half on Ragi—both jealous of resources. And they don't communicate with me, or haven't, since events you know. I did send them a letter saying I have materials and will deal with them. Now they send a letter wanting me over there immediately to *report and give account*. But if I do go, which I can't do at their date and time, I can't go under the terms they'd like."

"Oh, I've watched *this* brew for years."

"I know. And you know there's a particular reason I haven't renewed acquaintances over there since I came back from Reunion."

"Officially, *your* contact point *is* the State Department and has been for years. Adding the kids to that situation is no logistical problem to State. I'll make a call or two of my own, one to State, one to the University, and you—Do me a favor. Do go. Talk to them."

"I can't on their date."

"Tell me. What would you, yourself, consider adequate for those youngsters, and for the future of the Linguistics Department? I'm sure you've had thoughts about that—considering the changes in the last decade. What would *you* recommend—regarding future paidhiin?"

"God, Shawn . . ."

"Would you have the successorship under the University? Or tied to State?"

"State. It has to be. It may be political, but so is the aijinate. It *has* to be open to negotiation and subject to reasons entirely separate from University politics."

"My opinion exactly. State. The University's had the program, historically. It has the records, the library, the experts, but once the paidhi is designated, he's *not* subject to whims of the Committee. We've never drawn that line. We've never had it established and set down in law. We've never found reason. Maybe it's time."

"Legal moves will take time. And more committees. Problem is, we've got very young non-terrestrial kids facing a situation right now."

"Who are already spoken for. And therefore, as you suggest—given that status in international relations—they'll move under State. *They'll* help define how that all will work, beyond our tenure. All we need do is get them through undamaged. *They* have to prepare for another visit with the kyo, based on the work you've laid down. And how that sits with the sitting Committee or the current head of Linguistics is completely immaterial—since *these kids'* appointment doesn't involve a need for the Committee's selection, am I right?"

"You're right. They *are* the paidhiin the aiji will accept. There's no arguing with it."

"So?"

"I can't just dump the kyo materials in a box and give it to them. I've tried not to come in conflict with the University, considering the kyo materials *need* their cooperation—but I've scarcely gotten my feet on the ground. I've had no time to put things in order. And the Committee's already upset. I don't want this coming under political pressure, or to have any theories about atevi reluctance to hand them over. The materials aren't in Mosphei'. That's the point. They don't *fit* in Mosphei' without going through two layers of translation. And I haven't got the free time to explain it."

"State can propose and dispose that, too," Shawn said. "It's the impression of my administration that we are a three branch government, and the Committee on Linguistics is not one of those branches. The Secretary of State ranks well above the Committee where it come to the paidhiin, and the President ranks somewhere above the Secretary of State in making foreign policy—which currently involves protection of the relationship we have with Tabini-aiji, and disposition of the kyo materials. And if it comes to a contest between Dr. Koman, Mr. Wilson, and the Secretary of State, I'm not worried. The University President, frankly, has his own problems with the assumptions of the Committee. I hear you want Heyden Court. I hear the University is anxious to shed that bottomless pit of unoccupied expense, and I understand the Art Department can move its display to the downstairs of admin."

"You work fast."

"Tom works fast. I had a call from him. I suspect the missive that landed on your desk is the not too remote result of *his* conversation with the University President and Board of Regents. I also suspect the Committee on Linguistics thinks they can make a flanking attack in your direction, *if* they can get some independent promise out of you. I'll be seeing you tomorrow, at the legislative panel, which I hope won't extend too long, or be more than information-gathering. I think you could safely meet with the Committee on the 17th, and explain the situation to them. I'll send you over a draft of the agreement with the University for Heyden. So that will be a settled issue. I only wish I could be there."

Facing the dreaded Committee with State's complete backing for changes in the way his office functioned? There had been times he had dreamed of such an encounter with Wilson.

Right now it was not the most attractive item on his agenda.

But he might, he thought, warm to it.

15

It was not every guest who had permission to visit Uncle's basement. Amid all the anxieties in the house above, a frozen place, a noiseless place, a place where, in an odd way, time seemed stopped and voices should be hushed.

And it was a place to have a little peace, a little relief from the goings-on that still had a white cloth at the gate, a cousin still locked in, and the whole estate buzzing with phone calls and Guild talking back and forth with Headquarters, which had been going on all day, and did not directly involve him.

So one could pace, or one could try to read, or sit and watch people coming and going. Uncle at least had people to call. The only people Cajeiri knew to call were mani out at Malguri and nand' Bren over on Mospheira, and neither would have time for a pointless call, he was sure.

But there was the basement. He had his young aishid with him, detailed by the seniors to stay with him constantly—and not to let him do anything stupid, while his senior bodyguard were upstairs doing things that were much more critical to solving the Ajuri problem.

For him—it seemed a good time to go down to the basement and be absent for a while, and to think about things other than problems he could not solve. It was not as good as being out by the stables, or riding around the grounds. But it was distant from the troubles of the house, and full of a thousand things to see, much of it brown and plain, in the colors the earth gave, when it faded the glazes on pottery, ate up iron or faded the blues on an ancient bracelet.

There was so much hush down here, the moment the door to the upstairs closed. It was like visiting a tomb—which it was not, but almost. One could see up close, in the rows of glassed-in shelves, hundreds of items of brown and red pottery, some broken and some mended and some amazingly whole, the cups from which people thousands of years ago had drunk, over which they had laughed, or argued, or plotted, and carried on their lives. There were curious designs painted on them, now that he had time enough to spend. There were people, and gods and demons who surely had had names—one face with tusks like a mecheita, with war-caps, that was many times repeated on a display of what they called timber finials, that had used to cap the ends of beams, and another set he thought must be the moon, with a round face and strange stare . . . that one he thought of as a plump, pleasant lady, a ghost lady, pale and fixed on things nobody else could see.

Amid the cases of pottery stood one glass case taller than any other, holding a skeleton that dominated the collection, a fierce and primitive thing frozen in a posture of defiance.

There was a room of ancient porcelains, one of which was from the Southern Island, from before the Wave. It was very rare, and had its own case. He knew that one was incredibly valuable, more than things made of gold.

Antaro stopped, and took on a very serious expression, doubled in the reflection of the glass case, next to the Southern Island relic. She was listening to something—Guild communications. And so were the others, all stopped, all listening.

"Yes," Antaro said then, to empty air, and then said, to him. "Nandi, one has just heard—the kyo ship has disappeared . . . when, we are not sure. But we think yesterday."

Yesterday.

The kyo ship disappeared from the solar system. And nobody on the mainland thought it important?

"You asked to know," Antaro said. "Apparently, in the other matters—the notification did not get through the system. One believes a message is waiting in Shejidan."

It upset him. He was not sure why. The upset was too unfocussed. It went everywhere.

"I think it rather important," he said, "nadiin-ji."

"We think it important, too," Antaro said. "We regret, nandi."

"One has no doubt," he said, thinking that his father might know—his father might have been informed. Likely nand' Bren had been informed. Very, very likely mani knew.

But nobody had told him, until it happened to find its way through. *Father* could have told him—if somebody had bothered to tell Father.

"The assumption," he said, trying to find words, "that it does not matter—is *wrong,* nadiin-ji. The *assumption* that now that we are back and the world is still going on, the kyo are not worth noticing . . ."

"We know," Antaro said. "We do know, nandi."

"We are about to bring Reunioners down to the world. We have very nearly had a catastrophe in the heavens. And neither your Guild nor the Messengers seems concerned that I should know."

Their faces *were* concerned. They *did* understand. He was sure of that.

"I shall express this to the seniors, nandi," Antaro said.

Guild dealt with Guild. But for Antaro to go confront Rieni— who himself might not have gotten the information—that was no easy thing. But if she said it, she would do it.

"No," he said. "We do not yet know if they are staying. And they would *not* understand, because they were not there. The world does not understand. The whole world was involved in the troubles down here. The clans do not understand. I am not even sure my father understands, but I think he truly does, because mani does—I know *she* does, as well as nand' Bren, and

Banichi and Cenedi and the rest. I think *they* need to talk to the seniors when we all get home. I think we need to have our households all understand. I think—I think there are things that went on that none of us know, except nand' Bren and his aishid, and mani, maybe. She had it only from what nand' Bren would tell her, whatever went on, but nand' Bren was on that ship, and wrote the treaty, and made the agreement. Which is why our space station is still safe up there, because there is nothing we could have done to protect it. I cannot say these things to everybody—because scaring people is not going to help anything. The kyo *are* gone, and whatever happened when nand' Bren was on their ship that we do not know—that is not *going away,* in any sense. It is going *on* to somewhere else, to where the kyo live, and whatever happens after that, that is not just *going away.* Ever. So I do have to worry. We all have to worry. If something happens out there we need to know it. And I can never be the one to find it out later. That is what all our households have to know, even the servants, the people who take in the mail and arrange schedules and all that. I have to know. And I have to have confidence that I know, that I will be told first, and fast, or I have to worry about it."

There were nods. They themselves had not been at Reunion. They could not imagine the voyage. They could not imagine being there to see a strange ship and wait for the messages to creep across the screen while nand' Bren and the ship-folk tried to figure what to do next.

Or to see the kyo for the first time, when they knew how strong and how dangerous they could be, and how frail mani was, and to be with mani when she found ways to calm a person who might not be reasonable . . .

All that. All that, he knew. And the people handling his messages did not.

"We shall do better," Antaro said.

"I know you will," he said. "I know you already do the best anybody can. And you will not have to tell the seniors. We all should. I shall. And if they will not listen to me because I am not my father, then we should know *that,* too, should we not? They are doing all they can about the situation upstairs and we are too junior to do much about that, but they need to understand that something like this cannot slip by, either. Ever. We shall be respectful. But we shall have things understood."

"Nandi," Antaro said very quietly, and there were nods from all of them, there by the ancient beast, by the evidence of a world very different from the world they lived in.

"So," he said, and shrugged and walked on. "I wish them a good voyage. I wish their people to know *we* are important, too."

"The young one," Antaro said, "Hakuut. He was quite pleasant."

"He was. I do not think I could introduce him to Mother. But Father might see his character."

It was a cold thought, that the ship with Hakuut and Prakuyo had just . . . evaporated. Or whatever ships did when they just ceased to be where they had been and turned up somewhere else—through a space that had made that funny plant nand' Bren had had grow like mad.

Curtains of green plants. I should trim it, nand' Bren had said, but never had, not until the day they had left the ship for the station, and run, literally run, at points, to get aboard the shuttle and get down to the world to undo the things Murini had done and help Father get back in power.

The world had moved at a kind of breakneck pace, too. So maybe people in general had not had time to realize just how dangerous the kyo visit had been—they had had the Troubles, and families had been upset, and clans disarranged, Ajuri and Kadagidi had fallen—so, well, the world had been busy adjusting, too. People had had no time to learn new things. They had been trying to save the old ones.

So maybe he should not be too angry at the seniors, who were still trying to help patch what Murini and Shishogi had broken. He had to think about that, too, at least as much as he did about events in the heavens. He was *obliged* to think about that. It was all a question of where you were when things had gotten scary. And the seniors had had their own worries in those days, and still did. The seniors were doing what they could right now to see that the aishidi'tat stayed together, and that Shishogi ultimately lost.

So maybe, he thought, maybe he was the one who needed to understand what *he* had lost touch with, while he was out there in the heavens.

Maybe together—he and the seniors had a better vision than either did separately. He knew he had things to learn about what had gone on to unseat his father, and everything that still wanted fixing. Part of it, he knew, was because the space program had scared people, and upset their thinking, and crossed old feuds; but part of it, too, was because old problems had never gotten fixed. And meanwhile something had been going on for two hundred years that could have come back and killed them. But if the world had not gotten together—that thing would have never gotten fixed and they would have been like the Reunioners—attacked, with no idea why.

The rooms went on and on, like a house of shadows under all the lively, bright house above, two different worlds, past and present, one living, one lost in the past. Armor racks held the weaponry of ancestors and enemies, with heraldic colors fading, some of them maybe of clans no longer existing.

He had had his guests here, in this place where most servants feared to dust or sweep. Uncle had walked them through, showing them wonderful things, scaring them, too, but in a way that he liked to remember. It was the first time he had really, really understood Uncle, and a time when Uncle had become one of his favorite people. Anybody he meant to trust—should see this place. Should be here. And think about things that people he trusted should think about.

Mani said there was a ghost on the lake near Malguri—one

never knew if *mani* believed in ghosts, but he rather thought she wanted to, in spite of being practical. Maybe it was part of being smart—that one could make things exist that might not exist, because they were useful, because they let people think about things without thinking about today, and understand things without it necessarily being about Ajuri and Atageini, but about something else.

It was about all that accumulation of armor. And cups. People had worn that, and used those, and they were all bones, now, like that creature raging in the glass box. It was not *about* Ajuri, and yet Ajuri had, like a ghost, life that they imagined it had.

Maybe, between what he imagined, and what Nomari imagined, and what Uncle and the Guild imagined, they could shape it into something more like the cups, and less like the armor.

Uncle had made peace with Taiben, after two hundred years of people saying it was impossible, over a stupid little patch of woods around one of the world's oldest train stations, and an old lord who now was just an armored shell, with the colors fading. Uncle had imagined something different, because it had become practical to do it.

He found it practical to change some things, too, and to hold fast to others.

And to make associates who thought a pebble, a bare little rock smoothed by centuries in a stream, was a great wonder to hold in the hand.

There were *going* to be changes in the world. He had to stay alive, and be patient with people who saw things otherwise, and imagine ghosts into existence, just to test the ideas.

He had made associates of humans, and of Hakuut an Ti.

Could he not make one of a young man who called him cousin?

16

It seemed worth a question why, psychologically, dispensers of justice, human and atevi alike, wore black.

In the case of the atevi Assassins' Guild, Banichi and the rest, it was the occasional need for stealth, one supposed, that and the fact that atevi night vision was far, far keener than human—in an arrangement in which Guild might oppose Guild, given competing Filings of Intent.

In one's own species, perhaps the black robes were simply intended to convey solemnity and set the justices apart from other citizens. It was, in its own way, imposing. But none of the justices bore weapons . . . unlike the Guild.

Such extraneous thoughts filled a mind left too long during a minute—extremely minute—dissection of the treaty document.

"How," a justice asked, Justice White, ironically named— "are we to rely on the language of the first section, as interpreted by their authorities, when we cannot be sure of the basic content?"

"I was able to gain some acquaintance with the written language. I cannot claim a full knowledge of the kyo language, but I have worked with their writing, and do see a correspondence between kyo words the meaning of which I know, and words in the Ragi and Mosphei' sections of the document. The structure and length of the document seems similar."

"Appointing Reunion as a future meeting place."

"Yes, Your Honor, a site they do hold, and where they have apparently maintained a presence. May I make a short statement, Your Honor?"

"Do," White said.

"Initially there was some thought that we might be able to conceal our defenseless state from the kyo, that they might believe there were other ships abroad, and we thought that we could protect ourselves by seeming more advanced than we are. As I began to understand, and as I believe the ship-folk knew from the start, they will learn nothing by their possession of Reunion that denies the truth of what they observed of us at close range—steam trains, a limited access to space, in short, a young civilization, no threat to them at all, incapable of any defense against them. We destroyed the Archive records there, but very many other sources of information would have escaped that erasure. We also had a chance to observe the effect of their attack, on the physical structure of Reunion. It convinces us that the kyo might, at their whim, have laid claim to our entire solar system. Instead, they wanted us to agree not to visit them except at the appointed contact point, and they, reciprocally, will leave us to our own devices—leaving us free to develop in our own path, in our own way, and satisfying our own needs. This is the structural framework of that very simple document. We don't enter their territory and they don't enter ours, except by an appointed doorway. It's simple, but it answers all questions of access, identification, proper and improper behavior for us toward them and them toward us, and definition of our territories in a three-dimensional space. Nothing forbids us traveling in any other direction. And they are, without stating it, our buffer between us and any intrusion from a direction we know to be inhabited. In a very large and dangerous universe, Your Honors, disinvolvement and nonaggression is a valuable declaration. That direction is safeguarded. Simple as it is, it is a good agreement."

The justices leaned together, conferred at some length. Bren took a sip of water.

Then another justice asked: "Regarding the former inhabitants of Reunion, Mr. Cameron, can you explain *why* the plan to build a second colony is off the table?"

Change of direction. But a simple one to answer.

"Very simply, Your Honor, the plan never had substance. The materials to build would have to be mined, and the project would take decades, with decades more to show any return. The Reunioners are in the main not construction operators—of the five thousand, only about a hundred have that skill. The rest, including children, including older adults, have to be housed and fed somewhere, and their presence on the station, or on *any* construction yet to be built, demands, by treaty, an equal influx of atevi, which would send the population level soaring beyond anything the station can possibly support without its own considerable expansion. Five thousand people, including older folk and children, including clericals, scientists, technicians who know Reunioner materials, Reunioner science— are not a burden to a planet. Bringing them down offers them a comfortable life without shortages, and likewise frees the station of supporting them."

"They *can* tolerate living here."

"With medications as the stopgap solution. Some may have to go back. But we think it likely they can adapt. Our ancestors certainly did, after as long a time in space."

Another conference.

And a question from the third justice. "Mr. Cameron, regarding your own status, do you still claim Mospheiran citizenship?"

"I would not presume to instruct the court, but as I have never renounced it, I would assume I still have it. Whether or not I have it, I am capable under the law of the aishidi'tat of representing the President to the aiji or vice versa, but it was

260 / C. J. CHERRYH

recently useful for me to have that citizenship to represent the President to the kyo."

"Did you do so?"

"The transcript will show I did. Yes, Your Honor, faithfully so."

"The aiji has placed three children under his protection."

"Four, counting a boy named Bjorn Andresson, yes, Your Honor."

"And designated them to be trained for your office."

"That is his wish. It is easily possible to have multiple paidhiin at once, from the atevi point of view, and should they not wish to take up the office, that will be their choice. The aiji wishes them to be educated as Mospheiran, so that they may represent Mospheiran interests and explain Mospheiran opinions, but it does not preclude others being appointed at any time, from this side of the strait. What Mospheira may choose to do is, again, within the view of atevi law, up to Mospheira to determine. The aiji, being an ally, will receive any paidhi appointed to speak to him."

"Under which law are you currently appointed, Mr. Cameron?"

"At the moment, Your Honor, I know I am appointed by atevi law, and sent by the aiji, but I was requested here by the President."

"Have you been recompensed?"

Touchy question. "I have not received *salary* from Mospheira since two months after I returned with the Reunion mission."

Someone dropped a pen, which echoed in the chamber.

"Peculiar, one would agree," the justice said. "You no longer maintain an office here."

"And no longer incur expense here," he said. "I do still receive interest on the bank account I maintain, and on that interest I do pay Mospheiran taxes."

"The salary in arrears would be a considerable sum by now."

"It would be. But no sum of money dictates my loyalty, Your

Honor." He had no wish to go into detail on finance, or a bank account which during the troubles on the mainland had slipped funds to Toby, for reasons the State Department knew—and he suspected that the cessation of his salary since his return to the world had more to do with the State Department's operations, possibly even a simple clerical glitch. Clandestine operations involving Toby had found the absent paidhi's bank account a convenience during the recent troubles. It had let Toby get funds to obtain materials and information in various places neither the Mospheiran Foreign Office nor various atevi guilds would want to discuss.

And when Tabini had returned to power, and the flow of those clandestine funds had ceased—possibly some efficient accountant in State had simply closed off the flow of funds.

So, no, he had absolutely *no* wish to try to explain *that* situation to Revenue *or* the Judiciary Committee. It would need intervention by State to work that tangle out—a flow from funds the Foreign Office didn't itself discuss.

A nod from the justice, one of the older ones, whose views of the goings-on in space could be problematic, but not, he sensed, in this instance.

It was, as hearings went, relatively benign.

"I believe we have had," the Chief Justice said, "a fair and honest account. We will issue a ruling on your own citizenship and empowerment, but if my colleagues will consent to a finding—my own inclination is to rule it never lapsed. And if the aishidi'tat considers you to be a citizen of the aishidi'tat, that is its affair, and of no concern to Mospheiran law." The Chief Justice looked left and right, obtaining only nods. "Then we settle that technicality. As to the advisory on the treaty, we would have wished more precise language, but we understand that *any* language at all was an achievement, and we will create a special framework for it, so that no Mospheiran law creates a roadblock to its implementation or attempts to derive precedent from it in domestic law. It stands, in effect, exactly as written, and with binding effect on Mospheiran citizens. Only one thing needs to be written: a law defining what level of authorization it would take to make contact with the kyo."

"Or any other species," Justice White said.

"I would not go that far," Justice O'Hara said.

"Mr. Cameron?"

"Your Honors, in the venture of the ship to any other territory, it is a sovereign entity, but it has now entered a period of reassessment of its policies and actions. An agreement with the ship, with the aishidi'tat, with Mospheira, might carry that sensible restraint into generations yet to come—by treaty."

"That would be a decision of the executive."

"Yes, Your Honor. Be it noted, I would be willing to negotiate such a treaty if it were the President's decision to seek it."

"Will you recommend it?"

"I would certainly recommend it."

Benign, though he had had some concern about the mood of the Justices, and his own freehand treaty-writing. He was relieved . . . except the notion, potentially an issue for him or his successors, that he could not renounce Mospheiran citizenship . . . and evade Mospheiran law. Still . . . he had the power of the aishidi'tat to enforce its claim and get him back. That power would not surrender him to any other government, and in a time of peace, there was no problem.

The meeting on the morrow—he was sure would not be half so pleasant . . . or so cooperative.

It was a peculiar breakfast arrangement, a little service table set across the threshold of Nomari's room, with a servant at his shoulder, a serving before him.

Likewise Cajeiri settled into a little hard chair *outside* Nomari's confinement, and to a plate a servant provided.

There were no knives, but there were spoons and forks.

And two tureens of a fine order of porridge and jam, and crisp rolls with ama seeds atop.

"I feel I must be in your debt," Nomari said, after a sip of tea. "I have never eaten so well."

"I wish more than anything—well, more than anything convenient—that we might go riding," Cajeiri said. "For my birthday, mani and Uncle gifted me a mecheita, and I have only scarcely gotten to ride her once, and had one lesson."

"One does not believe your uncle would trust me with a mecheita, much less his nephew. And I confess I cannot ride."

"You cannot ride?" That seemed a sad situation. And not likely in a country house.

"Now, if you ask me how to switch a train to another track I can do that."

It seemed a very useful sort of thing to know. "How?" he asked, and by the time they finished the porridge Nomari had told him the difference between a stock rail and a switch rail and shown him, with one of Uncle's spoons and the berry fork, just how the Red Train could be sure it was going to Sidonin and not to Najida.

"That is," Cajeiri said, "the shift the train makes just as it goes past the hotels."

"Exactly," Nomari said. "That is the Bujavid Hill number three, or the 1113 if one is outside the city system. I have thrown that switch."

"Have you? Have you ever thrown it for the Red Train?"

"Several times," Nomari said. "I serve properly on maintenance, but they always have maintenance up if the Red Train is rolling."

"That is so amazing! I might have been on that train!"

Nomari was amused. "They never tell who is in the Red Car," Nomari said. "And I never had clearance to be up in the Bujavid tunnels. But I would watch it pass and wonder who was aboard. They never tell us, but sometimes you can guess."

"How do you guess?"

"Oh, by where it goes, and whether other cars are in the consist."

"What is a consist?"

"A consist is the number and type of cars that make up a train."

The Red Train had the Red Car and a baggage car. But sometimes it took a second car, if *Father* was going, or if mani was moving part of her herd across the high mountains.

"The Guild should think about these things!"

"That they should," Nomari said with a smile. "And I am sure they do."

"But you never have ridden?"

"I rode when I was very young," he said. "At Ajiden. But when I was ten, things changed. They moved the herd out. They moved others in. And I no longer had permission." Nomari had gotten serious a moment. Then turned more pleasant. "I remember enough to get on from the stable gate. That was how I got on. I was not the best rider."

"I can get on from the ground," Cajeiri said. "I hardly remember learning. I think I had to." That in itself was not the best memory. "Does Sidonin have switches?"

"There will be one a little distance out, that goes up to the northern towns, one that goes down to the south. If you go south, the next is Modigi. Are you testing whether I am Transport?"

"No. I want to know!"

Nomari gave a silent laugh, and helped himself to toast. "Do you?"

"I cannot learn these things in the Bujavid," he said. "But you know."

"You want to know everything, do you?"

"If I could," he said, "I would know everything. Everything is useful. My great-grandmother taught me that."

"Your great-grandmother. The aiji-dowager."

"Yes. Mani. She knows all sorts of things."

"You went to space with her."

"Yes."

"Did you ask questions all the way there, too?"

"Wherever I could."

"Then I imagine you already know a lot of things," Nomari said. "An impressive lot of things. I see why they call you a little scary."

"*Me?* Who calls me that?"

"People. Regular people. They say you are one part your great-grandmother and one part your father. I wondered, when I decided to try to talk to you, whether there was anything of your grandfather."

Now they were not talking about railroad switches. Now they were talking about family, and people he knew, and a grandfather who had been murdered, and he became very much more wary. He planned his questions now, not about such wonderful things as railroad switches.

"Did you know him?"

"No," Nomari said. "Kadiyi, Komaji—We did not even live at Adijen most of the time. We had a house in Puran. That is what I mostly remember. My father would go to Adijen. We were happy in Puran." The look on his face was not happy. "I've upset you. I was sorry about your grandfather."

He thought about saying, Be more sorry about my father's staff, my father's aishid, and *all* the people Shishogi killed. But he held that back, and let Uncle's servant provide another pot of tea.

He thought, watching Nomari lift the pot and pour himself a cup before the servant could provide an after-meal cup, I wonder if he ever knew my mother when she was there.

I wonder if they spoke. He's about as old as my mother.

She had left Ajuri when she was young, too. She ran away at Winter Festival, when everybody was in Shejidan. She saw the Atageini banner and went to it, and asked Uncle to live with him.

She had stayed a few years. Then went back to Grandfather, when Kadiyi was lord.

Why did she leave Uncle? Uncle hated Grandfather, that was one thing. And Mother had tried to live with both of them. But maybe the pieces would not fit.

"Did you know my mother?" he asked, adding two lumps of sugar to an after-meal cup of his own, and maybe it skirted propriety, asking serious questions at table. But they were sitting at a table that blocked Nomari into a room and blocked him out, with security hovering behind the servants.

"Not well," he said. "Her father was very protective of her. He did not want us to spend time together. We did meet. But my father did not get on with that side of the family, and I understood I was not wanted in her immediate vicinity. That was how it was."

"Do you think she would know you?" he asked, taking a sip.

"Tell her—tell her when she fell in the garden, I was that boy. She might remember."

"Why did she fall?"

"She was trying to climb the statue, out in the garden. I said stop, she slipped, and she probably never has forgiven me."

"I shall tell her," he said, thinking that, if his mother was Nomari's only hope for a recommendation, it was a thin hope.

He sipped his tea. Nomari sipped his. He was not used to thinking of his mother as a little girl. But that his mother had broken rules—that sounded possible. His mother had never liked to be told no.

"My mother has a daughter, now," he said.

"I have heard," Nomari said.

Of course he would have heard. The whole world had heard that. He had no tidbits of family news to give, nothing that he *ought* to say. The little table they shared barriered them from each other. But a lot more than that did.

He asked: "What else do you remember about my mother? Do you know why she ran away to Tirnamardi?"

Nomari shook his head. "Not exactly."

"Do you have any idea?"

"Benedi had died. Kadiyi became lord." Nomari turned the little cup on the table-top, looking at it, not at him. "I was gone from the house by then. My family was dead."

The conversation had gone to a horrible place. "Why?" he asked. It was his job to ask, with the Guild taking up every word; and he asked because it was *his* family, too. "Was it all the same reason?"

"I have no idea why she left," Nomari said, and now his face had closed down and become still. "I know my reason for leaving. I came to the guilds. I came to the one that would let me travel. That was my thinking. I was shut in for a few years, learning the basics, but it led outside. And that is where Ajuri have tended to go, to the guilds. Your mother had another place to go, and she went there."

Secrets. Things his mother never talked about. Questions she never answered. Maybe she had answered him for his father. Maybe when his father heard these things, a lot about Nomari would fall into place. Maybe Uncle knew.

But he was still without the answers. It was not an uncommon situation, that secrets flew about him, and none were within reach.

"Are any of your associates in the Assassins' Guild?" he asked.

"No. None of mine. That is the one place *my* associates would not go."

"But some did."

"No few did, from Ajuri." Nomari covered the cup with his hand when the servant attempted to take it, to replace with another. "I thank you for the breakfast, cousin."

He was not in a position to be dismissed. He was not of a rank to be dismissed, even if their relative ages could let Nomari assume the privilege.

"Please," Nomari said.

That was the right word. He accepted that and turned his cup so the key design faced him, ending matters. "My uncle is not angry with you," he said. "But he is careful."

Nomari nodded. "One understands that entirely."

Cajeiri got up. Nomari got up. On opposite sides of a doorway they each gave a little bow.

Only one of them could walk away.

17

"We shall go see the Committee on Linguistics," Bren said to his aishid, on the morning, as Narani was bringing his coat, "and we must expect certain people to be loud and improper. Do not react in the least."

"This seems frequent here," Algini remarked dryly.

"All too frequent," he said, amused, and thrust his arm into the offered coat, retaining a practiced and careful grip on the lace. It was dress to the maximum, court regalia, his second-best, however—he went no further than that for the Committee. "Wilson-nandi is not our only problem, but his seniority lies heavy on committee decisions—at least regarding the Foreign Office selections. And he will not be happy to be told he will *not* have absolute governance of the Reunioner children, and that their selection is settled."

"Will he know it by now?" Jago asked.

"He may." Second arm, and a shrug that settled the coat on his shoulders, atop the detested vest. "I truly wish I did have the good will of my predecessor. His detestation of me is emotional and deep, capable of overwhelming his common sense, and very unfortunately, he occasionally has a similar effect on me. I shall try to restrain it." He stood while Narani attended the details, the adjustment of his queue and ribbon. "Nadiin-ji, I have had my arm broken and I have been shot, and I do not bear those who did it any particular animosity. I cannot say the same of Wilson. Nor, certainly, will Tabini-aiji, in his dealings with the man. Yet television and its images led to aviation, both designs dropped on an unprepared public. Wilson maintains to this day that his notes were stolen. Others hold that Wilson surrendered the notes in fear for his life. But we should always remember that without Wilson's gifts, we would not have been prepared for *Phoenix* to return, and certainly we would not have been prepared for space. Wilson calls me reckless." He managed a smile. "I intend to give him all possible respect. Will he receive it graciously? He has not, in the past. But bear with him, even if he throws a water glass at me. He did, once."

The meeting with the Committee on Linguistics was *not* in Francis House. It was in Obert Hall, on University grounds, which required a car and driver—not that they couldn't drive on their own, but they were guests, and Francis House provided transport—a van, more elegant transport having too low an overhead.

It was, however, a comfortable van, more like a small bus, with ample seats. And in addition to the driver, it came with Francis House security, an earnest young man in a dark blue suit, with no visible armament. The young man might feel a little superfluous in the company of Banichi and the rest, armed as they were with visible sidearms, but he was polite, and zealous about watching around about as they all piled in and settled comfortably. Their young security agent sat up front next to the driver, and there was, they found, sparkling water and glasses, a healthy breeze from the air conditioning, and a fair view from the windows.

It was a chance to see the town—which had changed very little in the vicinity of Francis House, but past the iron fence, and beyond the boulevard of aged trees, they emerged into a district of fairly new buildings. "Offices," he said, "likely legislative offices and hotels. Restaurants." He saw several of those as they went. "The legislature is in session here for a third of the term. This is all similar to the gathering at the foot of the Bujavid. But without the antiquity." That area in Shejidan was quite old, dating, some of it, from before the aishidi'tat itself. "We should be turning to the right, soon. The University sits a little higher than this, in an older district."

The van did make the turn onto a boulevard. Older buildings swung into view, a well-manicured central parkway.

"There is a public park in that direction," Bren said, indicating the right hand, where an intersecting road descended toward the harbor. Water was scarcely visible from here, among the luxury homes, but the road did lead that way. "Quite popular for the view. There was an observatory on the ridge, but it has long since moved to the hills, because of the city lights . . ."

Familiar places, not a familiar circumstance. He had used to take the bus from an area far to the east, from a far humbler residence. He had an impulse to ask the driver, on their return, to pass that apartment, and see how it was, now.

But that time was past, there were no monuments, and the passing years probably would have worn on the building, which was definitely not on the historic list. He had a memory of it, vivid as it needed to be. He didn't need to complicate it with its current condition. There'd be no plaque on the corner saying Cameron House, not likely.

As it was, he saw they'd cut down a row of trees on University Drive that probably had gotten too large and heaved up the pavement, but, damn, they'd been good trees. And that godawful modern building on the corner, God only knew what that housed, but it had been the fairly comfortable student center. At the moment it looked as if a pile of construction sheets had gotten caught in a high wind. Modern? He'd seen modern, upstairs, on the space station. He'd seen a kyo ship look more familiar.

"You seem displeased," Jago said.

"We used to have a restaurant there, a sort of tea room that sold confections. They've cut down the old trees that used to shade the open-air tables. One assumes there is still a sort of tea room, but likely twice the price. With no outdoor tables."

"A sort of a park, then."

"On the edge of the district. It was a sort of park." The driver turned them toward the broad end of the oval, where trees did remain. Obert Hall still stood, a many-windowed fortress at the end of the oval of the oldest buildings, which he was glad to see remained, though Topp Hall had a too-modern portico leading to Mostander, for what particular reason one could not guess.

Instructions were coming to their security person, one guessed: he was holding an earpiece close to his ear and talking to the driver—and it was not surprising to have the van head onto a small drive that led around to parking and to a freight area. Celebrity and notoriety alike never got the front of a building: it was very commonly the loading dock and the underbelly of the grand building or the event.

In this case it was into a garage, and a place of concrete and old plaster, more historic, at least, than the portico at Topp, cracked and many times painted. The van stopped.

"I know this place," he said to his aishid, before their security person had time to turn in his seat and inform them they would use the freight access.

"I know it well," he said. There'd been the day, early on, when he *had* come in the front door to Obert, unremarked and unrecognized. That day was not this day, and when the driver and security got out and came back to open the van door, it was in Guild order they exited, Banichi and Jago first, then himself, then Tano and Algini, and that was the way it would be, side-arms and all.

"They *are* sending someone down," their security said—Burns, his name was.

"That's all right," Bren said. "I know my way. Will you stay with the van? If they want the space, the driver can move it, but on no account are you to leave the van, either of you."

"Yes, sir," Burns said, with a slightly uneasy look at atevi towering about them. "We'll watch it."

Burns was Presidential security, scant though the presence

was, in the Mospheiran concept of a secure guard. Shawn himself wasn't accustomed to having more. And one hoped it stayed sufficient.

The antique freight lift opened, let out a young man with a clipboard, who looked completely shocked. Confused. But who did manage to identify the one blond man in atevi court dress among the towering Guild security.

"Mr. Cameron?"

"You are?"

"Stockton. Aden Stockton. Secretary to Mr. Koman."

"I take it the Committee is on schedule."

"Yes, sir."

"I take it that lift will deliver us to third level, where we'll transfer to a regular lift."

"Yes, sir."

"Then let's go up."

"They—" A glance about, at four very tall people.

"They go where I go, Mr. Stockton. Always."

"They can't . . ."

"Regulations forbid them to be without weapons when abroad with me, Mr. Stockton, and if their presence doesn't alarm the President of Mospheira, it shouldn't worry the Committee on Linguistics. You can share the lift with us. I assure you you'll be perfectly safe."

"Yes, sir." Stockton didn't stir to do anything. Bren went to the freight lift himself and waited until Banichi and Jago had boarded. Then Stockton joined them, squeezed into the corner as Tano and Algini came in. Stockton started the lift moving, staying as close to the control panel as possible all the way to third, where the lift let them out in a dingy back hallway. From there, a doorway to the public corridor and the regular lift system gave them a quick ride to the fourth floor.

Oh, indeed he'd been here.

Mr. Stockton led the way—he needn't have. The end of the hall was a pair of doors, wood and hammered glass, and Mr.

Stockton opened one door of the pair. Banichi and Jago arrived and opened the other, before taking up guard positions inside.

Mr. Koman, Mr. Wilson, and assorted members of the committee at the half-circle table sat and stared in shock. Ogilvie, Beecham, de la Forte, Lundgren, Capu, and, old as Wilson, former chair Wagner.

Bren walked in, as Mr. Stockton worked his way along the wall, halfway up the edge of the room and Tano and Algini took up their posts outside the open doors.

"Mr. Cameron," Koman said. "This entourage is a little extravagant, if you please."

"It's actually the ordinary state to which your predecessor appointed me, Mr. Chairman. Thank you for today's invitation." He walked forward of Banichi and Jago and took up a posture he was prepared to keep for the duration, having no wish to sit. "I have owed you the courtesy of a formal statement for more than a year, but circumstances made leaving the mainland not only difficult, but irresponsible to my position. It did seem possible that I might still be useful, and I was very glad to resume my service to Mospheira in the recent emergency."

"With the same arrogance. With the same reckless procedures," Wilson said. "Your dress, your armed guard—you've fairly well gotten above your responsibilities to *this* government."

"I understand your views, Mr. Wilson. I won't debate you until you've had your say."

"That is *exactly* the issue, Mr. Cameron. You don't debate. You don't report. You engaged another species on your own, without consultation with this Department, you *guessed* your way through an encounter, gathered, we suppose, some pittance of information . . ."

He simply let Wilson run. He was not about to try to outshout a man with a microphone, quite the reverse of his situation with Woodenhouse. He simply took a non-committal stance, one hand at his side, one at his lapel, the sort of pose one could hold for quite lengthy public appearances, when hands in the pockets was simply not a pose one ever took and arms folded was not something one did unless one wanted a war. He listened, took mental notes, expression bland, and let Wilson wind down to:

"Now you wish to meddle with the composition of the Department. I can assure you, Mr. Cameron, that your design will not prevail, you will not simply *appoint* a set of juveniles, and foreign juveniles at that, as representatives of Mospheira, and as for their transfer to State, at their age, that is open to debate. You may manage to move the University to make a material grant and to squander funds on the Heyden mansion, with special staff and *servants* and whatever state you seem to have gotten far too used to, but this Committee still makes the rules, this Committee still governs language education, and this Committee makes the appointments."

He waited. There was silence. Wilson sought a glass of water. He was an elderly man, and working himself into a rage sent him an alarming shade of red.

"I will wait, if my predecessor is not yet finished, or if others wish to speak."

Wilson, addressed by Koman, said something under his breath and shook his head. Then he said, "I know your tactic, Cameron. You will then say you should not be interrupted."

Nandi, he almost said, mentally translating the respect he tried his best to accord the man. But diplomatically it worked out to, "Mr. Wilson, you may interrupt me as you wish and I will deal with it. May I begin to answer your points?"

"You may *attempt* to answer. We will not surrender the prerogatives of this Committee. That is our position."

"The appointment of the paidhi, sir, is one-sided, by whichever side sends him."

"And if the appointed paidhi is rejected by the other side, there must be another. In the case of these three children, Mr. Cameron, . . ."

"If the Linguistics Department rejects them, that is not a rejection by the government of Mospheira, Mr. Wilson, so we have that clear."

There was a moment of stark silence.

"Let me clarify my position. During my tenure, which is current *with* the aishidi'tat, and *with* the government of Mospheira, the nature of the office has shifted. I do communicate freely and verbally in Ragi, and in Mosphei', as appropriate to the situation. I am frequently employed *by* the aiji to represent him to atevi, and I am currently employed by him to represent the aishidi'tat to the kyo visitors, *and* to the Mospheiran government, which I have done. During the meetings with the kyo, I did, in consideration of the skills of the Linguistics Department, produce certain materials which can be translated into Mosphei', a task in which I am willing to assist, but not while in residence here. Indeed, I would think the Linguistics Department would have little trouble rendering them."

"Irony is unwelcome, Mr. Cameron," Koman said.

"It is not irony, Mr. Chairman, simply an offer of assistance regarding context, which may be helpful. The materials are designed to be a key to the language, and I did consider the Departmental approach. I'm well aware the Department would rather rely on its internal experts and I take no offense at it. But I suggest that a consultation with the individual who actually took the notes is a valuable crosscheck. There will be gaps in the record, partly because some of the visual materials involve persons who should not be portrayed in Mospheiran materials, namely the aiji-dowager and the heir. But the kyo were quite willing to provide keys to their language—in fact, I would characterize their chief negotiator as someone with a paidhi's skills and professionalism. I have a key to the written language, and to one of the very interesting aspects of their language, written indicators of emotion, which pepper their communication in sound, tone, pace, and volume, and which answer somewhat to facial expression, which they mostly lack. These moderate the meanings of the spoken or written word, much as our expressions moderate *our* language. You will hear it in recordings and see it in wave form analysis, and it can change the meanings of the spoken words. I have no desire to go deeper into detail here, but the material I have *is* in Ragi, which is the language the kyo find easiest."

"The language of *your* choice."

"Actually the language of the kyo's choice, but they were willing to learn both." An image welled up unasked, unwanted, and he didn't let himself go to that place. "The young children the aiji wishes to entrust to your care also met the kyo, as did their parents. It was a beneficial contact, indicative of peace, and it set a good tone for the moment. The children themselves speak a little kyo, which they learned from the aiji's son, who learned it in *his* face-to-face dealings with the kyo emissary. What I would like to put in your hands—is a fragile, easily misled contingent of young people, who do not deserve to be accused of the political sins of their remote ancestors, about whom they know nothing. These children love what they have seen of the planet, they have been exceedingly polite and respectful of things they don't understand, and they are above all eager and willing to learn. They are an asset to any educational endeavor, and they are already under the protection of the aiji in Shejidan as paidhiin in their own right. They and their parents will live here under the protection of the aiji, and may become the target of politics at its worst, so I hope you will look out for their welfare. You are educators, before anything else. I have every confidence your own conscience will guide you appropriately in their case. You will have students who want very much to learn. And if they are not Mospheiran youngsters, and if they have been through experiences no Mospheiran has had to face, they are good young people, very bright, very respectful, and they will be excellent and rewarding students. I hope you *will* take them as a responsibility and a trust, and not tangle this all in politics."

There was a little clearing of throats.

"Yet *we* have no say in their appointment," Wilson said.

"You have a major voice in their education, Mr. Wilson. Can there be any greater power? You are a voice for caution. Certainly they should hear that."

Oh, Wilson did not like him. The resentment of years burned in that look. Wilson didn't trust him, Wilson didn't respect him, Wilson took his dismissal as a lifelong mark against his service, hated the dowager with an abiding passion, and viewed Tabini-aiji as the devil who would bring Mospheira under atevi domination.

"You have no interest in teaching caution," Wilson said. "It's nowhere in your plans—assuming you have overarching plans of your own, Mr. Cameron, and maybe you do. You've perfectly well acknowledged what you represent, which is not Mospheira."

"Correction, Mr. Wilson. I represent *both* parties in a dispute. That is the nature of paidhiin *as* the office is defined by the people who created it. If you have mistaken the nature of the office, I am sorry. I am quite clear on it."

Several members of the committee found it convenient to shuffle papers or otherwise look at the table in front of them.

"Your presence with these armed assassins is an affront to a democracy."

"Strangely, the democracy asked me to include Mospheira in my negotiations with the kyo. I negotiated for both the aishidi'tat and Mospheira, which understands, officially, that the Reunion refugees are also Mospheiran citizens."

"*That* is yet to determine!"

"Not according to the President, Mr. Wilson, from whom I received instruction. I regret the necessity to disagree with you, but that issue was not left to my interpretation, by either government. The aishidi'tat has given official notice it considers the human population of the station to be out of balance, and while, by treaty, the aiji *might* move five thousand atevi citizens onto the space station, he has been quite satisfied by the President's declaration that the Reunion citizens, who have not passed screening for station residency, will be transferred to Earth in a reasonably expeditious process, in which the aiji has offered assistance. In short, sir, there is no way to regard the Reunion refugees as anything *but* human, and it is extremely convenient for both governments to see them settled on Earth in as rapid and efficient a fashion as possible. *In that light,* Mr. Chairman, I have proposed an expansion of the Linguistics Department to deal not only with the kyo language as of vital national interest, but also with the variant dialects of both Reunioners and the ship—as another matter of national interest, to help these people both contribute and assimilate, and to preserve that knowledge. The expansion I propose would be in personnel, in funding, and in physical structures. It can be done otherwise, but my first thought was to utilize the considerable expertise of the Department."

Funding. That magical word.

"Where does the finance come from?" Koman asked.

"Where it comes to the safety and residence of the first-down, the aiji will provide that, likewise assisting with the landing and transfer of cargo, which will be parachuted, thus freeing the shuttles for passengers on the Earthbound trip. This process will begin within a matter of weeks."

"Weeks!" That was Ogilvie.

"Weeks, sir. The physical conditions aboard the station have reached such a point that something has to be done, or risk adverse health conditions, and security issues. Moving that population now will begin to solve it. And it will be needful for Linguistics to move on the situation very rapidly, or the State Department *will* take it entirely under its own management. It would be very much to the advantage of all concerned to have Linguistics fully involved in a cultural study, and involved in interviewing these new residents, collecting their experience for study, and in arranging programs to see them safely integrated into various communities. They are as diverse a population as, say, Port Jackson itself, with individuals ranging from scientists to workmen to, perhaps, a small number who may bear closer scrutiny. As I indicated—these people were born there. They have been through hell. And they have survived by whatever means. The History Department will also find them an interesting resource—while I'm sure National Defense and the Judiciary will have questions for those in a position to observe what happened. What *will not* happen is to rush these people through a checkpoint, hand them a suitcase and put them on a bus to random locations. There has to be a process that records, analyses, preserves information, and makes humane and proper judgments on individual problems. Can Linguistics handle it alone? No. Should Linguistics be a major resource? Yes. In my opinion, yes."

There was another silence, but not a hostile one, give or take the glare from Wilson.

"If that will be all, I think I should leave you to settle the specific questions and advise the State Department exactly what you think you should do. I have received word that Heyden *will* be dedicated to the very first down, the three children and their parents. I would invite you to contact Dr. Katherine Shugart, who will be operational head of the Heyden center, or Dr. Tom Lund and Dr. Ben Feldman, who will be in constant touch with the University President and the Foreign Service."

A pause. A direct, though intermittent stare from Koman. "I think we have sufficient. We may be back to you with questions."

"I shall be happy to answer them. Thank you." He gave a little bow, absolute reflex, turned and left, in atevi order. Banichi and Jago shut the doors as they left, and Tano and Algini formed up with them.

"It went fairly well," he said in Ragi, as they headed for the lift.

"Wilson has aged," Banichi said, "and not well."

Of course. Banichi had seen the man, some years ago.

"Not well," he said. It occurred to him that, had he wanted open warfare, he might simply have addressed Wilson in Ragi—inviting a response. But he had not done it, and he was glad he had not. He was glad to have held out several civilized offers to the man. And he was not at all sure that Wilson could, even yet, reply in the language. It would surely be a matter of principle with the man not to do it.

He had launched one barb. He really wished he had not done that. But the Committee needed to know what Wilson did not seem to have accepted even yet, that it flatly didn't *matter* which side appointed a paidhi to go negotiate with the other. The paidhi's job, always and forever, was to represent both sides fairly, at whatever risk to his person.

Wilson never had understood that. And possibly the Committee never had, either.

Were the children already paidhiin? Not quite. Someone had to commission them, and that had not happened. There was a great deal they had to learn before they could serve. But were they qualified to serve? Once they knew how to serve both sides, yes, they would be qualified.

But Tabini was right. To do that, they had to know Mospheira as well as they knew atevi.

And he hoped he had put them in good hands. No matter what the Committee did or didn't do.

And if the Committee did monstrously badly—he had provided people with the initiative and resources to get the kids and their parents safely onto a boat headed for the mainland.

18

It was possible to *see* the stables from the upstairs window. That was as close as Cajeiri was able to get to where he wanted to be. He could see Jeichido. He watched her politick with the lesser members of the herd.

He thought about what Uncle had said about a separate herd, a separate stable—his stable. He was still not sure what he thought about that—but watching Jeichido nip and fuss at the seniors in the herd, he could see why Uncle thought it might be a good idea. If mecheiti were running wild—there were almost no places left in the world where they could do that—Jeichido would separate herself, and raid other herds for individuals she could manage. That was the way they were. Diegi was far enough she would not have the temptation to confront Uncle's herd; and if she came here now and again under saddle, with her own group, she would be far easier to handle. Compatible herds were a great advantage to an area. He could see that. Arranging to bring in a Taibeni presence was a good thing, too. It meant neighbors could cooperate, or just ride for pleasure. Or bring in new blood.

He thought, however, he should ask Father for an allowance, and a fairly large one, if he was going to have the stable, and a head groom, and maybe others. Uncle should not pay it. He insisted not to have pieces of his household under this management, and that management. He should give the orders. He should have the man'chi, with no one in doubt. It was the way his father ran his household. He knew of other people who were a little more tangled—Mother, for one—but he never wanted to wonder things Mother had had to wonder. He wanted to know.

He gazed out the window—the sill of which could do with a little dusting: he noted that little lapse in Uncle's ordinarily immaculate house—and thought of his little office, and his state of no mail, ever, and he was not happy to contemplate having to keep accounts and write letters to more staff. Some things about growing up were to look forward to. Letter-writing was not.

But it would gain favor from Father, he thought, if he did undertake to manage his own small stable, at least in the beginning. Mani said if one turned things over to staff without knowing how to do them, then one was surrendering authority, and giving it to somebody else. And he had little enough authority in the world, and maybe it was a good thing to run a stable and a house in Diegi before trying to run anything more ambitious.

His own household was expanding. He *might* need somebody on his own staff to deal with the seniors, their laundry and their off-schedule meals and such, and just to help them with whatever they needed . . .

Granted the senior Guild were going to stay with him. Which was also *theirs* to decide. Maybe they had rather not be burdened with a boy and a very young and very upside down junior aishid. They could say no and have, probably, any house in the aishidi'tat wanting them and willing to offer them all sorts of benefits if they would come.

He rather hoped they would stay. They did take a certain amount of his young aishid's focus away from him and onto themselves, but it all came back to him. It was just larger, was all. It was a good idea. It was useful now, when they had a threat at hand, and a situation that needed contact with Guild Headquarters. He did not now have any objection when his aishid asked for information. No one told the seniors something was classified.

He dusted the window sill himself, so some servant would not get the blame for his fingerprints showing it up. He wiped his fingers, thinking that this little window, this inconvenient nook, probably was the boundary between the upstairs servants and the downstairs servants, and found itself neglected. Boundaries— were always chancy places.

The order from market had gotten through this morning. *Eggs* had come in, along with vegetables. The grocer in Diegi had taken it on himself to make the estate delivery, and had come in besides with all the *mail* that had accumulated, a whole basket of it, which the staff had been sorting, which was why Uncle was in his office now, dictating answers to the ones that absolutely had to be answered. The rejection of his nomination had generated a flood of it, so this morning was full of unpleasant questions.

So they did have eggs for Boji. They had not had any to spare for treats, but they did have now.

And since they now had adequate bribes, if they got Boji into his harness, the only sort he had not yet escaped, they could go down to the storerooms and let him get a little exercise among sacks and crates he could not damage.

But even to do that, he would first have to ask Uncle when Uncle had finished with his correspondence, and *then* he had to ask his own senior Guild, who outranked all the Guild in the house.

His aishid was waiting for him in the hall just below this odd little window, waiting for him because there was nothing in the house to do but wait. He could ask for this. He could ask for that. But everything required permission from someone. He could ask permission to go down and talk to Nomari again. One part of him wanted desperately to do that. But he felt bruised, himself, from the last session, with questions asked in the open that led to other questions—and then no answers, because Nomari himself might not know.

Did his mother know these answers? It had disturbed him

most to know that the things they most wanted to know from Nomari—involved a time when his mother had been there, involved a time when assassinations had taken out key people in Ajuri. Lords, one after the other, had feared for their lives.

He did not *want* to ask more questions. He did not want to dig up things maybe his mother tried not to talk about, that was one thing. He *would* go back and ask, when he had sorted things out himself. But now the Guild was asking questions—and now Uncle was thinking about having Nomari to dinner tonight. Uncle had asked him how he would feel about it, and he had frozen on that answer, for fear of how that would go.

Well enough, for the dinner: Uncle was proper. But brandy afterward frightened him.

It would just be—hard—sitting at table with someone he felt moved toward—and knowing the questions this person brought with him might touch on Mother's relationship with Uncle, on Mother's past, and the things Uncle and Mother never talked about.

Was Uncle after something in particular? He had no idea. And he so wanted to go outside for a while, and just for an hour to escape to the stables, and not to think about dinner, and brandy, and questions that were edging on very uncomfortable ground.

He had come to rely on his young aishid. He had told them things, discussed things with them he would discuss with no one else, but now he felt as if telling them his fears would give them things they would feel they *should* tell the seniors, and they should not. For the security of his family and all the delicate man'chi his father and his mother shared, he *could* not. So he stood up here to be as alone as he could manage, and knew he could not escape dinner tonight, if Uncle was set on that notion. He could not tell them why this cousin locked in Uncle's basement upset him so. He could not explain his reasons.

He wished nand' Bren were here. He could sometimes ask nand' Bren things that he would not even ask mani, because nand' Bren sometimes thought of things differently, and gave him different ideas.

His aishid, however, stirred from the bench below, and Antaro came halfway up the steps toward him, bearing a troubled look. "Geri-ji." Geri-ji was the name that felt warm and good, but when he looked down he saw all of them on their feet, and worried, which had the feeling of ice about his heart. "People are at the gate," Antaro said. "We are asked where you are. We answered. Seniors say we should stay upstairs."

It was *not* the advisement they would get if his father had sent someone, or if it were a tradesman with a delivery.

At least there was a view from upstairs.

"We shall go to the west windows," he said, coming down the steps to join them. "What do they think they are? Nomari's associates?"

"They have brought a bus," Jegari reported as they headed off across the main level. "The colors are Ajuri."

That was not good news. Ajuri was here to visit, *his* relatives and Nomari's, not Uncle's, and he did not want to see them, because there was nobody in Ajuri with anything good to say to Uncle. That feud had been going on since Grandfather had run off with Mother at her birth.

Uncle was coming from his office. The seniors were coming up from downstairs.

And they were bringing Nomari up with them.

That was fairly scary.

Uncle surely would not let Ajuri arrest him or any such thing, not under *his* roof. But Uncle had a very grim look, grimmer than ever Cajeiri had seen him.

They all assembled in the sitting room, near the tall windows.

"Uncle," Cajeiri said, trying not to let his voice rise in distress, "have they said what they want?"

"They *want* to bring their bus onto the grounds, and we have advised them this will not be permitted. The visitors include an infelicity of two, your great-aunt Geidaro, who is acting as clan lord, and your aunt Meisi, who wish to talk to us, along with your cousin Caradi, whose function in the world we cannot determine."

"I have not met him."

"It is no loss," Uncle said. "The bus will stop at the gate, and if they intrude, we will stop them and we will *not* see them. If we disable the bus, they will *walk* home. We are sending the car to the gate, for the three, with two Guild of their company, and we anticipate a very brief meeting. Nomari, cousin of my nephew, welcome. Be assured you are under our protection."

"Nandi." Nomari gave a little bow, well-composed and quiet, with Guild outnumbering servants in the room. "Thank you."

"Have you committed any offense we should know about?" Uncle asked.

"I am in good standing with my guild. My clan will claim unanswered summonses. My principal fault within my clan, with apologies, nandi, is being the last survivor of my house."

"You are Sanari's son."

"Nandi, I am."

"Grandson of Anoji, great-grandson of Nichono, twice-great-grandson of Ajuno and Haro, and great-grandnephew of Shishogi, am I correct?"

"Nandi, you are correct."

Uncle nodded slowly. "You are aware of my history with Ajuri."

"Nandi, I am. I knew when I came here, no one has ever had to tell me, and I can only express regret. My own father, my brothers, my mother, my grandfather—all died at Shishogi's orders."

There was a lengthy silence then. Uncle's face was absolutely still. "You believe Komaji murdered my sister?"

"No, nandi. I suspect his bodyguard."

Uncle's sister was Grandmother. Muriyo. Mother's mother. Cajeiri stood still, hands tucked under his arms as if it were winter chill in the room.

"At Shishogi's order."

"She would not go to Ajuri," Nomari said.

"You are *extraordinarily* well informed on the matter." Uncle's tone was ice.

"Nandi, it was the center of everything that went wrong. Komaji was this way and that—the whole house rallied in the notion he was unjustly accused, but my grandfather, Anoji, suspected it was Guild, somehow. *He* thought it might be the aiji-dowager. Forgive me. But Shishogi was the one power our clan held. He *was* important. He held a tremendous power—we had no idea how great, or how important, or how extensive. Ajuri is a little clan. It always has been. And it has always been a conservative clan, and some of the elders more so than most—but nobody, *nobody* in my own family ever understood what Great-uncle was *doing* until he was dead. He was, we all knew, upset with the aiji-dowager being an Easterner, sitting as regent. He was upset with the aiji being a Taibeni woman's son—and I have no idea all that he did, except that he was putting his own agents where he wanted them, and moving people he wanted in power. In Ajuri, people did not criticize Shishogi. They just did not. When we were young, we heard how important he was. When Grandfather did speak against him, everybody was upset—but some were afraid, too. My mother was afraid. And Grandfather died. That was how it was. When I was thirteen— when Lord Benedi died—my father was deeply attached to Benedi—and my father was upset. He said it was Guild responsible, and it was not the aiji-dowager, and I think now that that was enough. It was the end of our family, nandi. My mother told me go to Shejidan, to her relative, and I went into Transport Guild training. That is what I know about the things Shishogi did. We know more now. Or those of us *outside* know. Geidaro is still not saying it. And I know she has heard everything people outside are saying . . . that it was *always* Shishogi. If a lord went against him, he died. There was always another. If he wanted a tie to Atageini, he ordered one. It was Komaji's fault he could not get your sister to go with him to have the baby in Ajiden. And Shishogi would never have trusted him if he had disobeyed orders, and stayed in Tirnamardi. *That* is the scenario I now imagine, behind the situation I know. I have had years to think it was a Guild plot. I have had the last several years to wonder why Guild would so concentrate its actions on Ajuri—if it were *not* the aiji-dowager in association with you, nandi. I do not now think so. So who else could order the Guild?"

Uncle sat down. There was a terrible stillness in the room, that went on and on. No servant moved. Guild did not move in the least. Cajeiri himself felt his heart beating hard, felt a massive sense of things utterly in suspension. *Nobody* talked about Grandmother. Nobody mentioned her to Uncle. And Uncle almost never talked about her.

But this stranger dared defend Grandfather, dared to tell Uncle and the Guild all about them that Grandmother had indeed been murdered, and that Grandfather *was* in a sense to blame, but that he had not necessarily been the murderer—that Guild had carried out an unFiled assassination, that Grandfather had stolen the baby—Mother—and carried her off before Uncle knew it.

Maybe it had saved Uncle's life, that Grandfather had gotten away with Mother as a babe in arms, and taken his guard with him. Maybe the feud had misdirected suspicions in Atageini *and* in Ajuri, so that more people were innocent than anybody might have thought, but that even Mother being born was Shishogi's planning . . .

Shishogi might have planned Mother's life, but he had done *nothing* that he knew to prevent Father marrying her. *Had* he? Had he designed Mother all along to marry his father?

He felt a need to sit down, too. His heart was racing. His thoughts were racing—over every scrap of half-heard discussion that had not involved him, things that Mother had said to Father, that one could, when they argued, hear through the doors.

Mother had lived her life in a state of anxiety and upset,

angry at secrets, angry at his father taking *him* away, angry at Great-grandmother—had she heard *that* in Ajuri? That Great-grandmother, mani, had had *her* mother killed? And did she even halfway *believe* it?

"Interesting," Uncle said in that cold tone. "These are not things we discuss in this house. Perhaps we should."

"Nandi," Nomari said, and gave a little bow. "I deeply apologize for anything I may have said which distresses you. My clan is troubled. It is troubled by the very people you have arriving to visit you. If you wish me to leave before they do arrive, I know a gap in the hedges, and I would rather not put this house to the inconvenience of defending my presence here. If I leave, you can very properly tell them you have no idea where I have gone."

"You will kindly leave my abused hedges alone, guest of mine. Do not dare suggest to me that I would face this harridan of a woman with any evasion. One appreciates that Ajuri is fallen on hard times and lacks a lord to see to the niceties of the situation, but by the less felicitous gods, I *hope* that woman gives me cause. Do you have *any* substantiation for your defense of Komaji, thin though it be?"

"Lord Tatiseigi, I have nothing but my memory. I know what was said in the house, and eventually, after the events in the Guild, among certain of us in Shejidan. I cannot prove any of it."

"Lord Komaji was coming toward Atageini lands when he was killed. And that killing, *killing*, I say, no Guild action, was itself unsanctioned. I have asked myself, had we met, what Komaji might have been so desperate to say to me, because it was not the safest direction for him to go. *Hiding* would have been safer. Any other direction would have been safer. I have asked myself—was he coming to gain my help? And how did he look to explain himself? What you say offers at least a rational explanation."

"Nandi." Nomari made a second bow. "If I can do anything constructive in the situation—"

"Sit down. And respect this house."

The car had arrived. Cajeiri heard it on the paving, which meant the lower doors had opened.

He had his aishid. He had the seniors. Uncle had allowed these people to come with two Ajuri Guild, which he wished now Uncle had not done.

He said, quietly, "Uncle. This is your house. But I do *not* wish Ajuri Guild to come onto this floor."

"The heir-designate *can* so order," Uncle said.

"Then I do," Cajeiri said, with a lump in his throat, and immediately, as if a switch had been thrown, his senior aishid moved toward the doors and down the steps, and his younger aishid took up positions on either side of his chair, Veijico and Lucasi behind and Antaro and Jegari a little in front.

There was the noise of protest from below. It did not continue. Uncle's bodyguard took positions at Uncle's chair. It was the house servants who went to stand by the doors, and Uncle's estate guard who came up the stairs with the visitors.

Cajeiri had not seen Geidaro or Meisi since Father had sent Grandfather home from the Bujavid and thrown all the Ajuri out with them, even Mother's nurse and her maids and her security. Everybody had gone. And now Geidaro came up the stairs, an elderly woman with a cane like mani, but always, always scowling. Meisi helped her, scowling to match. And behind them came a thin man in a gold-thread coat, a little ostentatious for a country estate. A gold-thread coat and lace. It would have been ordinary in the Bujavid. Here—it was a little in excess.

"Lord Tatiseigi," Aunt Geidaro began, a little out of breath, but that voice could penetrate doors. "This is an outrage. My aishid half barred and now held at gunpoint—this is entirely excessive."

"It was *my* order," Cajeiri said. "It was *my* aishid, Aunt. I take full responsibility for them."

Aunt was not expecting him to interfere, he was fairly sure

of that. Her face went from scowling to impassive and cold, and she stared at him in a way he was sure she would not dare do with Father.

But answer back? He thought she might, but he would remember. He would already remember her and hers, and if she thought she could make him flinch, she was wrong.

"We are not prepared for tea or hospitality," Uncle said, drawing Aunt's attention to himself. "We ordinarily receive notice of impending visits."

"We are not prepared to take tea with this renegade," Aunt retorted. "Clearly he has deceived you and made himself seem acceptable company. He is not. He has chosen to leave his house, to desert his clan, and to create a nest of opportunists and petty thieves. Clearly he is here because of your nomination of our cousin, which you well knew would meet a veto. Your political maneuvering has agitated this opportunist into making you an offer he can never deliver."

"Atageini is not accustomed to have unannounced arrivals criticize our decisions or attack other persons under our roof. You are treading close to the brink, Sister-in-law, and if you wish a *car* to take you and your niece to the gate, at any point, I would suggest you moderate your tone and reconsider your approach. Your son is quiet. Has he a voice of his own?"

"I have, nandi." That was from the middle-aged man and that was, Cajeiri thought, Aunt Geidaro's son Caradi. "And Ajuri requests you, as a neighbor, consider backing someone who can be an ally, someone within the line."

"Do you not think the aiji has noticed your existence?" Uncle asked sharply.

"Nandi!"

"I believe he has," Uncle said. "I believe he has fully considered a candidate even more directly descended from the last lord, but he will not expose *her* to the politics that have taken down her father. Likewise he has surely considered the vacancy and the candidacy of her son—"

"A minor child!" Aunt exclaimed. "The situation of Ajuri needs mature leadership. Someone trained in the lordship."

"Alas, they die. Benedi, Kadiyi, Komaji . . . all dead."

"I can manage this," Caradi said. "I offer you a good association . . ."

"With no fear of assassination," Uncle said. "Certainly the chances are less, now, since the scoundrels now sit in charge."

"You *have* the scoundrel under your own roof!" Geidaro said. "You *have* the faction that has repeatedly struck at Ajuri's stability! He sits there, smug and satisfied." In fact Nomari's expression was nothing of the sort. "And you accuse *us* of discourtesy. *You* have been no neighbor to us. You have abandoned the policies of your uncle, you have led the seven clans astray from our principles, you have associated yourself with Easterners and liberals, you have made peace with the Taibeni bandits, you have voted to admit the Edi pirates to the aishidi'tat, you have made association with the aiji's pet human, and you have sold our heritage!"

"Diplomacy," Uncle said dryly, "diplomacy, diplomacy, Sister-in-law. Caradi, you are standing there like a stone block, doubt-less wishing your mother understood discretion. The habit of being feared, perhaps, encourages her indiscretion. Easterners and liberals, is it?"

"You cannot stand without us," Aunt said. "Your power, such as it is, comes from your association, from the Padi Valley, and do you think you can replace *us*, pure Ragi, with Taibeni? With humans? Think again! Without us, you do not have Purani, you do not have Madi, you do not have Ardiyan."

"And without us, you do not have access to east or west or south. You think I will tremble?"

"My son is lord of Ajuri! It is his inheritance!"

"A lordship is *no one's* guaranteed inheritance. And I have yet to hear much from your son," Uncle said. "He seems a silent sort. Another Shishogi? Or is he simply shy?"

"Great-uncle was an infelicity," Caradi said stiffly. "We were more affected by his actions than any other. We do not know all that he did. Likely no one ever will know."

"That *would* be comfortable for some, perhaps, but we will continue to pursue it."

"Support my son," Aunt said. "You can *restore* a good relationship with Ajuri, nandi, by proposing him as lord, not some distant relation of Komaji's house. Ajuri will never accept an outsider."

"Your son seems incapable of speaking for himself."

"Do not insult my mother."

"Ah," Uncle said. "There *is* an opinion. Speak your mind, Caradi. I wait to be amazed."

"You insult me, a guest under your roof."

"You are no guest. Your *cousin* is a guest. You have turned up at my gates presenting demands. I have been courteous enough to invite you to make them here, rather than relying on messengers, but you have quite the same status as some traveler on the road. If this is the way guests arrive in Ajuri territory, I beg to be instructed."

"This person," Caradi said, "is a thief."

"I am not!" Nomari said.

"How," Uncle asked quietly, "did his family die?"

There was a small silence.

"I ask," Uncle said.

"There were unfortunate accidents."

Nomari made a move as if he would get up, but one of Uncle's Guild moved slightly to the fore and Nomari sank back with a clenched fist.

"Unfortunate accidents," Uncle said. "Like my sister's?"

That made a *dreadful* quiet.

"Leave my premises," Uncle said. "I will convey you back by car *only* to have you off these grounds. Delay, and I shall loose the mecheiti on you as trespassers."

"You are making a mistake," Geidaro said.

"I never Filed in the case of my sister's death. The agency was unclear. Do not try me now."

"You dare nothing of the sort."

"I *beg* you try me."

Uncle had never used that tone. Ever. The three Ajuri stood still a moment, angry—but not pushing further, either.

Meddling in the affairs of grown-ups was not usually a good thing. But these were *Mother's* relatives. And his. And Cajeiri stood up with all the height and calm he could muster.

"Leave," he said. "Now."

Aunt fixed him with a dark, sharp stare that grown-ups in Ajuri probably dreaded. He stared back, mad, on Uncle's account, on his mother's account, on Grandfather's and Grandmother's, because this woman, this one old woman, was their enemy, and his, and Uncle's. If Shishogi had acted inside Ajuri—he had a notion this woman had been his hands. This woman had been scary, and powerful, and had acted oh, so prim and proper when she had visited the Bujavid with Meisi and Dejaja—and Grandfather, who was newly lord of Ajuri and very soon dead, like all the others.

Geidaro kept surviving. Geidaro had blamed mani for everything, just the way Shishogi had.

Enemy? Among all his pins, he had never placed one. But he would now.

And Aunt stared at him last when she turned about, stamped her cane on the floor and said to Meisi and Caradi, "We shall go."

She was smart enough not to speak any threat, not against him, not against Uncle. But Cajeiri thought, she meant one. She very much meant one, as she turned and walked down the steps to the foyer; and he was shivering, not because he was afraid—well, he was—but mostly because he saw a danger he could do nothing about. He had his aishid on those steps, if the Ajuri Guild dared draw a gun, but they were not the danger. That was not the way that woman would work.

He looked toward Uncle, who looked to be carved of stone, still seated; and he saw, next to Uncle, Nomari, whose hands were clenched, whose composure was not as perfect as Uncle's. Nomari looked as if he would fling himself out of the chair and after that company . . . or bolt for the doors himself, in another direction. Nomari had not had mani thwacking his ear and saying, Face. Face. Stand still.

But was *he* the proper lord of Ajuri?

Better than Caradi, who dared not draw a breath if Geidaro disapproved.

Cajeiri sat down again, proper, waiting for Uncle, in Uncle's house. And shortly they heard the doors open and close again, and in due time they heard the cars start up and leave, carrying Geidaro's company and a good number of Uncle's guard toward the gate in the hedges.

"Tea," Uncle said, for which Cajeiri was grateful. He did not want to talk at the moment. He was not sure of the things he had done, and the things he had said. But he had thought he should say them, because he knew his father would have, not to mention what mani would have said.

"You shall stay," Uncle said to Nomari, "and take tea, if you will."

"Nandi." Nomari gave a little nod, unclenched his hands, let go a breath. "I am in your debt."

"No more of it," Uncle said. "Take tea. I do not say your quarters may improve. But I shall not detain you, should you wish to leave these grounds. That is as much as I will say at this point."

Uncle needed to think, too. So did everybody, Cajeiri thought.

Geidaro was a problem. He had no question of that.

19

The first set of meetings with the Mospheiran legislature had explained the kyo, the situation, and the treaty.

Now came the more worrisome part—explaining the future, in which the Committee on Linguistics' rules had to change, in which there would be—technically, there already was—more than one paidhi. There had been Yolande Mercheson. There was, currently, Jase Graham. And there were, now, three Reunioner children.

And the Committee on Linguistics had no actual role in any of those selections.

Explaining that the landings of other Reunioners—which had begun to be rumored in the media—would take place, and that they would start soon—was the next step.

Explaining that very soon Reunioners would not be a station issue, but a permanent and local one—was the job at hand.

It would be much more comfortable, Bren thought, to call Toby in, board the *Brighter Days* and be off to the mainland once this session was over.

But comfort wasn't the wise choice. The best course, the only reasonable course, was to be here to explain what was going on, and work out the attendant problems.

Today's hurdle involved a second joint session with the committees on Science, on Internal Affairs, and on Foreign Affairs—this time, however, in the Senate chamber, with the chairmen of the three committees at the rostrum, and the members of the various committees sitting in a sparse pattern across the chamber. Bren had a table in the well, with a microphone, facing the three chairmen, with his back to the other members. In the Senate chambers, *everybody* had a microphone. But to his great relief, Woodenhouse, who sat on Internal Affairs, had reported ill—if it had been on the mainland, his illness would have been suspect—but it was fairly certain Woodenhouse would be back.

It did, however, suggest that the Heritage Party might have urged Woodenhouse, who did not seem to excel in self-restraint, to call in sick.

If that was the case, Heritage actually wanted to hear the content of his testimony, which it could not get from any other source. Then it would decide its position. Fair enough, that, until they figured out a way to use it politically, and of all possible bedfellows in Mospheiran politics, that was not the set he wanted to have.

Corporate donors . . . perhaps a little interested in the Reunioner papers. That could make for interesting alliances. And maybe some restraint on the part of Heritage.

There was in this chamber a written agenda, which at least gave him some advance warning and the first item under question was his statement about changes in the paidhi's operational duties.

That one was not so difficult. "I can't say the most recent changes were ever planned," Bren said. "But there's been a shift in the aijinate, a major shift. Some years ago the aiji in Shejidan opted to make the paidhi-aiji a court official. This has had benefits. Principally, it has given humans a face and a voice to the mainland in general, has set up a greater acceptance of technology in many areas, and a more positive view of humans across the board. As a direct consequence, when *Phoenix* arrived, the aijinate was able to respond and cooperate with Mospheira in restoring the station, and we have been working together in everything that's followed—a cooperation which has turned out to be life-saving in the arrival of the kyo. I strongly suspect that, whether or not *Phoenix* ever had returned to Reunion, the kyo knew this world was here, knew it was connected to the ship and knew it was connected to Reunion. We have *very* likely been under observation by the kyo for decades, if not centuries."

That produced a stir. He had meant it to.

"You've made this claim before," Internal Affairs said. "But is there any proof?"

"A technological assumption, Mr. Chairman. *Phoenix* could do it. *Phoenix* evidently saw a kyo world at a distance, and injudiciously went there. I consider it safe to assume that the kyo, whose ships are faster, armed, and in general far more advanced than our single ship, could also do it. We do know that they were watching the activities of the ship, and likely knew its movements over a long sequence of time. I used to believe that we could conceal our lack of technology—and I thought that we could have remained unknown to the kyo and others, except for the ship. I no longer believe it was ever possible. And fortunate for us, again in my opinion, that we were able to go to Reunion, and that we were able to face the kyo with our Mospheiran experience of negotiating with foreigners and in cracking a language barrier. Initially, *Phoenix* ran from contact. That was a very wrong response with the kyo. *Mospheirans* have had the experience that says—go in and talk. It seems so simple to us. It was *not* simple or natural to Reunion or to the ship, but we arrived, we talked, we asked, and we were able to reach a mutually satisfactory conclusion. We *have* that very useful skill to offer the universe—but we *should* realize we are not technologically superior when it comes to ships, weapons, or science. The kyo are much more advanced in areas that have the ship technicians baffled. The kyo have stepped out of the dark, in effect, sat by our little campfire, and now they've gone back into the dark, headed home with a good understanding that we're not a problem and we don't represent another threat. They have a war going on. They don't want us in it and we assuredly don't want to *be* in it. If we're lucky, they'll settle it and reach a peace with their enemies. But eventually—they—or someone—could come here, and we can't predict when that will happen. We're perfectly visible to the whole universe. That's unchangeable. A good relationship with a good neighbor is a situation we've begun to enjoy on this planet, and one we hope we've established with the kyo. We need to be ready for others."

There was a small silence when he finished speaking.

"That's a grim future you paint."

"I don't think so, Mr. Chairman. I do not think so. Having dealt with the kyo, I can say they have good qualities. We may find them *very* good neighbors. But in that consideration—it is the aiji's position that the space station is essential, and that a settlement of the situation on the station is urgent. It *is* a crisis—but it need not be a source of tensions between the aishidi'tat and Mospheira. Over the past number of days, we have been discussing the treaty between humans, atevi, and the kyo. But there is also at issue the treaty that mandates parity between Mospheiran presence and atevi presence on the station, and *that* is seriously in question. That is the issue, besides my delivery of the treaty to the people of Mospheira, that caused the aiji in Shejidan to send me here to deliver a message. The imbalance must be dealt with. The process must begin immediately. The aiji recognizes the numbers of persons mean it will take time, but he will expect the *process* will get underway. He is willing to help. He is not willing to wait another year."

"Are you," Internal Affairs asked, "are you, Mr. Cameron, a representative of this government—or the other?"

"One thing that has been somewhat lost in translation, Mr. Chairman, is the definition of *paidhi-aiji*. Paidhi is a Ragi word. Even the Department of Linguistics has persistently interpreted the office as solely a Mospheiran representative. But let it be set in the record: a paidhi, in the Ragi meaning of the word, serves both sides in a negotiation. The Ragi definition of negotiation does not see two tables, two negotiators each exclusively representing their own side, but one single negotiator moving between the conflicting sides, fairly presenting each argument in turn until an agreement can be reached, often with the advice and input of the negotiator. I have accepted that definition of my office, Mr. Chairman, and I consider it my honor and my duty to express, passionately, as an atevi court official, the wishes of the aiji and the aishidi'tat. When I cross the strait, I will just as passionately represent the wishes of the Mospheiran people."

"It seems rather a definition as the aiji chooses it to be."

"The Treaty of the Landing mandated a paidhi, a Ragi term, and the aiji was fair enough to suggest he would accept your choice to fill *his* office. It's an ancient position I'm honored to fill, and I suggest there is a profound advantage to Mospheira in understanding this office as it's understood on the mainland. Under this original interpretation of the office, Mospheira gets to hear the aiji's request without interpretation, by someone fluent and aware of nuance. I would hope that Mospheira will also accept me as a negotiator in the other direction, since as a court official, I have confidence *I* will be heard. And I will present your point of view as you express it—but the aiji would strongly hope that with that expression will come a resolve to solve this problem together."

"Rather remarkable that a mistranslation would have persisted for two hundred years, and only now we hear about it."

"Not as surprising, sir, since paidhiin before me were forbidden to speak the language to atevi. We simply passed notes. No negotiation happened. You now *have* a voice you have not had before. I urge you use it. And ask me questions, as speaking *for* the aiji."

There was a little stir at that, as if no one had ever thought of that, or found the thought uncomfortable. Bren took a sip of water.

"What, then, *is* the aiji's position on assisting us in a solution," State said, "in the station situation?"

A much friendlier interrogator, State. A much more welcome question.

"The aiji understands the logistical problems, Mr. Chairman. And welcomes the President's statement that he considers the Reunioners to be Mospheiran or under Mospheiran authority. He will take the same view. Let me be clear: I do not represent the Reunioners as a group. I am not negotiating with them. I represent the aiji, who simply says they have tipped the mandated balance, and the aiji is entirely willing materially to assist the Mospheiran government in finding a solution. Shipping them to Maudit—a company including elderly and children with family attachments—simply won't do. It would be a death sentence for them, under any conceivable circumstance. Recall that during the construction of Alpha Station, *Phoenix* itself served as residence and safe refuge. *Phoenix* does not wish to make that commitment to a Maudit station, and we have no means to argue that point. Mospheiran authorities on the station will tell you that the Reunioners cannot be adequately housed or supplied up there. Their presence overtaxes the resources the station has, and endangers the health and safety of everyone, including atevi. In consultation with station officials both Mospheiran and atevi, the aiji proposes that five thousand individuals be brought down from the station to balance the human and atevi populations. He assumes it would be easier to bring down the Reunioners rather than to remove working personnel from critical jobs. The aiji *could* set up residency for them on the Great Southern Island, but his view is that fostering a second human population and rendering a human population politically distinct from Mospheira, whether in space at Maudit, on the station in quarantine, or on the Southern Island, only breeds future trouble."

There was a murmur in the room.

He chose to ignore it.

"Five thousand educated individuals, many with high level technical expertise in space age operations, are not truly a problem for a population the size of Mospheira's to absorb. In fact there has already been a scramble after the knowledge these people bring, for its economic value."

The central chair, State, gaveled the room to silence.

"It is not that simple," Internal Affairs said.

"The science," Science said, "is of incalculable economic value."

"The question remains," Internal Affairs said, "why should we absorb all the cost for a mutual problem?"

"As I've already stated," Bren said, and waited for the gavel to establish quiet, "the aiji is quite willing to aid in the process financially. He is willing to give free passage on atevi shuttles to the mainland, and to ferry them over to Port Jackson, at his own charge. The aiji will also cooperate with the effort to clear shuttle passenger space, by directing atevi station operations to provide materials to build landers to bring down cargo by parachute. He offers landing zones on the mainland, and the transport of cargo destined for Mospheira to its proper destination, either by Mospheiran ships, or air, or by ships of the aishidi'tat. These are not inconsiderable financial contributions to the process. In return," he began and waited again for the gavel.

"In return," he reprised, "the aiji expects a free flow of information gained on processes and science, understanding that patents may secure economic benefits to Mospheiran corporations for a certain number of years, but that understandings of principle will ultimately benefit both sides of the strait."

"The cost of development of these programs . . ." That was, again, Internal Affairs.

"Is known, sir. We have lander designs that have worked, as recently as the last few years, to set large payloads down on the mainland. The landers must be built in space, and they offer no-return salvage for the ground-based operations that unload them, so nothing will be wasted. We have the designs, we have the precise numbers—I am speaking now for the cooperative of Mospheiran and atevi administrations on the station—and it will not interrupt necessary station operations. We have a clear and practical reckoning of the number of flights and launches, and where and how these persons may be lodged on Mospheira during a period of orientation—which they will need—along with short courses through the University, simply on managing daily life. All these obstacles have been dealt with far more cheaply than any expedition to Maudit—or doubling of the size of the current space station. I can promise you that where there are difficulties, as yet unforeseen, the aiji will work with you in close partnership to share expense and effort. And he will share any science that falls into atevi hands as he expects you to share what you may gain. We *have* a solution to the station crisis. We have only to put it into operation."

"Beginning with these children," State said.

"Beginning with the children," Bren said. "The paidhiin to come after me. The aiji wishes you to teach them, educate them, inform them—and he will welcome them when they come to the mainland. But their home will be here."

There was quiet in the room.

State said, "Are there specific questions?"

One simply braced oneself for a long, long session.

If there were no reasonable questions, it was a certainty someone would find something to ask.

He was surprised when there was lengthy silence, and finally, from State:

"Chair moves to thank the paidhi-aiji for his responses and to commend him for his performance in recent events."

An official thank you that didn't come from a personal friend. It did a great deal for an exhausting session.

"Second," Science said.

"Motion made and seconded."

Three concurrences . . . graciously so, State and Science outnumbered Internal Affairs.

"Let the record show it." Gavel. "Do I hear a motion to adjourn?"

"Motion to adjourn," Internal Affairs said.

"Seconded," Science said, and the gavel banged down.

"We stand adjourned sine die. Thank you, Mr. Cameron."

"Thank you, sir." He rose, bowed to the three chairmen, and to the room as a whole. His aishid, again, was separated from him, waiting in the hall. That circumstance gave him an uneasy feeling, not helped when Science and State came down from the dais to speak to him, and members of the committees clustered around.

"Good job," State said, shaking his hand. "Damned good job."

He was, pending any other arranged session, free. He looked forward to that. He looked forward to being back in Francis House, in the close company of his aishid. He wanted to explain to them what he had said, he wanted news from the mainland, news from what amounted to . . . home. He'd used to catch the public bus, walk the street in the shade of old trees, have tea in the little shop just off campus, without a bit of fear.

But then he hadn't had a cluster of political powers around him, some praising him to the skies and others wishing he'd never been born.

Here wasn't home. He had that absolutely clear, now. He had a few connections left, people he'd, humanly speaking, call friends. But, God, he wanted to go home now. And it wasn't going to happen. He had work of a different kind to do—no more of these sessions, he hoped. But things to set up.

Things to make happen.

A shuttle to meet.

20

Uncle had invited Nomari to dinner—a country dinner, of a sort that did not require the utmost in dress, but certainly Nomari's mended coat and workman's trousers and boots were not what one would choose to wear to table at Tirnamardi.

It was, however, a trial of sorts, and dress was a minor thing under the circumstances.

Manners were not. And, Cajeiri thought, manners showed a lot of things, and communicated a lot of things. But even those, Uncle seemed disposed to glance past. They had no doubt now that Nomari was *who* he said he was. Aunt Geidaro had met him and known exactly who he was. Aunt Geidaro's emotional reaction alone might be reason enough for a dinner invitation. But Nomari had flaws, as well. Cajeiri had seen them. In his position, in Uncle's house, under Uncle's protection, he should have had confidence in Uncle. He should have shut down, and kept quiet, and maintained a quiet all about him. And he had not. That was a problem.

That had disturbed Uncle somewhat. But Uncle had asked him to take tea. And Nomari had settled and quite properly begged pardon.

Then Uncle had asked Nomari to dinner tonight. That was how it had gone.

But Nomari had not had a clan lord's upbringing, if one took Nomari's account for the truth. His house had never been that sort—had been, really, nothing except a bloodline a little too close to the lords of Ajuri. He could have gone off to study, eventually. He could have gone into, well, those things people of good education did, and made his own living and had a family to do much the same, on into generations . . .

Except they had lived for a time in Ajiden, a little too close to the lords, and Nomari's father had had an opinion about the way the clan's business was going. He might be only fortunate nine years, but he could figure that far. He could imagine that big house, with its two wings, and all of a sudden, they moved out one mecheita herd and brought in another.

Why? Incompatible herds. One, in which a child had ridden. One in which he was not permitted to ride. The second herd was *not* one with a mecheita a young child could handle. That said something. *That* herd was protective of the house, of the grounds. *That* herd was there to protect—against some threat.

And lords had died, one after the other, despite that. Nomari's father had spoken his mind—speaking out might run in the family—and died for it.

Nomari had to learn better than that, if he was going to take Ajuri. He had to be smarter and better than that.

Was he who he said he was? Aunt Geidaro certainly indicated he was.

But he could not be a fool, either. What was it mani had said? Principles make a good rudder, but a very poor sail. Do not fly them. Steer with them.

He really had not understood when she said it. But he thought about that now, and the position Nomari's father had been in— with no way to change what was going on, because he had not understood where the trouble was coming from. Ajuri had blamed mani, and Uncle. And Father. And now Nomari had come to Uncle for help.

That was a change in everything.

He wished he could ask Mother. He had never been in a position to think that, but he really wished Mother could meet Nomari. And maybe then things would be clear.

"Nandi." Eisi brought one of his pretty collar pins, a bright topaz jewel, but he declined it.

"Our guest is in work clothes," he said. He had picked his own plainest brown coat, and he was sure Uncle would dress down, too, though the food would be the best in the midlands. "I shall just take the plain pin, Eisi-ji. Please. And no, Boji, it is not a toy. You may not have it."

Boji was bored, stuffed full of eggs, and bored. He hung on the filigree flowers of the cage and stretched out an imploring hand.

"Poor fellow," Cajeiri said. "We are freeing one prisoner tonight, but it cannot be you. What would you like? Liedi, his mirror. Give him his mirror. He wants a shiny thing."

Liedi brought it. Boji took it and retreated to a perch, where he alternately looked in it and flashed light with it, and bit it.

Sun was leaving the windows, so the rain spots showed clearly against the fading light.

It was a gray evening becoming a soggy night.

And tomorrow the grounds would be green and wet with last night's rain, and despite any understanding with Nomari, they would still be as caged as Boji, unable to ride, unable even to go near an outside door.

They had heard from Aunt. They knew the bus had gotten back to Ajiden.

They did not know what it might have left in the neighborhood. But Taibeni were out in this cold rain, looking for any problems—notably Antaro's and Jegari's parents were on that mission, skirting far across the meadows beyond the gate, with mecheiti senses to be *sure* there were no Ajuri lingering in the neighborhood.

Did Father know?

Senior Guild would have gotten that word to Guild Headquarters, and probably straight to Father as well.

So would the next train through Sidonin shed any additional Guild presence?

It was very possible.

He settled the collar pin to his satisfaction, looked at the time on a very ornate clock that had, he was sure, told the time for mani, and took a little comfort from that, because he felt his nerves unsettled, counting all that was at stake tonight.

"We should go," he said.

Nomari *had* managed a nice shirt under his travel-worn and mended coat. Uncle had surely provided that. Nomari's hair was in a tight queue—it was a little unruly, but he had a nice non-committal ribbon, green satin, and a very quiet manner as he stood behind his chair, unattended except for one of Uncle's staff.

Uncle came in last, as he should, and they both sat down, a table of three, which needed no extra felicity; but the arrangement on the table was significant, flowers of the season, which spoke only for themselves, but grain stems and green reeds and white sprigs, too, which were Atageini, a red flower that was Cajeiri's own color, and a sole blue flower, which honored their guest.

Could Nomari read it? Surely.

Wine arrived—fruit juice for Cajeiri's glass. And everything went quietly, pleasantly. Uncle asked safe questions about Nomari's travels, and made safe comments about the wet weather, and about the pleasantness of the season, which he often spent in the capital.

Nomari answered. He did not ask. They went through course after course, delicate things, that tested knowledge Nomari might not have used in years. Or, being a boy in a minor branch, might never have used. He wisely watched what Uncle did, and chose that utensil, but the fact he was watching carefully, and once mistook a small gold spoon—and changed it—that said something, too. It was a trial, a test, subtle as it was. Najida never turned out such single-purpose utensils. Mani's table might, but rarely—nonsense, mani called it, though mani could manage any of it.

The Padi Valley clans were the heart of Ragi ways. Atageini

was the very heart of the Padi Valley. And there *was*, indeed, a small pick precisely to move tiny pickled berries, a regional dish, from a condiment tray to the fish. Nomari did that with no difficulty at all, and laid the pick precisely across the stand, where it belonged: one never put the sticky thing back into the holder.

It was *not* an etiquette ever called for in the Transportation Guild.

But it was clever of Uncle. It was, Cajeiri thought, very clever.

And Uncle never mentioned it. They finished with a nice meringue and curd, and Uncle, rising, proposed brandy.

That was the scary part.

"Honored, nandi," Nomari said, and amended it, "One is honored."

"Nephew, you will join us."

He said: "One would be pleased, Uncle," and they all went out into the grand sitting room, which was larger than Father's by twice . . . not that Uncle had ever planned such an excess: it had always been that large, from the time of cavalry and armor, when the Atageini lords had used to stand at the head of the hall and give orders.

Now there were brocade chairs and little serving tables, and servants to move about pouring this and that on request.

For him, there was still more fruit juice, which he was not inclined to drink: he simply took a sip and set it down still full, so the servants would not pour more.

They sipped slowly, and the level in Uncle's glass declined. Nomari's matched it. And all was peaceful.

The servants poured another glass.

"I must say," Uncle said, "that Atageini greatly regrets the incident today. We do not regularly subject guests to such behavior."

"Nandi," Nomari said, "I am only sorry my clan was the occasion of it."

"*Are* you still Ajuri?"

That questioned man'chi. It questioned feeling. It questioned attachment. And Nomari nodded slowly.

"Yes. Yes, nandi. I am."

"It is a fatal attachment. Have you wished it otherwise?"

"No, nandi. My mother's clan is Purani. Puran was a pleasant place, while we were there, but, no. Purani folk sheltered me when my family died, but they could never warm to an Ajuri. And I told myself I could become clanless. But I was my father's side of Ajuri. I could not look away from it, ever. I could not go in. But now that things are as they are—now that everybody outside Ajuri knows what was going on, someone has to do something. Someone has to set it right. If there were anybody between me and Ajuri, I would follow that person. But there is not. I will not follow Geidaro. I will never follow Geidaro. And there are hundreds who think the same."

"Hundreds."

"Hundreds, nandi. People still inside Ajuri, who have been too quiet to be thrown out. And outside. Outside. In the trades, in the guilds, in whatever living they can make. I am not the only one."

"But you came here. To talk to my nephew. Have you found any satisfaction?"

"I have found my cousin," Nomari said with a little nod in Cajeiri's direction. "I have found one relation I am glad to meet. And my host, nandi. You have been more than generous."

"I take it you ask my support."

"I hope, nandi, that you will at least consider my claim on Ajuri. That you will at very least, take a position against Ajuri being broken. Somewhere, someone, surely must take the clan. And I would try. If you would do no more than recommend me to a hearing by the aiji's staff, I would be grateful."

That was the beginning of a hearing of a legal case. Father's staff started an inquiry. And held a hearing, with staffers gathering evidence and taking testimony and piling up papers and documents. Hearings could go on for a long time.

"How do you think you shall live," Uncle asked, "and, more, stay *alive,* during that process?"

"Nandi, I have associates."

"One is obliged to stay visible and accessible to an inquiry. How will you manage that?"

"Nandi, I shall manage."

"By going back to Transport and riding about the aishidi'tat hoping to make appearances on schedule? Cousin of my nephew, you underestimate Ajuri's capacity, reduced as it is. There are, I understand, a number of Guild that Guild Headquarters is quietly pursuing. They are not *in* Ajuri—if the Guild knew where they were, they would settle the problem. But they are a festering wound on the aishidi'tat, and you propose to go in singlehandedly and cauterize this untidy situation?"

"Nandi, no. I would not go *in.* If I were named lord of Ajuri, I would not go *in.* I would not be that easy to find. And I would know the people I *can* trust, who *can* operate inside. And I would hope to engage a bodyguard of my own."

Uncle's right eyebrow went up slowly. "You are not naive, then."

"I hope I am not naive, nandi."

Uncle nodded slowly, and Cajeiri drew in his breath.

"Do not hasten to leave this house," Uncle said, and set his brandy glass aside. "There are questions yet to ask. But do not despair of a favorable answer."

Nomari carefully set his glass aside. "Nandi, I would be more than grateful."

"The upper floor is more comfortable," Uncle said. "One trusts you would prefer it."

"Nandi."

Uncle gave a wave of his hand. "A good dinner, a fine drink, and a pleasant conversation. I think we are for bed, are we not? Nephew?"

"Uncle," Cajeiri said. He had hardly said a word, things had gone so rapidly in a direction he was sure now Uncle had pushed them.

Scarily fast. And they were going to have Nomari on the same floor as themselves.

But that was all right. Guild was going to be watching. Very closely.

Fried fish. Tano was pleased.

And a very good dinner.

There was a note from Tom and Ben, which outlined considerable progress. More, there was a message from Gin Kroger.

The shuttle schedule is attached. We look for an on-time launch and as on-time a landing on Port Jackson runway as the planet affords. The kids are excited. The parents are terrified. Well, so is Irene, as I understand, but she is excited. Lord Geigi says even the parents are acquiring enough fluency to ask for food and towels, and to deliver basic courtesies.

Glad to get the messages from Tom and Kate in their respective venues. I understand you're winding down the legislative appearances. I hope you'll take the chance to rest a bit and maybe have dinner at Lolo's.

That wasn't on the horizon. An armed attendance was not quite the thing to settle Mospheiran nerves.

But interviews, news appearances. He could arrange that.

We're going over the plans for the first landers. When you get back to the mainland, if you can get a firm commitment on the landing zones we'll be able to get the numbers in order.

Give my regards to everybody. We're making progress on the Reunioner sections. We've had a few set-tos that don't amount to much, have tagged a few petty thieves who've just put themselves on the very bottom of the landing list, right along with you know who.

On a more serious note we have now had our first lottery, and we're starting our first ten on an orientation program that will at least prepare them for domestic living. Some seem a little daunted by the notion they'll be cooking their own food and washing their own clothes, but we'll break the Port Jackson transport system to them very gently.

What the lottery has done is take the pressure off. Reunioners are generally relieved at not going out to build a station over a barren, airless rock and Mospheirans are glad there's now a timeline for getting the shortages solved. I'm not sure Reunioners have ever lived without shortages, but they're now seeing pictures of beaches and forests, and living spaces where the furniture doesn't fold up to let you access your closet, and where you get a choice of colors.

Me, I'm loving it up here. Though now that I've booted Tillington out of his apartment my furniture doesn't fold. I'll be delaying his return to Earth until we've finished the hearings up here, and that's fairly indefinitely.

Enjoy whatever rest you can get. We're doing fine up here.

Moving Nomari to a bedroom upstairs was no great complication of baggage and servants and such—he simply came upstairs, attended by Uncle's security, and took the first suite by the stairs, at the end of the hall. Uncle assigned two servants to be there, and wished him good night and good rest.

Then Uncle walked along with Cajeiri, with their aishids around them. Uncle said absolutely nothing about cautions or distrust.

But one noted that there was a bench on the landing, and that two of Uncle's guards had lingered in that area—likely to take up position and to be relieved at intervals through the night.

It made Cajeiri feel a little less anxious.

"He is no fool," Uncle said, as they were about to part, on opposite sides of the hall. "He likely would not be alive if he were."

That was surely true.

He went to his room, and he was glad to have both aishids

with him, the younger one, and the seniors. But he felt a little uneasy, in the seniors' company, considering the things he had done today, and the orders he had given.

Did they think him afraid of Geidaro?

Did they think him too trusting, or too simple, regarding Nomari?

He was reluctant even to meet them eye to eye, for fear of detecting that disapproval that his own aishid dreaded. He simply addressed himself to Eisi and Liedi, and paused at Boji's outstretched hand. He had brought a little tidbit, a wrapped sweet, which was probably not a good thing to give the little wretch right at bedtime, but it was not a very large one, with a dried fruit inside. He gave Boji his bribe, and stood still while Liedi untied his queue and put the ribbon aside to be pressed.

His aishid had gone into their area of the suite, to have a conference with the seniors. He truly hoped the seniors were not telling them he had been excessively stupid today.

Eisi slipped his coat free, in the cool air of the room. He undid his own shirt buttons, and Liedi took that, too, to have the night staff launder it. He had gotten off without once spilling gravy or letting his cuff into the soup. He could say that for himself.

He sat down and let Eisi pull off his boots, stood up, unfastened his trousers and stepped out of them, glad, in the cold air, that Eisi had his nightrobe ready to fling about him.

"Did everything go well at dinner, nandi?" Liedi asked. "Was it a good outcome?"

"I hope so," he said, and found it was the truth. He really hoped that. But it was not going to be easy, and there were a lot of ways for it to go badly. Geidaro was not physically imposing. But there was a meanness about her that had always made him uneasy.

He went into his own bedroom, beyond an arch with massive doors that could be closed if one wished. He did not. He liked the doors open, liked not to be alone.

Even if it was just Boji in his cage.

He listened, for a while, to Boji moving about in the dark. He listened to the patter of rain against the glass, a shower with a bit more vigor than the one before dinner.

He thought over everything he had said and that Nomari and Uncle had said, rehearsing it in his mind, looking for more clues than anyone had given him.

It was frustrating, being young, and stupid, and missing clues. He was sure they were in there, that Uncle had delivered a message with the centerpiece, with the servings, with the brandy—he could not judge that. He had had one experience with alcohol, and he truly did not like to remember it—a night that had not left him able to judge the quality of what was served, but it had looked like a really old bottle, of several on the counter, and old was good, where it came to that sort of thing.

So he thought Uncle had treated Nomari really well. And Nomari had been modest in asking Uncle for help, after all that *might* have encouraged him to ask for Uncle's help outright.

And Uncle had answered that without answering much, certainly making Nomari a guest—but not saying what he would do. It was still a puzzle.

But he had learned, over time, that Uncle was very, very smart. He had not used to think so. *That* was how smart Uncle was. He had been many things to many people, and he had never told anybody but mani what he was really up to.

He began to slip toward sleep thinking that.

Boji chittered in the dark. One really hoped he did not get up to that. And that the sugar had not been a mistake. He had chided Eisi and Liedi about just that matter.

Boji changed perches, and jumped up on the cage wall.

Settle, Cajeiri wished him.

Then Boji let out his alarm shriek.

That would wake the dead.

And it might *not* be the sugar. Cajeiri kicked the covers,

heard feet hitting the floor in his bodyguards' quarters only a little ahead of his own, and his immediate thought was that Nomari had lied to them, Nomari was up to something.

"No lights," he heard Rieni say. The Guild had rather work in the dark. "Keep him quiet, someone."

Cajeiri moved to the cage, put a hand on it. "Hush," he said, "hush," aware that his aishid was moving about, shadows in the scant light from the window, and he saw the muted quick gleam of an uncovered instrument of some sort.

He heard, then, very faintly, the ominous low complaint of mecheiti.

"Someone outside," he whispered, "or they heard Boji."

"Boji may have heard *them*," Veijico said. "We have a call from the Kadagidi path. The sensor is tripped."

Cajeiri shivered. "Are we in touch with Uncle? And Nomari?"

"They are aware," Rieni said. "There are a number of people. They are not Guild. They were on the path that leads to the gap in the hedge. There are twenty-one of them."

Twenty-one. "That is just—"

"Odd," Onomi said. "That is much more than odd. They are armed—they have rifles and pistols. But they are stating that they wish to see Lord Tatiseigi."

"News people?" Liedi wondered.

"News people do not carry rifles," Rieni said.

"We had better advise my uncle," Cajeiri said. Boji was becoming quite excited, bounding about in the dark. He put a hand on the cage to find a furry hand and quiet him.

"Your uncle is aware," Rieni said. "He wishes us to bring these people to the foyer, without the weapons. He wishes Nomari set under close guard and a guard in the second and third floor halls, as well as the stableside door and kitchens."

Uncle had been through this before. The rain was still spattering against the windows, a fairly energetic rain, now, and whoever was out in it would be soaked.

"Give Boji an egg, Eisi-ji. He has earned it. I shall dress. I

318 / C. J. CHERRYH

think Uncle will be dressing." He shivered in the dark, in the madness of the hour.

Twenty-one people.

"Rieni."

"Nandi?"

"I think we should ask Nomari who *he* thinks these people are."

"Likely a very good notion," Rieni said. "Haniri, uniform. Go make that inquiry."

"I shall dress," he said. He was still shivering, with bare feet on the floor. "We all should dress. I do not think this will settle quickly."

"Juniors," Rieni said, "uniform. Quickly."

Eisi and Liedi brought trousers and a shirt. And stockings. Cajeiri put them on, and pushed his feet into boots, standing, while Eisi braided his hair in the dark—knowing that he shivered, there was no helping it. He hated that.

A coat helped. It was one of his outdoor ones, *because* he was shivering, he was sure of it, but it was a comfort. Boji making another fuss did not help anyone's nerves: Liedi kept trying to soothe him, even gave him an egg, but Boji was too upset to care.

Haniri had left a time ago, and now came back. "The inquiry with Nomari-nadi. Lord Tatiseigi also inquired. Nomari says they may be his. Lord Tatiseigi has ordered them gathered up, will hear their explanation, and Kadagidi is lending its bus."

This intrusion onto the grounds had run into an armed sensor, that was clear. They had *not* gotten as far as the orchard.

"We shall go down," Cajeiri said, when they all were dressed. And to his servants. "I think we may turn on the lights, may we not? But stay away from the windows. Calm Boji. I think we are all right."

Uncle was already in the hall, and the hall lights were up. Nomari was called from his room into the hall, wrapped in a nightrobe, the servants likely having taken his only clothing away to launder. He bowed, embarrassed, clearly, and probably was chilled and worried.

"Well," Uncle said, "we shall see what the night has given us. Come, come down. Let us identify these people. The bus will be here and we shall know."

Down the stairs, then, Nomari making at least an effort to braid his hair after they had gotten to the bottom. They gathered in the sitting room as they heard the bus on the drive. Uncle's bodyguard and Rieni and Haniri went down to the doors. They heard the lesser door open, a silence, and then heard it open again, and the Guild who had gone down came up again, bringing a very wet young woman.

"Lord," she said, but not first to Cajeiri, or to Uncle, but to Nomari.

"Peja," Nomari said with emotion in his voice. And the young woman did bow, deeply, in their general direction.

"We take it they are indeed yours," Uncle said.

"They are mine, nandi," Nomari said. "I claim every one of them. I stand responsible for any damages they may have caused."

"I shall hold you, nand' Nomari, good only for three evergreens, in some future time. Will you identify all of these people? And may we find dry wraps for them? Kindly stay to the marble, nadi. Avoid the carpet."

"Nandi." The young woman bowed a second time, dripping onto the marble flooring, shivering massively. "Young aiji," she guessed correctly, and bowed again.

"May we have tea?" Uncle said in a voice that echoed, there just above the foyer, and servants, some in every evidence of very hasty dress, moved to arrange it.

It was a sodden and shivering group of people who came up from below, one by one, to present themselves and bow. Uncle's servants brought sheets and towels to wrap in, they brought five benches from the servant hall, to give these wet, desperate folk a place to sit, and they provided large cups of the sort the servants used, to serve steaming hot tea.

"We shall lodge them in the lower hall," Uncle said, and left matters to his major d', to have staff go out in rain gear, to mop the bus dry, and to arrange warm baths and a way to dry coats and clothes.

"Nandi," Nomari said, "I cannot express my gratitude."

"We do not turn people away dripping and cold," Uncle said. "We are old-fashioned in this house, and we trust that you do know them all."

"Every one," Nomari said. "They are all Ajuri, from Puran, from Ajiden, from Ara. This is my second cousin," he added, of one of the young men, who had taken a position near Nomari, who had said things to him, "Teiachi. Of the Messengers. They saw Geidaro arrive today—they feared I might not even be here. So they came to intercede."

"Intending to go through my hedges," Uncle said. "I swear I should establish a second gate, except the gap faces Kadagidi. You risked Guild over there, young man, and worse, you would have risked the mecheiti."

"Nandi," Teiachi said, still shivering from the cold. "We thought—in the rain—we had a chance."

"You had a chance to be soaked," Uncle said shortly. "And to end your night in my fruit trees, which are planted there as the *only* safety if the herd goes on the hunt. It has caught burglars before this. Well, well, you did not get *that* far."

"We are not criminals, Lord!"

"That you are not. The next time you may use the front gate, given you identify yourselves. We are not prepared for hospitality at this hour, but we have water heating, we have food preparing, we have hot tea, and staff will do their best with your laundry and your boots. The young women may go to the laundry, you young men may go down to the stableside storage and be served a supper, which I doubt you have had—"

"No, Lord," Teiachi said with another bow.

"And you may wrap in sheets and blankets while my staff attempt to do something for your clothes. Do not stray into the halls, mind! We are not a boarding house! If you have need of something, ask staff."

"In order, all," the major domo said, "Up, up, you have heard! Women to the laundry with the maids, in the north wing, men to the stableside, east wing. Up! Leave the cups on the benches! There will be more!"

Twenty-one people, wrapped in sheets and blankets—surely Uncle was having every sheet and blanket in Tirnamardi brought out—and likely all the prepared food in the kitchens. Every one of the intruders managed a solemn general bow, heads ducked, profoundly and long, as they sorted themselves into order—three women taken in charge by the laundry staff, eighteen men headed down the broad steps to the lower hall, with the night maintenance staff, and cook, likewise, mustering his staff, the night baking staff *and* the day staff, toward the main-level kitchens. It had become orderly, leaving five deserted benches, and teacups on them, and puddles on the marble, which the cleaning staff would have to deal with.

"Nandi," Nomari said, "this—I shall never forget."

Uncle said wryly: "This house has seen all manner of guests. And we manage. We always manage. You wish my endorsement? I am leaning to it. *They* recommend you, these people. I do not say they have good sense, but they are a recommendation. You will stay a little longer in Tirnamardi, and *make* me sure, nandi, before I commit my name again to a nomination. I daresay you *will* gain my confidence, in due course. In the meanwhile, we shall interview your young supporters, and if they have information bearing on the case, we shall be glad to hear it and relay it to Shejidan. Belief and enthusiasm are not enough. There must be facts. And substance."

The door below thumped shut, and the cold draft eased. Cajeiri masked his own shivers, hugging his arms about himself. He ought to feel uneasy with so many strangers in the house, unproved and unchecked, but a glance about him showed his younger aishid, and Rieni and his older one, and Uncle's own— Guild of whom they had no doubt, Guild that would keep them safe.

Someone should tell his father what was happening. Somebody should talk to Taiben, too, and let their Taibeni allies, camped out as they did in all weather, know that they had found one reason for disturbance in their woods.

But he was relatively sure that, behind the quiet attendance, Guild was talking to Guild and that was *exactly* what was going on.

There were, too, he remembered, all those news people, in the hotels over in Diegi and Heitisi, and wherever else they could manage to be, all interested in Uncle's politics.

Had they noticed the Ajuri bus at the gate? That was not exactly a major piece of news, but it was in connection with Uncle's nomination. And the veto. Both of those were in the news.

Had they just noticed that the Guild occupying Kadagidi estate had sent a large noisy bus over to Kadagidi's bitter enemy, the Atageini house, at an hour past midnight?

If the news people were camped out in the area getting as wet as Nomari's people, risking Taibeni and stray mecheiti, they might know it.

And if they knew that, they would be beside themselves trying to find out why.

Uncle might signal them. Or they simply might be asking the grocer who would have a very large order upcoming, because they had twenty-one more people to feed, fairly hungry ones, by the look of them.

Father was going to want him to come home, that was what. And he did not want to come, not now. He had protection. And Uncle needed him. Uncle needed his extra bodyguard right now.

He *did* matter. And he was not just a boy to be pulled home when things went on. He was the heir of the aishidi'tat. And *he* did not run.

21

It was a brisk morning, not yet into the daytime heat in Port Jackson. And with the morning breeze blowing from the open balcony doors, and after a generous breakfast sent up from Francis House kitchens, arrived news from the mainland . . . not much of it, the Guild not having secure communications on the island, and even Shawn's best assurances not being able prevent certain agencies from listening to phone calls.

There was, first, a Mospheiran news report this morning of unrest in the Padi Valley, a name a good many Mospheirans actually did know.

It would be a rare day there was not. But it was a little unsettling. Banichi launched, via phone, relayed from Port Jackson to the space station and down again to the aishidi'tat, a coded inquiry.

There was, within half an hour, a phone call from Bren's own apartment in the Bujavid, from his valet Koharu, whom he had left in charge. Koharu said simply that he had just gotten a letter from next door saying that Uncle had found a replacement.

And that was all.

"How are you doing?" Koharu asked, then, on to courtesies.

"We are doing very well. Everything has gone very well. How are things there?" *That* was a signal, wanting more information.

"We are well," Koharu said. "We are all very well."

"Excellent," he said, thinking, damn, and knowing there was

not a morsel else he could get. Koharu knew nothing more to tell him. "Am I needed?"

"One does not think so, nandi."

"Good. Very well. Thank you, nadi."

Next door was Tabini-aiji. Tabini had no uncle. Damiri did.

A confirmation on the nomination that was never intended to succeed? That made no sense.

Unrest in the Padi Valley? Unrest there was decades old, but it could get more insistent.

And today, following their inquiry, Tabini saw fit to send that fact across the strait?

And nothing more?

God, he wanted to be home.